Louette Harding

Louette Harding is a journalist as well as a writer. She is married and lives with her husband and their daughter in a 17th century thatched cottage in Cambridgeshire. *Two into One* is her first novel.

Two into One

Louette Harding

CORONET BOOKS
Hodder and Stoughton

Harding, Louette
Two into one
1.English fiction – 20th century
I.Title
823.9'14[F]

ISBN 0 340 65446 5

Printed and bound in Great Britain by
Cox and Wyman Ltd, Reading

Hodder and Stoughton Ltd
A Division of Hodder Headline PLC
338 Euston Road
London NW1 3BH

For Bob and Holly

Acknowledgements

I would like to thank the following for their generous help and support:

Alexander Carter-Silk, solicitor

Geoff Wilkinson, photographer

Maureen Mullally, barrister, who specialises in family law and is the author of the excellent layman's definitive book, *Law And The Family, A Practical Guide*, also published by Hodder & Stoughton

My agent, Caroline Sheldon

Sue Fletcher and her 'team'

And, of course, my husband Bob and daughter Holly for putting up with me and having a highly developed sense of humour

Chapter One

It was early, about eight, but already a bright March sun was up, pouring through the windows like warm treacle, coagulating in thick puddles on the floor. It was a hopeful sort of a day, not the sort when you wanted to stay indoors.

But it was also a Friday, the day on which Chris felt obliged to tackle the housework. It had been Chris's mother's optimum day for cleaning, so that 'everything would be nice before the weekend', as she always put it. Marjorie Greene had acquired a husband, a small detached house and two children in the 1950s and a part-time secretarial post in the early 1960s. At that point, Marjorie had reduced her life to lists, hurtling around an unvarying routine. Clean on Fridays. Shop on Saturday mornings. Iron on Mondays. It was ridiculous. Chris stuck with Fridays for entirely different reasons. Without a job, part-time or otherwise, he found the housework stacked up at the end of the week from his having avoided it earlier on.

The detritus of family living lapped at the walls, lay strewn across the floors and beached on tables and chairs; toys, clothes, newspapers, magazines, coffee

1

cups and, underneath a chair where it had lain undiscovered for two days, a Benjamin Bunny mug of juice, with a crust of powdery green mould already flowering upon its surface.

'Do you think there are magic pixies to tidy up after you?'

From her bedroom under the eaves, Emma laughed. She was six, just old enough to detect irony and respond in kind.

'I hope so,' she called back.

She smiled up at Chris who loitered in her doorway for a moment, before she returned her attention to the two chubby plastic ponies in her hands, whose heads she was rhythmically banging together.

'They're fighting,' she announced. 'They're a mummy and daddy.' She turned back to the lurid figures and raised one above the other. 'This stable's a shit heap,' she yelled.

In the bathroom, a dune of magazines was collapsing by the loo. Chris sat down on the edge of the lavatory, his burst of energy replaced by exasperation. At that moment, Annie appeared, in a morning hurry, as usual. She glanced with momentary surprise at his sitting on the loo with his jeans still fastened.

'Haven't you forgotten something?' she asked dryly, tugging a brush through her dark hair.

She gazed critically into the mirror, turning her face from side to side as if something was not to her satisfaction. She had a lovely face but she never looked in a mirror with anything approaching complacency. Long ago, while attempting to persuade her that she looked fine without make-up, he'd remarked on this. She'd said lightly, 'Anyone who admires their reflection is a man. It is against

2

the laws of nature for a woman to like what she sees in a mirror.' Now he wondered why she wasn't satisfied with her lot.

'Do you think you could stack the magazines on the shelf when you've finished with them?' he snapped.

She looked at him.

'Don't bother with those,' she said, and there was a note of irritation in her voice. 'Just pile them in a corner. You know what needs doing? The kitchen floor. It's filthy,' she added. 'And could you take that dry cleaning in today?' It was more of a command than a question. 'I'm desperate for my blue jacket.'

He seemed to remember that when their roles had first reversed – when she had taken up her high-powered job and he had metamorphosed into a house husband – her requests had been sweeter, prefaced by emollient phrases such as, 'Darling, would you mind? – Is it too much trouble?' For a month or so, he had taken some pride in her never having to empty a dishwasher or plug in the iron. And she had been amply grateful.

For a month or so, playing at keeping house had worn some of the borrowed charm of novelty; he had cracked robust jokes about it. But soon even this had faded and he had realised all too well why his mother had wanted that two-bit job, had been prepared to rush, so flustered, from chore to door in hanging on to it. He had never been so bored. The day stretched before him, limitless in its sameness. His life was ticking by but he was incapable of filling the time: he simply grew more and more listless, as if he were boring himself. He did not even have entry into the female support groups of the village; the coffee mornings and the art classes which replaced the mother and toddler groups as the children grew.

He was isolated. How he missed the male banter of the office!

He looked up. Annie was rifling through a heap of jewellery on the windowsill, searching for something. Automatically, although she had not said a word, he felt guilty, as if he had mislaid her trinket. As far as he knew, however, his only responsibility towards the jewellery pile was to slide it gently a few inches to the left each week as he wiped the woodwork.

Real men buy their wives jewellery. Wimps dust under it.

But he was being trite and self-pitying.

'Oh my God,' he moaned in a daft voice, 'I'm turning into my mother.'

Annie gave a little exhalation, which was half a laugh – she still laughed at his quips – and half an expression of sympathy. She smiled down at him, her head on one side. She understood that he felt diminished. He could read in her dark eyes her concern for him and also the opposing reflex to catch the train, get to work. She was probably resolving to talk tonight when there was time.

He knew her so well, could track her thoughts as if they were a pattern on an exotic silk scarf that floated behind her, or as if they were the bright gaseous tail of a shooting star trailing in her wake. She had intelligent eyes, big soft pools above a pointed chin, and a quick, hesitant smile. There was a soft American lilt to her voice – even now after fifteen years of living in England. That was Annie and once he had loved her from the top of her head to the tips of her toes.

She had moved him so much because of the contrast between her gravity of manner and her vulnerability. She seemed reserved, but it was easy to see that this was a disguise for her real self, which was artless and impulsive. He remembered, when they were first married, catching her unawares in the kitchen. She'd been pretending to be – who could it have been? – Ginger Rogers? Rita Hayworth? Anyway, she was tap dancing – except that she did not know how to tap dance, so it was a bit of a pastiche – on the hard vinyl tiles of the floor, which clicked when she walked over them in her favourite high-heeled shoes. When he had interrupted her, she had continued, putting on an inexpert show for him. And he had realised, at that moment, while they were both laughing, how this was to be the shape of life from now on, that there was someone with whom to share private silliness, with whom you did not have to put on a wider act. What on earth had happened to them?

She had no time, and no wish, it seemed, for moments of madness now. She had things on her mind. He sometimes wondered if she'd be better off without him. Their delight in each other – the honour that somehow, in day-to-day life, they had done to each other – seemed to be in the past. With the collapse of his business, his self-assurance had withered accordingly. But Annie, in becoming the breadwinner, had grown brisk and confident.

They regarded each other across their exasperation. Frequently they argued – rowdy, emotional, uncontrolled arguments – nine times this year already. He knew because Emma had told him: he had been startled and ashamed to discover she was keeping count. They fought over money. They fought because each felt unappreciated. They knew why they did it but still they fought.

He knew perfectly well that they would not talk when Annie got home from work. They'd be too frightened of starting another argument. And besides: what was there to say? I can't stand the containment of my life? A life turned flaccid with embarrassing suddenness.

'I've got to go,' Annie called from the bedroom.

She reappeared looking down at him, with a little smile which could not hide – not after fifteen years of marriage, fifteen years of interpreting her moods and thoughts – how sick at heart she was. Chris kicked himself for the worry he was causing her.

'Back to the salt mines,' she said. She was having a hard time at work currently.

'Don't knock it,' he said, before he could stop himself.

Her face crumpled.

He heard her voice in Emma's room, calming and light and funny. He heard her cooing at the collie. 'Be a good boy, Ben. Do good guarding.' Footsteps on the stairs. The door closing. She was gone.

Chris sat still for a moment, listening to the quiet. I'm relieved, he realised suddenly. Relieved she's gone.

In the mirror, his face stared bleakly back at him. It was one of the saddest moments of his life.

Annie always allowed several minutes to get the car started: she was wise to its caprices. She had never before owned such an old car, normally replacing them before seventy thousand miles. It was unfortunate that she had had to hang on to this one, which she had never liked – this sensible family motor she had dutifully bought second-hand when pregnant, despite her yearning for a silken red Japanese sports car. As if sensing her resentment, her old crate was growing curmudgeonly and needed tactful treatment.

Oh hell! Annie brushed a strand of hair from her mouth. I've become expert at coaxing and cajoling. It's my major role in life these days.

The car wheezed but stubbornly fell silent. Annie turned off the ignition. She would have to wait five minutes to avoid flooding the engine. Intending to extend the aerial, she stepped from the door.

The outbuilding which they used as a garage, and which they rather grandly called a barn, was, in fact, where the village fire engine had once been kept, years ago. It was dilapidated now, its pantiles awry and the tarred wooden planks slipping. At the back stood two tall, bulky forms, half hidden by the shadows and by dust sheets polka-dotted with blobs of paint, blue and green and white. She stared for a moment. Chris's statues! She had stopped seeing them long ago. She cautiously manoeuvred past the car, the ladder, the buckets, the old paint tins and brushes which Chris insisted on keeping, although he took great pleasure in buying new ones whenever he decorated a room.

Shafts of sun, in which the dust soared playfully, sliced through the gaps in the roof. Cobwebs, furry with grey dust, garlanded the old beams. The air smelt of warmth and familiarity. It was still. Somewhere above her a bird scuttled across the tiles, the only sound except her own breathing. She took a fold of a sheet gingerly between thumb and forefinger and tugged it back.

Two plaster horses, almost life-sized, wild, muscular, stared sadly at her from their blind eyes. They were beautiful.

'Hello, boys', she whispered, because they did seem half-real to her. 'How have you been keeping?' But she could see they were cracking and crumbling from the damp. It was such a shame.

These part-finished statues were the means by which Chris had once measured his talent. Crafted during his time at art college, they had been the unwieldy but stirring proof that he was a cut above the rest. Today, they were all that remained of his youthful dream. She had a vivid memory of his telling her all about it the very first time they met. Indeed, in the early years of their marriage, he'd still had plans to brush it off and set it gently moving. Chris had wanted to be a sculptor.

With her fingertip Annie traced the contour of an eye socket, of a flared nostril.

She had been seventeen when they met, at Jim's party in a prettified area across the bay from her home town of San Francisco. Jim was an artist, at least ten years older than Annie, and gay. Annie was inordinately impressed that someone so Bohemian should wish to be her friend. But Jim collected people. He was gregarious and loved to entertain.

Chris, twenty then, was in San Francisco for a vacation before returning to art college in London: he had been included in Jim's typically expansive invitation because he was the friend of a friend. She first spotted him perched on the windowsill with a can of Bud resting on the knee of his jeans. He had a quizzical, amused expression. He was funny, and the uneven tilt of his smile, and the flop of his mid-brown hair on his forehead, which he pronounced furrid – his Newman blue eyes, each of these disparate components made her like him. Of course, his accent reminded her of her father. Someone mentioned her being half-British, assuming this would interest Chris, and he was smitten enough to pretend it did. She remembered, with a smile, that frisson of mutual attraction.

The music was too loud. Half a dozen figures

quivered to its beat in a darkened room where the chairs were pushed back, the men self-conscious and gawky, as dancing men always are. Annie and Chris removed themselves and two cans of beer onto the deck outside, but it still pulsed to the music, and a group – two men and three women, their nude bodies alarmingly pale in the half-light – was raucously enjoying the hot tub.

Annie and Chris negotiated the steep steps to the lawn below and stretched out, the warm lights of the house washing the shadows behind them, the bay glittering with its hard glamour below them, and above them the stars, bright, distant and unimaginable.

Annie lay on her back as she talked. She talked to the stars in the sky. She talked about her childhood, which she never did. Normally she affected to remember very little about it, as if she had clipped it neatly from her memory, just as she had scissored around the ghastly business of losing her virginity six months earlier, under the influence of Quaaludes and the brashest of the boy jocks at school. But lying on the lawn with Chris beside her, a foot away, not even looking at her but gazing resolutely into the inky bruise of the night, she told him about her father, the English father she adored, who had left San Francisco when she was ten and gone, with the hateful Patricia, to live in New York, from where he sent her extravagant Christmas presents and floral arrangements on her birthday. So inappropriate, everyone said, which was why, of course, she loved them the more. He had never sent flowers to Mom. As far as she knew, he sent flowers to no other female.

He called her poppet. Her mother called her Annie or darling, but to her father she was poppet and that endearment, like the flowers, was a sign. It meant that, no matter what, she was the special girl in her father's life.

When she was thirteen, she went to visit. By then, Henry Bradshaw was an executive at the New York branch of the company and he was busy, busy, busy. Patricia, a bottle blonde who wore carefully applied but heavy eye make-up, was dispatched to meet her at the airport. Annie was unprepared for this; in her mind's eye she had been swept into her daddy's arms. She was sullen during the cab ride into the city, head down. Patricia's left arm, artificially tanned and glinting with fair downy hairs, rested within her field of vision. Patricia's engagement and wedding rings were bigger, flashier, chunkier, than her own mother's had been.

Patricia settled her in the apartment, which was on the east side, in the mid-fifties, into the cramped spare room. The bedspread was blue; a Snoopy lolled against the bolster. Her dad had always loved Snoopy, and when she was very small had read the cartoons to her, so the toy's being there cheered her. But somehow she had feared, even then, that the visit was not going to be a success.

He came home late, about eleven, and said, 'Hello my poppet,' in his quirky accent, and hugged her tight. He asked her a few questions about school and about Louise, who had been her best friend when he had left three years ago, but wasn't any more. Each day, Patricia took her out, shopping to Bloomingdales, to the Empire State, to the Statue of Liberty, and tried to make conversation; each night her father came home late, but ebullient and affectionate.

Even with the blinds closed, the city lights infiltrated her third-floor bedroom. She lay with Snoopy in her arms looking around the strangefamiliar room – Patricia called it 'her' room – distorted by the artificial yellow glow, just as Patricia's bottles altered her hair and her skin. One night, towards the end of the week, she heard their voices in the adjacent master bedroom; she heard Patricia say, 'Look, hon, couldn't you take just one itty bitty day off to see your kid? For Chrissake! She worships you,' and she heard her dad say, 'Don't nag!'

That was all. There was silence after that. Silence in the luminescence washing 'her' bedroom. They weren't going to argue over her.

'So which did I mind most?' she asked herself, and Chris, as they lay on their backs on Jim's carefully tended lawn. 'Was it my father's indifference? Or the humiliation of Patricia taking my part? I still don't know. I remember realising, in a flash, that the bouquets had been sent by Patricia. Only another woman would have known the effect they would have on a little girl.

'And I lay there all night, stuffing the pillow in my mouth so they wouldn't hear me crying, wondering what I had done, because I must have done something, to make him stop loving me.'

'Did you tell your mother?' he asked the sky.

'Nah. Never. Raved about the visit. She acted happy for me. Underneath she was jealous. I wanted her to feel like that. It gave me back some power.'

Chris's hand stretched across the foot between them and took her fingers briefly, and squeezed them. But all he said was, 'Do you want another beer, Annie Bradshaw?' for which she was disproportionately grateful.

And that was it. Chris went home two days later. But she kept his address which he had scrawled in blue Biro on an airmail envelope. The pressure of the pen had perforated the thin tissue paper in places. She placed it between the pages of her much thumbed, hardback copy of *Pride And Prejudice* – all her heroes, even the fictional ones, had been English – and never forgot that it was there. And when she was planning her own trip to Europe, she spent a ludicrous amount of time and thought phrasing a note to him.

She felt that she must remind him who she was, in case he had forgotten. She decided she must not sound over eager. It was, she thought, even as she posted it, a very gauche and transparent note. Months later, when he showed it to her, preserved in his wallet, they had laughed the conspiratorial laugh of lovers enchanted by their past uncertainty.

For at the spring break, she'd left college and never gone back. She had thrown over the course at which she was doing so well, slated for a magna cum laude, at the least, so the professor had roared when she telephoned him from London, England, to tell him. Chris had asked her to marry him three weeks after her arrival. Two months later, Mom flew over for the ceremony, rumbling menacingly, not about Annie's foolhardiness or their haste, but with some feminist rhetoric. They'd met her at Heathrow to wheel her recalcitrant trolley through the spiky ankles of the crowd, and she surprised them by suddenly blurting out: 'You won't submerge your identity, will you, Annie?'

'Excuse me? Mom, I'm getting married, not reinventing myself as a little woman.'

Chris looked as if the wicked witch of the west had alighted at his side. Ever since, he had examined her from time to time – usually during arguments – for traces of her mother.

The horses, which then stood in a corner of their first flat, had stared at her sadly, as if they knew the fate to which her arrival had consigned them. For at that point, life had demanded sacrifices, and the plunging uncast horses were the first offerings. He was not to be a sculptor, not yet. Later, they told each other. Not that Chris had ever minded. He was as generous with money as he was with his time. Too generous as it turned out, for he was no businessman.

Initially, he took a job in the graphic design studio of a lesser advertising agency with a convoluted name, paying the bills while she studied journalism at an English college. Later, he set up his own design business because he could earn more by working all hours for himself. In this way, he funded the endless treatment, the shuttling from doctor to doctor, when it had seemed she couldn't have a child.

In a coffee bar, in central London, they had both laughed and cried on the day she told Chris she was pregnant. The man at the next table gave her the rose from his buttonhole. The waitress wouldn't take their payment.

So they had their baby. She knew now the fierce passion to hold tight to the velvet skin.

They moved to the Cambridgeshire countryside, for Emma's sake. Their cottage was a cliché, thatched and idiosyncratic, its beams curling under the weight of the years. The textures of rough lime plaster, polished beams, handmade Tudor bricks, delighted them. That and the unfussed half acre of grass and apple trees, in one of which they slung a swing.

The village expanded to accept them, even the old-timers like Burt, who told them in his rolling accent that he had never been further than Cambridge in his life, not even to London, and they realised he was proud of his quirky insularity.

It was a good place to raise a child. The old plots were infilled now, often unhappily, but the village was still compact, contained by fields that spread their crops to ripen before the infinite domed sky; corn, rape and linseed. Old Dora, next-door-but-one, filled a wheelbarrow with produce, her knobbly cucumbers, red, fragrant tomatoes, sweet peas in their season, and sold it from the pavement in front of her house, putting out a jam jar for the money. Then the takings disappeared. Teenagers from the other side of the village, it was said, meaning the bunch of council houses. After a few months, Dora gave in. She moved to sheltered accommodation and the cottage in which she was born was demolished, giving way to three executive houses in the mock-Tudor style. But still it was not a bad place to raise a child.

Annie worked as a freelance journalist but only part-time, to dovetail with the school day. If, on occasion, an interview demanded longer hours, which happened once or twice a month, there was always a congenial mother of one of Emma's school friends who would have her to tea. These other women envied her the balance of her life. They said, 'How interesting your job must be! And you can work the hours you want! It's worked out so well for you. You're so lucky.' And she said, 'Yes, I am, touch wood,' and tapped her skull lightly three times, just in case. She remembered once, driving home after an interview, going to collect Emma, thinking, 'I'm so happy. I am completely happy.'

Emma was the light of her life, and if she never had another child, she would not mind. Emma insinuated herself into Annie's side of the bed in the morning, and she said, 'You know something, Mummy? You're the best.' She picked ragged bunches of hedgerow flowers for her which they stuck in jam jars on the windowsills. When Emma was crying over a graze on her knee, it was Annie who could silence her with a kiss. Through Emma, Annie held the magic to make everything better.

Then Chris came home looking worried, saying he needed to speak to her after Emma was in bed and, most alarmingly, refusing to answer her questions until then.

'I think I'm bankrupt,' he said.

'How much for?'

'Twenty thousand.'

And she had laughed, because in her mind she'd said to herself that she would remain calm if his answer was less than twenty but not if it was more. A queer thing. She didn't know why she'd picked that figure, any figure, and she'd picked the exact amount.

But they had fought off bankruptcy. Annie had found a job, a well-paid and therefore a demanding job, which took her away from her home and her daughter for twelve, fourteen hours a day. She had had it all and Chris, poor thing, had taken it away.

She reached out and stroked the rough-smooth muzzles of the dream horses. Time had altered her just as it was changing them. She had been moulded, kneaded, extruded. Time had smoothed and roughened her; worked her into a new shape, until she was unfamiliar even to herself. The Annie she saw in her memory would never have forgotten these statues; she had cared too deeply for Chris. His plans were always in her mind.

She was going to be late.

Patting the nearest horse as if it were real, she drew the dust cover back, and picked her way back to the driver's door. The car spluttered testily before conceding to her pumping foot.

Chapter Two

'Buongiorno.' Stella hung up her coat, wheeled on one heel, and strode to her desk, shaking out her red hair. She wore maroon lipstick and a tart's tight dress in which her breasts and matronly belly were bobbing and shoving like apples in a bucket.

'Free for lunch?' Annie asked, dropping the mouse of her computer.

'Planned to go shopping. Something up?'

Annie smiled, hoping to look rueful rather than self-pitying.

'Walk with me to the coffee machine,' Stella suggested.

Annie fished in her bag for her purse and together they strolled from their bank of desks, up the corridor.

Stella's walk was humming and happy. 'Phil pulled off a deal yesterday. Earned five hundred quid,' she confided. 'It's amazing how sexy that made him.'

Jubilant in her unsuitable clothes and her afterglow, she sashayed up to the coffee machine, clicking her fingers, jiggling her hips and breasts to some interior rhythm.

Annie lent on the side of the machine and pretended to bang her head against it in frustration. 'Oh, boy! Sex! What's that?'

'Had a row?'

'No. No. Not exactly. In fact . . . it's worse than that, if you can believe it. We've got nothing to say to each other, Stella. We've said it all. How sorry he feels that so much weight is on my shoulders. How sorry I am that he's bored out of his mind. And you know what? It's become easier to avoid each other. If we keep out of each other's way, we don't get the chance to row.'

She drew her coffee from the machine's mouth with care, the hot liquid burning her fingertips through the flimsy plastic.

'It really worries me. We don't enjoy each other's company any more . . .' She tailed off. She was fond of Stella and regarded her as her closest friend in the office, but even so, she sensed it was an artificial closeness, caused by regular proximity. She couldn't bring herself to finish her sentence, because that would be disloyal to Chris. She would not reduce him, or her fears, to the level of office gossip.

She had worked here on the features desk for almost two years. She had contributed pieces to the review supplement as a freelance, and when Chris had ceased trading and she had telephoned to say she was looking for a staff post they had conjured one up for her. This was flattering. Nevertheless, she mourned, each evening at eight, as she sat on the train home, her separation from Emma. Eight o'clock was Emma's bedtime.

She propped an elbow on the machine. 'You know, Stel, when my parents split up they sat me down and told me they both still loved me but they had grown apart. I was ten. And I kept wondering how you could grow apart. Why didn't you realise it was happening and grow back together again?'

'Oh yeah,' drawled Stella. 'And let's have the meaning of life while we're about it.'

Annie laughed. 'Did you read that report in the papers this morning? That divorce may be passed down the generations, all that stuff? Jeez, Stel. I feel like I'm up against the researchers as well as the bank manager and the role reversal.'

'It's tough, isn't it?' Stella grimaced sympathetically. 'God knows, Phil and I have rowed so much since Thomas was born . . . . Oooh, I dunno! Most days I could pull 'is balls out.'

Annie laughed again. Stella was the daughter of a doctor, had gone to private school and normally spoke with the sort of accent which Annie now realised placed her firmly in the educated classes. But when she talked about sex she tended to adopt a camp manner and a council estate accent, a trait that amused Annie. This inability to talk seriously about sex seemed charmingly British. Some years ago, in a northern seaside resort, she had first seen revolving racks of 'saucy' postcards, each spattered with bawdy jokes and bulging bosoms, and been amazed. This attitude to sex was one of the national characteristics that reminded her she was not really of this place. Generally, she was at ease here. She slipped between the nuances of the culture; her speech reflected the idioms and rhythms. She no longer noticed imperfect, National Health teeth. She was accustomed to her husband cheering on a different team in the Olympics; indeed, she had begun to cheer for his side, too. And she particularly liked brassy, intrepid, outspoken Englishwomen like Stella.

Stella was one of five women in the office who were

in a similar position to Annie; their husbands or partners earning little or nothing. Stella's Phil was an opportunist, a doer of cash-only deals. Initially, for Stella, this lent him the gleam of the gambling man. Neat men in ironed underpants and nylon socks worked nine to five. She wanted none of them.

Later, she decided to try for a baby. She was forty-four. The tick tock in her ears had risen way above the agreed decibel limit. Phil had been delighted by this sudden change in her priorities. He had always wanted a child, dreaming of a son, but he had never pressured her. He was an admirable man and by any standards, a good father. As a provider, though, he was intermittent.

But, Annie noted, none of the other women, including Stella, were in quite the same boat as she was. Stella and Phil were not weighted with debt as she and Chris were. None of her colleagues lived as she did. They spent their fat salaries on themselves and their whims. Stella and Phil had a social life; they went out for dinner, they entertained. Annie was accustomed to a weekly menu of chicken, mince, vegetables and pulses, the ingredients unvarying because they were cheapest. Stella did not think the hundred-and-fifty-pound skirts in the newspaper's fashion pages ridiculously expensive. Annie's working wardrobe was bought in sales and carefully revolved, different blouses, different scarves, same three skirts, same two trousers. The magazine articles on 'clever capsule clothes' never taught her a thing. She was an expert in make do and pretend.

As for Chris, who had no job to make demands of his appearance, he wore threadbare jeans and faded T-shirts. The previous winter, which had been the worst period, when they had thought they might lose the house, she noticed his socks were inexplicably blackened. It emerged that there were holes in the soles of his only shoes, which were beyond repairing, so he was wearing them anyway, trying to combat the seeping cold and rain by lining them with cardboard. They were middle-class people of the 1990s, and they lived like characters out of Dickens.

As a child she had loved the mail arriving, the expectation always that it would include a postcard from her father, although it rarely did. As an adult she had grown to fear it. It brought nasty letters, from the tax collector, the hire purchase company, the bank manager. 'I would think that by now you would know my attitude to unauthorised use of an overdraft on your account,' he once wrote, the pompous prat. He was in his twenties and very supercilious. But of course we are overdrawn, she wanted to reply. We had to pay the electricity bill or we'd have been cut off. Why are you so irate? You are making ludicrous amounts in fees and interest from my misery.

Pay a bit here, pay a bit there. People like Stella did not understand the grim and faintly farcical juggling act which consumed her time and emotions. Stella might bear the responsibility for paying their mortgage, but she had never been in arrears. In any case, she and Chris had never told anyone the full indignity of their daily, middle-class poverty. It wasn't something you talked about.

Stella lobbed her empty cup five feet into a waste bin. 'It's conference time,' she said.

Annie lightly slapped her own cheek. 'I better get my mind into gear. Alec's back from that seminar thingy today.'

'How is he, this morning? Have you seen him?'

'No. But I've sensed a life form in his office.'

21

Stella smiled. Alec was a tyrant, a misogynist and a Right-wing bigot. It was astonishing that anyone so quick could be so obtuse.

'I think I might actually have some hot ideas for conference this morning,' Stella trilled. 'It's amazing how creative I feel. I'm in love with the father of my child!'

'Don't worry,' Annie said, patting her shoulder. 'You'll hate him again tomorrow.'

Chris wiped some crumbs from the breakfast table with a damp cloth and painstaking care. Nevertheless, a light storm cascaded over the edge. He knelt to wipe the floor, realised he was using the wrong cloth, thought he'd mentally redesignate it as a floor cloth though he already had one, rinsed it under a running tap, sprayed water onto the Aga, wiped the Aga, smeared crumbs on it.

He put the kettle onto boil.

The coffee jar was almost empty; there was no granulated sugar. He took a mug from a hook, shook the last grains of coffee into it, and spooned in some icing sugar from a packet on the top shelf. After adding the hot water and a gulp of milk, he took a sip and grimaced.

Emma, off school with a cold, wandered into the kitchen. 'Cheers!' she said cheerfully. It was her new habit whenever a cup was raised to lips, following a week's stay with his parents at Christmas when the gin and tonics and festive humour had captivated her. He suspected that she thought the very word made people happy, some kind of terse spell which magically restored the atmosphere between Mummy and Daddy.

'Get your shoes on, Emlet. We're going shopping.'

'We went shopping yesterday.'

'I know we went shopping yesterday. I forgot a couple of things.'

She looked at him over the jam sandwich she had retrieved from a sticky plate by the sink. 'OK,' she said, inexplicably cooperative.

Chris felt absurdly pleased, as if he was not such a failure at instilling discipline as he had thought. He might hate most of his inside-out life, but he delighted in being a father.

He parked his old jalopy in the school car park to avoid the thirty-pence charge in town, held the seat forward while Emma extricated herself from her seat belt and clambered out, locked the door, realised Emma's coat was lying on the back seat and banged his head on the door frame in the process of retrieving it.

'Shit!'

'Dadd-ee.'

'Sorry, sweetheart.'

Leaving the car park brought them behind the church, a stolid turn-of-the-century building whose architect had remained steadfastly uninspired by the infinite glories of God. It resembled an elongated house, with pebble-dashed walls, painted ivory, and a steep roof of orange pantiles. The windows were leaded but not stained, except for one which showed the martyrdom of St Thomas of Canterbury. For some reason, the saint and his assassins wore togas, and when Chris had first seen it he had assumed that for inexplicable reasons, it depicted Julius Caesar on the Ides of March.

A notice board on stilts by the entrance declared the Mass and Confession times. Chris glanced at his watch. Weekday mass, at 9.45 a.m., had only just started. Despite sending Emma to the attached

Catholic primary school, he had not attended Mass since her christening. The truth was, he was no longer sure of the truth. How odd it was that great changes could occur without your noticing or minding very much. You looked up from your perpetual, insistent worries and discovered that the old landmarks of your life had been bulldozed away, like the village cottages, first one, then another, but it was all so gradual and piecemeal that you hardly realised how complete the transformation was.

Chris's certainties were everywhere replaced by doubts. He had been a reluctant Catholic as a child, an inattentive altar boy, but as he had grown older he had found a new dimension in his faith. He had wanted to marry in church. It held a significance for him. And Annie who was not a Catholic, whose mother was an atheist and whose father may not even have possessed a soul – such was his self-centred materialism – had agreed because she was touched by his sincerity. She had attended the meetings with the priest and vowed to bring up any children in the church. She had been so sweet in her seriousness that, Chris realised, Father David entertained hopes of converting her. Annie's mother had been outraged. She saw the Catholic church as a sinister conspiracy against women, and Chris's membership of it as further proof that he intended to keep her daughter barefoot by the kitchen stove.

Chris wondered what Martha Bradshaw made of their reversed roles today. He wondered if she knew of his present agnosticism. Better not to think of her. He shook her from his head.

There was an aura of neglect about the church that mirrored Chris's lapsed attendance. The once white paint on the entrance door was blistered and yellowing. Straggly weeds grew in the cracks between the paving flags that led, in shallow steps, towards it. Flakes of old, damp confetti were glued to them. Emma knelt down and picked at one with her nail. She was fascinated by the paraphernalia of weddings, like all little girls. They seemed to recognise so early that the sacrament was a flowering of eternal feminine power. He saw Annie behind her veil. He never forgot their vows: 'all that I have, I share with you; all that I am, I give to you.'

Suddenly, on a whim, he took Emma's hand, like a soft efflorescence in his, and climbed the steps. She looked up at him but said nothing. Her silence was a token of her understanding.

The inner door creaked softly, alerting those inside to late comers, to intruders. Six or seven figures stood in the front pews, amen-ing a prayer. Chris led Emma towards them, genuflecting in a perfunctory, embarrassed fashion, as one who feels they must observe the social niceties. He sat down with Emma nestling next to him, three rows from the front, as the sparse congregation sat, too. The woman in front turned round: she had long grey hair fastened into an untidy bun with a thick strip of leather and a wooden peg, round metal NHS glasses, and a benevolent air. She wore an AIDS ribbon pinned to her crocheted waistcoat. Chris interpreted her glance as a welcome rather than as disapproval. It relaxed him slightly, for he had immediately noticed that he was, with the exception of the priest, the only male here. Apart from Emma, he guessed he was the sole person under sixty.

A tall, thin woman, also with glasses, but these dark-rimmed and disapproving, her hair an iron grey, rococo, permanent wave, climbed onto the lectern. She tapped the microphone three times with her finger very deliberately, and leaned her lipsticked mouth towards it.

'The first reading is taken . . .' Her voice was blotted up by the vast, cold, grey spaces of the church. The sound system was switched off.

Chris bit his bottom lip hard. The Gorgon continued the reading, bending towards the microphone like the etiolated mustard and cress that Emma grew on blotting paper, and that always leant, pathetically, towards the window. The prophet Elijah was virtually inaudible.

What did I expect to find here? Why did I think it would feel comfortable or smell reassuringly of childhood and safety and certainties? How dumb – as Annie would say – can you get? He couldn't leave now, though. It would be impossible to slip away unnoticed, avoiding the alert, squealing door and the hurt disappointment of the happy-clappy pensioner in front.

The women rose again and Chris jumped to his feet a second too late. 'We believe in God . . .' They recited the creed from memory. Chris looked around for mass sheets but in vain. He began mouthing wordlessly to the tum-te-tum rhythm. He hoped he looked convincing. The priest, a corpulent man, shot him a look from his sharp, dark eyes. Chris was suspicious of fat priests. It was prissy of him, he felt sure. After all, he disliked very thin priests even more.

The weekday morning mass went briskly, thank God. No, no, he didn't mean that. Kneeling, he tried to focus his mind, form a prayer to coax God into healing his poor, bruised marriage.

Chris did not pray in words but in pictures. He envisaged the object of his thoughts and elevated them into a beam of light. He was sure this was both sentimental and ineffective. Even now, at thirty-eight, he felt there was a right way to pray, that the response was somehow dependent on the deftness or sincerity of the petition. He tried now to picture Annie, but the figure in his mind was not the Annie he loved, tap-dancing in the kitchen, sniffling over the video of *Dumbo* when she watched it with Emma, but weekday Annie, dressed in a trouser suit, clutching her briefcase, a business woman who was disconcerting because she was not his. He revolved her in a shaft of light, but it was hopeless. He was reminded of the transporter on the starship *Enterprise*; he and Emma had been addicted to the re-runs of *Star Trek*.

The priest elevated the host. The ladies bowed their heads devoutly.

There was no bell. Chris had expected a bell. But, of course, there were no altar boys during the week.

The priest raised the chalice.

'Cheers!' declared Emma, voice chiming in the silence, dropping like a stone into the dark pool of the church.

Chris buried his face in his hands. He hoped no one saw his shoulders heaving slightly.

A group of ten adults of uncertain ages filed through the heavy wooden door into Alec's office, each nurturing a childish flutter of apprehension. The Features Desk – Annie's desk – were led in by Callum, an aggressively amusing young man who wore Armani suits and an air of confidence. He was the Assistant Editor (Features). Stella went by the title of Features Editor and Annie by Assistant Features Editor. Stella had more hard experience and was a better operator than either of her immediate superiors, Callum, and David, the Deputy

Editor. Before having her baby, she had worked on the features desks of several nationals in the middle market and then moved to broadsheets, each time poached with a promotion and a fatter salary. Having Thomas had blunted her ambition. She left daily newspapers for lesser jobs on weekend supplements, because she didn't want to work the hours, nor on Sundays.

Stella and Annie sat down on the sofa in the corner, side by side. There was a place next to them but Callum ignored it, placing himself at the table in the centre where the other men of the office – the production editor, the managing editor – gathered together.

As the door closed, Alec leaned forward over the expanse of his desk. 'This is Jane Williams,' he said abruptly, gesturing to a neat woman in a cheap suit, her elbows clamped to her side, who was perched on a chair next to him.

'Good morning, Alec,' said Stella. 'How are you? Did you have a productive conference? Yes, I did thank you, Stella. And how have you all been in my absence?'

'Good morning, Stella,' said Alec gruffly. 'As I was saying, this is Jane Williams, from the Association of Social Studies. There must be an acronym here, up which I would like to stick market research in normal circumstances.' His paunch heaved at his own witticism. Jane Williams looked down at her shoes with a slight smile playing on her lips, a smile that Alec could interpret as amusement but Annie read as contempt for the male. She giggled. Alec shot her a glance, gratified.

'Jane,' he continued, 'has come to give us a talk on demographics. She gave much the same talk at this think-tank balderdash our parent company thought fit to send me on this week, when I could have been here putting together the review and avoiding bloody awful covers like the one that's gone through in my absence, Rachel.'

Rachel, the Art Editor, gave him a look of abhorrence but he ignored it. 'Anyway, the subject matter of Jane's talk was so effing rivetting I've asked her here today to let you lot in on the secret.' The euphemism was a concession to a strange woman's presence; normally Alec fucked and blinded with impunity. He gestured to his guest, 'I'll let her do her stuff, first.'

Jane Williams rose, pulling down her short, crumpled jacket. There was an overhead projector on a trolley by the table and after several minutes of fiddling with blinds and locating light switches, she launched into her talk. The first slide showed the readers of the Saturday section of the *Daily News* 'by age, class and gender'. There followed three flickering graphs. Age peaked at thirty-five to forty-five, as it always had. Class peaked at B, average spending power around £20,000 a year. A pie chart was coloured 58 per cent blue, 42 per cent pink. Annie picked up her pencil, put it down again. We know all this. Why has Alec asked her here to tell us what we know?

'We are living in a period of change,' Jane Williams announced portentously. 'In the last decade, the number of women working full-time has increased while the number of men working full-time has fallen.' Figures appeared on the screen. 'By the year 2000, more women will be working than men. Some forecasters say women will be filling 90 per cent of new vacancies. There are a growing number of families in which the woman is the main or sole breadwinner.

'A lot of people seem to think that as the economy improves, everything will revert to how it was before, to "normal". This isn't so. The days of father working nine to five for the same company until retirement are over. Men's career patterns will become interrupted, they will have to accept short-term contracts, for example. Women are used to career insecurity because of taking time out to raise children, so they are better prepared for this. Mentally, they can cope with the erratic career course. Men can't.

'This, of course, has many interesting ramifications for society. From your point of view, it is a factor you must address.' She fiddled with the celluloid sheets in front of her, and the ominously blue pie chart reappeared on the wall. 'This is obviously something that your Editor will wish to discuss with you, but our recommendation would be that you look carefully at the appeal of your review to women.'

The whirring of the projector ceased as she flicked its switch. There was a heart beat of silence in the darkened room, before Callum turned the lights on.

Alec said, 'That's where the money's going to be then. That's where advertising's going. Wealth is with women,' he announced, in a lugubrious tone from his jowls.

Annie suppressed a smile but could not resist meeting Stella's eye. Rachel doodled a power-woman on her pad, one foot resting on a played-out male. She was a beautiful, rounded, olive-skinned woman, with a severe crew cut and a penchant for black jeans and alley-cat footwear. Her journalist husband had been made unemployed at the depth of the recession. They discovered they could meet their bills on her salary alone. Now he was writing the biography of an obscure eighteenth-century scientist on the kitchen table, which was stretching to 250,000 words as day followed amiable day. 'The harder I work, the more fascinating this bloody dead boffin becomes,' she muttered once, before retreating into her habitual, loyal silence.

'I don't think this news comes as such a shock to us women,' Annie ventured. 'We seem to be living proof of the statistics.'

'Bloody women,' muttered David, the Deputy Editor. 'Taking over, they are. It's like a fucking science fiction novel.'

'Heh, heh, heh,' Alec mirthlessly approved the comment from his jiggling belly. 'We may fight them in the corridors, lads, but with an eye on our circulation, we've got to put some more female stuff in. Fashion. Shopping. Stuff like that. You girls,' he said, turning to address the sofa, 'I'm putting you in charge of this.'

'Thanks, Alec,' said Stella. 'Something told me you would.'

Alec's barking infiltrated Annie's mind only in fits and starts, though he waffled on interminably about viewing this analysis as the key for redressing the disappointing fall in circulation, blah de blah. Annie was thinking of the additional work required by the repositioning of the supplement, calculating where she might steal the time. If she caught the seven o'clock train, she would arrive at her desk at eight thirty in the morning. But she would leave the house before Emma awoke, as well as returning after her bedtime.

How ironic! She was one of an army of women whom men now envied, because, unlike them, she had a job. She was one of an army of women who had reduced motherhood to a weekend treat. This was not as she had foreseen. Instead of feeling smugly triumphant, she felt sad and spent, as cross and bewildered as Alec and David and Callum. Chris joked that he was becoming Mr Mom. But as for her, she was turning into her father.

Chris knew the first law of supermarkets: that the trolley you picked would be unsteerable. His listed so violently to the left that he felt as though he were undergoing a work-out while he shopped.

He picked out a medium-sized jar of supermarket brand coffee. It took him some time to find the granulated sugar, which had been moved during a 'reorganisation to rationalise your store', as the notice informed him. He added a large bottle of gin because it was 'only £18.99' and Annie, on occasion, enjoyed a gin and tonic in the evenings: moreover, their finances were growing healthier, or so she had told him. In a weak moment he treated himself to a four-pack of beer. He felt guilty, like a dypsomaniac caught taking a swig. He quickly scooted Emma up the aisle to find her fizzy drinks, ice creams and crisps.

The bill came to £37, which was unexpected. He extracted the joint cheque book from his breast pocket. He felt guilty at spending unnecessarily, as he always did. But they didn't have many treats. They deserved the odd one. He had a vague feeling that the account was sliding towards the zero figure. He had better be careful next week. He didn't tot the figures up on the stubs, never had, it seemed mean-spirited and fuddy-duddy. Moreover, he was ever conscious that he was spending Annie's money, and he really preferred not to know the sum total that he felt, by his own code, that he now 'owed' her.

* * *

Stella swept the curtain back from the changing booth.

'Da-daa!' she trilled.

She was wearing a stone linen halter-neck dress that was so quiet it screamed money. The price tag dangled heavily from the neck. Annie examined it, whistled.

'Phil's paying for this,' Stella smiled. 'Though he doesn't know it yet.'

'It's wonderful,' said Annie.

'Why don't you get one in another colour?'

Annie looked at her. 'Are you growing horns and a tail? How can my nice girlfriend turn into the tempter and father of all lies in the twinkle of an eye?'

'Aww! Whose money is it, Annie? Loosen up, girl. Live a bit.'

'I do need cheering up,' she said, smiling. 'I'll just try one on,' she added, sweeping a black version from the nearby rack.

Annie sat at the kitchen table sipping her gin.

'You look lovely, Mummy,' said Emma who was allowed to stay up late on Fridays to see her mother. Annie had rushed upstairs to change into the halter neck when she got home, to show Chris. He whistled appreciatively when she reappeared.

'It was real expensive,' she said, as if she expected him to bluster.

He was frying omelettes on the Aga. Tipping one onto a plate with a waiterly flourish, he brought it to the table. 'You haven't bought yourself a dress in eighteen months. You look great. You deserve it,' he said.

Emma snuggled into the crook of her arm. Annie kissed the top of her head. Her hair was mouse coloured, silky soft and smelled faintly of medicated shampoo. She wriggled, gazing out of the window at a bright moon hanging in the clouds above the dark garden.

'If I could have an adventure, I'd go to the moon,' she said. It was Emma's favourite wish to have an adventure, and Annie had been planning a quest for her birthday in August, hiding clues in the country-side that would lead her to some magic piece of treasure. She thought this would be her last chance. Next year, Emma would not believe in magic any more. But when she had mentioned it in the office, someone had rolled their eyes to heaven and said, 'You can't do that. She's got to live in the real world.'

'What would you go on?' Annie asked her.

'A silver unicorn with unfurled wings. A silver unicorn with a golden horn.'

'I knew equines would come into it somehow,' Chris said.

'If I went to the moon, I would dance along a gossamer thread spun by a sorcerer's spider,' said Annie.

'You'd take me, wouldn't you? You wouldn't leave me behind?'

'Of course I'd take you, as long as you held tight to my hand.' Annie squeezed her.

'Bleu-uh! Don't strangle me first.' Emma pretended to gasp.

Chris began to crack more eggs into a bowl one-handed, keeping up a television chef commentary. Annie settled back in her chair and sipped her contentment. There was nothing so very wrong between them, she thought. Nothing, after all, that they could not work out.

Chapter Three

Annie folded the soft sheets of newspaper up, and returned them to a brown envelope marked, 'Boyd, Susan (née Wright), Athlete; married, 1981, Andrew Boyd'. In three envelopes, all the articles ever written about Susan Boyd were stored by the cuttings library. Not a bad quantity, Annie thought. After all, some lives were contained in one slim, little-thumbed envelope, and the previous folders on Susan Boyd had been fat, for the late seventies and early eighties had been the years in which she was successful, a gold medal winner.

She had faded from the public consciousness when she retired, as they all do, until finally she had dwindled into a figure who appeared occasionally on second-rate television quiz shows, sitting in a booth reading her scripted spontaneous remarks. She was grateful when they asked her on.

Then, last month, her photographic likeness had stared anew from the front pages, but unsmiling now, unimpressed by her fresh importance. Her husband and three children under ten posed with her. Susan Boyd, the one-time golden girl of British athletics, was fighting her last brave battle. Susan

Boyd had incurable ovarian cancer.

'This is a great story,' Alec announced. 'A real womb trembler. Women will love it.'

Annie had written her a letter: Susan wrote back. Yes, she would do the interview if it would help other women. Annie was due there this afternoon.

She packed her notebook, tapes, recorder, spare batteries.

Al, the photographer, lingered by the lifts. 'Come on, Mrs Greene,' he yelled in his estuary adenoidal whine. 'Let's go and cheer ourselves up with this jolly job. Anything's better than being in the office.' Then, as Stella passed him, 'Hello, gorgeous, will you commit adultery with me?'

'Not now, Al,' she said. 'Ask my secretary for an appointment.'

Al was in his mid-forties. You knew that without asking because his appearance was caught in a time warp. His hair was curly and shoulder length, he wore an earring in one ear and an Indian, beaded necklace twisted twice round his wrist. It was the uniform of his heyday, in the seventies, and he clung to it still, labouring under the misapprehension that this made him look young. In fact, he looked like a fat and sagging roadie for a sixties rock group, in his rumpled jumpers and camouflage trousers with lots of pockets to hold the small fiddly paraphernalia of photography.

He was a nice ordinary blokish bloke who was doing better than he had ever anticipated so that, incongruously, he lived in some style in a sprawling 'tween wars mansion in stockbroker belt Surrey. He had five children, the eldest twenty, the youngest two, and a jolly round wife whom he adored. The elder girl teased him about his growing bald spot and made it clear she considered him as much of a dinosaur as he had ever considered his father. He told Annie this in mild surprise. Annie was fonder of him than any of the other men she worked alongside.

Now, she sat silently as his Volvo inched patiently through the London traffic. 'All right, kid?' said Al, amiably, and was happy to turn his concentration to the road when she murmured, 'mmmm,' distractedly. Annie was trying to put herself in Susan Boyd's position, imagining how her tuned and trimmed body had betrayed her, the cancer threading through its channels, like silent mould in a house.

Susan Boyd was dying in a bungalow in Kent.

An hour and a half after leaving London, Al turned into the road that led to Radhurst, past an old lodge house that was being restored, past an oast which had long since been converted, past playing fields where a mongrel gambolled, unattended. The sun was out again, a mild but milky yellow warmth, transforming the muddy English countryside with its promise, sending light and shade frolicking under the trees with their fresh green leaves. Pale-faced daffodils in the verges bobbed before it, like coy crinolined girls.

Annie had interviewed Susan Boyd many years previously. She recognised the scenery, the yellow-brick bungalow with the gravel drive and the garden with its preponderance of conifers, some golden, some blue, some shaggy, some dwarf. There was a rock garden and fish pond round the back.

The front door was of 'obscured' glass. It was opened, before they rang the electric bell, by Andrew, Susan's husband, her manager, too, though the title had always seemed an honorary one in that his duties were few and far between. He smiled. He'd always been a friendly man.

'Susan's in the lounge,' he said nodding. And there she was, also smiling, only a little thinner than Annie remembered her.

The interiors didn't seem to have changed in the ten years since Annie had last been there. The Boyds were careful people, and kept all their possessions so meticulously that they did not seem to wear out or become stained or discoloured. Susan had never amassed as much money as some of her male contemporaries. She had a sharp, rather unphotogenic face, which had affected her earning potential: she had never appeared in a television advertisement, for example.

Somewhere in the early eighties, the Boyds had bought a three-piece, velour suite and a cabinet with leaded lights and Georgian-style moulding. The carpet was fitted and beige. Somewhat incongruously juxtaposed with these items were the shiny, ostentatious medals and cups by which Susan measured success. These sat next to a flotilla of family snapshots in silver-plate frames, behind the fake, leaded lights, for ease of dusting.

These last fifteen years in England had made Annie familiar with the rules by which people like the Boyds lived. So, when she was shown to a chair and handed a cup of coffee, she knew better than to put it down on the leather-topped 'occasional' table until a special circular mat, intended to protect polished surfaces from heat rings, was fetched from its drawer.

Susan Boyd was dying as she had lived. She ate frugally, drank hardly at all. The Boyds had raised parsimony to an art form.

'We don't intend to change our life style now,' Susan explained. 'We've never been ones for going out much, socialising, that sort of thing. I've got my routine. I get up every morning at nine, bathe, and rest in a chair with a magazine, or I watch the soaps on telly. Books? No. I don't have much call for books. And then, mid-morning, Andrew dusts and vacuums round me.'

'She's always kept a nice home,' said Andrew from his corner. 'I'm not going to let her down now.'

'I have my standards,' said Susan with a laugh.

'Did you do it all, then?' asked Annie, keenly. 'When you were competing – did you still run the house, do the cleaning?'

'Ooh, yes,' said Susan, surprised at the question. 'I believe in a man helping but I'm no feminine whatsit – what do they call it? – no women's libber. Oh, I don't mind him helping with the washing up and the shopping. But I draw the line at ironing, don't you? And laundry. I couldn't fancy a man who washed my knickers. Most women couldn't, could they?

'I don't mean now of course,' she added quickly, nodding to her husband. 'Now is different. Needs must. But I still try to help him with the ironing. He'd burn great holes in the children's clothes otherwise,' she said with an explosion of a laugh, as if she had said something funny.

She fell silent. The gas fire hissed from its central position in the fake, stone fireplace. It was stifling in the room, but Susan appeared not to notice.

'Can you cope, Andrew? Will you be able to cope? With the children and the house . . .?' Annie didn't know how to finish the sentence.

'I'm teaching him,' Susan interrupted proudly. 'I teach him a new recipe every night. You've got quite a reper-tree now, haven't you? Not just things like beans on toast or fish fingers, neither. He does a lovely curry. Really tasty. With raisins and things innit.'

'You should try it sometime,' Andrew averred from his corner. "Course, we don't do much entertaining now.'

'No,' said Susan bleakly. 'Not much to celebrate. Mind you,' she added firmly, 'we never did.'

Annie talked with them for an hour, two, changing the batteries, flipping over the tape. 'I hope to die in my own home, in my own bed,' Susan said. 'I have a Macmillan nurse coming in now to give me pain relief, and she'll be with us till the end. I've got everything organised. I feel I have to tie the ends up. I've told the children. I don't know if the youngest understands. She said, "How long will you be in heaven, Mum?" Little love. Anyway, we're keeping to the usual routine.'

Al, as always, sat in a corner meditating, until Annie finished and then he sprang to his feet, shepherding his subjects into his artificially assembled photographs. Al would never win an award and probably didn't aspire to; he simply wanted to earn his living and keep his family in anglo-bourgeois style.

On the return journey, they were uncharacteristically quiet, the pair of them. Normally, after completing an assignment, they were merry and chattering. Today, Annie was trying not to cry.

'How can they do it, Al? How can they spend her last weeks so domestically? Why don't they go, and see, and do, and laugh, and drink into the night – all the things you'd want to do if you knew time was running out . . .'

'Each to his own, kid. Everyone copes with it in their own way.'

'I suppose so. I suppose you're right. Other

people's marriages are incomprehensible, aren't they?'

She turned back to the scenery flicking by. She felt as if she had seen apparitions in the room that the Boyds themselves affected not to notice; as if the Angel of Death strode into their neat little bungalow and stood in the corner of their lounge, his terrible wings unfurled; and Andrew Boyd said to Him, 'Please move your feet. I want to Hoover under them.'

Annie had looked at the dark face of the angel and it was implacable. He could not be dusted away. Death was always a mystery, not a problem of organisation, not something so banal, try as you might to reduce it with frantic activity. She shivered.

'All right, kid?' Al asked.

'What? Yes. I'm fine . . . I suppose I was just thinking how lucky I am.'

Al smiled and patted her knee. He was one of those rare men who could pat a knee platonically. 'Yeah,' he said with a bleak laugh, 'I don't suppose I'll beat the missus up tonight.'

It was a difficult article to write. Annie asked Alec if she might take the office portable home and work on the kitchen table, where she transcribed the tapes and fretted over each word, weighing them not only for their impact on the readers but on Susan herself. Annie was conscious of her responsibility to Susan, of not hurting her further by misinterpreting her. And there was the problem of Susan herself, in many ways. Her approach to death was not the stuff of high drama, not the 'womb trembler' Alec had envisaged at all. It was something much sadder than that.

Annie interpreted what Susan had said and hadn't said as sensitively as she was able. Her satisfaction had been in the composed pleasures of everyday life, like all women, she was much prouder of her children than her own achievements. It seemed to Annie that Susan's chief fear, which she was trying to avoid by being as normal a mum as possible, was that her children would not remember her. Given their ages, this seemed entirely likely.

When the feature appeared, it seemed to strike a chord with the readers. The cancer charity Annie had mentioned received £3,000 in donations which they ascribed to the publicity. And Susan wrote to Annie, a warm, grateful letter. 'Andrew's going to keep the article safe, and when the children are old enough they can read it and see what I was really like and what I really wanted for them. Thank you, Annie.'

Annie was touched by this letter but it also left her feeling achingly sad. It seemed so pathetic that when Susan's children asked, 'What was Mum like?' the answer would be provided by a journalist who scarcely knew her because their own father was too inarticulate, too vacuous, to describe Susan to them. It was difficult, too, to decide whether Susan was aware of Andrew's inadequacies. Was she tolerant, forgiving, especially as she looked into the moist, black mouth of the grave? Or did she sometimes wonder why she had married him and wish that she had shuffled him off earlier, to wreak fun with someone sparkier?

Annie admired magnanimity. It was a quality she craved for herself. She wanted to wipe Chris's slate clean. She made a private resolution. She would be generous, like Susan. She would close her eyes. She would bite her lips. She was going to mend her marriage.

There was a week in which she bit back every

comment and tried to be as nice as pie. It was a particularly trying time. Chris had a heavy cold and like most men seemed to exaggerate his discomfort. At the end of the week, she realised that he hadn't registered her efforts to be considerate.

One Saturday morning, in April, when she was lying in, Chris picked all the red tulips from the garden, where they made such a brave display, and placed them in a vase by her side of the bed. She said thank you and awarded herself a pat on the back.

'Don't say I never give you flowers,' he said lightly, kissing her on the forehead.

She was suffused with optimism. 'Chris,' she said, sitting up in bed, sipping at the coffee he had also brought her, 'I think we should talk.'

His stance altered. 'Oh, God. What about?'

'Don't be so defensive.'

'Normally, "I think we should talk" is a prelude to a row,' he said.

The tide of irritation rose within her. She managed to control it and continued. 'I was looking at the horses in the barn the other week and it set me thinking. Why don't you go for it? Why don't you start sculpting again?'

He stared at her. 'Er, what with, Annie? Where? It's not exactly something I can do on the kitchen table, like you.'

She rushed to interrupt him, enraptured by her vision of the happy future, trying to infect him with it. 'We'll rent somewhere. I'll help you get started. When I've paid everything off, I mean. But that would be the aim. The dream. As it once was. After all, what is it the Chinese say? Something about opportunity lying on the other side of disaster?'

'Don't patronise me, Annie,' he said curtly. 'I

thought you would have realised that running my own business again doesn't hold a lot of appeal.'

She subsided, hurt and angry.

'And don't you be so damn ungrateful, Chris,' she told his back as it retreated down the corkscrew stairs. 'I was only trying to help. And,' she couldn't stop herself from adding, 'I prefer the tulips growing in the garden.'

A curious thing happened then. When she was away from him, most usually on the home leg from work, she looked forward, just as she always had, to seeing him again. But when she was with him, she avoided looking at him, averted her eyes from his. Even when she kissed him hello, she looked over his shoulder. And he hers.

She felt spent. For the past two years it had been her responsibility – to her own mind, anyway – to stoke him with spare enthusiasm which she would dig out from her own heart. But she had never been able to lift his spirits for long, and now she was tired out by the effort. She was tired out by him.

At weekends, she took Emma on walks, took her to the local swimming pool, read *The Borrowers* to her. 'I must spend time with Emma,' she said, and he agreed. It was his Achilles heel, the one thing he could not deny her. In the deepest parts of her mind, however, she knew that this brand of diligent motherhood was not completely what it seemed. But she didn't stop to look or to analyse. She was frightened of what she might discover.

They niggled each other. It was astonishing, really, how petty they could be. Annie was aware, because of her parents, that this was how marriages disintegrated. Two adults, seemingly mature and making a convincing fist of self-confidence, reduced to point-scoring. Many a time, as a teenager, she had wondered why her mother hadn't pulled herself together. She was such an intelligent woman and she had behaved so childishly. Well, now she knew. There was nothing you could do about it.

Some of her grievances were worth the stating. But others? How could she grow so peeved over such trivialities? 'This house! Can't find a damn thing in it!' She flounced from room to room, dramatically. Mom had had a tantrum about a lesser domestic disorder at least once a month, shouting and slamming drawers and doors, hurling cushions across rooms, and, in extremis, breakable items. Annie had never expected to be offering a parody for her own family's entertainment twenty-five years later. She hated to think what Emma would make of her when she was older, objective.

As a child, she herself had felt sick with fear at these sudden thunderous maternal outbursts; as a teenager, contemptuous and judgemental. She lay on her bed beneath her arty posters and her shelves of earnest fiction and she fingered the edge of sour thoughts – how it was no surprise that Dad had left them for Patricia; how it was Mom's fault that he had fled to the other end of the continent so that she, Annie, never saw him.

It was dusk. She snapped on the lights in the sitting room and one of the bulbs pinged like a bell and went dark. Annie sat at her desk and massaged her temples. She was looking at a photograph of Emma, a smile smeared across her face like chocolate ice cream. There were no photographs of Mom on display, not anywhere in the house. Odd, that. If she could somehow profile herself she would find the omission telling.

The local newspaper lay in the wastepaper basket

next to her. One of the situations vacant had been circled in blue pencil. Even this had caused a quarrel. It was for a post as a care assistant, working with handicapped adults, which – Annie could quite see – would suit Chris, with his wry compassion and his ability to make people like him, but although it was only for twenty hours a week, it involved night and weekend working. The advert was unequivocal.

'You can't go for a post like that,' she had wailed. He knew her job expanded late into the evenings and into weekends, sending her abroad from time to time, brusquely, at a moment's notice.

He had crumpled the writing paper in his hand with a violence that perturbed her. 'Do you know the only jobs I can go for then, Annie? If I'm to be here to take Emma to school and fetch her home? Cleaning jobs. That's all. There's nothing else in the paper. Take a look.'

He spun it across the desk towards her.

She bridled. 'It's not my fault, you know. I didn't choose to take this goddam sixty-hour-a-week job. A job that means I hardly see my daughter . . .'

Annie flinched at her memory. Emma had been upset. They had caught her lingering at the sitting-room door, listening to them, frowning, her face worried, as a child's face should not be. Chris, in his attempt to divert Emma, had been a little too brisk.

'What are you doing down here? You're supposed to be tidying your pit,' he had roared.

And he had marched Emma up the steep spiral of the oak staircase. Annie had listened, cringing rather, to his realistically stern amazement at how little had been done. Then they found a bowl with the remains of a stash of play dough made with flour and salt and water and dyed with cochineal. It was rather old and going off.

'What's that?' Chris asked appalled, as he gingerly slid the bowl from under her bed. He turned his head away from the smell.

Emma pulled an exaggerated face, mouth pulled wide, bug-eyed.

'It's life, Daddy, but not as we know it.'

After that, Chris had pretended to cuff her and they had both laughed and Emma had returned to her task, tunelessly warbling the *Star Trek* theme music.

So it had turned out quite well.

Annie began to slice open a stack of brown envelopes with the edge of a pair of nail scissors which were not supposed to be used for cutting paper but often were, because the scissors for the job had disappeared. Emma said she thought they might have Borrowers. Annie said she thought Borrowers would have taken the nail scissors – 'more their size' – and left the paper scissors for the human beans. She found she entered her daughter's imaginative world without effort, returned to childhood by her, slipping from one world to the other, observing the conventions of either automatically. It was one of the best things about parenthood.

She wrenched her mind back to the matter in hand, spreading the statements and the month's bills in front of her. The old sick feeling of panic gripped her hard on her elbows, punched her in the stomach. There must be some mistake.

She pulled out the right-hand drawer in which she kept the calculator. It wasn't there. She scrabbled under papers, in the middle drawer, the bottom. There it was, inexplicably perched on the telephone directory.

For half an hour she sat punching in numbers, impartial numbers that had the power to shake her like the gusting wind. Clickety-click: the printer whirred. Each month, she sat here and went-through-the-finances: it was her ritual, her proving to herself that things were improving, that the years of sacrifice were bearing fruit. When Chris had ceased trading they had made a pact to pay off all his creditors themselves, and so they had done, month by month, the small firms first. It was a matter of honour to them. One of the reasons for their own predicament was because he had not been treated so honourably by others, people he had trusted, some of whom were supposed to be friends.

Each month, Annie sent a cheque here or there and the debt – she regarded it as an alien growth, a malignancy to shrink steadily, drip by drip – was reduced, so that now it was down to around £5,000.

But now, here, these figures – this inflated electricity bill, this credit card statement informing on her silly shopping spree, the unexpected overdraft – these meant she had already overspent her salary. A letter from the tax man told her he was running out of patience. She had been stalling his latest payment. It had all gone wrong.

Chris appeared, placing a coffee by her left elbow. The steam rose, coating her cheek in stinging moisture. He returned, a moment later, with a new light bulb. When he had screwed it in, she handed him the joint bank statement. She felt her resolve falling, spiralling, spinning away, as if she had dropped it from a great height.

'How the hell did you manage to spend so much?'

They stared silently at the figures on the page: £1,172.45 OD. The precise sum to the last penny, stated so smugly, as if the computer that printed it was flaunting its mathematical ability. He said nothing. He looked like a schoolboy caught smoking behind the bike sheds. Once, she had found that habitual expression of his endearing. Now, she wanted to hit him.

'How could you? How could you?'

'I haven't been squandering money on myself, Annie,' he protested.

She remembered the pack of beer he had been drinking, and suddenly resented each thick, bitter drop trickling down his throat: she hurled the memory at him as if it were a glass.

A little voice at the back of her head said, calm down, Annie, you're blowing this up out of proportion, deal with this rationally, but the little voice was drowned by a loud angry voice that sounded like Mom's.

It expanded, this argument, as their arguments always did. She was so cold, she never showed her affection, never held him.

'Of course I don't hold you. I don't want to fucking hold you. I feel you're like . . .' don't say it, Annie, don't say these words you'll regret . . . 'like a dead weight round my neck.'

The words lay between them and both were aghast at their ugliness.

The words travelled upstairs to Emma's room where she was now drawing. She put her hands over her ears and rocked back and forth for a while. This did not work. After a few minutes, she began to write on a clean page in her children's sketch pad. She tore it out, with difficulty, so that its edge was drunkenly saw-toothed; then, carrying it in her hand, along with the mug of milk she had been drinking, she crept down the stairs.

The enclosed staircase was steep and winding and she had been told to always go carefully on it as it

49

had been built many hundreds of years ago when people did not know so much about safety. She went slowly now, but because she was frightened. She was frightened to stay in her room to listen to the shouting and she was frightened to come down in case they began to shout at her.

At the doorway she paused.

Emma darted into the room in the silence which now seemed unbreakable between them, into the pool cast by the light above them, as the gloom deepened outside the windows. She lay her piece of paper on the rug and scampered back to the door, turning to look at them. The milk in her mug slopped over the edge and dribbled on to her bare foot.

On the paper was written in bright purple felt pen, 'Dear Mummy and Daddy please dont argew. I am sorry.'

Both of them turned to look at their daughter. Tears streamed down her face, pale except for the bulb of her nose which was red with her crying. Her shoulders shook. She raised the mug in her fist, which was still dimpled, the bones seemingly still soft and pliable.

'Cheers,' she implored them. 'Cheers, Mummy and Daddy.'

'Oh, God.' Annie's heart stung.

Chris picked up the sheet of paper and stroked it smooth, as if it were Emma herself. Afterwards Annie wondered why he didn't go to her, why neither of them did for that first moment.

Chris looked at her across the pool of light, across the sitting room. She was keenly aware of the distance. He looked inexpressibly sad.

'This can't go on, Annie,' he said softly. 'You know this can't go on.'

Chapter Four

''Ere you are, dear.'

The thin, painted door swung open, revealing the dim inner world of bedsit land. Stella marched into the room, screwing up her face. 'Bet you never thought you'd be flat hunting again,' she muttered.

'I've never done this before. When I came to England I moved right in with Chris,' Annie said. She had never before lived alone. She had lived with her mother, then, at college, in the square buildings at the back of the campus, then with Chris. Perhaps she wouldn't handle this well? Had she considered that? Of course not. She hadn't thought anything through properly; not in the way she assumed adults should or would; other adults, that is, people one saw on the subway and in buses, people who looked, and presumably acted, their age.

'Good bit of carpet that,' said Mrs Harris, the owner of the house, following them in, indicating the swirls and whirls in busy browns and bronzes. 'Handy, that pattern. It don't show the dirt.'

Annie had not heard that expression in years. It was the more surprising as Mrs Harris was not old. She appeared to be fortyish and was lumpen, with a pale face, a fuzz of yellow permed hair and a tight short skirt. She should have looked jolly but the jowls of her face contrived not to.

Annie turned her attention to the rest of the room. A crowd of plates, pictures and statues adorned the white pearly anaglypta wallpaper. The pictures, in cheap wooden frames, were amateur oil paintings and watercolours that looked as if they might have been executed by Mrs Harris or members of her family, and featured a preponderance of odd cats; misshapen, lumpen as their mistress, posed in anatomically impossible positions. The commemorative plates featured royal weddings, seaside towns and Jesus walking on the water. Several large crucifixes, with ketchupy blood on palms and feet, hung in focal positions. The contrast between Mrs Harris's worldly appearance and the excessive, forbidding religiosity of the flat she offered for rent was startling.

A divan, pushed against a wall, with cushions ranked along it, served both as bed and sofa. In addition, there were several armchairs in green moquette, and a battered oak table by the French windows. A tessellation of heat rings marred the surface. Clearly, Mrs Harris did not fish out the coasters when she had visitors.

Outside, Annie could see a rectangular patch of grass surrounded by a narrow flower bed in which orange marigolds, magenta busy lizzies and silver wormwood marched in consecutive rows. A revolving washing line was planted in a block of concrete in the dead centre of the lawn. This was the cheapest of the flats in the classified column which she had marked and the first that she had looked at. She knew that Stella was anticipating a long afternoon driving her from one to another.

Mrs Harris opened a low cupboard. 'Sheets,' she said. 'Blankets.' The sheets were nylon. Annie bit at a snag nail on her left forefinger. She hated nylon sheets.

Mrs Harris sashayed up to a door. 'My peese dah resistance,' she announced as she opened it and ushered them through into a kitchen, and thereby, by the narrowest inner lobby, to a windowless bathroom. Both were poky, both cheaply fitted out.

'Seventy-five a week. Cash,' she said. 'You won't find cheaper than that around here.'

'I'll take it,' Annie replied, and registered Stella's astonishment on the back of her neck even as she ducked out of the room to pay the £300 deposit that Mrs Harris now requested, apparently against her future self making off with the threadbare moquette chairs or daubing graffiti on the sheeny-shiny walls.

She had left the cottage a week previously. They had sat for hours, she and Chris, that night, after they'd settled Emma in their double bed upstairs, with the lamp on as she had asked.

'I can't bear to see her like that, Chris.'

'I know.'

'We're screwing her up with every row we have . . . This is it, isn't it?' Her voice wobbled.

He nodded. That really threw her. She had not quite expected him to endorse her pessimism.

'I thought you were going to tell me I was wrong,' she said. 'It sounds crazy but I hoped that things are not as bad as I think they are. I've been living in the hope that one final crisis will clear the air. The emotional cavalry thunders over the hill.'

Chris looked at her with fellow feeling, the first sign of empathy between them in weeks. They were both looking at each other. They no longer needed to avoid each other's eyes, wondering what they would see there, or what they might betray of their own shadowy thoughts.

'I think we should separate,' he said. He sounded so calm that she recoiled. But she was being ridiculous. Did she want him hysterical? Immature?

'I don't mean permanently,' he continued. 'Or I hope not. But I think it may be the only way we can restore some sense of perspective.'

'But who will look after Emma? I'll have to work, still . . .'

'Annie, that's why I think it should be you that moves out. Practically, it can't work the other way round.'

'But I can't leave Emma.' She blurted out her first thought. She hadn't mentioned leaving him. Until that point, neither of them had realised where her fundamental loyalty lay.

To his credit, he did not respond. 'You'd be here at the weekends. We actually need to be apart. For Emma's sake,' he added. 'Annie, think about it. She probably won't realise you're gone. You leave before she gets up. You get back after she's gone to bed. I know, I know,' he held up his hand. 'It's not what you want. It's not what I would have wished on you. But it's the pattern she's used to. It's much less disruptive for her than if I suddenly move out.'

There was no arguing with that. To do so would be to put her own wishes above Emma's welfare.

They had talked for hours after that, into the darkness of the night and to the aloof, indifferent jubilation of the dawn chorus, but they kept repeating the same words. How they felt, what they wanted, why it wasn't working. Understanding why did not actually help. They could trace the construction of their misery but they could not dismantle it. She was angry with him, and *wanting* to forgive him did not lead to forgiveness. She was angry for the past, that for a year or more, as his business dwindled, he had kept the failing figures a secret from her; month after month had hidden the bank statements and the business accounts. He had explained why a dozen times. He hadn't wanted to 'trouble her'. He thought 'things would get better'. His stupidity enraged her. He had left her to pick up the pieces. Each time she skipped off early only for the train home to be delayed, she swore at him. Each missed school nativity play and sports day was added to the list of grievances. She hadn't been ambitious. She hadn't wanted to emulate her father.

The new employment trends were beginning to attract comment elsewhere in the media. There had been an optimistic article in one of the broadsheets about the way in which men and women would share work and family responsibilities in the future. Young people, it said, were eager for the compromises involved. Annie wondered how they would react when they got there. Certainly, she was not trailblazing a path for others to follow. She was behaving like a man, the sort of man she had once despised, who attached importance to his pay cheque. There was an equation at the back of her mind. Chris should earn his share of her salary. Her dinner should be on the table. She was a replica of the man her mother had wanted to divorce.

Chris used to consider her with blind partiality. Now her husband – her other half in the apt English colloquialism – regarded her with objectivity. Once, seeing herself as he saw her, as someone worth loving, she had felt confident and optimistic. At the moment, she did not want to know what he thought of her.

So, Annie had telephoned Stella, who was the only

person in London with whom she could stay while she searched for something to rent on a short-term lease. They stressed those words. Short-term. Temporary. Won't last forever. When Emma woke, she kissed her and said brightly that she would be working so hard she would not see much of her this week, but they would go out somewhere special, to see the dinosaurs, perhaps, one weekend soon. Emma was clingy and suspicious. In the end, they had both assured her that nothing was the matter between them.

Annie had to take the train to Stella's because the car was finally inoperative. Two hours later she had stumbled from a taxi to Phil standing at the door, a barrow boy blond with a wide smile and a stiff drink in his hand which he passed to her immediately. They had been watching for her from their window. She had howled and howled and howled. She was crying for Emma, she was crying for herself, she was crying for her wasted hopes and her marriage, and for fear of the future. And a part of her was still crying for her mother and father and their wasted marriage.

For the course of the afternoon, Stella and Phil fed her gin and tissues, until they had frog-marched her to their spare bedroom. She lay in stupor until her dry mouth and heaving stomach woke her abruptly in the middle of the night. She tiptoed around the strange stairs, finding the bathroom, where she was sick, and the kitchen, where she opened every cupboard door before finding a glass for water. When she returned to bed, sleep had given way to more tears. The white pillowcase was soon alarmingly stained with whispers of black mascara, imprinted with the smudge of her lashes. Annie wondered if the stains would ever wash out. She could not even cry or puke without wondering if she was inconveniencing her hosts.

Stella and Phil had been staunch and dismissive of her thanks, but it was time to leave them. She was an intruder into the private world of a couple. It was only decent to get out swiftly, leave them to their right to nag, to loiter naked between bathroom and bedroom, to belch, to fart. To leave them to their mutual subjectivity.

She tried to explain this to Stella, sitting in the front seat of her tinny, battered hatchback as they left Mrs Harris's and the outer sprawl of the city, heading towards the newly smart borough where Stella and Phil lived.

'Of course you're a bloody pain in the neck,' Stella said directly. 'Much as Phil and I like you, you are an imposition. But, honestly, Annie, there's no need to hot-foot it out of our place into the first half-clean flatlet that turns up. And it's the back of beyond. What sort of a life are you going to have in the Tudorbethan suburbs?'

'I don't want a life,' said Annie, and her voice trembled out of her control once more. She gazed resolutely out of the window at an Asian supermarket next to the traffic lights where they were stopped. Newspapers in wire racks, fruit in crates, bags of smokeless coal were beached outside it. A pale labrador, tied to a ring near the door, whined persistently for its owner inside.

'I don't care what the flat looks like. The only thing that matters is that it's cheap – I can't believe that it's a bit less than my train fare. It's the right end of town for me. Once my car is fixed I'll be up that motorway every Friday evening.

'And the rest of the time, Mrs Harris and I can comfort each other. What a pair we'll make – she's renting out the bottom floor because her husband's left her. Here we are, two estranged women, sharing the creepiest house in north-east London.'

'You're not estranged,' said Stella firmly, 'You're going to work things out.'

'So we are. I'm glad you reminded me of that. Don't patronise me, Stella, I told you I'm in a foul mood.' She folded her arms and slouched in the car seat, feeling miserable and cold. 'I even talk like Chris. That's one of his phrases. "Don't patronise me." I heard it so often I thought I'd scream.'

Stella kept quiet for a mile or two, then pulling up by an off licence, said, 'And no, I don't want any money for your bleeding keep. But you can buy us a bottle of wine for tonight, instead.'

'OK,' Annie managed a smile. They both felt the need to mark her going with a social rite.

Unexpectedly, Mrs Harris made a ceremony of her moving in, as well, unlocking the flat's glass-paned door, which was round the side of the house, with something of a flourish. She carried three keys, which, together with a card label, were strung on a loop of twine. She handed them to Annie and said, 'These are yours now. For the duration.' Annie took them and said, 'Thank you,' as if they were a gift. She examined the label. It was blank.

'Why don't you unpack your bits first, and then come round for a cup of tea? Just to welcome you, like.'

'That's really kind of you.'

After Karen Harris left, she felt as lonely as a lost child. She dumped her two bags by the chest of drawers, resolving not to sit down, so depriving herself, she hoped, of the chance to work up a head of self pity. Instead, she examined the room, removing a plate of Charles and Diana from above the divan. In its place she pinned her last home-made mother's day card, a splodgy watercolour of a smiling stick woman, in garish colours, with the inscription: 'Youre the best'. She stood a framed photograph of Chris and Emma on the table. She did not wish to do more. The prospect of trying to make the room more like home offended her. She wanted it to feel alien. She wasn't going to belong here.

Chris and Emma, wearing paper hats from the Christmas crackers, pulled silly faces at her from the table. She hurt for Emma.

She unpacked her two cases of clothes, laying her shirts and underwear in neat piles in the chest of drawers. At home, there wasn't enough cupboard space for the both of them, and everything grew higgledy piggledy despite her best efforts.

So here is one benefit of single life . . . .

The flippant, random thought shocked her. How could she? How could she possibly think like that?

She got a cloth and 'creme' cleaner from the sink unit in the kitchen and began to scrub the bathroom, the lavatory seat and bowl, the taps and drains and plugs. She emptied the purple kitchen cupboards of their haphazard stocks of crockery and odd unmatching saucepans and cutlery, and wiped them inside and out, although they were spotless. When she had scrubbed away her thought, she had a back-ache and red hands.

Suddenly, Annie remembered Mrs Harris's invitation. Forgetting it was not the best way to endear yourself to your new landlady. She raced to the hall, the door, and through the alley to the back garden. She rapped at the kitchen window. 'I'm sorry I'm late. I was just . . .' She decided not to say what she had been doing in case Mrs Harris inferred some criticism. 'I was just sorting things out,' she finished lamely.

'Tea's stewed,' said Mrs Harris, pouring a mahogany stream into a mug for Annie, nevertheless. She took a tentative sip. It was bitter and lukewarm.

'Welcome to number thirty-nine,' said Mrs Harris glumly.

Annie sat down while Karen Harris slapped an iron over a basketful of dry clothes. Steam hissing, appliance gurgling, she prattled as she worked, telling Annie about herself and her situation, assuming her interest. Of Annie, or indeed, of anyone else, she seemed not to have the slightest curiosity. The dominant tone of her conversation was a complaining indignation, which did not vary to reflect the relative importance of each calamity. The bossiness of Mrs Watson next door was related in the same snivel as the infidelity of her husband, Ken, who had left with another woman after his business, as a carpenter, had 'gawn bust', in the recession.

At least Chris didn't do that.

'You say what you like,' said Karen Harris, though Annie remained silent throughout, merely nodding from time to time, which proved a sufficient prompt for renewing the stream of information, 'You say what you like, but if 'is business was going on, 'e'd still be 'ere. It's the government's fault. All this unemployment. Still, it was under the Tories we got to buy this 'ouse,' she added. 'Never have dreamed of it under the Labour.'

Ken had hacked the flatlet out of the reception rooms of the ground floor before running off. He'd sold Karen on the idea by playing on their need for more money. Perhaps he'd been planning it all, and the scheme eased his conscience.

There was a teenage daughter, called Tiffany, who was away with her nan out Epping way but would return next week. There was a twenty-year-old son called Daryl, who lived with his girlfriend, her children and her parents in the next postal district. But above all, there was trouble with the neighbours, who, Karen felt, looked down at her from the smug perches of their lower middle-class superiority.

'Why do you think they don't like you?' Annie hazarded a question.

'They think I'm common, that lot do. Well, you say what you like, but I'm not having it.' She slapped the iron down on an outsize pair of jeans and a seething curl of steam made its way, complaining, to the ceiling. She leaned towards Annie self-importantly. 'I know I'm common,' she announced. 'I know I'm common, but let nobody else tell me that.'

Chris didn't laugh when Annie rang him and recounted her day – not properly, though he gave a chuckle for form's sake. He was being polite, she realised, with another little contraction of hurt and fear; as if she were some stranger.

She had emphasised the awfulness of the statuary and pictures, which Karen Harris had picked up in a job lot when the old lady down the road had died – so Annie had discovered without asking. She had told him of Mrs Harris's lack of irony. But Chris had seemed awkward rather than amused. It was only when she put the receiver down that it occurred to her that he felt guilty about her being there. Perhaps he thinks I'm blaming him?

She considered dialling him again, but what to

say? Why should she worry about him and his feelings? Was he worrying about hers? The truth was that she did intend his discomfort. She didn't want him at ease with the idea of her in this shoddy place, where Emma wasn't and wouldn't even come visiting.

She hated him at times.

She sat on the divan/bed sawing fiercely with a long file at her splitting nails. A fat cat looked sleekly down at her. She knew, now, from Karen Harris's jabbering, that it was one of a tribe of cats, generation after generation, ever growing with adopted strays and new matings, that the lady from down the road had doted upon. Before her death, she had commissioned an artist, discovered through an exhibition in the local library, to paint her favourites, her petted darlings. How nice to be a cat. How simple and unworrying.

She thought of Ben, whom they had rescued from an animal shelter five years ago. No one else had wanted him, a middle-aged dog with bad breath and a habit, so the label on his cage said, of chewing up the post, shoes and other objects of his own choosing. Chris had said, 'I can't bear to leave him, Annie.' And she'd been glad. 'Neither can I.' They'd cured him of the chewing habit in a week, just by standing by the front door whenever the postman was due and flinging a quarter bucket of cold water over his back as he grabbed the letters. Messy but effective. This room, with all its feline faces, felt horribly undoggy.

Finally, Annie gave up the battle she had been fighting all day, all week. Through her mind, she ran a film of Emma, what she was doing now, at this instant, what she would have done this morning. She envisaged her getting up, the red pyjamas she would have worn, the smell of her, the feel of her winged shoulder blades through the warm brushed cotton. She imagined that she was holding Emma as she often held her in bed, side by side, one arm over her, their knees bent companionably in the same shape, like an interlocking puzzle.

Noticing the carpet, she registered that she had bent her head to her knees. She did, in fact, feel sick, the awful sick-with-fear that she had known as a child when her parents parted and her life was set spinning into a new shape over which she had no control. The twist in the stomach, the weak elbows, the dry throat, that sort of sick.

She was overwhelmed with a sense of waste. It was so unbearably sad. She and Chris had been such friends. They had lusted for each other, too – they had needed each other – but she did not regret the loss of those feelings, or not so much. What she deplored was that above and beneath every other attraction, they had been such good friends that they had had Emma, and then this regard had just withered. It was so pitiable. It was sadder than death. Andrew Boyd would not grieve more than she did.

But every time they had tried to form responsible plans, they'd been thwarted by schizophrenic personalities who seemed to dwell within them, and popped out, yelling obscenities, at the worst moments. They just weren't big enough to rise to the occasion. The trouble was that she could not work out how to be the wife Chris now wanted. Because he seemed to require some ultimate woman who would go out into the big tough world to work, yet be an unchanged girly at home, who, though tired and perhaps frightened – as she had often been when caught between Alec and the bank manager at their most bullying – would be cheerful at all times. Where was this woman? Go and try to find her, Chris, and if you do, please introduce her to me.

She realised now that she had been investing a sum in their coupleship. The hours she spent at work, the money she earned, these she had been giving to the idea of Mr and Mrs Greene. In return, she felt that it was now his job to provide emotional sustenance. He should be second guessing her moods because that was what a woman would do. A woman who is financially dependent on a man tippy-toes around him, carefully considerate. Annie was being her father, and Chris, despite his wry comments, was simply being a depressed man without a job. He was absorbed with his own failure.

The divan cover smelt of aniseed, of moth balls. She remembered lying in her father's spare room. She remembered both wanting her mother and resenting her, thinking, if I pretend I'm happy here, will it affect her more than if I tell her I'm lonely? How do I extract the most satisfactory response?

She hadn't been able to forgive her mother and she wondered if the capacity was beyond her. It might be a warp of her character, to flee rather than to forgive. Perhaps her love for Emma was the only pure and generous love she would ever feel? In which case, where did that leave her?

As far as she could see, she was no nearer to enlightenment than she had been a week and a half ago. She doubted that the distance between London and Cambridgeshire would provide it. The only benefit of their separation was the impossibility of arguing over an expanse of fifty miles.

The mattress was more uncomfortable than she

had anticipated. It was a narrow bed. She had not slept in a single bed for fifteen years.

At two forty-three in the morning, she got up and scrabbling in yet another unfamiliar cabinet in another unfamiliar bathroom, found her small phial of sleeping pills, and took two, seeking oblivion.

Chapter Five

Emma sat on her haunches under the boughs of the maple tree, swaying slightly through the effort of trying to keep very still. She was watching a thrush hammering a snail on one of the paving stones that marched across the lawn. *Crk, crk, crk.* A sharp sound. She bit her lip. She was not sure she wanted the shell to crack and the snail to be eaten. Poor snail! But the thrush was working so hard: he deserved a reward. Every now and then he stopped, and he cocked his head, his shiny, dark eye revolving. Emma knew he sensed her somehow, was waiting for her to move, and that if she did he would drop his meal and fly away. But she didn't want to frighten him, to make his little fluttering heart lurch. Birds were delicate, she knew.

There was the baby robin they'd kept in the box in the kitchen, feeding it at half-hourly intervals with meal worms. They had done so well. Five days it lived in the kitchen, growing bigger and stronger. And then, on the sixth day, when Daddy was talking about letting it go, it had died. She had watched Daddy feed it, the beak opening, a kite shape, a greedy shape. She had gone to put on her shoes. And in that space of time, while she was gone, the robin had died. When she returned and looked in on it, Bob the Robin lay stiff on its back. Daddy had said, 'Birds are delicate.' And Mummy gave her a stock cube box with cotton wool in it and dug a hole with the trowel and stayed for the funeral.

The shell gave with a crack. The sharp beak stabbed the plump moist flesh. The thrush flew away. Emma unfolded herself and paddled over to the stone, on which lay half a shell, mottled on the outside, smooth and golden on the inner surface. All that was left of the occupant was a trace of slime. Emma felt like crying.

Mummy had gone back to London just before tea in her car which Daddy had just mended. Mummy came home on Fridays and went to London on Sunday evenings. She had, Emma knew, another family in London. Another husband, another child. She wasn't sure what the husband was called, but the other child was a boy called Thomas, because Emma had heard Mummy mention him to Daddy. She had said, Thomas was teething and screamed all night. Although Emma knew that babies teethed, she still imagined him as an exact recreation of the only Thomas she knew, a boy in the class above hers, who was tall and broad and faintly frightening because he kicked his leather football at you hard and on purpose.

Mummy had gone back to Thomas. Emma did not understand why Mummy did not want to stay here any more. She did not know what she had done. She knew that Mummy had wanted a boy, because once before there had been one, or one expected. They had sat her down and said she was going to have a baby brother or sister, not for a while but by the time of her next birthday. But Emma knew her next

birthday was yonks away. She had tried to imagine
this baby; she tried hard to imagine loving it. But in
her dreams, she was on a beach with her parents
and the baby, and she began to cover its arms and
legs in the sand, the way Daddy did hers, but
somehow she did not stop and the baby was buried
in the sand and she couldn't find it. The dream was
mixed up with Mummy going to hospital and coming
back but without a baby. She asked where it was but
Granny, who was staying, said, 'Not now, Emma,'
and Mummy said, 'Leave her alone, Marjie,' so that
Granny had set her lips into a thin line before
stonking off to the kitchen to make a pot of tea.

Perhaps the baby had been in London all this
time? But it did not seem fair that he saw her five
days a week compared to Emma's two. The threat-
ened tears plopped down her cheeks onto the slab.
Daddy came out and found her and asked what she
was crying about. 'The snail,' she said, 'The poor
snail got eaten.' Daddy laughed and put his arms
around her and said, 'You soft heart, you,' in a kind
voice. And by the time she had had her bath and
been put to bed with a story, Emma herself almost
believed she had been weeping over the snail and not
over Mummy.

At the top of the hill, Annie paused for a moment,
pulling over to the side of the road, to look down at
the fields which cascaded away before her – the luminous, vivid rape, the young, green corn making
obeisance before the breeze. The wind blew the
stalks in waves, dark and light, dark and light, like
an invisible hand stroking a velvet nap. At the edges
of the fields, and in the verges, cow parsley tumbled
in the long grass. It had been a warm Easter and
although it had grown cooler and wetter since then,

already the silence buzzed with bees. In the distance, the village church bell tolled for evening service.

How quickly the inconceivable grows familiar! She was already accustomed to arriving on a Friday evening to Emma and the dog's rumbustious greeting, aware that tucked in her bag was a treat for both of them, as if she were a visitor. She picked her way around Chris's embarrassment: whole swathes of her life seemed out of bounds to his questions – he never asked her about her flat, how she was adapting, if she was lonely. The same guilt that clamped his mouth when she first moved out, clamped it still. These days, she talked about her personal life in the office, to Stella, and with her husband she discussed her work.

Annie favoured the idea of their seeing a counsellor.

Chris found it abhorrent.

It was his English male reticence, she told him, and he should try to overcome it. She was criticising him again. She subsided.

After that, she didn't press the point.

They slept in separate beds. The first weekend of their restructured lives, she had arrived wondering if they would still climb into their double bed. The idea was unsettling. During their last months together, they invariably fell asleep maintaining a distance between them. Once Chris actually said sorry when his arm accidentally fell across her as he turned over. It had got that bad. The idea of it continuing was awful.

On the other hand, the idea of it not continuing was awful, too. Because many a time she had lain there, on her back, the darkness pressing on her eyes, wishing that he would put his arm around her, wondering whether she should risk a rebuff by

reaching over . . . Whereupon her indignation would
bubble up again. Who was he to climb upon his high
horse? Why was she always the one to proffer the
olive branch?

On that Friday night, Chris said he wasn't tired
yet, and she should go up first. She was wrung out
by the week and fell asleep much quicker than she
had intended, with the lamp still on, as if she were
Emma in need of reassurance. In the small hours,
she woke. The neighbours' cockerel was crowing in
his coop, a muffled but persistent sound. The bed
was empty. She turned the yellow light out and lay
listening for the rooster. The sky bleached, to a
luminescent grey.

She was accustomed, by now, to insomnia. After
ten minutes, she got up, throwing her robe around
her shoulders, and padded onto the landing. The
guest bedroom door was slightly ajar and within she
could see the humped shape of Chris, curled under
the duvet on one of the single beds, the dog in the
crook of his knees. He was sound asleep, a deep,
rhythmically purring sleep, as if he didn't have a care
in the world. His ability to sleep throughout crises,
including those he had caused, had always
infuriated her. It was so male and so callous.

Don't brood, she told herself, do something. She
went downstairs and made a cup of coffee and sat
on the sofa she'd paid for – she did not forget to
remember that – and extracted from her briefcase
three articles which she had commissioned. But just
for a moment she sat in thought, aware of her
surroundings, looking at her sitting room with the
eyes of a visitor. Once, the appearance of this room
had been a source of pleasure. She had assembled
its components over some years, the massive royal
blue sofa with its plump cushions, the thick bright

71

rag rugs on the matting, the quilts over chairs, the North American primitive art, the photographs, the decoy ducks, which were massed on polished surfaces, crammed into the quirky corners of the inglenook, and on the shelves, the stacks of much loved books.

It had been a very carefully composed background to domestic bliss. Of course, now it was a little shabby, what with the scuffed paint, like the rest of the house. The money had run out before she'd gotten around to the kitchen or the bedrooms and today, even the rooms which she had so lovingly transformed were in need of further attention.

It was a very American room, she thought, and it was also – even she was aware of it – the statement of a child of divorce. The perfection of clutter was an attempt to impose order on life, to gather possessions and arrange them, just so. People could not be arranged so neatly. They fell from the place you had allotted them and they bled on the carpet. They were not there when you looked for them. According to the proverb, you couldn't take it with you. But it lied. Possessions were permanent, they went with you wherever you strayed. People were temporary. There wasn't a heap of difference between her and Susan Boyd in their mania for their interiors. Susan's mother had died when she was six, also of a virulent form of ovarian cancer, so the parallel was clear.

Sighing, she turned her attention to her work, firstly to a feature on single mothers. These were not, out of respect to the *Saturday News*' far Right readership, high-rise, teenaged mothers on benefit, but nice middle-class women who'd been left in the lurch by divorce. She pencilled a working headline on the copy: 'Is This The Future of The Family?'

There followed the usual case histories of fathers

losing contact with their own children. As an expert in the field, she recognised the truthfulness of the children's accounts. The women seemed to be coping well. Annie considered how she herself would deal with the practicalities if she and Chris divorced. Juggling the job and Emma would not be easy, but she would manage somehow – women always did. It occurred to her that for the price of Chris she could afford a trained nanny. Even Mary Poppins could not leach more money from her purse than Chris and his endless debts.

But she was being bitchy. He had wanted to find a local job, selling, driving, anything to make a contribution, but the best provision for Emma they could afford was a childminder. They sent off for the list approved by the local council and visited the trio who were near to Emma's school. The one they liked, the cheerful, open woman, with cheerful, open children, had no vacancies. Of the others, one was tired and wheezing, the other flushed and distracted, and both their television sets were babbling though it was first thing in the morning. A little girl being left by her mother began to cry. 'I don't want you to go,' she wailed.

So that was that. Chris had searched for a part-time job, but the posts available were uniformly for women. There was a bias here as forceful as any which excluded women from top positions. 'I make them feel uncomfortable,' he said after one interview with the woman who ran the local riding stables. 'They don't feel at ease with the notion of giving me orders. They think that if they gave a man a job he'd try to boss them around.' Annie felt sorry for him. She felt exasperated with him. She oscillated between familiar love – the wish to be reconciled – and fresh anger.

She knew she could manage on her own. She no longer felt disloyal for the hypothesis. The only twinge she suffered at revolving divorce in her mind was the thought of a future Emma in her future home, painstakingly acquiring her possessions and putting them on display. Somehow she found the idea heartbreaking, though she had never regarded her own behaviour as sad.

She had worked on the articles until Emma woke, then turned herself into a normal, happy mother, or as close an approximation as she could manage. Since that day, the pattern of her visits had become established. Various items of Chris's moved into the spare room permanently – his radio alarm, his combs, shirts, socks, underpants. She suspected he slept there during the week so as not to make her arrival so disruptive. But she didn't ask him.

In other ways, though, there was an improvement. They were able to discuss money. She felt ridiculously proud and adult about this. There was a gradual but steady diminution of The Debt, as they called it in an ominous tone, which matched the monstrous size and shape it had long held in their minds. Now it was dwindling into something tamer. Maybe when the weight finally left their shoulders, they would suddenly spring back into their former selves again? Standing tall, regaining the dignity they had lost? She lived in hope.

She was thirty-five. When she was little she had imagined being big meant feeling accordingly big. How much we think we'll change and how little we do. . .

She pulled her mind back to the present. She had better get back. She had all the Saturday and Sunday newspapers to read before tomorrow's conference. She had to wash her hair and iron her clothes. There was even less room for spontaneity in her life since she had left home.

Chris found it bruising to see Annie so bravely bright in her parting from Emma. He knew the true cost to her. Annie's love for her daughter was something beautiful. Sometimes, he wondered if they had loved Emma too much. They spun their world around her, the both of them. It was odd how much a child could distort the warp of your marriage. He had never realised, however, that he had been secondary to Annie until recently; the second-best object of desire, not the one loved equally. He had not, indeed, realised that she was now subordinate to Emma in *his* affections. *Quid pro quo.*

The nature of parenthood is to be vulnerable. You strip yourself bare. You have no defences. Should the child prove ungrateful, you will wither. Should the child – God forbid – die young, you yourself will no longer inhabit the earth, not in the same way as you did once. The best part of you is gone. There is no other link that you tie between yourself and another which is as brutally simple.

Marriage, he had come to believe, depended for success on wilful not thinking. The happily-married alter the truth; they doctor it. They render themselves blind. Otherwise they will see that it is a selfish business. They are adding and subtracting. Am I getting enough from this? And if the sum works out neatly, with a positive, they will quietly potter on. Substantiated by their spouse, they are reassured. But what a little thing it takes to make the sum come out differently! The having of a baby. The losing of a job. The telling of a few white lies.

Chris had once felt that he had let Annie down. He had been intensely guilty. But that is such an uncomfortable emotion with which to live. It is easier to hate than be shamed. So he had begun to hate Annie. He succumbed to little bouts of rancour, flipping his emotions. Now, the clarity of his love for her was pock-marked with pungent patches of anger.

He cooked some sausage and egg and ran a bath for Emma. It was easier without Annie around, that was the sad, plain truth. Practically and emotionally, he coped better without her demands.

The oddest thing was that he had no expectation of the future any more. Unemployment had drained off his plans as well as his confidence. If Annie had made her suggestion that he become a professional sculptor three years ago, his heart would have leapt with excitement. But she was too late. The timing was wrong. He couldn't do it any more. He didn't have the self-belief. He was not oblivious to her sporadic attempts to raise his morale; it was simply that he knew they were futile. He could quite see how irritating his listlessness must be, but he was unable to rouse himself. The fact was that he was frightened, pig sick at the idea that he was facing a lifetime of unsatisfactory labour; selling life insurance perhaps, or double glazing, like John from down the lane, fifty-two years old and made redundant, grasping at the first paid employment he was offered and loathing every minute of it. It seemed quite clear to Chris that at some point – when they could sort out childcare or no longer needed it – he was going to swap the drudgery of dusting for the unctuous monotony of a service industry job. He couldn't bear to look at his future self.

Being dissatisfied with himself made him querulous, yet he was the only company he had. Apart from the school run, he could quite easily spend his day within the cottage, seeing no one. There was as yet no place in the social life of the village to accommodate the house husband. He was not invited onto committees where doughty women reigned. So he was forced onto his inner resources just when these were at their lowest. And the solitude only increased his lethargy. He did not want company. Unexpected visitors were unwelcome and made to feel it.

There was a rap at the door. He answered it with a towel in one hand and one sleeve rolled. It was Pamela Henderson, a neighbour, a woman in her fifties who wore chain store leggings and market stall T-shirts despite having the backside of an elephant. This was a rock of a woman who helped out on the parish council and with the church flowers and the fund raisers, who sewed, did patchwork, knitted and made collages, who brewed wines, baked breads and bubbled jams on her hob, and generally lived a life the village judged so constructive and admirable that they forgave her the sharp edges to her personality, her gossiping tongue, her habit of searching for a put-down in their every innocuous phrase, for she suspected, in her heart of hearts, that they didn't really like her. A village really is the best place to be for a woman with no job and no real, substantial self-confidence. She could fill her long, lonely hours, and pretend she was important, by living as Pamela Henderson did. All the same, Chris took his hat off to her. He knew how hard it was to muster the energy.

She had come to borrow some salt, she said, to assemble help for a village clean up – 'everybody out with a bin bag next Saturday' – and mainly she had come to ask after Annie. Chris was accustomed to the querying inflections in their voices when the neighbours mentioned her. 'Haven't seen her around for a while? Not ill, is she?'

There was little malice involved in this. The village simply wondered about one of its own. He felt rather churlish in denying them the information. But it would be far too painful to make their unresolved situation the subject of kindly gossip. The prayer group would doubtless include them in the weekly petitions. The young mothers would offer to help him in some way. And those who considered themselves intimate enough, which would probably extend to Pamela Henderson, would ask him solicitously how 'things' were going.

Chris gave Pamela the cup of salt and the cold shoulder. She looked disgruntled. 'Look, Chris,' she began officiously and he wilted. 'I know there's some would say it's none of my business but I'm worried about you two. I know I'm old fashioned. I like Ian working and me at home. I appreciate that young people today are different and Annie's ambitious, but I must say I think she's driving herself too hard. What about Emma? You two seem to have dropped out of village life completely. We never even see you down the Green Man anymore.'

Chris was struck dumb. He and Annie had hidden the real reason for their reversed roles so well that scarcely anyone knew of their private struggle. Even Chris's sister, Jan, had rung their parents to complain tearfully of his unfriendliness, how he and Annie refused invitations consistently. The truth was so prosaic yet no one guessed it. They could not afford the petrol for the drive to see Jan and her boyfriend. Moreover, they could not afford to return the hospitality. Unemployment left you unable to afford normal social communion. It left you so completely isolated that you came to prefer your own company.

'So we'll expect to see you and Annie on Saturday? Ten? Village Hall?' Pamela was intrepid as she stepped on your heart.

Chris smiled but did not acquiesce. He manoeuvred her from the door. He felt the urge to strike back.

'Love the leggings,' he called after her waddling behind.

She flushed. Chris felt like a right bastard. He had always regarded himself, intrinsically, as a good bloke, a chap's chap, straightforward, benevolent. He felt uncomfortable at his own transformation. And without his even being aware of it, somehow, in some way, he chalked up another grudge against Annie.

'Chris, I have some news.'

'I was just about to ring you.'

'Is everything OK?'

'It's nothing to worry about . . .'

Annie's hand tightened on the telephone receiver.

'Emma's had a virus that's going round. She was sick last night. High temperature. She's fine now. The doctor says lots of fluids and doses of Calpol.'

'Oh, my God. When you say she was sick, do you mean she threw up? Is she OK? Can I talk to her?'

'She's asleep. I'll ring you on the portable later so you can talk to her. Honestly, Annie, there's nothing to worry about.'

'Make sure she drinks a lot. And when she starts to eat, make it something light like chicken noodle soup. Or an egg. Lightly boiled.' She knew that she was questioning his competence but was unable to help herself. 'Shall I come down? I could drive down tonight?'

'What on earth for? I told you she's fine. I can manage.' He sounded irritated, but changed the subject. 'What was it you were going to tell me?'

'Oh. It doesn't matter. It was just . . . I paid off the major outstanding bills today. The tax man. The overdraft. They're both clear. I only have to pay off the loan account now. And the credit card. But I should be able to do that the month after next. Then we won't owe anything to anybody. That I'm aware of.' She added this from superstition, but it occurred to her that Chris might think it a dig. She added hurriedly, 'Well, you know the slimeballs are bound to claim some more,' and she laughed a fake laugh, an appeal for a truce.

'That's great, Annie.' He sounded genuine but curiously subdued. 'That's really great. Well done.'

She accepted his congratulation, as if it had been a single effort. She wondered why he wasn't as joyful as she had expected, why she herself felt a steady satisfaction but not the mad, capering relief she had imagined. She put it down to concern for Emma.

'I'll call you later so you can speak to Em.'

She put the phone down. It crossed her mind that if Chris wasn't testy, he was scrupulously polite to her. And she hardly knew which was worse.

Chapter Six

He was the most beautiful man she had ever seen, and he stepped out of the lift on the seventh floor. He had black hair, swept back, and very high cheekbones; his skin was a rich, dark gold. He walked past her, preoccupied; she doubted he even registered her presence.

Annie watched his grey silk shoulders disappear through the swing doors, as he passed beyond her awareness. She entered the lift and pressed the button down to the fourth. Formerly, she suppressed even a passing interest in other men, but that day, which was dull and drizzly to match her spirits, she allowed herself to carry his image back to her desk, and to describe it, giggling, to Stella, who sat opposite her.

'It's like a frigging hen party on this desk,' said Callum. He was leaning back in his seat at an extravagant angle that anyone less poised would not dare to attempt, smirking. Each of his thumbs were hooked through his red braces which he tugged, rhythmically and seemingly with great satisfaction.

'Red braces were right for the eighties, Callum. Wrong image for today's boy wonder,' she retorted.

'Gordon Gecko lives, heh, heh, heh,' he said.

Annie shook her head. She didn't understand him, he didn't understand her. The barrier of age and gender was fortified and impassable. The annoying thing was that he didn't care a jot that this was so, whereas she was non-plussed. Why? Why did she care?

Because, she thought, it's a sign to me, a little cryptic hobo's puzzle scrawled on the wall, comprehensible only to others of my type: you're turning into a woman of a certain age. To young men you're part of the scenery, not worth the noticing. You're on your sell-by date, girl. Soon only fiftyish men will think you worth making a pass at. Soon you'll be grateful that they do. These men with flabby paunches and noses reddened by broken veins, these men who don't apologise when they fart in bed.

At lunchtime, she went out and had her hair chopped off.

'So Teller Stella, give us the low down on Annie Greene's love life, then. Has she given the house mouse the elbow?'

'Jesus, Callum, you're so tough. Not.'

Stella sat down opposite him at the cheap Chinese where she had joined the 'lads', as they dubbed themselves, for lunch. She cast off her coat to reveal a V-necked shift and an expanse of ageing cleavage. Of the women in the office, she was perhaps the only one with whom the men socialised, tolerated because they saw her as a parody of womankind, recognisable, pigeon-holed as the bawdy wench who was raucous and lippy but ultimately obeyed her superior male. In this way, inappropriate clothes had been Stella's passport into the man's world.

Tony, the production editor, David and Al pulled

out the remaining chairs. Callum crooked his finger at the waiter and ordered two bottles of wine.

'First, Stella,' he continued, 'little Miss Married Bliss has never before got the hots for another man. As she expressed so fulsomely today in my hearing. Second, she never talks about the hubby and the brat any more. Ergo, something has happened.'

'Oh, you're smart, Callum, you're smart,' said Stella sarcastically, munching on a prawn cracker. She swallowed, took another one, weighing her options. Mendacity wouldn't slip past him. Also, the plain truth was that like all good journalists she loved to gossip.

'Well,' she said, 'if you must know, she moved out about two months ago and is now living in a gruesome bedsit in the far and unfashionable reaches of north-east London.'

'Hah!' said Callum, triumphantly. 'I knew it.'

'Hoo-bloody-ray,' said Stella. 'One person's tragedy is another's entertainment.'

'Yeah, Stella,' sneered Callum. 'I'm a rubberneck, craning out of my car window at the scene of motorway pile-ups. I'm one of the crowd when an aircraft crashes.'

Al swilled his wine around his glass, looking injured. 'She never told me.'

'Al, I don't even think she's told her own mother,' said Stella, glad for the chance to ignore Callum. 'Especially not her own mother. She's in denial. Thinks she's gonna get back together with him. Transitory troubles, then happy ever after.'

'She should get shot of the bugger,' said Tony gruffly, adding, in an exaggeration of his own northern accent, 'a ne'er do well, we call his kind, oop where I come from. This wine's a bit bloody dry, Callum. Did you see England on the box last night?'

*   *   *

Chris loved the sweet freshness of early summer. Field poppies and daisies danced in the verges of the main roads, from seed scattered specially by the council, a reminder of the glory of the corn fields of Chris's youth. In the evenings, a family of bats, which roosted in the church tower, swooped over the back garden ponds, inhaling invisible insects. But down the lane, the county council workmen bull-dozed into an ancient river bank, where kingfishers darted, bright and quick as fairies, to widen the lane where it was judged too narrow for traffic. When the crew left so, it seemed, had the kingfishers.

One afternoon, when Emma was at a friend's for tea, Chris sat on the bank with the dog for an hour, watching, waiting, but there was no blue flash, no still moment of wonder, only a fat trout which had been thrown back in the river by some of the lads who fished upstream, by the bridge. With damaged gills, the trout gasped near the surface, mindless, near death. Chris found himself feeling sorry for it. He had always been a sucker for a sob story. He took off his desert boots and his socks, rolled up his old cords and waded through the shallows. Mud embraced his feet in an oozy squeeze. Sharp stones punctured the soles of his feet. Round his ankles the water tugged like icy silk. He stumbled, recov-ered, grabbed the trout by its mucus-slippery tail. He put it out of its misery on a patch of the new tarry road, and was narrowly missed by a car taking the corner too fast, as they all did since the improvements.

He padded home gingerly, his boots in his hand, at six, later than intended. A cheap red hatchback was sitting on the gravel. In the garden, Emma and her friend were skipping barefoot – 'Dadd-ee,' she called, waving – and a young woman was perched on the kitchen garden wall, watching them.

'I'm so sorry. You said quarter to, didn't you?'

'That's OK. Been paddling?'

'Animal rescue,' he said, dropping the boots. 'Would you like a coffee, Becky's mum? I'm Chris, by the way.'

'Fiona,' she said. 'Love one.'

She was tall when she unfolded herself, slightly taller than him. She moved in a way that reminded him faintly of Annie, the same graceful posture, though Fiona's movements were sleepy. Her hair, mouse brown, was tied back in a plait and she was almost pretty. In the kitchen, he caught himself assessing her and needed to distract himself with the stirring of mugs and proffering of biscuits.

She sat at the table, dunking the edge of a digestive in her mug, making small talk. 'Your wife's a journalist, I hear?' She said it like a question.

'Mmm hmmm.'

'And you're holding fort here for now?'

'Something like that.'

There was silence. Her cheeks coloured faintly.

'I'm sorry. It's a moot point,' he said. 'Actually, we're separated. The strain of her big job and my unemployment had its effect.' She looked up and managed to convey sympathy by wrinkling her nose. 'As a matter of fact,' he added, 'you're the first person I've told about this.'

'You probably sense the fellow feeling. Been there. Done that. Got the T-shirt. My husband had to follow his job to Scotland. Supposed to come back at weekends. Didn't work out. We're divorced now. It's been hard on Becky but we're coming through it. Touch wood.' She tapped her head. That was something Annie did, too.

He had been standing, the pose of the busy person, intending to convey to her that she should finish up quickly and be gone. Now, abruptly, he sat down opposite her, wanting to talk as he hadn't done in quite a while. It would be a relief to talk to someone who did not know them, did not know Chris-and-Annie, did not have an emotional stake in their partnership as friends and family and village seemed to feel they did.

He placed his arms, palms downwards, on the slightly battered pine table, with the crayon marks and the word Emma gouged clumsily into the top. 'I've been meaning to sand it down,' he said, looking at it. 'But I can't bring myself to do it. When we found it and confronted her, she said, "It wasn't me. It was the dog." She was two. She didn't realise why the excuse wouldn't wash.'

She smiled. 'You know the good times don't get sanded away from your memory. After a while, you can actually remember when you were happy together. I wish I'd realised earlier, admitted we weren't happy earlier. I clung on too long, trying to fool myself,' she added, pulling a face.

'How do you know when too long is?' He was surprised at his own question.

She shrugged. 'You know.' There was a pause. 'You feel better on your own and you can't hide it from yourself.'

Chris felt something inside him tear from top to bottom.

'Still, every case must be different,' he said.

She looked at him. 'I'm sure. And having said all that, there's no getting away from the fact that being single is lonely. Terribly lonely. But it just seemed better than being constantly undermined. My husband ended up by criticising everything I did. He made me feel like a complete moron.'

Chris ran his nail around the edges of Emma's name. Fiona was touching raw nerves with every sentence. Thankfully, she did not try to force his confidence further. When she left, she squeezed his arm in a gesture of fellow feeling. She was nice, was Becky's mum.

He closed the front door. He felt a flutter of interest, the delicious rush of blood. Becky's mum had warmed his loins and his ego. This is dangerous, he cautioned himself in his head, though he wasn't sure why. Momentary fantasies are, after all, meat and drink to married men the world over. He failed to see why they should be significant just because there was a marital hiccough. But then, he failed to see a lot at that time.

'Look, a fuck's a fuck and nothing to make a fuss about.'

A gale of laughter rippled through the room. The speaker, a slight teenage girl with a tangle of rebellious hair, was perched on the corner of a table in the common room of the village college to which Annie had driven with her tape recorder in her bag.

In the corner, the headmaster, a florid man in a loud bow tie, laughed, too, a little self-consciously, parading his tolerance. He was showing Annie how informally he wielded his authority, how effortlessly in tune he was with his pupils.

He had agreed very readily when Annie had called to ask if she might see his pupils for vox pop interviews which aimed 'to capture the thinking of today's young people' – this was Alec's summary when they had refined Annie's original idea in conference.

'Who're you going to commission?' he'd asked her.

She suggested the names of some of the freelance

writers they used regularly, but Alec rejected each in turn. Some were not good enough writers. Some not sensitive enough interviewers. In the end, she had volunteered. Alec looked pleased but guilty. 'You're doing an awful lot of writing as well as your desk duties,' he said. She had gone from scapegoat to teacher's pet in a matter of weeks.

'I enjoy it,' she replied. Callum made a slight but unmistakably rude gesture at her from the other side of the room.

Callum would have approved, however, of the fact that she planned to skive off early today. Of all those in the country, she had chosen this particular college from the Yellow Pages for Cambridgeshire, because she planned to finish here at two thirty latest, and meet Emma at her school gates. She had arrived at eleven thirty, at a single storey, pale brick building on a wide grey forecourt which was situated at the edge of an ancient village.

The headmaster, Mr Thomas, came out to greet her. He was smiling and hearty, anxious to make a good impression, his ego straining for national publicity. He insisted on 'filling her in on the background' for three-quarters of an hour in his office, telling her about the history of the school, its past as a grammar school, its national curriculum and GCSE results, none of which she would use in her piece. Her watch ticked. The prospect of missing Emma crossed her mind. She hoped she was not being unprofessional. Eventually, he had trotted her along the vinyl-tiled corridors to this bland room with thirty selected teenagers sprawled across it.

'The difference between your generation and our generation is that you thought you could change the world and we know we can't. You were idealists –

Woodstock and all that – and we're pragmatists,' announced one alarmingly thin and white young man.

'I was a little young for Woodstock, actually,' Annie interjected gently.

The boy struck himself on the head. 'But you understand my point?'

'Yes, I do,' Annie said. 'Tell me, are you as "druggy" and "sexy" as we were?'

That was when the girl on the table, in black T-shirt, black jeans, and black platform boots, made her point. Annie must have looked baffled because they laughed when they registered her expression.

The young man, who was called Jonathan, interpreted their feelings to her. 'It's like, sex is a big deal to our parents' generation but it isn't to us. We don't set as much store by it . . .' There was laughter and lewd comments about mater and pater's ravening sexual appetites.

Jonathan continued: 'It's nice if you can get it but it's not like we monitor every girl here for the likelihood of a sexual encounter. Or vice versa. We grew up in co-ed schools. For us, the middle classes haven't been divided by gender at the age of eleven, or even younger, like our parents were. They invented the sexual revolution because they were so repressed. But we talk the same language, we wear the same kind of clothes, the uniform is the same. It's actually possible for us to be platonic friends. We hang out together. Girls aren't strange, mysterious beings to me. Like, you know, sex isn't the ultimate issue.'

The girl in black concurred. 'This is the face of equality. This is why feminism is redundant. Girls of our age just don't need it.'

'That's fascinating.' Annie glanced at the recorder

to make sure the spools were still revolving. 'Do you all feel like this?'

A hubbub of voices rose and she began to take shorthand notes to reinforce the taped record. The school nurse came in with trays of pizza from the canteen. The boys handed round the wedges, called for seconds; many of the girls tore their slices in half, sharing them.

'There's a more fundamental reason for our not needing feminism,' said a fat girl in a corner with ginger blonde hair. 'Out of the thirty or so of us here, hand-picked by Mr Thomas, the brightest and best,' – there were whoops – 'half us are likely to get higher grades in our exams than the other half. That is, we girls are going to score consistently better than you boys.' There were more whoops, also jeers. The girl made a quieting gesture with her hands. 'We all know the statistics. Girls are now outperforming boys across the board, including the sciences. We're in the ascendant and we know it.'

'How does that affect your view of marriage?'

'Who says we want to get married?' the girl replied swiftly. 'I'm not sure I do.'

'We told you: a fuck's a fuck,' muttered the girl in black.

'All right, all right, don't get stuck on a theme,' bellowed Mr Thomas, his patience wearing thin. He had begun to envisage what a hostile report could make of her.

Jonathan looked at Annie from the centre of the mêlée, shrugged and smiled. 'R I P passion,' he said amiably. 'You see why romance is dead.'

Al took Annie's elbow and steered her around a deep puddle rainbowed with oil. The narrow streets behind the office were cobbled and grew slippery when smeared with a slick of rain and today was unseasonably wet and blowy.

Garages and greasy spoon cafés clustered under the railway arches for warmth. Annie and Al negotiated their way around a placard that read, 'MOT while you wait, and Body repairs – phone a quote'. At the end of the street, a plate-glass frontage had been inserted into the semi-circle formed by the red-brick bridge supports. Behind it, a new wine bar had opened; music leaked through the gaps and hinges. Al held the door open for Annie and they stepped into a blast of tropical warmth. It was all metal tables and chairs, blackboards chalked with the day's specials, inexpertly spelt, and pretty, gay waiters in jeans and wine-bar logo'd T-shirts.

'Not very us,' said Al, as if they were a partnership, as he pulled out a chair for her.

'Very chi chi,' said Annie, looking around.

The waiter who came to take their order looked about fifteen years old, with his acne, his orthodontic braces and the slow blush that sucked up his neck when Al looked him in the eye. Al asked for champagne and a plate of smoked salmon blinis. Annie was surprised and touched; Al had insisted on taking her out for lunch and he was treating her in the way she assumed he treated his teenaged daughters when they wanted to act grown-up.

She took a sip of the champagne. It was very good.

'So what's the matter, our kid?'

She swallowed the champagne and her fizzing feeling of well-being went flat.

'Oh boy, Stella couldn't keep her big mouth shut. God! And I thought I could trust her!'

'Whoa!' Al put his hand up, palm towards her, as if slowing a vehicle. 'It wasn't entirely her fault. Callum gave her the third degree.'

'Callum! Oh, great! Who else knows? Why doesn't she just publish a report in the sodding review.' Her lower lip stuck out, like a sulking child's. She didn't care.

Al made a pacifying noise and rubbed her arm. 'What's 'appened? Why didn't you tell me?' he asked.

Annie looked across at his big, open, blunt features and felt bad for having worried him, which was ridiculous. He had suffered a recent haircut under the influence of his daughters, from Kevin Keegan to short back and sides. His ears, rather large and slightly protruding, were suddenly dominant. Blondish spikes rose at the crown of his head. It all contrived to give him a boyish, earnest air, endearing when contrasted, as your eyes travelled downwards, with his nascent paunch under its married man cable-knit. They had worked together for five years, on assignments when she was freelance, and she had liked and trusted him, both professionally and personally, from the start. He was friendly without being garrulous, sometimes paternal, rarely patronising.

Even so, she didn't particularly want to talk about it, especially not to a man, at least not about the rows and the break-up. But she told him about the interval at Stella's, the bleak flat in suburbia, also how Emma had been ill the other week, nothing serious, but it had broken her up. She should have been there. It was a mother's place to spoon medicines into the rosy mouth, to bed-bath the child-shaped body with its skinny arms and teddy tum, to pile pillows behind her back and read her Roald Dahl. That had been the worst yet. The worst not-being-there.

'And when I got down there on Friday evening, she

was right as rain, happy as Larry.' She adopted an exaggerated English accent for the English idioms. 'She didn't miss me, you see. And half of me is glad because she's settled, she's not hurting like I am. And half of me is childishly torn to pieces. I'm so easily dispensed with and all that stuff.' She tore her paper napkin into small strips and began to scrunch them into tight balls.

'And what about Chris?'

'How do you mean?'

'Is 'e 'urting like you are? Or are you dispensable,' his index fingers described quotation marks in the air, 'to 'im, too?'

A little worm of warning squirmed in Annie's stomach. She didn't like the turn the conversation was taking. She pushed a tissue ball round and round the rim of the heavy glass ashtray which lay between them, half full of Al's stubs. Had he touched a raw nerve? Or was it simply that he had strayed over an invisible barrier of loyalty? That must be it. He had walked past one of the keep out signs which hedged around Chris, marking the bounds of her allegiance. She didn't want to talk about her husband. There was a limit on how much of a marriage and its problems should be revealed, even in crisis. Once you start talking about the problems to outsiders, there is no mending it. Airing his faults to a stranger, even one who says they will help to put things right, breaks some fundamental code of fealty. Perhaps Chris had been right about the counselling.

'My great tendency,' she said, lightly, jokily, 'is to believe I'm dispensable to every one. It comes of being a child of divorce. I remember I really hurt someone once just because I hadn't realised how

much he cared for me. Women don't break hearts
from selfish cruelty. They do it because they haven't
a clue how much emotion they've aroused.'

He smiled broadly. 'I bet.' he said. 'I can see you
as a *femme fatale.'*

He took her hand from the ashtray and held it
between his, rubbing her fingers between his,
massaging them, from palm to tips. He held them
quite tightly, so that to withdraw them would have
been a definite act, a moment of contention.

He lifted her hand to his face and lightly brushed
his lips against her fingertips.

The seconds pulsed and extended.

The message was silent but crude.

She withdrew her hand, her eyes on his face. 'You
and your silver tongue,' she said brightly. He hadn't
settled the bill. She couldn't sit here making small
talk with him. 'I'll just find the loo,' she announced,
as she had often heard hearty Englishwomen do. It
was something she would never normally have said.
She scraped her chair back and walked very slowly
in the direction of the miniature skirted figure
painted in glossy white on a matte grey door.

Oh, Al, Al, I don't believe it. Through the swing
door, she ran the cold tap and splashed the water,
which smelled unpleasantly of chemicals, on her
neck and wrists, as if she needed to sober up. Her
reflection, with its unfamiliar gamine hairstyle,
looked suitably bewildered.

He was the one man she had been certain was safe
in taxis, safe in restaurants, safe full stop. She
counted him a friend. A mixture of indignation and
grief – at losing him, effectively – rose in her. And
embarrassment, too. The cheeks and neck of the
mirror image were diffused with startled pink.

She was back on the market. That was how they

saw her, these opportunist, predatory men whose wedding rings slipped from their fingers so quickly, in an illusionist's tricksy trick.

How dumb can you get? How can you misjudge someone so totally?

She sat in front of her computer for the rest of the afternoon, ear phones on, tapping out the transcript of her tapes, consulting her notes. And all the time she ran the scene in the wine bar through her mind again and again. She examined Al's gesture, replayed his caressing her hand and kissing it, making certain she had not misread it. She doubted herself now, so thoroughly had she believed in him. But there was no fooling herself. He had intended the frisson of sexual interest.

Was it her fault? Had she inadvertently led him on? Then she got annoyed with herself. That was a typically female reaction: he hit me, it was all my fault. But Al's in-your-face propositions were a feature of the office. It was precisely because they were delivered loudly, in public, to every woman except the vulnerable secretaries or juniors who might have been embarrassed by them, that she had trusted him. She had never thought him capable of quiet innuendo.

Her own reaction puzzled her, for she had connived with him to save his face. She'd pretended he hadn't done what he did. She had acted as if there were no trace beyond the platonic in that kiss. She hadn't slapped him down. She hadn't made him feel small or silly. But he knew that she knew.

Of course, she had to work with him, still, which was a powerful restraint. But there was more to it than that: a reflex of hers to be grateful, even in some small and flinching way, for male attention. That had been learned a long time ago, from her father. That had been learned at high school where she was considered pretty and the other girls envied her her popularity. The man who paid you a compliment might be pock-marked and leering but you said 'thank you' sweetly and were properly obliged. It was an age-old feminine lie; Scarlett O'Hara flirting with the squirts while secretly despising them.

Marriage had protected Annie from all of this. For years she had been cocooned in the safety that went with being Mrs Greene. Of course she had known that if word spilled out of her new uncertain status, she might be regarded, in some coarse male mind, as being in need of a lay. What surprised her was discovering that after everything, the marriage, the child, the job, she still reacted with the conditioned response. To women of her age, sexual appreciation was your currency, you were given an illusion of power by it, and if you had to rebuff it, you did so gently.

The girls at the sixth form college had broken free. They dressed in androgynous clothes; they talked bold and brash, they negotiated their own path to better treatment by degrading the importance of sex. Perhaps it was simply that in an era of AIDS they had no choice.

For some reason, she thought of the man in the lift. Perhaps this is just a matter of piqued pride? she asked herself. Perhaps you just want an approach to be made by someone under forty, with a young man's buttocks?

She laughed out loud, which was cheering.

'What's so funny?' asked Stella eagerly from the other side of the desk.

Annie looked at her, friend and incorrigible gossip. She was too fond of Stella to hold a grudge over such a small matter. 'Male bums,' she said.

Callum groaned. She punched the button of the recorder. The voice of the etiolated Jonathan declared that platonic friendship between the sexes was the norm for his generation. Lucky boy! Annie thought. Let me introduce you to Alan and Callum and David.

Chapter Seven

Phil wrapped his lips around Stella's left nipple, tugging it gently with his teeth. I'm going to make you so horny, you whore, he promised her silently.

Stella, arm around his back, looked down at his blond curls buried in the soft sagging mound of her breasts. She thought, Shit! I must buy some after-bath body moisturiser.

'Get off, Phil,' she implored. 'I've had a hard day and I'm knackered.'

He rolled off and lay on his back beside her. His penis shrivelled and slumped. It looked foolish and rather sorry for itself.

'You love your job. Don't whinge,' he said sourly.

'Correction. I used to quite like my job. At the moment it's a waking nightmare,' said Stella. She prodded at his sulking sex organ with a red dagger of a nail. 'So you can put that away, mate, and lump it.'

There was a speaking silence as he turned, presenting her with the faintly spotty expanse of his back.

She flopped back on her pillow.

'Oh mother!' she crooned. 'Why didn't you make me a lesbian?'

Phil muttered something that sounded like, 'Are you sure she didn't?' but Stella chose to ignore the provocation.

She wasn't quite sure what had gone wrong at the office. Alec was being an absolute bastard. The plummet in circulation had slowed but it hadn't reversed and he was banking more and more on their new changes. Stella, as the woman in charge of them, was bearing the brunt of his anxiety. In addition, Callum was baiting Annie with a feverish energy. There was something distasteful in the erotic charge he seemed to achieve in humiliating her; it was like watching Caligula in his court. Al was chilly towards Annie, too, which was unheard of.

At the moment, however, Annie was the favoured darling of Alec. Three months ago, when she had refused to work one Sunday, he had embarked on a campaign of alternately belittling or screaming at her. Now, she had redeemed herself in his eyes by devouring the workload, volunteering for assignments. She was in the office at eight and the last to leave at nine, ten, in the evening. They all, except for Alec, knew why.

Poor bitch, Stella thought with a squeeze of sympathy. No matter how bad things are for me, they're a hundred times worse for her. She's going to do something really stupid soon. I can see it coming a mile off.

Emma and Becky grew close during the remaining weeks of the summer term, caught in the sudden intensity of childhood friendship, which burgeons and withers so quickly. Chris watched them, amused. Teenage love follows the same erratic pattern. It was a wonder that at some point, you learn constancy.

He felt sorry for Fiona. He admired her proficiency as a single working mother. She held a part-time job, which she enjoyed, a minor post in a local estate agency. During the summer holidays, she took two weeks off, and had arranged for Rebecca to stay with her mother in Walsall for the remaining weeks. When Chris learned of this plan, he volunteered to have the child. It was a convenient suggestion. Fiona's mother had not been well. The children were eager to spend time together. And naturally, Fiona had been quietly dismayed at the prospect of seeing so little of her daughter.

As he saw her, for brief spells but on an almost daily basis now, Chris grew fond of Fiona. She was always cheerful and as a consequence, cheered him. One day, picking up Becky, she said that she would like to thank him by taking him to a performance of *Twelfth Night* which was being held in one of the Cambridge college gardens.

'My treat,' she said, turning pink.

Once again, it provoked in him the wish to ease her embarrassment. 'Great,' he said, subduing a flare of unease.

It was a matinée. Fiona arranged an afternoon off work and a teenaged babysitter, whom she transported, with Becky, up to the cottage in her car. Chris swapped places with the teenager, folding himself into the front seat, easing it back. Fiona's driving was erratic: he had to stop himself from wincing or stamping on an imaginary brake pedal during the journey. Finally, when they arrived, she stopped by a space between two cars. 'Will you park it for me?' she said, looking a little fey, 'I'm no good at reversing.'

She had brought German wine in a padded freezer bag, crisps and chocolates, too. The bag and its contents were very different from the picnics he was accustomed to extracting from Annie's wicker basket. Fiona had even packed baby wipes for their hands and mouths. It would never have occurred to Annie to buy such an item.

He lugged this bag through the streets to the appointed college. It was another hot day. Fiona was wearing khaki shorts and a white T-shirt. Chris noticed she had nice legs, pale and a little plump, but nicely shaped. He could see the shadow of her nipples through her white T-shirt.

Wrought-iron gates, high and intricate, with painted heraldic devices, hung in the archway at the entrance to the college, as beautiful an obstruction as a spider's web in a tale of magic. Chris felt, on stepping through into the cool shadow of the archway, as if he had stepped across an invisible boundary and had come within an enchanted realm.

Fiona's sandals made clicking noises on the stone. She proffered two tickets to a student standing by a trestle table, and Chris bought a programme for a pound. Buying something unnecessary, even for pocket money, reminded him, in an unpleasant context, of Annie. He hadn't told her about this outing; he couldn't be bothered to explain.

'How are things?' Fiona asked, as they placed themselves in the front row of the foldaway chairs which were arranged in an expectant half-moon facing a lawn backed by a hedge. Swathes of fabric had been pinned to the shrubs. These, together with a variety of garden benches, served as scenery. Chris and Fiona were the first there.

'How are things?' he repeated. 'No change to report, I'm afraid.'

'That bad, huh?'

They both laughed, one rather nervously, and the motives of the other could only be guessed at.

Chris looked round at the elegant college buildings behind him, red brick with oriel windows, at the perfection of the gardens before him. The plants hummed in the buxom borders, pink phlox billowing prettily against spiky blue thistles. The swish of a sprinkler was curiously soothing. For an afternoon, at least, he might be a member of a world of privilege and known rules.

'It's not just being without a job,' he added. 'It's . . . well, it's Annie and me. We're miles apart. We don't talk.'

His voice tailed away. Nevertheless, this was the first time he had confided in her. Fiona was acutely conscious of this new departure towards intimacy.

'Have you tried to talk?' she asked. 'I could babysit Emma one night if it would help?'

He was surprised. 'Thanks. Erm, I don't think it will come to that, but I'll bear it in mind.'

She reached out a hand and stroked his wrist. Having established her willingness to help him repair his marriage, this gesture was now open to her. He clasped her hand, as if in appreciation, removing it tactfully, letting it go. He turned his face to the sun, not because he was relaxed, but because he was not.

Nevertheless, he found himself saying, 'I thought it would get easier. We – she – has paid off most of our accumulated debts, you see, which were massive. I guess we had both assumed that would take some of the pressure off . . .'

Instead, Chris felt that their differences were now stripped of excuses. He and Annie seemed to irritate each other more than ever. Chris had assumed that

Annie would willingly return to freelancing now, enabling him to pursue a full-time job, but it seemed there was a moratorium on commissioning at the *News* and she did not dare to. The circulation was falling. Budgets were tight. It was not the best time to turn your back on a reasonably secure job. Chris could see the point but still he felt a pang of disappointment.

Every penny of their expenditure remained under scrutiny. Annie was now obsessed, so it seemed to Chris, with saving a nest egg against possible misfortune. She saw bad luck around every corner. He knew that when her parents had divorced she and her mother had had to move to a smaller house in a new district. He knew that Annie was frightened of such changes. He explained to her why she was over-reacting. She exploded. 'I'm just saving for a rainy day. You're so irresponsible. Even now. After everything.' And because she controlled the purse strings, there was no compromise to be had. They would do it her way.

They were a pack of two, hunting for malicious intentions. As a teenager, he had despised the parents of some of his friends, whose marriages bristled with snide digs and public put-downs. He had always promised himself he would never be party to such unpleasantness when he grew up. But last weekend, when the brake lights on the car had gone, and he had been trying to fix them with the help of the mechanic who lived in the council houses nearby, Annie had fluttered around.

'Is the bulb screwed on correctly?' she'd asked.

'Oh, shut up,' he said.

He had never spoken to her so viciously either in private or in public before. He remembered the look on her face. She'd gone indoors.

'I didn't mean it,' he'd told her afterwards, brushing it off. But he had, and he had felt a sense of renewed power at being able to humiliate her. Now that she held all other power in their relationship, it was the one avenue left open to him.

He should have been ashamed of himself but he wasn't. He rebelled against Annie's wanting him to feel ashamed.

Fiona, on the other hand, regarded him as a normal, decent sort of bloke. She said that she admired his patience and good humour with the children. He took them out into the countryside to gather twigs and stones, teaching them to make 'nature sculptures', he made bubbling-over ice-cream sodas with them; he played rough stuff with them in the garden, hurling them into the air and catching them, swinging them into dizzying rotations of fright and laughter. And when Becky reported on the 'brill' day they'd had, Fiona would smile, and once she said that it was so good to meet a man who wanted to spend time with his child; if only her husband had felt the same way.

He should admit it: he had been aware from the start, by the alchemy with which a woman signals these things, that she found him attractive.

A Japanese tourist and two Germans joined them on the front rows. An assortment of women, some white-haired, some in their twenties, all unmistakably bookish, arranged themselves, their cushions and their wine, on the remaining seats.

It was a good production, but the fact that it was in modern dress unsettled Chris. Viola, in her disguise as the boy, Cesario, wore a double breasted man's suit. It was not unlike one of the outfits Annie wore to work when she, too, in order to protect herself in the aggressive atmosphere of a competitive office, masqueraded as a male. The trouble was she had grown accustomed to it. She never took the pretence off, not even at home.

'I am not what I am,' Viola told Olivia in their most ironic scene.

'I would you were as I would have you be,' Olivia replied.

Chris had forgotten she said that – the eternal cry of husbands and wives.

Afterwards, he and Fiona walked companionably to the car, and she asked him what he would really like to do. So he told her about his dormant ambition, and when they arrived at the cottage, he led her into the garage-barn, uncovering the plaster horses, his masterworks which were crumbling before him. She was effusive in her praise.

'They're brilliant. Oh, Chris, they're absolutely brilliant. You really do have talent,' she told him with obvious sincerity. 'You mustn't let it go to waste.'

He smiled at her. He allowed himself to accept her flattery. Her words stroked him, oiled him, warmed and relaxed him. He felt able to accept her belief in him whereas he was no longer able to accept Annie's. Why was this so?

The sun knifed through the hole in the roof and assaulted Fiona's eyes. She squinted and stumbled trying to trace a path through the accumulated debris. He caught her by the elbow. And it seemed entirely natural that he then kissed her.

She smelt of cheap perfume and tasted of cheap wine. Even as he held her, he decided that the kiss should be brief, a dry-lipped kiss that he could pass off afterwards. But her tongue darted into his mouth, slippery as sin. There was nothing subtle about Fiona. She fancied him and she wanted to make it clear.

He was tetchy and perverse with Annie that weekend. To his surprise, she did not guess why. He had assumed the episode was written on his face, but she didn't read it. She may have been preoccupied. She may simply not have cared enough to look. The latter premise seemed somehow to justify his betrayal. And he learned a new lesson. It was easier to hoodwink your wife than he would have guessed.

Annie, sitting on the tube, decided there was no God. The halitosis of the pudgy man on the adjacent seat, the jingly buzz of the personal stereo of the leather-skirted girl with purple beehive who sat opposite – no God could have created these people; nobody, not even God, could love them. The sight of so much humanity, in all its unloveliness, testified to the random and horrible results of the matings of indifferent genes.

Most particularly, God could not be held to blame for the existence of Callum Rogers, who was strap hanging in front of her. Normally, they did not travel on public transport together: Callum preferred to drive to work in his classic MG, his babe machine, as he called it, but today it was in the garage for its annual service.

The doors slid back and the majority of the occupants dispersed. The seat next to Annie was empty. Callum flopped into it.

'Good feature on modern youth,' he said without preamble. It was the first pleasant phrase he had addressed to her in weeks and she was instantly suspicious. 'No, I mean it,' he added, unscrewing the top of a bottle of mineral water he carried and taking a swig.

She decided to risk a conversation with him. 'At first, I thought the kids' attitude was healthy and different, but now I'm not so sure.' She became conscious once more that he was ten years younger than her. 'In my day we were sexual predators.'

He looked her up and down. 'Yeah, I can imagine you as a babe in a mini-skirt.'

'Hot pants,' she said. 'By my very early teens, it was hot pants worn under a long skirt slit all the way up to the waist. With white linen boots,' she giggled. 'Anyway, it seemed refreshing that the girls today did not trade in the same currency. But in retrospect I suspect they're just scared of sex. You know, AIDS, political correctness. So they've decided to ignore sex. I think they're rather tame really. Pretending the wild and fierce doesn't exist.'

She ended on a questioning note, seeking his concurrence. She had a nagging feeling that she did that a lot with male superiors.

Callum swirled another mouthful of water around his mouth and looked at her without commenting. Then he tipped his head back and gargled noisily before swallowing.

His yobbish habits were deliberately at odds with his oleaginous appearance. Callum's hair was cut very neatly, and carefully Brylcreemed, swept back from his forehead. There was a hint of a shaving rash under the shadow of stubble on his young cheek. Annie knew he used colourless mascara because he applied it, quite openly, in the office. He smelt, faintly, of an expensive aftershave.

Callum never smiled openly or gave himself over to a belly laugh. At some stage in his life, he had constructed a mannered image and hid himself behind it until his real self, the boy who could not have started out so smug and smart and derisive, had entirely evaporated. It had not surprised Annie when she discovered that he was the child of very rich parents, who had managed to marry and divorce three times each during the course of his childhood.

'I don't see much difference,' he said eventually. 'Take you, for example. You're scared shitless of sex. They're scared of catching AIDS, you're scared of being "wild and fierce" – as you put it with your typical verbal exaggeration. Big fault in your writing that,' he added. 'You should do something about it.'

He smiled at her as she bridled.

It was the stop where she changed lines. She got up, wishing for a biting riposte when only the crude came to mind. She never normally swore in public but she gave into the temptation, particularly through the desire to seem as hard-boiled as he was.

'Screw you, Callum,' she said and the remaining passengers shifted themselves deeper behind their newspapers and examined their feet with a new consciousness.

She felt rather pleased. The door slid open. She got out.

It was a mistake.

He looked her up and down and up again, very deliberately, his face a mask. 'I don't think so,' he drawled.

The doors slid shut. The train carried his complacent face away. Already he had turned his attention to the newspaper on his lap.

'The prize for the best entry in the vegetable class goes to Ian Henderson for his courgettes. Any of us who has tried to grow them knows how hard it is to find two that match, and I must say Ian's pair was practically identical, a nice size and with the flower attached. So, jolly well done, Ian . . .'

There was polite applause as Audrey Benbow, chairman of the horticultural society, leaned down from the village hall platform to confer a battered silver cup on the sandy-haired, freckled man who had edged to the front. He looked absurdly pleased as he bore it away.

It was the last of the prizes to be presented. Ian returned to his position, near the back, next to Chris, to whom he had been chatting.

Around them, exhibitors removed their flowers, pot plants and vegetables from the trestle tables lining the room, children carried off their collages of pasta, the WI ladies their pots of jam and jellies. Beneath the smiles and the pleasantries, a vein of true competitive spirit ran, particularly amongst the retired men. There were those born-and-bred in the village who never exhibited, so convinced were they that no incomer could grow a superior vegetable and so frightened at the chance of being proved wrong publicly.

Old Arthur stood beneath the wooden board on which were carved the names of the village men who had lost their lives in the two world wars, a list of fifteen, an astonishing, heart-breaking figure for such a small forgotten place. He sucked his teeth as he examined Ian's courgettes dubiously.

'Oi prefer a cucumber, meself. A good old-fashioned sort of veg-tee-bule. There's an art to growing a good cucumber,' he told Ian.

'Oh, I agree,' said Ian disarmingly. 'There's no art at all to growing a courgette. And it's pot luck if two are similar.'

Arthur looked at him suspiciously, examining his words for condescension, but Ian was so good humoured there was no offence to be spotted. 'Still. You done well. For a townie.'

Chris liked both men and was amused by Arthur's

perpetual baiting of Ian. 'Don't praise him, Arthur. He might get above himself.'

'Chance would be a fine thing.' Pamela Henderson, in a tangerine-coloured kaftan, which Chris recognised as a £4.99 market stall 'bargain', swept by, with a loaf of bread and several jewel bright jars in her arms. Ian looked sheepish.

'You haven't heard, yet, have you?' he asked Chris, as Arthur strolled away in the company of other old people, with whom he had been to school in the days when the village roads were dusty tracks and the water was collected from the pumps that still stood on the verges, though now only for appearances' sake.

Chris saw Annie, who had arrived the previous evening, admiring Emma's vegetable lady on the other side of the room. It was a sultry day and she was wearing a long blue cotton dress over a white T-shirt. Her hair stood up in spikes around her face. She looked pretty, young and vulnerable. The sight of her discomforted him.

'Haven't heard what, Ian?' he asked.

'I was made redundant. Almost a month ago. Called in one Tuesday morning and told I was surplus to requirements. Firm doesn't seem to want people like me, anymore. It was my life,' he added simply. And it had been. He had worked for the same pharmaceutical firm for twenty-seven years.

His face worked itself into a philosophical smile. 'Still, I've got my redundancy. We won't starve. We're a lot better off than most. I can spend a bit of time on the garden now.'

Both Pamela and Annie materialised at their shoulders at the same moment. Chris could tell that Annie had heard the tail-end of the conversation.

Her face assumed a concerned expression. She was good at conferring sympathy on other people, Chris thought rather bitterly; one of the skills acquired in her job.

'What about Michael?' she asked softly. The Hendersons' younger son was at university.

'I'm going to work to pay for that,' Pamela announced. 'I've landed a job as the secretary at a high-tech firm in the science park,' she said. 'I'll be giving up my village duties, of course. Time for younger blood to do their share.'

Chris felt as though the Queen had abdicated – as a mild republican he should have been exhilarated, but instead found himself transfixed by dismay. The village had been her reason for being.

Ian examined his cup carefully. 'I went to see the employment agencies, of course. I went to the job centre. See if I could find something. But they more or less shrugged. A man of my age doesn't stand a chance, you see. Pammy was lucky, but she's got proper shorthand. Most of the young girls don't have it these days.'

'Can't spell either. They were ecstatic to find me. The only applicant for the job who knew how to spell "receive" apparently. Can you believe that? I voted for Major, last time around. Well, we all did, didn't we? I'll never vote Tory again . . .'

This was perhaps an even greater shock than her withdrawal from village activities. 'But Pamela! You're a party stalwart. You ran the fund-raising "hog roast", didn't you?' Chris remembered the amusement of the villagers at the sight of fat Pamela manhandling the butcher's best suckling pig from the boot of her car. 'You certainly canvassed for them last time around,' he added.

'More fool me. You should see what it's done to

112

him,' she said, gesturing to her husband. There was a wobble in her voice. Suddenly, her face crumpled. She made a supreme effort to master her emotions. 'I found him crying. Crying. Downstairs at six in the morning, looking at the photo of the last office party.'

The Hendersons were the last people on earth that Chris ever expected to weep. He found himself remembering what Pamela had said to him about the preferred role of men and women. But no sprite of vindictive glee twirled within him. Things like this shouldn't happen to people like the Hendersons.

'Not sure how I'll stand it,' said Ian, shame-faced. 'Got to do something. Anything. I've applied to be a traffic warden, in town.'

'A traffic warden!' whispered Pamela. 'He's a scientist. He's been a scientist all his life.'

As a group, they began to walk towards the doors, Annie helping Pamela with a boisterous pot plant. 'A third of the lab has gone,' Ian said. 'All the people of my age. The younger men are on smaller salaries so they've been retained. And it's assumed that they're more in touch with scientific advances.'

'But what about company loyalty? Reliability? Assets like that?' Annie asked.

'Companies don't want loyalty, any more.' said Ian. For the first time, he sounded bitter. 'They want people to move on. Join young, leave early. It's cheaper. Then, when they're my age and earning a top flight salary, they'll be someone else's problem. That's the ethos of today.'

'Do you know,' said Pammy. 'At my new firm there are five women whose husbands have been made redundant. Five! That's half the staff. We're each of us the breadwinner of our family.'

'Not so long ago,' said Ian, 'I used to think I wanted to retire early. Didn't think I wanted to soldier on till

I was sixty-five. The way things are going everyone's going to be retiring early. Forceable retirement.' He looked out over the trees which lined the opposite side of the road. His pale eyes were watering, whether with the sun or emotion, it was hard to tell.

Annie and Chris looked at him. Neither of them knew what to say and he very quickly sensed it, as the redundant do. Chris could read the signs.

'Well, mustn't go on about it,' Ian said. He smiled at them.

'Nice to see you *both*,' Pamela added pointedly.

Ian's slight arm, with its red hairs glinting, clasped Pammy's broad, padded back. Through the thin fabric of the kaftan, Chris could see a roll of flesh protruding above the torturous grip of her large and sensible black bra. Ian steered her towards their Volvo as if she were the most breakable object in the world.

Chapter Eight

Chris navigated his way around the curving roads of the council estate to which divorce had reduced Fiona, pulling to the kerb twice to check the local map. It was hot. He wound down the window. The heat ricocheted from the pavements to the pale pink terraced walls of bank after bank of cheaply built housing. He rubbed his brow with his shirtsleeve. There was a children's activity week in the town hall that week. Chris had dropped Emma and Becky off, Fiona had promised to collect them. Four o'clock, she had said. Pick Emma up from my house at four.

There had been an awkwardness between them since that evening when they had kissed. Their conversations had been stilted largely because he was deliberately confining them to essential arrangements. But he kept thinking of her in her shorts and T-shirt, her round white thighs. He kept thinking of what she would be like in bed. He told himself he hadn't had sex in God-knows-how-many months, so it wasn't surprising.

He examined the glass front doors for street numbers. At last he saw hers. Number 13, unlucky for Fiona, who had, presumably, once lived in a middle-class house in a middle-class area with the husband who had had to go to Aberdeen and had never returned. He thought of the jiggle of her breasts, the dark shadow. More fool the husband, Chris said to himself.

Fiona was pink, damp with the heat, looking uncomfortable in her office clothes, a white blouse and navy skirt, both now crumpled after a day at a desk. She had kicked off her shoes and was barefoot. Her little toes curled under and the joints looked rubbed and sore. Chris noticed this and rather than repelling him, he found it endearing. All her imperfections seemed to attract him. They made a welcome change after the perfection of Annie, her glossy executive exterior, her perpetual, tedious being in the right.

The glass front door opened straight onto the sitting room, which was full of cheap and ugly furniture, net curtains fluttering at the wall of windows, little ornaments and school photographs of Becky arranged carefully on teak veneer surfaces.

It was quiet. He followed her through to the kitchen where she was delving in the fridge. The small patch of garden beyond was empty.

'I tried to ring you,' she said, 'but you must have gone. I got it wrong. They don't finish till five. I could run Emma back to you later, if you want to go home. Or stay and have a glass of wine with me?' She waved a bottle of Liebfraumilch at him and wrinkled her nose coyly.

It crossed his mind that she was lying, but he decided he was being self-important.

'How could I resist?'

She made a play of uncorking the bottle, trying to camouflage her embarrassment with activity. 'Chris,' she said. 'About the other day . . . .'

He put his hand up to interrupt, but she continued, 'No, No. I want to say . . . I just want to make it clear that I know things are difficult for you and, well, I don't regard a kiss as a statement of intent or anything.' She circled a wineglass in one hand and a tumbler in another. 'I wouldn't like you to avoid me because of it,' she finished.

She looked so appealing.

A fly reverberated in the flaring air.

He moved across the distance between them and guessing his intention, she put the glasses down abruptly, and reached her hands around his neck, stretching to kiss him. Her eagerness was just the solace he needed.

He tucked a hand around her bottom and pressed her groin to his. He felt a schoolboy urgency. With his free hand he undid the buttons on her blouse, fumbled with her bra which would not open, which needed two hands, and then, at last, massaged her round breasts and the harder, puckered, port wine nipples. He had forgotten the sensations of soft- nesses and curves and bones pressed against him.

He pulled up her skirt; she unzipped his jeans. He felt her fingers fumbling. He pulled down her pants and the rub of dark, springy pubic hair against his skin was added to the sensations which overcame him. Slack dampness of her mouth, sweat between her breasts and in her prickling armpits – the very vulgarity of her and her fleshiness was arousing. He pushed himself into her and rocked her rhythmi- cally, and as he opened his eyes and nuzzled her neck he caught sight of their half-clad hips against her Formica and chipboard kitchen unit and of the fly settled on a patch of goo nearby.

But by that stage he was past caring. He only wanted the ultimate selfishness of climax.

*   *   *

Chris's father had worked in the City. Every morning he left for the station on his bicycle with his clips fastened around the ankles of his suit trousers. Every evening he returned home on the five forty-two retrieving the cycle from the concrete stand with the galvanised iron roof. Chris and his sister, Janet, used to watch for him from the sitting-room window, then bowl from the door to greet him, taking it in turns to perch on the saddle as he pushed the bicycle up the drive.

That had been when they were very young. By the time Chris was six, they had a Morris Austin with the number plate OGW 986. Chris still remembered the number of that first car. When his mother took her part-time job there were two cars and holidays abroad.

His father had said, 'Are you sure you can manage it all?' and when Marjie had said that yes, of course she could, now the children were at school, she had been permitted to accept the post.

Each evening, his father dried as his mother washed the dishes. She said he was a good man, a marvellous husband. She was so grateful to him for picking up a tea-towel and for pushing the mower across their quarter acre of Buckinghamshire lawn.

In his teens, Chris chafed against their cosiness. He looked at the neat houses with their hybrid tea roses growing by the lawns to be mown each Saturday, and the cars on the drives to be washed with a special brush attachment on the hose every Sunday, and thought that he could not bear to emulate them. Waking at midday on a Sunday morning after a Saturday night out with friends, he would peer from his bedroom window at the quiet lives of suburban Britain and wonder how people could settle for it. Were their aspirations so small that this was sufficient for a lifetime's achievement? Did they never long to travel the world, to create something memorable, to place a small marker – Chris Greene was here – on the impassive face of history? Seemingly not. Seemingly they craved only a colour television, or a fridge-freezer. These people measured the years in acquisitions.

Only now did he see something heroic in their quiet decency, these family men. On the whole, they were liberal, tolerant, especially in comparison with the aggressive ignorance of the swaggering men who replaced them in Thatcher's Britain. Now, he found himself nostalgic for the innocence of the country of his childhood. He found himself appreciating the better points of the white collar classes just as they disappeared for ever.

He had never extended his teenaged scorn to his parents, though the same day-to-day industry governed their lives as their neighbours', the same paying of bills, the same buying. His mother had converted to Catholicism when he was very young, still in short pants, and he was aware of her intensity as she prayed in her Sunday morning pew, struggling towards the infinite in a snatched hour of a busy week.

He was fond of both his parents but particularly his mother. She treated him differently from Jan, of that he was aware. There was a secret partiality for the son that manifested itself in small but significant ways, the bigger portions of favourite foods on his plate, in the licence he was allowed and Jan was not. He was given £25 on his birthday, and Jan was given £20. They said it was because he was older. Sometimes Jan said, 'It isn't fair.' And it wasn't.

His mother did not talk to him, though, the way

she talked to Jan. Marjie told her daughter the facts of life herself, but neither of his parents told him. When Annie had suggested counselling he had recoiled at the idea of talking to a stranger, particularly a woman, and small wonder that this was so. Today, as in childhood, he did not talk much to his parents about anything consequential, including his own situation. His father's comments were confined to 'How're you bearing up?' and his own answers to 'Oh, OK, considering'. Every now and then an advertisement from the *Telegraph*'s appointment pages would arrive in an envelope; usually for some totally inappropriate post that Marjie had seen and cut out specially, under the misapprehension that Chris could suddenly metamorphose into a marketing consultant or an account manager.

'Well, it's the same sort of line, dear,' she would say during her fortnightly phone calls. 'It's all in advertising.' Or, 'Well, try for it, dear. Just try.'

They hadn't an inkling. Chris knew that they worried about him. He hadn't been able to bring himself to tell them about his crumbling marriage. He knew that if he did, they would make an effort to drive over, make the supreme effort of having a 'serious talk' with him. They would say, 'You've got to think of Emma,' and other platitudes, as if he were still a boy who hadn't considered every repercussion.

This was why he and Annie were faced with the ordeal of masquerading as a happily married couple at the wedding of Janet to the man with whom she had lived for the past ten years. In any case, this was a moment of supreme relief in Marjie Greene's life, her daughter finally agreeing to the sacrament of marriage, so it seemed cruel to puncture her contentment. After the wedding, he told himself, he would clear the air with Annie first and foremost. He was finding the subterfuge sullying and could not bear it to continue: on the other hand, he hardly knew what he wanted to say. To confess his infidelity? To tell her he thought he had fallen in love with another woman? Had he?

In preparation for the journey to Buckinghamshire, he checked the vital signs on the car. As he bent under the bonnet, he heard the scrunch of a bicycle behind him.

'Morning, Chris.'

It was Ian Henderson. A little gawkily, he held out the daily newspaper. 'I'm delivering the papers for the shop,' he said, in answer to the question on Chris's face.

'What about the traffic warden's job?'

'Didn't get it. They thought I was a bit of a martinet, I gather. Too likely to stick to the letter of the law. They gave it to a woman I believe, on account of her improved communication skills. Asked Else at the shop if I could do this instead, they've had such trouble with kids saying they want the paper round and then not turning up on time, not turning up at all if it's raining . . .'

'Jesus, Ian.' There was no point in beating about the bush. 'It's a bit of a comedown, isn't it?'

'Kids' job and all that? Yes, I know.' He hung his head, plucking at the ginger fuzz on his own fingers with their bony, freckled knuckles. 'I don't care. I've got to do something.'

'What does Pamela say?' Chris didn't like to think of Pamela's reaction.

'She's a game old girl,' said Ian. 'Of course she's worried what people will be saying behind our backs. But she knows I've got to do something. She keeps a brave front up in public.'

Chris could imagine Pamela's inexpert attempts to pretend she didn't care.

'I expect people understand,' he said. 'I certainly know how you feel.'

'Thanks, Chris,' said Ian, handing over the paper. 'The Newson boy said something. But that's all the unpleasantness, so far.'

Chris tried to place the Newson boy in his mind, finally settling on a blond pre-teenager who rode his expensive bike around the village in extravagant, unlaced trainers. He was the boy suspected of having stolen old Dora's vegetable money.

'What on earth did he say?'

'Said I was pinching a teenager's job by rights. Of course they wouldn't have given it to him, even if he'd wanted it. Still, it stung a bit.'

'What's the pay?'

'One pound fifty an hour.' Ian sniggered. 'Derisory even for the Newson boy.'

Chris looked at him. 'I admire you, Ian,' he said simply. 'I really do.'

He found himself admiring Pamela, too. The old battleaxe was showing hidden reserves. In all, the Hendersons were displaying far more grace under pressure than he and Annie had managed. The English middle classes were unsung even as they were forced to their knees in a brash, competitive world.

'Help yourself. Don't be shy.'

Annie's father-in-law waved towards the trestle tables at one side of the marquee. She didn't feel hungry but obliged him by spooning a slice of cold poached salmon onto a plate. She examined the bowls of salads, each predictable and bland – rice with cubes of red and green pepper and tinned sweet corn; potato in an acidic mayonnaise with chives; lettuce, some of the leaves red-edged and crinkly. She manoeuvred three slices of beef tomato onto her plate and returned to her seat.

Chris's cousin, who was seated next to her, shifted a fat and dribbling baby to a different hip and inspected her plate. 'I can see why you're so slim,' he guffawed. 'Keep an eye on Sebastian for us.' He deposited the infant on the grass by his chair, as he headed for the buffet.

It was cold. Goose pimples stood up on Annie's arms. After a glorious week, the weather had turned grey and blowy for the Saturday of the wedding. Jan wandered past, her train smearing along the grass. She smiled and nodded at her sister-in-law, but took the elbow of a friend Annie didn't recognise, the pair talking and laughing with great animation. Annie had never been particularly close to her in-laws, and during the past years of working full-time had avoided them as much as possible. In a way, she blamed them for Chris's predicament. It was easier to censure them for his faults than to censure him. They had brought him up. Why hadn't they managed to teach him how to deal with money?

Sebastian's father reappeared with a laden place. 'I went to a company do last week, bit like this. Nothing like good grub and a bit of bubbly, eh? I'm in computer software by the way. Educational games, that sort of thing. We're looking at games which will tie in with the national curriculum at the moment . . . Seb! What are you doing? Oh, shit! Hey, Ali, can you get this baby's nappy changed? I've got my plate full. Where's Chris, by the way? Haven't seen him since Aunty Mary's funeral which is all of five, six, years ago. Or was it? Let's see. I had just met Ali but we weren't engaged or anything because she didn't come to the funeral. I think we were going steady, though . . . .'

'Excuse me,' Annie murmured. Once upon a time, she would have tolerated a bore at a family function. It was only to be expected. The one went with the other. But now her nerves were stretched too tightly to take any more twanging. She indicated her empty plate, implying that she wanted to get more food.

'Seconds, eh?' said the cousin, talking with his mouth full. 'That's more like it. See you in a tick.'

Annie slipped her plate onto the side of a trestle table and dodged through the hubbub to the bar where a number of waitresses, grey-haired women in improbable frilly nylon aprons over black dresses, were serving champagne. At least Chris's father had ensured it was a decent label. Annie took a tall flute and threaded her way to the tent's opening, passing her mother-in-law in the process.

'Oh, Annie!' Marjie trilled. 'You've cut your hair.' There was a pause. 'I think I preferred it longer, dear. It suited you.' And she turned back to the friends with whom she was chatting. 'My daughter-in-law,' she announced. 'I can be honest with her and she doesn't mind.'

Emma was playing on the pub lawn with the other bridesmaids who comprised the latest branch on Jan's husband's extensive family tree. They were a tribe. There was a unity of purpose, manner and speech about them. They were a brood who knew their pecking order. Emma stood on the edge of their group. She was dressed, like them, in a floral, cotton, hand-smocked dress, but she did not belong. Her smile was a little hesitant, a gesture of ingratiation. The Thompson children raced around her, noisy and certain of themselves.

Annie watched and her heart went out to her

daughter. She saw herself, her own awkwardness, reflected in Emma. Was Emma formed in the womb with the same folds and fault lines in her personality? Or was Emma growing shy as she sensed the fracture in her parents' marriage?

'Emlet,' Annie called. 'Do you want something to eat?'

Emma trotted over to her, pleased to be offered an excuse to abandon her forlorn attempts to join in. Annie steered her into the tent, stooping quickly to pat her bum.

The truth was that she felt much as Emma did. The Greenes and their relatives were a unit from which she was excluded by the subtleties of a shared history and common signals. However, although she did not fit in, she would forever be linked to them – because of Emma, because she had mothered a blood member of the Greene family group. Should her marriage fail, she would still have responsibilities towards Marjie and John. They would still harbour expectations of her.

She took an immoderate swig from her glass.

Great! You lose the husband but you're lumbered with the effing in-laws.

She was losing the husband. His ill temper could no longer be ignored. This invitation, so long marked on their calendar, was unavoidable, but driving here it seemed obvious to Annie that she was the last person in the world Chris would have chosen as his day's companion. He had not commented on her appearance. He did not look at her: indeed, his eyes avoided her, so that he spoke occasionally and sullenly while looking out of car windows, or examining flecks of nap on his suit trousers.

Since the ceremony, he had been missing from her side. She spotted him on the other side of the marquee, moving between groups, laughing, having such a good time, it seemed, with everybody else. On occasion, sensing her observation, his eyes would catch hers, then flick quickly away. It was like a replay of her father's retreat. She still didn't know what she had done.

She put several dollops of custardy trifle in a bowl with a spoon and placed it in front of Emma whom she sat at a table that wasn't supposed to be theirs. She couldn't stand listening to the details of Sebastian's father's life once more.

'That'll put hairs on your chest.' John Greene appeared next to them.

'I don't want hairs, Grandpa,' said Emma through a mouthful of jelly and cream.

'I do,' he said. 'But on my head. Will you share yours with me?'

Emma crooked her arm around the bowl by way of reply.

'Well,' said John, addressing his attention to Annie, but more at a loss for conversation with her than with his granddaughter. 'You look very nice, Annie. How have you been keeping?'

A defiant whim grew within her. 'Badly,' she said.

He looked a little startled, evidently deciding he had misheard her. 'I'm sorry?' he said, straining forward.

'So am I, John,' she replied, finishing her champagne in a movement, 'So am I.'

She got up, took Emma's hand and led her through the marquee, out into the drizzle which now speckled the car windscreens. Behind her, John Greene sat for a second or two, murmured, 'How astonishing,' to himself, and was then sidetracked by his duties as host.

The car keys were in Annie's purse. It had been

agreed that she would remain sober for the return journey.

'Where are we going, Mummy?' said Emma, surprised but acquiescent.

'Where do you want to go?'

'To see the dinosaurs.'

'Then that's where we're going.'

'Is Daddy coming?'

'Nah. Daddy has to stay here, Emlet, but we can go. We're kind of secondary.'

It was one o'clock. She guessed it would take her an hour to reach central London from this corner of Buckinghamshire. Nevertheless, she was nosing into a parking space in South Kensington before Chris noticed they were gone.

Afterwards, her memory of that afternoon possessed a clarity which surprised her; she who had always been so skilled at blurring the unpleasant. But she remembered the pleasure she had taken in Emma's fellowship, and how this was interspersed with a blind and juvenile fear of the retribution awaiting her.

There was a special exhibition in the Natural History Museum, for which they queued. Emma was so excited and apprehensive she did not notice the curious glances that others were directing at their formal clothes. Once inside, the room darkened and there was a loud roaring. Emma took Annie's hand with alacrity.

One of the tableaux of mechanical models depicted a sad, herbivorous dinosaur in the process of being devoured by a crowd of rapacious carnivores. When the lights came on Annie and Emma discovered they were both near to tears for the victim.

She bought them hamburgers and chips and they ate in the car.

In the evening, she drove Emma back to the cottage where Chris was already waiting. That was the one detail she forgot. She knew she asked him who had chauffeured him home and that he told her but she couldn't remember the name.

She had expected Chris to be livid but he was measured and polite.

But after Annie had put Emma to bed and come downstairs and was embarking on an apology in the kitchen, Chris had interrupted her.

He told her he wanted a divorce. He said, 'Annie, I think we should get divorced,' quite softly, and right in the middle of her sentence, which was very similar to the way he had once asked her to marry him.

How strange that even though a part of her had been expecting it, it was still such a convulsing shock.

And again there was the sense of waste, of casting aside something that had once been strong and whole. She did, in fact, say, 'It seems such a waste,' which was a silly, lame way of putting it.

But Chris shook his head, almost as if abashed.

Afterwards, she also remembered how, in the middle of this, a spasm of suspicion passed through her and she blurted out, 'You haven't found someone else, have you?' She phrased it like that, the negative question, to invite the negative response.

And she remembered that he shook his head and said, 'No, of course not,' in a shocked tone, and she thought that she had once again misjudged him and even then, she rebuked herself.

Chapter Nine

The building was a haunted place at six in the morning. Annie walked down the corridor towards the open plan area and the lights above her flickered into life automatically.

Voices rose and fell ahead of her. As she pushed through the swing doors, a security officer and a cleaner sprang from two of the swivel chairs which they had pushed in front of the television set clamped high on the wall. This had been installed as a background source of news stories and occasional ideas for any of the features desk journalists who had a minute to stop before it. The remote control was supposed to be kept in the secretary's drawer: clearly, the cleaners had tumbled to that one.

Annie ostentatiously wheeled her chair, which had been one of those purloined, back to her desk. The cleaner had altered the height and angle of the seat, which irritated her. She pressed levers, tugged at the metal trunk but the mechanics defeated her. She ended up perched too high, her thighs squeezed under the lip of the desk, an extra indignity.

Annie switched on her computer and the printer. She opened some files and began to edit copy, the keyboard's staccato dance the only noise except for the hum of the machinery. The copy was not taxing. She finished it in twenty minutes.

What time will Alec be here? How long do I have to play these games of concentration? She thought he would be in early. He had taken to getting in at nine. There was a memo in her in-tray, calling all staff to an additional afternoon conference. The circulation figures had dived again. Alec was worried. He wore the cowed, panicked look of a man who fears for his job just as his two children have settled happily at their expensive private schools.

Annie opened the morning's papers and scanned them each, cover to cover. For stretches of time she could disappear into her tasks, but as each ended, or her concentration wavered, the sharp blows in her heart broke out anew.

I can't believe this is happening to me. Doctor, doctor, I'm in pain, do something.

What do you give a woman with a broken heart? she wondered. Prozac, probably. She thought about making an appointment with her GP when the surgery opened, but realised that she had never registered with a London practice. Officially, she was still on the books of nice Dr Trevor in Cambridgeshire.

Would Prozac dull the pain? Would it turn down the volume of her anguish to background levels, so that the rest of life would be bearable?

I'm a big girl now. I'm getting divorced just like Mommy.

She and Chris had felt so adult when they'd first seen the priest to arrange a date for their wedding. They had laughed about it in a pub afterwards: this is real, this is something grown-ups do.

TWO INTO ONE

If it's six thirty in London, what time is it in New York?

She did not work out the sum, but dialled the long, musical international number regardless. There were five rings before Patricia answered.

'Patricia, it's Annie.'

'Annie! Whassa matter?' Annie only rang her father to announce births or deaths. Was a divorce in the same category? She was struck dumb by the sudden realisation that no social etiquette applied to this pronouncement. She imagined the greetings card companies plugging the gap in the market, tasteful floral covers opening to the nice, neat platitudes inside: *'We feel sad that it has ended this way, but it is better for all those concerned.'*

'Annie? Annie?' Patricia sounded alarmed. 'Shall I wake your father? Will you stay on the line while I wake him?'

'No.' Her voice answered. She was half surprised to hear it. 'No, Patricia, I was ringing you.'

'Me, honey? Whassa matter?' she repeated.

'I'm getting divorced, Patricia.' And she added, melodramatically, 'My husband doesn't love me anymore.'

'OK. So he's gotta 'nother woman?'

'Nope, nope. There's no one else. It's just us, we've grown apart.' She had started to cry.

Patricia's voice with its brittle Noo Yawk accent crackled with incredulity. 'Don't you believe it, honey. When a man asks for a divorce there's always another woman. They always set up the next one to run to.'

Judging others by your own past performance, Patricia?

'Annie, you get yourself a lawyer. Quick. And a

good one. You wanna speak to your father now? I'll
go wake him.'

She heard Patricia retreating. It was odd. What
was odd? Annie frowned. There was a picture in her
mind. Patricia had to go to another room to wake
her father yet the phone was by the bed. Suddenly,
Annie realised that her father was sleeping in a separate bedroom – undoubtedly as it was only a
two-bedroom apartment, her old room, the one with
the ineffective curtains and the Snoopy on the
bolster. The toy lay there still, in her memory, bathed
in sodium yellow light.

Before her father came on the line, she replaced
her own receiver very softly.

Why on earth should I want to speak to him?

*If it's six thirty in London what time is it in
Buckinghamshire?*

She dialled the number. There were twelve rings
before Marjie answered it. Nothing so louche as a
telephone in the master bedroom of 'Grove House'.

'Annie, do you know what time it is?'

Annie glanced at the clock on the wall above
Callum's chair. 'Six forty-three precisely,' she said. 'I
was phoning you, Marjie, to tell you that just as
I have paid off his debts, your son has asked me for
a divorce.'

There was a silence. 'Annie, what do you mean?'

'That was a pretty unequivocal statement, Marjie.'

There was a strangled sound from Marjorie's
throat. Annie realised that her mother-in-law was
crying. She had misjudged her totally. Her hostility
evaporated. 'Don't cry, Marjie. Don't cry. I didn't
mean to sound so argumentative. I just thought,' she
lied, 'that you should know what's going on.'

'I'm calling Chris,' Marjorie announced eventually.
'Ask him what in heaven's name he thinks he's

playing at. I'll get Father David to talk to him.'

'Don't do that, Marje. Please don't do that. It will make things worse. It will affect your relationship with him. I wouldn't like that. Let him tell you. Act shocked when he tells you. *Please*.'

They talked for another ten minutes. Afterwards, it struck Annie as ironic but appropriate that it was she who had spent the time and energy in consoling Marjorie.

If it's seven in London, I don't even want to consider what time it is in San Francisco.

Annie returned to her in-tray, until finally, at eight thirty, Alec's shambling figure appeared outside his office door, fumbling with the keys, his briefcase and a cup of coffee. Annie only realised how red-eyed and wan she looked when Alec exclaimed, 'Good God, what's happened?' as she walked up to him. She followed him into his big cold, impersonal office and asked him if he would guarantee her work should she return to freelancing because she was getting divorced and she needed to be at home with her kid now. And Alec walked round his desk and clamped her in his arms against his plump bosom, to the string vest tangible beneath the drip-dry, poly-cotton shirt which smelt of cigars and sweat and aftershave, and said, 'Don't you worry about anything. The minute you need it we'll put you on a retainer. If it's the last thing I do.'

And at that point, even in the midst of the selfishness of misery, she realised just how scared Alec was for his future, too.

Chris attributed his symptoms of shock to the accident. It happened when he was returning from dropping Emma at school on the first day of the new term. She was subdued and anxious: he had had to

133

struggle to control his short fuse when she had spent fifteen minutes washing her face but had still emerged from the bathroom with egg yolk encrusting her mouth. He was thinking about her when, as he sped up the village by-pass, the Vauxhall in front of him pulled out to overtake a lumbering cement lorry. It took some long, cushioned seconds, during which his mind refused to come to terms with what he was seeing but remained resolutely entangled in his personal problems, until, with a rush, he was in the present, awake and aware.

'You idiot!' he said aloud, addressing the other driver.

A stream of traffic was rushing towards them, spear-headed by a dark green saloon with feverishly flashing headlights. The lorry trundled on, obstinately refusing to be deflected from its course or speed. The Vauxhall accelerated, its left indicator winking its desperate intention.

Even as the Vauxhall whisked itself out of danger, the green saloon, edging to the left, struck the high kerb and left the road. It cannoned over the grass verge and flew into the ditch beyond, muddy debris flicking from its spinning tyres.

The lorry and the Vauxhall beyond continued impassively onwards, hurrying towards their banal appointments.

Chris decelerated, quickly and smoothly, mounting the kerb, stopping. He checked the road and hurried across. The occupant of the saloon, a grey-haired woman, was slumped over the wheel. There was blood, shockingly bright, on her forehead. She was almost hanging in her seat belt but there were no other obvious signs of injury. On the bonnet, in front of the passenger seat, impaled on several long shards of glass, a small black poodle was shivering. A trail of slime and long white strands of translucent flesh escaped its soft, pale belly. It made no noise. As Chris went to it, wondering what on earth he could do to help it, it simply stopped moving. He knew it was dead.

Petrol was trickling from the engine. He had better get the woman out. A figure appeared above him, a young man in shirt sleeves and tinted glasses, another driver who had stopped who knows where? At the lip of the ditch, he paused and seeing the dog, grimaced.

'I'll call the emergency services,' he said, with a faint questioning tone which was directed towards Chris, as if he had somehow been nominated crisis leader through the dubious distinction of having reached the scene first.

The young man was reaching towards a mobile telephone slung at his belt.

'There's leaking petrol! Go further away!' Chris urged him.

'Oh! Yeah! Sparks!' The figure duly disappeared.

Chris turned back to the woman, whose eyelids were now fluttering. He wrenched open the car door and knelt next to her, calming her, distracting her from the dog, which, nevertheless, she seemed to have some knowledge of, for she kept her eyes fixed on his; nor did she ask after it. When she seemed more or less conscious, and could tell him that she was not in immediate pain, he gently extracted her from her seat belt and helped her out. Struggling, sliding, he carried her up the bank to a safe distance, where two or three concerned spectators wrapped her in a plaid rug.

She did not seem to be badly hurt, though, of course, when the ambulance turned up, sirens whooping, it spirited her off to hospital. Chris gave his details to the police. He had caught the number plate of the Vauxhall and gave that, too. He thanked the man with the mobile, who slapped him on the shoulder, their shared experience breeding instant camaraderie. He took it very slowly as he drove home.

All the same, when he turned into the lane, he felt the bile rising. He stopped the car abruptly and cast himself from the door, retching. Jesus, what a week! He knelt on the verge collecting himself and his mind flew back to Annie, to the divorce, to the great matter of his life . . .

'You all right, boy?'

It was Arthur, returning from walking his fat, black labrador across the stubble fields. His face, sagging from the weight of the years, reddened by beer and fresh air, and the nose thrown as if by an inexpert potter into the rough centre, in size and texture like an overripe strawberry, wore an expression of cautious concern. Arthur was not one for nosiness and would not like to be thought of as prying.

Chris straightened himself out. 'I'm fine,' he said but he wasn't. He held his head in his hand, as if that would hide his distress from Arthur. His shoulders shook uncontrollably.

'This is ludicrous,' he announced, more to himself than his unwanted companion. 'Sorry, Arthur,' he added.

'What you got to be sorry about?' said Arthur, with his bucolic logic. The question was unsettling in its pertinence.

Chris took a deep breath, steeling himself to the village's knowing his business, to being the subject of its small talk and its well meaning.

'Annie and I have split up. We're getting divorced.'

'Aah,' said Arthur. There was a pause during which he might have been digesting the news, or weighing his words, or simply clipping the lead on the labrador to stop it running into Mrs Manningtree's garden which was her pride and joy and open two days a year under the Yellow Book scheme. 'Oi don't agree with divorce meself,' Arthur said. 'Not good for the littl'uns, is it? And whose idea was this divorce, then?'

'Mine,' he said, frankly.

'Mmm.' Arthur looked at him. 'You've lost a good 'un there,' he said. Muscles in Chris's throat and jaw were twitching beyond his command. Arthur continued to measure him with his slow glance. He seemed unabashed at Chris's contained distress. 'Sad business,' he added kindly. 'Oi daresay you know what you're doing.' Somehow, Chris had the impression that this statement was an exact contradiction of Arthur's private thoughts.

Chris slid into the car and drove slowly home, monitoring his queasiness. Once inside, he made for the fridge, pushed his thumb into the silver top of a pint of milk and drank it straight from the bottle. The coolness soothed his stomach.

The telephone stood on the chest of drawers, next to the tank of Emma's terrapins and beneath the blackboard that said, 'Bleach. Don't forget wedding present!!!' He walked over to it, picked the receiver up, put it down again. He rubbed the note about the wedding present from the board with the cuff of his shirt.

He felt terrible, which was only to be expected. He had an odd sense of unreality, as if his senses were blurred by downers. He was trying to juxtapose what his life had been until quite recently with what it was now. Sitting at the kitchen table, he looked back over the years and was astonished.

It was only three, four years ago that he had been a dynamic, self-employed scion of successful Britain. He had had a good job! He placed an exclamation mark after this statement even in his own head. It seemed so novel to him, now. He had earned a comfortable salary. He had taken considerable pleasure in spending his disposable income on his wife and his child. Indeed, he had felt so secure in his slot, so sure that the future would continue in much the same vein, as his father's had before him, that he had completely failed to see the signs of imminent financial disaster. Thus he had regarded his mounting overdraft, the growing debts, merely as temporary hiccoughs which would be conquered.

Even when his business had failed, he had somehow not understood the effect it would have on him. Of course, he had been shattered. But he had thought he would bounce back within six months or so. In the meantime, running the house while Annie worked had seemed sensible. He had never subscribed to mindless blokishness: he was as able and as willing to pass a vacuum cleaner over a carpet, stack a dishwasher, concoct a meal, as Annie was. It was only as the months dragged past, like burdened mules, that he found himself diminished by his new role.

There had been a defining moment. Audrey Benbow, standing by the post box, her teeth displayed in a teasing grin, had said, 'What's it like to be a kept man, then?' This facetious remark had oppressed him.

The irony was that Audrey Benbow was a kept woman. She was forty-two, had one child at school and a husband in a recession-proof business: Rod

Benbow was poised dizzyingly high in the management structure of one of the major supermarket chains. A cleaner did Audrey's housework. An ironing service pressed her sheets. A gardener mowed her bowling green lawn. Audrey used her time to learn pottery (not very successfully) and also dressage, during very expensive private lessons on a gleaming chestnut warmblood which she kept in livery at a cost to her husband of £70 a week. No one felt compelled to rib her about the structure of her life. Her parents did not send her positions vacant clipped from the *Telegraph*, although they certainly bored all their friends with accounts of her agreeable days.

The real difference between Audrey and Chris was that he had not become 'kept' by choice. And this fact had weighed so heavily on him that it seemed to have flattened him. The Chris he saw in his memory was resilient, resourceful, producing admired and innovative work. If he had to meet a client's impossible deadline, he worked all day, all night and all the next day, until he was hallucinating through sleep deprivation. But underneath it, there was always the steady satisfaction, the feeling of purpose, of meeting his promises.

He had always been a man of his word, in day-to-day business transactions as well as the more important promises. He would have thought it impossible that he would ever be unfaithful to Annie, but he had been drawing away from her for a long time now, walking a bitter and bewildered path, it seemed to him, absorbed in his own thoughts. When he had finally looked up, it had been Fiona who'd been standing in front of him, offering sympathy.

You haven't found somebody else, have you?
No, of course not.

He couldn't quite face telling Annie about Fiona at the moment, after all. It would be like hitting her, a final obscene abuse. He had a vague, and probably a vain, hope that they would be able to settle their differences in a friendly manner. Quite suddenly, it occurred to him that this was unlikely in the extreme. His picture of the future was of him and Emma, as they were, not of his leaving her. He wanted custody of his child.

And so would Annie.

It came home to him that he could lose everything. For didn't the courts always favour women?

Officially, the hours were ten to six, but in practice the office filled and emptied much later. The secretaries and the researchers arrived first because they left first. At ten twenty-three Callum strolled in, with a coffee in a polystyrene cup in his hand and a gamey-smelling sandwich tucked under his arm, grease smearing the paper wrapping. Shortly afterwards, Stella arrived, uncharacteristically late and tight-lipped.

'How are you?' she said in an off-hand manner to Annie.

'Terrible. Chris wants a divorce.'

Stella's coffee cup was poised half-way towards her mouth. 'Ah,' she said.

Everyone else was studiously occupied with creating an impression that they hadn't heard.

At lunchtime, Annie went to the loo. As she tried to apply some semblance of composure to her face with the aid of her polka-dotted bag of cosmetics, she decided that she needed a long and alcoholic lunch. Although she was not often invited to join the 'lads', and, unlike Stella, was far too reticent to push herself forward, today she knew that they would expand to include her. David had squeezed her shoulder as he'd walked past. Even Callum had brought her a cup of coffee without being asked.

The make-up did not camouflage the red veins in her eyes. She gave up trying.

She pushed through the swing door, turned the corner. The desk was empty. While she was in the lavatory, they had fled. She flopped in her chair, imagining their flustered alarm at the prospect of having to comfort a distraught woman for an hour or two; their relief when she gave them an opening for escape.

Normally, being excluded from the magic male circle did not disturb her unduly but today she really did not want to be left alone with a sandwich. She did not want to feel like an outsider or be driven to question her popularity. The men felt comfortable with Stella: why didn't they with her? You see, she was growing maudlin already.

'Ah, there you are.' Stella emerged from the direction of the lifts wearing her coat. 'I thought you'd gone. Come on, Annie, you're coming to lunch with me. A long lunch, OK? The lads have scarpered,' she added, gesturing to their empty seats.

On the first bottle of wine, when Stella told her Chris was a prat and a bastard, Annie began to sob. On the second, she herself declared him a blisterous outbreak of pus-headed pox and good riddance to him. 'I'm better off without him,' she crowed.

'Atta-girl,' said Stella.

She emptied herself of her emotions, and then, by the end of lunch, when Stella put her in a minicab home, she found that they had somehow replenished themselves. The anger, the pain, the bitterness had regrown from the roots. She was reduced to visiting

Karen Harris in her kitchen, repeating to her all that she had said to Stella.

'God,' she said, 'he must hate me. He must really hate being with me. He's prepared to give up everything, which is what it will come to, to cut me out of his life.'

And Karen Harris said, 'That's men for you. They all go off without a look behind them. I s'pose you won't be needing the flat much longer then? Not if you're going home to your kid?'

Talking, as if the outpourings of a dozen repeated conversations would ease the pain, became the pattern of Annie's life over the following days. She knew she was being a bore but she couldn't help it. She fastened onto each listener as if they might provide an explanation for what had happened, but the truth was she didn't listen to a word of their proffered advice unless it coincided with her own thoughts.

Rachel bought her an artistic bunch of flowers, pale lilies and grey eucalyptus leaves, to which she had pinned a note. 'You will feel better, Annie. This is as bad as it gets.' A letter arrived in the office with a Cambridge postmark and the words 'Private and Personal' in unfamiliar handwriting in the lefthand corner. It was from Pamela Henderson.

'Dear Annie,' she wrote,
'I was so sorry to hear that you and Chris are getting divorced. I hope you don't mind me writing, but I felt so upset. I can understand the pressure you have been under now that I find myself in a similar position. Of course, I appreciate that my job isn't nearly as high powered as yours, but I do now know what it's like to try to deal with a husband's depression' – and here she had inserted the word

understandable in brackets – 'while there are a million and one things to do oneself.

'I hope we'll still see you around, Annie. You're still a part of the village to us. I'll never forget that when we had the burglary you and Chris spent hours clearing up the mess so we didn't have to. I remember saying to Ian what a lovely couple you were.

'I don't know if it will bring any comfort to you but you're in my thoughts and prayers.'

Strangely, Annie *was* comforted by this letter. She folded it and kept it in her personal organiser. To be remembered was important. It reassured her that that part of her history which belonged to the village, years which included the best and worst of her marriage, had not been a waste of time.

After that, she was able to concentrate more on her work, resuming the punishing schedule she now thought of as normal. She wasn't eating much and she was drinking far too often. Stella, trying to support her, took her to lunch again. Annie looked across the table at Stella's dyed red hair, her brave attempts to defy the monstrous tyranny of time, and she felt a huge squeeze of affection for her. It was odd how close they had become during the past few months.

'Stel, why did you break my confidence and tell Callum and the office I'd left home?'

Stella took a sip of wine. 'I didn't mean to hurt you, Annie. You know me. I love to gossip, I love to impart information. It makes me feel like the centre of attention. It's one of my big character defects, as Phil is forever telling me.' At the mention of his name, she grimaced with distaste.

'We had a row this morning,' she said. And leaning forward, she explained how Phil had declared that he couldn't possibly 'operate' as he termed it, with the baby in a buggy by his side. Annie vaguely imagined Phil doing faintly questionable deals with faintly shady characters, his street cred hopelessly undermined by Thomas's voluble interjections.

It had been agreed between Stella and Phil that they would find a nanny, and Stella had duly set about finding one, 'though why the responsibility should fall on me, God only knows.' She had interviewed five and they were all unsuitable, 'raving, with nervous tics', Stella exaggerated merrily. 'You couldn't, in all conscience, leave these women to potty train your infant.'

The solution had presented itself yesterday evening. Mark held qualifications, an impeccable reference and was the only candidate who had gone down on his hands and knees to play with Thomas.

'It was male bonding at first sight. Phil hit the roof when I said I was going to hire him. Said he wasn't having some other bloke acting as surrogate dad to his son. I said, "But it's all right for some woman to act as surrogate mum in my stead?" "Oh, that's different," he said. Have you noticed how it's always supposed to be different for us? Anyway, that's how it was left this morning. Unresolved. *Big* bone of contention.

'He's jealous, of course. He fancied having a slip of a girl wafting around the house in her Marks and Sparks lingerie, and now there's going to be a slip of a boy in his – or may be. His other big fear is that Mark's gay. His big neanderthal head can only believe that any man who wants to look after children is gay or a paedophile or both. Said he's not having his son being turned into a "woofter". I said, "You looked after Thomas and you're not gay." That was different, too, of course.'

Annie took another sip of Sancerre. She hadn't eaten much the previous evening or anything for breakfast and it went straight to her head. Stella's domestic problems could not divert her for long. The pain began to saw across her heart.

'Chris and I couldn't afford a nanny,' she said, returning to her theme.

A flicker of boredom crossed Stella's face, her good intentions slightly askew.

'Play fair, Stel,' said Annie. 'At this crisis in my life, we're going to talk about me and my problems. How come you always manage to turn the conversation around to yours?'

Stella thought it a good sign that Annie's sense of irony had re-emerged.

'Oh, I'm unparalleled at that,' she agreed. 'So egotistical. But I always admit my faults right out front and everyone likes me anyway. I learned that trick from Phil. He always twisted me round his little finger by acting the boyish scamp. And I thought, if men can do that, I can, too. So now when I'm caught in the act I just stand there looking helpless and lovable. Good, isn't it?'

'Brilliant. Why can't I do things like that?'

'Oh, Annie, you're far too lady-like. It's one of your big problems. You're always worrying about the impression you're making.'

Annie digested this assessment. It seemed fair. 'Can I blame my mother for that?'

'Why not, darling? I blame mine for everything.'

Emma hadn't gone to the lavatory at last break. She hadn't wanted to then. Now she sat on her chair fighting the bloated, full-up feeling in her tummy. She knew it wouldn't be long until the end of school and then . . . the hot rush of the urine was audible.

Luke Smith put his hand up. 'Miss Caroll. Emma Greene's wee-ed in her pants.'

The class giggled. Miss Carroll said, 'Emma! How could you? You're a big girl now, you're not in the baby classes any more, are you?' Emma's scarlet face stilled her. 'Come along, then,' she tutted more kindly. 'Let's get you into something dry.'

Emma was ushered to the school nurse's cubby hole, where some thick cotton knickers were found, and her own rinsed in a basin and placed in a Tesco's carrier bag.

'Are you all right, Emma dear?' Miss Carroll asked.

Emma looked at her. 'I don't think my mummy loves me,' she said.

'Oh, Emma! I'm sure she does. That can't be true.' Miss Carroll looked shocked, as teachers rarely do. 'What makes you say that?'

Emma tried to think of the words that would let out the feelings within her. 'She fought with Daddy.'

'Ah,' Miss Carroll sounded relieved. 'Don't worry, dear. Grown-ups often fight, but it doesn't necessarily mean anything.'

Feet pounded the corridor, voices babbled. It was the end of the school day. Miss Carroll had to get on. Emma made her way back to her classroom. She was glad to see it was empty, except that she had wanted Becky to wait for her.

Miss Carroll helped her find her reading book and her coat. Emma slipped out of the heavy metal and glass door into the playground.

'I told my mum about you.' Angela Jones's round red face materialised a foot in front of her. 'She said you were a nasty, smelly little girl.'

Emma stared stupidly. She couldn't think what to say. If a grown-up said she was nasty, it must be true.

TWO INTO ONE

She saw her daddy at the edge of the playground, his eyes screwed up, looking for her.

Emma wanted her mummy. Where was Mummy? Why was Mummy never there? She trailed her shameful bag across the grey tarmac, painted with white hopscotch pitches and child-sized snakes-and-ladders boards, towards her father.

On the way, she saw Becky arm in arm with Sophie Howard, whispering something. She made for them, but Becky pretended not to see her and the pair flew off together.

Chapter Ten

The ambulance with its flashing blue light stood in the lane. In the driveway, a police car was parked, its radio sporadically firing messages at the indifferent air.

In her modern house in the cul-de-sac, built in the seventies on a mediaeval field, Pammy Henderson had realised that summer was loitering this year like an obtuse guest. She normally looked forward to September ripening. Heat sapped her but she loved a slight chill to the morning, the poetry of early autumn glistening on hedgerow cobwebs, lighting the leaves with glowing golds, cracking in the conkers that spilt onto the paths, luscious mahogany kernels against their acid-green minecasings. She liked the way the dew lay on the neatly clipped grass, dripped from the conifer hedge that marked the boundary of their patch with the fields beyond, sparkled on the Japanese anemones and the roses and glossed the brown earth which Ian so carefully manured each October. This year, however, was different. For the first time ever, she did not anticipate autumn with pleasure.

She washed up at her sink overlooking her garden,

the vegetables mostly harvested now, after the bullying heat of high summer, except for some late sweet corn and the greenhouse crop of reddening tomatoes.

In her apron pocket was the letter from Michael saying that he had had enough, university was not for him, he wasn't going back. It had arrived yesterday and she had telephoned him immediately, at his girlfriend's up North, pointing out how impaired his prospects would be without a degree, just look at his brothers.

'It didn't do Dad much good,' Michael had replied.

She'd tried to argue with him but Michael had grown irritable, as he always did when she fussed. Her sons were the only people she allowed to cow her and Michael quashed her now.

'Look, Mum, I've told you a million times. Don't try to organise me.' And then he put the phone down. Michael had been her last hope of the three of them. The other two were unemployed, one sharing a squat in London, the other shacking up with a girlfriend in Glasgow.

Ian was out on his paper round. The cats had been fed.

Pamela wiped her hands on a tea towel, and got a frozen bolognese out of the freezer for Ian's tea. Dinner, she meant. She still called it tea in her mind, a throw-back to the lower-middle origins that she prided herself on having eradicated from her speech.

Once, they had been invited to the Manningtrees' for luncheon and she'd scattered the salt all over her food. Then, when she'd seen Fleur Manningtree's neat little pile on the rim of her plate, she'd remembered, too late, the correct way of doing such things. But she and Ian had learned. They had got married in 1970 with an eagerness to better themselves

150

lighting their eyes. They worked hard and they mimicked. Only occasionally now could you hear the lower social whine in Ian's carefully phrased speech; most of the time his clipped vowels and idioms were a dead ringer for the Brigadier's.

The simple lines that marked out life in the seventies and eighties she craved now. You set your sights on the horizon and by dint of hard work and application you would get there. You shopped at Sainsbury's and gave dinner parties. You learned how to cook and eat artichokes and yams and mooli, though you didn't really like them. You paid the mortgage and bought shares in the newly privatised utilities. You sent your children to private schools, confident that they would go on to university, that, with these advantages, they would do even better than you had done.

You became middle middle class. You voted for Thatcher, though you rather liked that nice Dr Owen of the SDP, though your thickening and aging heart beat even faster at the mention of Gorbachev. There was something rather sexy about him, really, quite apart from the fact that he was a visionary bringing peace to the world.

She had been so proud of what she and Ian had achieved, how far they'd come, how well they were thought of in their community. Oh, she knew that some of the younger people looked on her as a bit of a busy-bodying do-gooder: fat old Pam, good for a snigger behind her back. But she also knew that the village would fall apart without her.

Only it hadn't. Younger blood had stepped into the breach she'd left behind her when she'd given up her duties. And she and Ian had worked and risen and now seemed to have fallen back. Pammy's father had been a clerk and they had lived in a terraced but respectable house in the suburbs, a terraced but respectable life. But her sons were content to meander through the benefit culture, to indulge in casual labour when they wanted cash, but otherwise to remain resolutely unemployed. What a waste! What a waste her life had been! Of course, Ian adored her, she knew that. He called her 'Mummy' still, as he had referred to her when the boys were small. And in truth, it reflected their roles.

She wiped the breakfast bar with a J-cloth, tipped the soapy water from the bucket down the stainless steel plughole in her stainless steel sink. Then she found the rope from the garage, climbed the steps to the landing, tied it firmly – she had been in the Guides and she knew all about knots – one end to the banisters, one looped round her neck. Then she jumped.

Unusually for the seventies, it was a solidly built house, and the thick teak planking stood firm as her fourteen stone thrashed below. Which was why, when Ian Henderson came home from his paper round, he found, firstly, an odd note by the defrosting evening meal on the kitchen table – 'Darling Ian', it read, 'See you again. My love till eternity.' And when, calling her name, he wandered into the hall, he was confronted by her bulk swinging, contorted, the tongue lolling, blackened, don't look.

He dialled 999. He fled next door and old Tom Gardiner rushed over with a scythe of all things, and cut her down. But it was too late. They knew that.

A crowd gathered outside when they saw the ambulance and the police car. Old ladies, mothers with pushchairs, Arthur on his way back from buying his weekly lottery ticket, they gathered and

they speculated. Then they saw the vicar arriving
with a pinched face in his tin can car and they knew
it was bad.

The word filtered out from Tom Gardiner's wife.
Fat Pammy of all people had hanged herself from the
stair banisters.

It was a wonder they took her weight.

Inside the house they had called Field View despite
the impervious conifer hedge, Ian sat at the kitchen
table while a young female police constable made
him a cup of tea.

'Thank you, dear,' he said.

He pulled at the ginger hairs on his knuckles.
Pammy had always told him off about that habit. He
sipped his tea. The constable looked out at the
garden and thought how bloody awful for the poor
old geezer.

There was a cry from the table. 'Mummy! Pammy!'
cried the funny little ginger-haired man in a cracked
and piteous voice. 'Why? Why? We could have seen
it through together . . .'

And he began to sob into his hands.

Annie wore charcoal to the funeral. She had considered the options for some time. Black might look as
if she were exaggerating her closeness to Pammy. On
the other hand, she wanted to show her respect. She
wanted to show Ian that his wife's death had the
power to move her neighbours, that Pammy was not
as easily dismissed as she herself had once
suspected she might be.

Annie sat towards the back of the ancient stone
church – Norman? Saxon? She had only the fuzziest
knowledge of pre-Tudor English history. She knew
only that the stones were as old as the earth and that
simple people had worshipped here for year after

calamitous, burdened year, bringing the same problems into the silence and straining for an answer.

In another century, they would not have permitted Pammy to be buried here. She had died by her own hand, committing the unforgivable sin. A more tolerant age allowed her to be mourned by the village with full pomp. It was a good turnout. Pammy would have been thrilled to see the Manningtrees, and the Brigadier and Lady Newlan in the pews. By her side, Chris was fiddling with a key ring, turning it over and over in his palm. Be still, she felt like saying. Be still and listen. The choir rose to their feet. The vicar appeared in his black cloak like a bat's wing by the pulpit at the front.

The choir would sing Pammy's favourite song, the vicar said. The organ wheezed and warbled. Doo-de-doo-de-dee-dah. Doo-de-doo-de-dee-dah. The choir broke into 'My Way'. They soared towards the high notes and missed. One by one, their voices strained and cracked. It was a shambling, maudlin rendition but overcome by emotion, members of the congregation began to snivel.

Annie stared at the stained-glass window. She thought of Pammy and her spoiled hopes. She thought of her own. She thought of the girl she had been and the woman she had wanted to be. She was just thirty-six and she had achieved nothing. She was thirty-six, perhaps halfway through her alloted span, and her life was barren. Except for Emma. Emma was her one source of joy. Emma was the fiercest of loves. Emma was her only attempt to reach towards the infinite distance. She would wish to spread the glittering sky before her feet.

Conventional hymns were sung. The vicar gave his sermon. Although in life he had kept Pammy at one remove, wary of her ability to take offence, he was an articulate man, and once again he said the right things. He painted a picture of Pammy that was true. He said how impossible it was to think that she had succumbed to despair.

'But I believe in a God of forgiveness,' he declared. 'And I do not think Pammy is condemned by Him. There is always a danger that we make our God into something that is less than ourselves. If we, flawed as we are, can understand her action, and feel, in the most pure way, human pity for her, then how much more does God understand her and, pitying her, has saved her.'

Forgiveness and redemption. *I'm so sorry, Annie.* But sorry wasn't enough. She had wanted penance to be done. And the doing of it had altered Chris for ever. They were both changed, but not for the better.

The service concluded. With Hugh Manningtree acting as fourth bearer, Pammy's trio of big strapping sons, their crew-cut hair and their earrings incongruous against their dark suits, carried her coffin down the aisle. Their podgy pink faces were impenetrable. Annie could not guess their thoughts. Ian followed them. His hair was greasy. His shirt collar was frayed. There was no one to care for him, now.

The hearse swept off to the crematorium: 'Mum's a burner not an eater,' one of the sons explained to the dumbfounded Brigadier. Only the family followed in the varnished black limousines. The rest of the mourners, including Chris and Annie, picked their way past the lichened tombs and spilled through the lych gate onto the lane.

It was early afternoon.

155

'I'll come back with you. See Emlet,' Annie told Chris.

He looked awkward, but she ascribed it to his anticipating that she wanted to talk, to settle the arrangements for the ending of their marriage. She intended to broach the subject with him shortly; not today, but at the weekend. He would have to leave the house; she to return to it. She had to tell him she was planning to resume freelance work. They had to discuss access and money and solicitors. She hoped it would be a civilised divorce. It had been an uncivilised marriage of late, let it be a civilised split.

But there was no need to discuss it now. A training day at Emma's school meant that she was at home. Annie gathered that it had been difficult for Chris to attend the funeral. She knew that eventually he had asked the mother of Emma's friend to babysit.

A red hatchback was parked on the drive. Annie walked in the front door. Ben hurtled down the stairs towards her, barking, picking up a shoe to offer her. She patted him, resting her face against the warm dogginess of his fur. Emma ran from the sitting room and Annie enfolded her, feeling her velvety skin next to hers, smelling Emma's special smell, stroking her shoulder blades, bony, like nascent wings, patting her round, soft bum.

A tall, full-figured, pale woman stood in the doorway, looking a little uncertain.

Chris said, 'Er, this is Fiona. Becky's mother.' A blonde girl wearing a Boyzone T-shirt was clinging to her skirt.

'You must be Becky,' said Annie, smiling. 'I've heard a lot about you.'

Fiona relaxed perceptibly. 'I'll make a cup of tea,' she said.

The proprietary undertone rattled Annie.

As Fiona turned, the dog detached itself from the group and padded after her. For a moment, Annie was confounded by this. There was a beat of time. Suspicion flooded her. Why was Fiona so familiar to the dog?

Alert now, she followed the dog, her dog, following Fiona.

She stood in the kitchen doorway and watched. Fiona spoke over her shoulder, 'Was it awful for you? Was she a very good friend?' she asked.

She stretched up to the cupboard and retrieved the tin in which Annie had always kept her tea. She opened the drawer in which Annie had always kept her teaspoons. She knew where everything was without asking.

And then Annie knew. Fiona Carr was completely at home in Annie Greene's house.

In the gloom and the smoke of a subterranean wine bar, baskets hanging from beams, sawdust on the flags of the floor, oak casks upended as side tables, on which were posed careful arrangements of dried grasses, Annie sat with a long glass before her. The thick crimson tomato juice was ribboned with spicy Worcester sauce; ice cubes sounded like wind chimes as she stirred the Bloody Mary with a long plastic implement. She'd walked out of the kitchen – her kitchen – encountering Chris in the dining room.

'Liar,' she'd said. He knew exactly what she was talking about.

She left. Emma cried out, 'Mummy!' but she hadn't stopped, couldn't stop – *one day, Emlet, you'll understand.* And then she found herself in the lane with no method of transport because she'd come down by train and taxi, so she'd done something very foolish – she could hear her mother's admonition – she had hitched a lift from a passing van to the station. The man in the van was young and tattoo-ed and had obviously fancied his chances when he stopped, but as she had sat and sobbed next to him, he had undergone the conversion from masculine excitement to male bewilderment. He dropped her in front of the ticket office and said, 'Don't worry, love, it may never 'appen,' which provoked her to long and bitter laughter. Even he, thick as he was, heard the bitterness in her laugh and drove away quickly, startled.

The train was delayed. Something wrong with the points at Hitchin. It ground into King's Cross at six and she negotiated the underground in a daze, pitching up at the office so late that everyone had gone home, except that the lads always had a 'quick one' in the wine bar after work. Annie had never before joined them. In former times, she had always been making for a train. Thereafter, she had been working late. She had been down here only twice before, and then during the lunch hour, for leaving parties. Afterwards, she thought that she was probably trying to run to Stella, but at the time she was hardly aware of her motives. Stella was not in the wine bar, of course, but Tony and Callum were, and for once they put on a good show of accommodating her presence.

'Bastard's got another woman,' she said.

Callum was unsurprised. 'And you only just twigged?' he said.

But he and Tony took it in turns to supply her with Bloody Marys, which she rarely drank.

The day swirled in the red lubricant. She saw again the pink faces of Pammy's piggy sons and tried to decide whether they were adopting a collective brave face or whether they were unmoved by their mother's funeral. She imagined the pall of smoke that Pammy made at the crematorium and she watched Ian watching the plume as it floated into the sky, never to return. Thin-skinned, thick-waisted Pammy had inspired a true love in her prosaic, meticulous husband.

'I'm prettier than her,' she told the side of Tony's head but she was referring not to Pammy but to Fiona. He and Callum were continuing with their office bitch, uninterested in her misery, but every now and then she addressed them and they humoured her, checking if her glass was low. 'Get the woman some more anaesthetic', one of them said at one point. And the other dipped for his wallet and made for the bar.

You wouldn't have looked twice at Fiona Carr in the street. Smash a glass in her plain face. Scratch out her eyes. There was no such thing as a civilised divorce.

Fiona Carr. Fiona Cart. Fiona Tart. Slapper. Bitch. Cow.

Six months ago, Chris had read one of Annie's letters. It wasn't a letter she'd received, but one she'd sent by fax, which was why the original was on her desk at home, awaiting filing. It wasn't an important letter, just a quick note to a friend on another newspaper. But he made reference to its contents so she knew he had come across it, perused it, as if being her husband gave him the right. It had rankled. She had felt him steal inside her mind. His breath was on the back of her neck. Was there no privacy inside marriage?

She hadn't said anything aloud, for once, but in her head she had berated him. I don't read your mail, she had silently told him. I allow you to retain some private portion of yourself.

Hadn't she just. She should have read his letters, read the signs, read his retreat from old loyalties.

She took a sip from the glass, imbibing bravado. Vodka made your troubles slip down. How many had she had?

'How many have I had, Callum?'

'Not enough,' he said and went to get another one at the bar.

Tony pushed back his stool. 'I'm going for a leak,' he said.

'Have one for me,' she said for some reason, and then giggled.

She saw Callum at the bar, silhouetted against its spotlights; next to one of the oak casks, as he fiddled in his breast pocket for something. He lit a cigarette, inhaled and blew a long trickle of smoke into the thick throbbing air. He was a burner but he'd eat you up. He was a carnivore. He was a flesh-eating worm.

Tony appeared by Callum's side and the two heads bent towards each other, the one balding and bearded, the other with its sleek hair and full lips, which coarsened an otherwise OK sort of face. She watched them giggle, then glance at her. Huddled together like boys behind the bike shed, they were discussing her, that much she surmised, but the alcohol and the pain of her day washed her curiosity away. Like an ice cube dissolving in the warm viscous juice, she was liquefying, rotating into a smaller and smaller version of herself, until she would disappear.

Callum returned with another glass for her and a glass of claret for himself.

'Where's Tony?'

'Had to go home to his loving wife,' said Callum with his habitual sarcasm. Single and very footloose, with no girlfriend to claim his time, Callum's attitude to the exigencies of marriage, particularly when affecting his drinking buddies, was unenlightened. He was unevolved man; but at least he was transparent.

'Ss funny,' Annie said. 'I thought my husband was a nice new man but he was a meat-eater just like you.'

'Huh! So this is all the thanks I get for playing nursemaid to a menopausal woman.' He rapped her knuckles lightly with the plastic stirrer.

'Don't leave me on my own,' she said.

He slipped round the stools and put his arm around her shoulders. There was a shine of sweat on his cheek. There were two red spots on his neck. She twigged his game.

'D'ya know that Al made a pass at me?'

'Did he?' Callum's eyes glittered at the acquisition of gossip. Even in her stupefied state, Annie recognised that this was the most intense interest he had shown in anything she had said. He would use the information somehow or other, and she wished to swim away from her statement. She headed off in her mind, across the red lake, but when she opened her eyes she was staring at the rough pine of the wine bar table.

'Oh,' she said, surprised.

'Come on,' he hauled her upright, and manhandled her up the stairs and into the street, where people jostled and taxi engines ticked and traffic roared still. A couple was snogging in a doorway. Callum pulled her around a pile of dog shit. He wrapped her arms around a lamp post, and she stood with her forehead against its cool, hard, surface, and began to bang her head against it, one, two, three.

Then she was inside a taxi, resting on Callum's

shoulder, and she wondered if he was taking her home or back to his place, and when they pitched up in a strange studio flat, with a mattress festooned with a charcoal grey duvet positioned in the centre of the room, its seagrass flooring littered with glossy magazines, newspapers, ashtrays and the odd discarded shirt, she knew the answer.

'Oh, look!' she said. 'I mas-tch your bed.'

Curiously, even as he undressed her, she had in mind that he was putting her to bed before retiring to the sofa, himself, like a gentleman. She watched articles of her clothing flicked onto an ever growing pile at her left. Then there was silence. She closed her eyes. She opened them. The main light had been switched off, a side light had been switched on. He was standing next to the bed, nude, his penis only slightly engorged, so that it swung over his scrotum like a comma between two full stops.

At this thought, she began to giggle, because it seemed to her to prove she was a journalist first and last.

After that she was aware only of fragments of reality, the weight of his body on hers, the pause and fiddling when, she realised dully, he put on a condom, the raw stinging between her legs because she was not aroused, the interminable in and out and grunt and puff of him, the sucking noises of lubricated rubber within damp flesh, until finally he breathed, 'I'm coming, I'm coming,' and she thought, 'Oh, hurry up and be done with it, I want to go to sleep.'

He emitted a groan and rolled off her, satisfied. He padded off through a lighted door, and there was the flush of a lavatory and the sound of running water. She knew he was fastidiously washing his private parts. She was glad there was no trickle of him

between her legs. She did not want to share that intimacy with him.

It went dark. She was aware of his bulk pushing
under the duvet next to her, his back turned to her
as he sought a selfish and separate sleep.

Before she began to snore, the vodka took effect and
she fell into a deep and dreamless stupor herself,
which was a blessing.

Chapter Eleven

A feeling, almost of elation, of liberation, soared in Chris. Somehow, Annie's knowing about Fiona had a finality about it which his request for a divorce had not, probably because he was always so aware of his unfinished business, that there was more to tell Annie which he had withheld.

He drifted through the afternoon. *She knows. She knows.* Yet in an instant, sorrow would knee him in the groin, double him up. *She knows. She knows.*

My marriage is over. The ultimate failure.

He walked down to the kitchen garden, watched the hens scratching at the dusty earth in their coop. He looked at the young leeks standing like so many phallic symbols in their neat rows. He whistled up the dog and took him for a walk because he did not want to talk to Fiona or, indeed, to anyone at that moment. She watched him go, perturbed. He knew she wanted him to rely on her at this of all moments.

He pitched up, without intending to, at the churchyard which he had left so recently. It was deserted. There was a crisp autumnal scent to the air which exhilarated him. He felt as though he were soaring over the grass, as though he were running with winged ankles up the winding stone steps that led to the top of the tower. Hands in pockets, he turned his face to the clouds. Without warning he was in the grip of a stabbing grief.

It was ridiculous to seesaw between such extremes of emotion. Was this a normal reaction? Did others facing divorce feel like this?

On the otherside of the yard, there was a kissing gate which opened to a farm track. Chris tied the dog's lead to the black painted iron of the gate, conscious that the dog should not really be here. He had no wish to re-enter the church itself, that route had lost its momentary promise all those months ago, in the ugly building next to Emma's school in town. Instead, he wandered around the churchyard, which was bounded by low flint walls against which the pale skeletons of hemlock scratched in a whispered breeze. In the high summer, they had foamed like a wave breaking against a barrier.

A few bleached willow leaves beneath his feet made a dry rattling sound. A blackbird began its liquid song from a tree above and Chris was caught by its beauty, until it was drowned by the drear drone of an aeroplane. The tombstones drew him, their inscriptions had always fascinated him.

The grass that he walked on rose and fell in telling undulations, most of the swellings marked by a headstone, but not all. In this corner they were old, flowering with lichen in ochre and luminous blue-grey, like bright ink splodges on a solemn parchment document. The inscription on the nearest was quite worn away.

By the next, he knelt and read, 'Example to her sisters, in humble faith, she, white flowe᛫ of a blame-less life.'

A blameless life. The two words were incompatible. You cannot live and yet accrue no blame. Whoever she was, this woman who lay beneath her gentle hummock, her bones as colourless as innocence, she had not lived, not truly. He imagined her passing her years in spinsterish composure, lacking the opportunity to test her righteousness. For if we are presented with the chance, how few of us refuse. He passed on.

There is a sameness about grief; it can be broken down into its component parts. There are stages through which you must pass – oh, maybe not in the exact order of your neighbour, but near enough so. There was a sameness about the inscriptions: 'Always remembered,' they avowed. 'Gone but not forgotten.' And some of the stones on which these words were carved stood above graves thick with weeds, bare of flowers. The dead departed had been remembered only until the rememberer died in their turn.

Still, we cannot kill our memories. He might cut the ties that bound him to Annie but they would remain, like silken cords tied around their waists, the ends flopping free. And Emma would remember when they had been joined: but not Emma's children. That, he supposed, was what he was mourning.

Sister lay next to sister in this village churchyard. Husband lay with wife. The stark dates and ages on the stones told their stories. Of a man who died within six months of his wife, though both were only in their sixties. It was so easy to imagine the swift decline of the bereft widower. Of a woman who outlived her husband by twenty years, and chose, at the end, to be buried, not next to him, or near him, but in the same hole, coffin resting on coffin, until wood rotted and bone rested on bone, in death the one cradling the other, as in life. How onerous had those remaining years been to her? 'Together now and forever,' their epitaph read.

Chris was reminded of the note Pammy Henderson left for Ian. 'My love till eternity.' Such a lavish phrase for her run of the mill passion. He imagined her watching Deborah Kerr carried away on the sand, in black and white, in the old films on television. He suddenly understood the romance with which Pammy had tried to invest her quiet compromise of a marriage. As we all do.

There was a chocolate bar wrapper and some polystyrene supermarket packaging scattered between two of the graves. He picked up the litter, scrunching it into his pocket, annoyed. He had read in the parish council minutes, posted on the village notice board, of a best kept graveyard competition – he had thought it a dazzlingly vulgar development. However, the judges, whoever they were, had shown an unexpected sensitivity, not assessing by the criteria of neatness and manicured grass, but awarding high points for sympathetic habitats for wildlife. They were, Chris supposed, politically correct graveyard judges. It had never crossed his mind that people might leave litter in a graveyard. Did they eat a picnic as they laid flowers on the tomb?

He had almost passed full circle round the stone church and Ben began to whine as he came into view again. In this section, the recently buried were clustered – people who had died since he and Annie had moved into the village, Dora's husband and the little boy who'd been killed by a drink-driver. And here a freshly turned rectangle of earth spoiled the uniformity of the lawn, with vases of flowers arranged in a spine down the centre of the grave, gaudy above the soil. Timmy Chapman had died, aged eighty, four months previously.

Grief caught Chris by the throat, not for the old man whom he had hardly known, but for the sudden cadence of memory. When they moved to the village he had imagined that here they would stay; that he and Annie would grow old in their cottage, in their village; that one day they would lie in the same grave in this churchyard. Yet it was not to be.

The haphazardness of being was something monstrous; the chances taken that had led him to where he was. He stood appalled before the random events which had steered him to this unforeseen ending, so that he found himself standing alone, and the possessive pronouns he had applied to all manner of words – my wife, my house, my village, my child, my future – might no longer be his to use.

The dog cried loudly and Chris started.

Grey clouds banking above them heralded rain. He had been a long time here. He should get back. To the cottage, to Fiona – who was his . . . what? There was a new possessive pronoun coming into use but he was as yet unwilling to define the noun to which it attached.

Self disgust came with consciousness, and was mirrored in her pounding headache and in the churning acid in her stomach. Annie lay for a moment or two as still as could be, trying not to touch the man she loathed lying next to her, straining to ascertain if he was asleep or awake. She detected no noise and very little movement. She decided, eventually, that he was pretending to be asleep.

She hazarded rolling from beneath the duvet onto the floor, crawled a few steps, and raised herself to her feet with the aid of a chest of drawers. Pulling in her sagging stomach, just in case he should open an eye, she progressed, naked, with as much poise as she could muster, to the bathroom. Ten minutes later, dressed in yesterday's underwear and yesterday's clothes – she felt perhaps more sluttish about this than anything else – she clicked Callum Rogers' front door quietly to, and hailed a taxi.

It was past ten when she reached the office. Tony, in conversation with David, raised his head, as if studying her would provide the answer to his impertinent question. It would be all over the office in an hour once Callum arrived. She would have to witness him giggling in corners with his cronies. It would be better brazenly to grab the initiative.

'Hey, Stel,' she announced. 'You know you said I needed a good lay? Well, I didn't get it last night.'

'Who? What? Where?' Stella asked. 'Do we know who was such a wash-out in bed?'

Annie nodded her head towards the corridor leading to the coffee machine. Stella and Rachel followed. She saw Tony turn to David.

Callum had not anticipated having the piss taken out of him for screwing Annie Greene, rather the opposite. He was wrong footed, too, by Stella taking him to one side and telling him that from the account she'd heard, his behaviour came perilously close to date rape. He became eager to hush the story. A sexual scandal would not go down well with the management. He was, at present, mesmerised by Alec's precarious dance on the high wire, was waiting for the next stumble. He aimed to have the editorship, and from there the editorship of the mother newspaper.

It had been stupid to take advantage of the drunken cow.

'This is the phase,' Stella said to Annie, 'when you will, with an unerring instinct, pick the wrong man. Admittedly, there cannot be a man more wrong for you – or for any sentient woman – than Callum Rogers. You have started with a bang.'

'I have started with a whimper. Oh, Stel, I'm never going to drink again. I'm going to become a nun.'

Stella more or less ignored this comment. 'Uh huh,' she said. 'You realise, don't you, why he did it?'

Annie was sitting on a squashy chair in Stella's sitting room. Thomas sat on the floor, straight-backed, his legs protruding at ninety degrees from each other, forced into yoga poses by the bulk of his enormous nappy. A string of iridescent saliva swung from his mouth as he chewed on the corner of a flash card. Dog, it said, under the picture of a furry, grey and white, bearded collie who looked a lot like Ben.

Annie was used to monitoring her conversations for their suitability for childish ears. It was useful Thomas being so much younger. She did not have to doctor her phrases, or alight upon polysyllabic words. 'I assume he wanted to get laid,' she said.

'You're so naive,' Stella wailed. 'He did it, my dear girl, because he was jealous of you.'

'Jealous?' Annie was aware that her incomprehension was everything that Stella could want.

'Mmm hmm. He's reasserting his power over you, because, since you left home and gave your life over to work, you've been outshining him. Well, you've been outperforming each and every one of us. What's more, everything you've written has some heart.

171

Callum's ideas, the stuff he's commissioned, has wit, but none of it has any feeling. It's feeling the readers want, these days.'

'Why didn't you tell me this before?'

'How was I to know you were going to bed the bastard?'

Annie folded her arms around her legs. The truth was that she had been working frenetically because her confidence had been so battered by her marriage failing. She had needed to be a success at work, the one area of her life where she hadn't screwed up. She was a mess.

Another Annie, who seemed to be floating in a corner of the ceiling above her, watched the Annie in the chair curl around her pain in an approximation of the foetal position. She hadn't drunk any alcohol for two days, and was sober, but the sensation was not unlike that which she had experienced in the wine bar.

'I feel as if I may be going mad, Stel. This all seems to be happening to somebody else, and I am observing it, like a spectator.'

'Oh, Annie,' cooed Stella. 'That bad, huh?'

It was very bad. She became a witness to her own routine over the next few days. She knew that Annie felt affronted by people in the street who smiled or laughed aloud. How could they continue so placidly, unaware of her calamity? She would like to draw black blinds down, scatter sawdust around her, as they did in the old days to warn the indifferent passer-by to hush, please hush, for they stepped near raw feelings.

The days dawned clear and lucid and Annie wondered how the weather could be so crass. At a bus stop there was almost a scene. The young woman next to her, in jeans and tartan jacket, her hair cropped around a pretty, bored face, was running out of patience with the little girl with her, who was persistently unclipping herself from her buggy.

'Kelly! Don't do that! I told yer!' she yelled. She lit a cigarette.

The little girl, she must have been three, maybe four, unclipped herself once more and scrabbled backwards. There was a moment of suspension and then the buggy and the little girl toppled over. Flesh hit concrete. There was a wail.

The woman grabbed the child's arm and swung her to her feet. 'I told yer not to do that!' she shouted. And she hit her, hard, on the side of her head.

Annie gasped. 'Oh, no, you mustn't do that,' she said. She wanted to explain . . . to explain what? To tell her of the fragility of the bonds of motherhood?

The woman wheeled round. 'Mind yer own fucking business,' she snapped.

Annie was out of kilter with everyone else.

The Annie on the ceiling watched herself place TV dinners in her wire basket at the supermarket. She even managed to feel sympathetic towards herself, selecting her sorry little meals for one when surrounded by family portions – the chops in fours, the steaks in pairs, the yoghurts in sixes and eights. She knew that Annie might not eat these tin foil ready meals; oh, she would place them in the oven at gas mark seven, rest them on a tray and fork some of the chicken or a little of the pasta into her mouth, but she was likely to lose interest before she finished. These expensive meals were due to be dropped in a bin.

On the third day she woke up and, walking to the bathroom, she sensed she was encased. It was as if she were contained within an invisible bubble, or a shell. Outside of this, the world continued, unaware of her presence. There was nothing she could do, no frantic gesturing, no screaming, that would draw their attention. The pod could not be broken.

This was so frightening, so reminiscent of what she had read about nervous breakdowns, that she telephoned a local GP's surgery and made an appointment even as she had herself transferred to his list. By good luck, he was pleasant. He was dark haired, intelligent, kindly, the sort of man for whom she invariably harboured a soft spot. He had keen blue eyes.

'What you are describing is quite normal,' he told her gently, 'a mechanism for self-preservation, I suspect. I could prescribe you something . . . But I'd rather not. I'd rather you took care of yourself. That you ate sensibly and that you did not work quite so hard.'

This so touched Annie that she burst into tears. 'I thought I was going mad,' she sniffed, in relief.

But even as she said this, the watcher on the ceiling thought she was a dork.

It was after the appointment that she telephoned Chris. She found the will to do this because the doctor who had been so compassionate had superficially resembled him. She also wanted to arrange new access to Emma, now that it had become ludicrous and untenable to stay at the cottage for the weekends. She wanted to pick Emma up on Saturday mornings and return her on Sunday evenings. To her surprise and indignation, he refused, insisting instead that Emma spend one day of the weekend with him.

'You have her during the week,' she cried.

'After school!' he protested. 'There isn't time to do anything.'

'There was when I looked after her. Oh, God, what a fool I've been! All the time I've been working in town and you've been screwing your floozie.'

'I haven't . . . it only started . . .'

'When? When did it start?' She was greedy for the history which would wound her.

There was a pause. 'Only just before I asked you for a divorce,' he said gently, as if this made it better. 'Only just before Jan's wedding.'

'You lied to me, Chris. You lied to me. I only left home because you said it would give us a breathing space. You talked about putting things right between us. You said it was a truce.'

'I'm sorry, Annie. I meant it at the time. It happens like that lots of times.' He tailed off.

Immediately, Annie knew who had told him this. Somehow, she had assimilated the information that Fiona was divorced. Annie could imagine her pouring over a self-help manual. This realisation, the fact that there was someone else to whom he listened now, the fact of having to listen to her husband ape the opinions and thoughts of someone she hated, made her want to retaliate.

'I should have known when you covered up your business collapse, that you were capable of covering up so much more,' she said.

'Oh, God, Annie. It wasn't like that.'

'Oh? Really? What was it like?'

'I was just . . . It was just . . . I saw a lot of her when I began looking after Becky in the holidays. I felt sorry for her, she wanted to see more of her kid . . .'

'You felt sorry for *her*! What about *me*? I wanted to

see more of *my* kid two years ago when I had to take this job. I want to see more of her now . . .'

'Annie, I'll call you back tomorrow when you've calmed down. This is getting us nowhere.'

The line went dead.

The Annie on the ceiling watched the Annie by the telephone. She dug her nails into her palms until they were pitted with livid indentations. It was so unscrupulously male to invoke the unanswerable put-down of feminine hysteria.

She was going to have to settle for Saturdays with Emma. Chris held all the advantages. He held Emma.

The Annie on the ceiling told her other self to locate a good lawyer immediately. Wasn't that what Patricia had said? Patricia was hard-nosed. She knew about these things.

The rumour spread. Was it true? Was it true? The editor of the parent newspaper had been sacked. Alec appeared by his office door. He was silent but there was a grim triumph in the set of his jowls. It was true, then. Alec surmised that the newspaper's editor would be carrying the can for the dwindling readership, and that he himself would be likely to survive.

The king is dead. The name of the new editor was now in circulation. 'Oh, great!' exclaimed Stella, when she heard. She had worked alongside him before. 'He's wonderful, really upmarket, he's got flair. No, no, he won't start sacking people for the sake of it. He'll want to assess the talent that's here.'

Her good report led to a noticeably optimistic swing to the staff mood. This could be the superman who would restore their fortunes. Callum milked Stella for information. The Annie who hovered above the group observed that Callum was flushed with more fever at this moment than he was when engaged in sexual union.

Ten minutes later, Alec was called to the eleventh floor. He returned with two security guards flanking him. One of them was old Bert who was normally so cheery when he was on duty in the entrance foyer. He looked now at his highly polished black boots, not meeting their eyes. He and the other guard waited while Alec cleared his desk and then they escorted him from the building. So cruel, the way it was done. There wasn't time to say goodbye.

Some of the staff gave up all pretence of work and regrouped in the wine bar. Annie and Stella were among those who remained in the office, though huddled into groups. The telephones trilled sporadically. If a regular contributor called, the staff would immediately embark on repeating the news, straining for the mixture of avidity and fear in the questions of their listener. In this way, the staff eased their own insecurity, using the simple device of comparing it to someone else's. It was even scarier for the freelance. A new editor might dislike their writing, and there was no cushioning payoff for them.

When they reasoned that Alec would have reached his home, they tried his number. They needed to express their sympathy and, though they did not admit this, to hear his version of events: who had said what? Did he hold any clues as to what would happen next?

But the answerphone was on. 'Alec and Joyce and family can't come to the phone at the moment. But please leave your message after the tone and we'll get back to you just as soon as we can.' Poor Alec and Joyce and family.

'Alec, it's Stella. I just phoned to say how sorry we all are. Please call us when you're able to talk.'

Alec's secretary, who was weeping, went to buy a card in which to express her condolences, as she might if some relative of his had died. They'll soon make cards for redundancy, too, Annie thought. *So sorry to hear you have lost your job, but please remember: on the other side of disaster, opportunity lies*. Trite cheer-ups she had parroted at Chris.

It was odd the solidarity of feeling that grew suddenly towards Alec, now that he was no longer in a position of power. During his editorship, there had been scant affection for him, nor even much respect for his talent or his methods – his tactic of abusive yelling, his coarseness and his pomposity. It was easy for the staff wilfully to muddle their pity for his humiliation with fond loyalty.

The next morning they learned who Alec's replacement would be. The managing director materialised at one end of the office, by the windows, to make the announcement.

And there, at his shoulder, stood Stella.

Chapter Twelve

Phil ordered a bottle of champagne. 'Tonight,' he said, 'you are going to get rat-arsed.'

Stella smiled. She was not, because she had a heavy day tomorrow, but to contradict him aloud would appear churlish. It was congenial of him to book a table at this, one of her favourite restaurants. He would not escape with much change from £120.

He raised his glass. 'Here's to you, me clever darlin',' he said.

It had been a heady twenty-four hours. She had taken the call from James late the previous evening and slipped off quietly to meet him. Alec had been autonomous, but as the incoming editor of the parent newspaper, James had insisted to the board that he wanted to appoint and oversee the head of its supplementary section. This was no problem to Stella. She and James respected each other professionally.

They met at the Ritz. James ordered drinks, asking for her views on the review. Stella was glad to parade the opinions that she normally muttered into a lunchtime glass with the lads. The truth was that Alec's supplement was a curious and unappealing hybrid, mixing, as it did, low budget analyses of current events, from wars to true life crimes, with cutesy wildlife stories and Alec's lumbering, limited attempts to appeal to the women's market. She told James that she would like to leave the analyses to the newspaper in order to concentrate her resources on creating a section which was both warmer and wittier, aimed primarily but not exclusively at women. This accorded with his private thoughts. He offered her the job formally.

It was all very satisfactory. Somehow, at some point over the last six months, the ambition which Thomas's birth had suppressed had stealthily regrown. She was surprised to find herself eager for new horizons. There was a metallic taste in her mouth when she considered promotion.

She was quite sanguine when she considered all the problems she had inherited – the 'challenges' as she had termed them to James. She might have to sack some of the lacklustre and disgruntled men over whom she had leap-frogged. David's face, when the MD made his brief announcement, was as sour and disbelieving as she had anticipated. Callum poured his oleaginous congratulations over his disappointment. She had to admire his single-minded professionalism, even though she knew that the instant her back was turned, he would be crudely but predictably putting it about that she was sleeping with James.

In a way, their reactions reinforced the decisions she had reached over night. David must be sacked and Callum promoted, a tactic which would reconcile him to the new status quo considerably. Whether she should promote Annie to features editor was a moot point. There was no doubt she had the talent, but she was also likely to be considerably distracted at present. It might also be wise, given their ill-advised one-night stand, to sandwich another person between Callum and Annie in the structure of command. Stella was pleased to be making informed decisions, as a party to insider gossip. Soon, she knew, she would be as oblivious as Alec had been to the office passions and hatreds. She would be exiled from the circle of matiness by reason of her power to hire and fire. Gradually, she would lose even her friendship with Annie.

She mentioned all this to Phil, now, as they waited for their first course to arrive. It was a long time coming. Phil began to fidget and to smoke. She censured herself for being a crashing bore. After all, aside from Annie, he knew none of these people – what would he care?

Her thoughts ran on. She wanted his opinion, his approval. She knew her image needed altering to complement her new title. At long last she had risen high enough for her idiosyncratic appearance to need curtailing. Of course, there were female editors who bore their warrior queen breasts before them into every boardroom battle, but she would not be one of them. She was going to cut her hair and buy a new wardrobe.

'I can't afford to look as tarty as I look now,' she told Phil.

'Why not? I like you looking tarty,' he said stubbornly. 'James knows what you look like.'

'No, the boobs were useful once, but the moment has arrived to stow them away. If you're lucky, I'll bring them out for you occasionally, for old time's sake,' she added.

Her humour didn't appease him. He took a forkful of sun-dried tomato risotto and chewed it, his face rancid.

Irritation rose in Stella's throat. This was her evening of celebration and she was spending it walking around a male ego, as if it were a lump of modern sculpture at an art exhibition. Here she was scratching her head and making the right noises of comprehension. Well, the fatuous object simply wasn't worth the bother.

On the other hand, whenever Phil was in the process of setting up a deal, he rabbited on for hours about the characters with whom he was involved. Each night she was informed in detail of his every phrase of clinching patter. For her part, she put on a good pretence of admiring interest, nodding in the right places, managing a question or two. Why could he not reciprocate, at this stage in her career at least?

They were still at loggerheads over the nanny, of course. No better candidate than Mark had presented herself. Phil had a talent for bearing sullen grudges which infiltrated all the other areas of their life. For hours and days he would sulk when he chose, his tactic for getting his own way. Stella didn't have the energy to spoil the atmosphere so relentlessly. But it was amazing how many men were masters of the art.

Stella looked at Phil's surly lips silently devouring his starter. She toyed with the idea of stealing his strategy and remaining speechless until he made some effort at conversation. After approximately thirty seconds, she snapped.

'Christ, Phil, you don't have to be so bloody pleased for me.'

His face was a picture of injured innocence. 'Whaddya mean?' He bridled. 'Well, this is the last bloody time I treat you to a champagne dinner for two.'

Halfway through the main course, simply because she couldn't stand his brooding any more, Stella apologised. She knew that it wasn't her place, not this time.

'I should think so, too,' said Phil, only half-jokingly, but yielding to the uneasy truce.

She had been right about the bill. It came to £117.15. Phil, to the waiter's surprise, settled it with cash, which was the only commodity he dealt in. Stella saw the restaurant staff holding the notes up to an angle-poise light by the maître d's desk, running a strange, fat pen, which she supposed detected counterfeits, over each one. Trust her to land a man who couldn't cope with a credit card.

The next morning, he asked her if she'd mind coughing up for the groceries this week, which he normally bought. 'I'm skint,' he said unabashed. 'You cleaned me out last night.'

Silently, Stella handed over the money. It seemed to her very much as if in one way or another, she had paid for her own treat last night. When she reached the office she had her secretary telephone the employment agency.

'I'm taking Mark,' she told them.

Chris was perplexed at the anger other people felt about his and Annie's divorce. Friends, family and village acquaintances were as often hostile as supportive when he broached the subject. Why should this be so? Did they fear that the condition was contagious, like a disease? There was supposedly an epidemic of divorce spreading across Britain, which appalled the government if not the Church. Yet his experience was that your circle was as disturbed by your commonplace decision to part as they would be if you had announced you were a secret cousin of Saddam Hussein.

Mike, Chris's oldest friend, and his wife Cherie drove up from London and took him to the pub in order to tell him how stupid and selfish he was being. Chris had the impression he would decline into a name on their Christmas card list now. We choose our friends, Chris thought, because their lives reinforce our own, reassure us that the decisions we have taken – marriage, mortgage, cradle – are correct. In divorcing, he had inadvertently thumbed his nose at Mike's marriage as well as his own.

The animosity was somehow preferable, though, to those who pretended they had always believed he and Annie to be incompatible. 'Saw this coming a long way off,' said Georgie, one of Chris's cousins, on the telephone. 'You were never suited, you know.' Chris envisaged battering Georgie's smug face into pulp. How dare this casual observer of their marriage, someone they had seen bi-annually at best, imply he had spotted cracks they themselves had failed to notice. How dare he thereby invalidate the years of happiness. How dare he invalidate the present pain.

Chris's mother had seemed anguished when he told her, which was not surprising in itself, though mercifully she hadn't burst into tears, as he had been certain she would. However, at the end of their long telephone conversation Marjorie suddenly swung round like a weather vane.

'She was always a bit different, not quite one of us, was Annie. She had a bit of a chip on her shoulder, didn't she?' Marjorie suggested.

'She's not dead, Mother,' he said.

He knew why she did it, she was seeking to absolve her blue-eyed boy from blame: but the indecent haste with which Annie was being ejected from the wider family shamed Chris. And his mother's comments hurt him, too, hurt him on Annie's behalf, but he did not really know why this should be either.

Fleur Manningtree stopped Chris in the lane and said, without preamble, that she was sorry to hear about the divorce.

'In my opinion, the justifiable reasons for ending a marriage when there are children are very few and far between,' she added. She looked at him from under her fine arched eyebrows for a second or two, as if hoping she would detect some hint of regret, but he remained silent, not offended but clearly willing her to shut up. She changed the subject.

Fleur was a patrician to her fingertips. Occasionally, she strayed to the fringe of being impertinent, but she always retreated before she arrived, and with good grace. She was a tall, remarkably handsome woman in her sixties, her white blonde hair pulled back into a bun. She wore her country tweeds and floral prints with a style most of the village women lacked. Annie had once half-mischievously and half-admiringly declared her an object lesson in growing old gracefully. He remembered at the time thinking that Annie would grow old gracefully, too.

The mind was an unruly instrument. It capered away from him, like an insubordinate imp, flaunting sad, stirring memories before him. If only it would leave him in peace.

'Come and see the barn,' Fleur Manningtree was saying. 'I want to talk to you about it.'

Whatever it was she wanted to discuss would provide a welcome distraction. He had noticed, as he lingered by her gate, that a yellow typewritten sheet, signifying that she had applied for planning permission, was tacked to one of the struts with a drawing pin. But this did not necessarily mean much. The manor was four hundred years old. Fleur needed listed building consent if she so much as wanted to change a lock.

He followed her up her drive, turning left under an arch between two high, dark, yew hedges. Tracing a path through Fleur's garden had the mystery of entering an ancient maze, and the same promise of delicious time-wasting.

The great tithe barn stood in a corner of her acreage, next to the kitchen garden and the lines of cold frames where Fleur nursed cuttings of herbaceous plants. The tarred planked walls and the great thatched roof were holed here and there, and ivy had taken one corner in its strong green embrace. Inside, the thick beams rose and met above their heads. The air was sprinkled with sanctity. Long, unruly strands of ivy hung down through gaps in the rustling thatch, so that the light was faintly green, like the sea. Time was when Fleur stacked hay in the barn, row upon orderly row of rich, aromatic fodder for her hunters, and still there was space; but since her children had left home and the horses had been sold, she had used it for nothing more than storing old furniture and garden implements.

'What a magical space,' Chris said.

'It is, isn't it?' Fleur agreed, looking round companionably. However familiar this place was to her, she still took pleasure in standing, quiet and small, in its arching vastness.

'I'm converting it, did you know?'

Chris's heart sank. 'No. Into what? Why?'

Fleur smiled. She knew what he was thinking. 'The council has been agitating rather. Well, it is in need of repairs, as you can see. It's grade two listed and they were quite rightly concerned about its future. I'd have done something sooner but, well, we had a few Lloyd's losses, between you and me.'

Chris nodded his head to imply that he quite understood and that the matter would go no further. He longed to tell . . . well, there was no point telling Fiona. She did not know Fleur.

'I wonder why I saved this?' Fleur exclaimed, walking towards some abandoned objects and examining an old washing machine. She shrugged. 'Anyway, I've decided that as I must restore the barn, I shall also put it to some use, try to recover some of the costs, which, as you can imagine, are enormous.

'I want to turn it into an arts and crafts centre. I envisage installing little sections – units – which will be let to artists and craftsmen. Those will serve as work rooms, studios, and then,' she continued to one end of the building, her footsteps distinct, and raised her voice, 'here, say, there will be one large area in which exhibitions can be staged. What do you think?'

'I think it's brilliant. Absolutely wonderful. And the units need not be obtrusive. They would fit well into this place if they were restricted to partial divides, perhaps in wood, like stalls for horses.'

Fleur smiled at his answering enthusiasm. 'That's just what the builder was suggesting. I've found someone very good, recommended by the listed building people. The council is rather keen to support the venture so I think the permission is a formality.'

Chris bet it would be. No one local would want to offend the Manningtrees.

'How much,' he was almost scared to finish the question, 'how much will each unit cost to rent?'

'I don't know as yet,' Fleur said. 'You used to

sculpt, didn't you? I remembered. You see, Chris, I want to proposition you,' she smiled, and there was a distinct nuance, whether she was sixty-something or not, of flirtation in her voice. 'I do not actually want to choose the artists, set the rates, organise the exhibitions and so on. I'm far too busy as it is and I'm thinking of opening the garden more often. I thought it might be rather fun to have an open day to coincide with each fresh exhibition, don't you think? Monthly, perhaps. Or once every two months. And I was wondering if you'd be interested in being barn manager, as it were.

'The catch,' she said quickly, 'is that I cannot pay you. But what I could offer you, in return, if you were interested, would be one of the units. If we said that you spent a few hours a week on organisation as required, initially filling the units with the right calibre of person, because I think we would want a certain standard, don't you? And in time, it would be chiefly a matter of collecting rents and organising advertisements for our exhibitions in the local papers – I can't think that that would take more than four hours a week, do you? And in return you would get one unit, gratis. What do you think?'

'I think I want to marry you,' Chris said. He knew there was a grin spreading on his face from ear to ear.

'Well, you can't,' she said, archly. 'I'm not getting divorced. Not last time I checked.' She had a soft spot for Chris, and though he did not guess it, one of the reasons was that he treated her like a woman, not as something sexless, but he light-heartedly complimented her, from time to time, on her appearance. She appreciated the fact that age had not put her beyond his young man's gallantry, as it usually did.

She was also favourably inclined towards him

because of the energy and enthusiasm with which he had supported village activities. The majority of incomers took no part in the hard slog that produced the harvest supper, the horticultural show and the church fête. Nor, it had to be said, did most of the indigenous villagers – the retired farm workers and their children, the old working families who had once inhabited the thatched cottages and now dwelt in the yellow-brick council houses with their satellite dishes pointing to the sky. The village instead depended on a small and active middle-class core. Some of these gave their time for motives of self-importance, to be sure, but there were others, and Chris among them, who were genuinely public spirited.

If Chris seemed lacklustre now, Fleur owed it to him to give him a helping hand. Her inclination was not wholly altruistic, though. The Queen herself could not have believed more unquestioningly in the concept of gentlemanly duty. It was through the exercise of social power – of acquiring obligations – that Fleur persuaded herself that her class, the squirearchy, was still robust and necessary. Which, Chris would have said, was exactly the game played by the House of Windsor.

'Come and have a cup of tea and I'll show you the plans,' Fleur said.

As he followed her through the nestling compartments of her garden, under pergolas and through gates, and into the warmth of the flagged manor kitchen, Chris felt heady with excitement. It seemed to him as if the past was breaking cleanly away, and before him there lay a happy and fulfilling future.

It was odd, sitting in a chair opposite Stella in what was still, to both their minds, Alec's office, discussing work – especially as it was so soon after they had sat opposite each other in Stella's sitting room, discussing sex and stupid mistakes. During the last months, they had become fast friends. Annie knew that things would never quite be the same between them; she had gained an inspired and talented editor, but essentially she had lost a confidante. And it was up to her as much as to Stella, to maintain the distance between them. Both their positions would be untenable if they did not.

In Annie's experience, this propriety of manner was peculiar to professional women. Indeed, office men cultivated shady areas. Callum, for example, worked as hard at the consuming business of internal politics as he did at his desk duties. He loved to be owed favours, even though he did not always collect them. Annie had never been in his debt, which was probably one of the reasons he had resented her, at least until that night. Annie brushed the memory away.

She found herself unmoved by the information that Stella was going to advertise the vacancy as features editor. Climbing the ladder did not fall within her designs, which were now dominated by her visions of life as a single parent.

'Before he was sacked, Alec said he'd arrange a retainer for me, so that I could return to freelancing but with some sort of guaranteed monthly income,' she ventured.

Stella looked at her over the top of a cup of tea. 'Aargh and treble aargh,' she said.

'It's a problem?'

'It's an impossibility. No budget for it. Newsprint is going up and up and I'm having to cut back at every turn. I'm not filling Callum's old post,' she added by way of explanation.

'I see.' This was a blow. Annie imagined paper mills in Canada, lumberjacks in tartan jackets wielding screaming chain saws, rafts of pine logs floating down icy brown rivers: why was it that the product of such an unchanging industry was suddenly twice as expensive this year as last? This year of all years. Did that lumberjack even begin to think how the price of paper was helping to shape the life of Annie Greene in London, England?

'Alec,' said Stella, 'was panicking about the budget. He'd overspent horribly. It was one of the reasons the board agreed with James that he had to go.'

Annie remembered the feel of Alec's string vest, his hug as he gave her his empty pledge. He must have known even then that he hadn't a chance of swinging her a retainer, but it was easier for him to hold out hope than it was for him to be honest. No doubt he would have presented himself to her later as the man who had valiantly tried but gallantly failed. The more she learned of men the more untrustworthy she thought them. At least Stella told it straight.

Stella was leafing through a pile of cuttings on the desk blotter in front of her. 'You saw this story about Andrew Boyd?' It was a rhetorical question. No journalist worth their salt would have missed it.

Susan Boyd had died two months previously, a death marked by reports in all the popular papers and by obituaries in two of the broadsheets. There had been photographs of Andrew at the funeral, looking lost. They played 'Lady in Red' at the service whereupon Andrew broke down in the arms of his children, so it was written, wracked with sobs. Annie was reminded of Pammy's funeral and the playing of 'My Way'. No one wanted hymns played at funerals any more: she supposed it was because they didn't really believe in God or in an afterlife. Or maybe it was simply that no one knew the words.

Annie took the proffered cutting from Stella, though she had already saved it herself, the story that Andrew Boyd was engaged to be married to a family friend who had been comforting him since Susan's death. It was headlined: New Joy for Tragic Susan's Hubby.

'I tried to ring him this morning,' Annie explained, 'but there hasn't been a reply. They may be in hiding.'

'They may have been signed up,' Stella said gloomily.

The supplement's resources did not stretch to paying for exclusives; nor did they possess enough staff to enable them routinely to doorstep potential subjects. They might lose the story for the lack of either. On the other hand, Andrew trusted Annie. She had written him a letter of condolence when Susan died and he had replied, grateful for the extract from DH Lawrence's 'Phoenix' which she had included.

Annie returned to her desk and made a note to complete successfully three telephone calls by the end of the day. The first was to Andrew Boyd. The second to Chris, to arrange the Saturday access to Emma. And the third was to a solicitor who had been recommended by the company's libel lawyer.

By lunchtime, she had ticked each line of the list. Andrew and his new fiancée would see her tomorrow, in Kent, for an exclusive interview. Chris had been cooperative over their arrangements. And she had arranged an appointment to meet the solicitor who specialised in family law.

Chapter Thirteen

Annie had expected Andrew Boyd's fiancée to be a bottle blonde with a fake tan, like a footballer's wife. It was only when she met Diane that she realised her preconceptions had been formed by Patricia, the woman who, to Annie's mind, would always epitomise the second wife. In person, Diane was small and stocky, with dark, curly hair and a pleasant open smile. Nevertheless, there was something unsettling about the ease with which she comported herself in the Boyds' bungalow. The resemblance to Fiona Carr in the cottage was too sharp.

Diane got the circular mats from the drawer in the display cabinet and laid one on the table before positioning Annie's instant coffee upon it. She and Andrew settled themselves on the small velour sofa, self-consciously holding hands. The photographer, who was a freelance, had thoughtfully decided upon a stroll around the garden. Annie was grateful for this display of tact, relieved, too, not to be working with Al again. His umbrage seemed to be permanent. Today, though, he had been summoned to a meeting with Stella.

Annie flipped open her notebook. 'Ask the

questions every woman wants to know,' Stella had said. They both knew exactly what she meant.

'So did this start before Susan died? It's all very sudden,' she said.

'Oh, no. Diane was more Susan's friend, right up until the end,' Andrew replied. He looked a little embarrassed. Poor Andrew. Annie felt a twinge of sympathy for him. He, naturally enough, was expecting Annie to be as she was before, and while she would always have asked that question, she would have slotted it tactfully into the middle of the interview and given it a disarming prefix, such as: *some people are bound to wonder . . .* He was not to know that the Annie sitting opposite him carried new perspectives to her job. He was not to know that he may as well have agreed to see a different reporter, a stranger to him.

Diane gave his hand a visible squeeze and jumped in, eager to protect him. Between them they told their story, falteringly at first, but with increasing confidence as their own blind happiness swept them on. Andrew, indeed, grew garrulous.

Susan died in her own home, Andrew said, as she had wanted. The nurses came in daily and towards the end they showed him how to administer morphine through the patient's rectum. He referred to Susan in this way, as 'the patient', and Annie wondered why. She imagined him, self-important in his medical rituals, the activity sheltering him from the sight of his wife dying. Just as she had found an adequate role for him in life, pretending he was useful to her as her manager, so Susan had found a role for Andrew as she died. She had helped him to pretend, to the end.

He had coped well, he said, when she died, and so had the children. They'd all cried a few times, noisily, in each other's arms, but they hadn't been too bad. The worst times were the evenings when the kids were in bed: he was lonely, then, so very lonely. Diane squeezed his hand again.

Annie saw him, sitting on his beige sofa, unoccupied, with nothing to shield him from the dark prospect of the angel, until Diane had so opportunely inserted herself between them. A divorcee, she had taken pity on him, managing so bravely on his own.

'My heart went out to him. I took to coming round of an evening,' she smiled. 'Well, he'd just talk and talk about Sue and about the good times, and then, after about three weeks, I realised I was falling in love with him. Because he was so devoted, I think,' said Diane thoughtfully. 'I'd always liked him. Maybe, when he was married, I just didn't allow myself to think about it.'

Yes, said Andrew, he had felt guilty when he realised how much he looked forward to seeing Diane. No, he didn't think marrying again so quickly said anything about the depth of his love for Susan. 'It was your poem thing, that persuaded me, Annie,' he said brightly, as if she would be pleased to hear this, or as if he might shuffle off some self-reproach onto her. 'You know when it said about clouds covering the sun? And it's our fault if we don't realise that the sun is still there? Well, I thought, that's it! Diane is my sun and mourning Susan is the cloud. But I can't pretend the sun isn't there. That's how I took it anyway. Is that what it's supposed to mean, like?'

'I've never heard of it interpreted that way,' said Annie, but quite gently.

They would get married soon, no point waiting, they said. They'd told the children the same evening that Andrew had proposed to Diane and she had, without a moment's hesitation, accepted. The two girls were really excited, they were chattering about being bridesmaids and having a lot of fun choosing the dresses, their style and colour, with Diane.

Diane had moved into the bungalow already. 'I'm not going to change anything,' she said. 'It's important for the children that it all remains the same. No, it doesn't bother me. She was my friend and I feel quite at home here. Except,' she added, 'we bought a new mattress. It was silly, really, I didn't know what to do with the old one. It didn't seem right to throw it away because Susan had died in it. So we burnt it, up the end of the garden, and scattered the ashes under the apple tree.

'We take the children up to Susan's grave once or twice a week. We talk to her, Andrew does it and me, too. I was close to Susan and I know that she'd have wanted this to happen.'

'How can you be so certain?' said Annie sharply, looking at Diane from across the room, but also – she knew this – from across the cottage kitchen and Ben's faithless back.

Andrew interrupted. 'I feel certain of that, too,' he said. 'I know that Susan's looking down on us now and she's given us her blessing.'

Was Susan that selfless? Would her desire to protect Andrew have extended to pleasure that he had found an acceptable substitute for her, who would bring up their children more or less as she had wanted? But Susan lay under an unbearable weight of earth and was now a matter of interpretation – either Annie's, which might be coloured by her own jealousy, or Andrew's, which was weighted with excuses.

Annie beckoned through the plate glass at the photographer. Mopping at his brow, he came in from the garden to take the pictures of Andrew, Diane and the children, the new and happy family.

While they were standing in the playground, waiting, Fiona told Sophie's mother that she and Chris were now together. 'Of course,' she stressed, 'I had nothing to do with Chris and his ex-wife breaking up.' She referred to Annie in this way, though she knew that strictly speaking it wasn't true. She said, 'They'd separated long before Chris and I got together, it was just, well, they didn't want to broadcast the news, did they?'

'Well, she was never here, was she?' Sophie's mum said. 'Never came to a play or a parents' evening. And when she did, she seemed a bit aloof, like she thought she was a cut above everyone else. Anyway, I think it's lovely you've found someone for you,' she added. 'If anyone deserves some good luck, it's you.'

Fiona was touched. At last, she felt that her life, and Chris's life, too, were taking a turn for the better. He had telephoned her, last night, to tell her of Mrs Manningtree's offer, which sounded like the answer to their hopes. Today, he had gone to a meeting with the architect that Mrs Manningtree had asked him to attend. Fiona was dying to see the barn herself. She was looking forward to taking her place as Chris's partner in the life of the village. But she appreciated that he wished to tread carefully. After all, he wasn't divorced yet and village people could be funny about these things.

The only shadow on the sunny skies of the moment was Emma being a weeny bit off with her. It was only natural, of course. She was bound to be distressed by her parents' splitting up, and when Annie had just walked out, without a word of a goodbye, after the Henderson woman's funeral, well,

Fiona said to Sophie's mother, it was hardly surprising the kid was upset what with her mother acting so selfishly.

She did not explain that Emma was being abrupt, quite rude really, to her. This was not a nugget she wished to reveal to Sophie's mum and thereby, over the course of a week or two, to the rest of the playground. Personally, she thought that Annie should have behaved in a more adult way for her daughter's sake, but she didn't say anything, not even to Chris. She was intuitive enough to grasp that the familiar loyalties had withered but were not yet dead. She did not want them to row over Annie, of all people.

It was handy, she thought, that she was picking up Emma today, as well as Becky. It would give her a chance to smooth things over with Emma, show her that she understood and that she would not be thrown by bursts of hostility. On the evening of that woman's funeral, when she had said, 'Time for bed,' to Emma, the child had thrown herself against her, flailing with her fists and yelling, 'You're not my mummy.' Annie had a lot to answer for. Fiona, remembering something she'd read in a book at the time of the divorce, had taken a firm hold of each whirling arm and had said, with a smile, 'Of course not, Emma. You can only have one mummy. But I'm your big friend. OK? Fiona is your big friend.' She'd quietened down after that.

'Over here, sweetie!' She saw Becky emerge from the classroom and waved to her. Emma followed a pace or two behind. 'Hurry up,' she called. 'We're doing something special.'

'What? Where?' they asked, but she kept mum until they were at home and she ushered them into the kitchen where she had already laid out a saucepan, the scales and the vanilla essence. She had read in her surviving divorce manual, as she called it, that a useful device in winning over stepchildren was to teach them something. The process of instruction established new bonds. And, Fiona thought to herself, teaching Emma would subtly help to reinforce her authority. Of course, Emma wasn't her stepchild just yet, but she would be at some point. Fiona was sure of that.

'I'm going to teach you how to make butterscotch,' she said.

Becky was unimpressed. 'I know how to make butterscotch,' she whined. 'You've made it with me before.'

'Well, Emma doesn't know how to make it,' Fiona said firmly.

'You don't know much, do you?' Becky said to Emma.

Fiona ignored her while wondering to herself if Annie had ever done much with her daughter. She put an apron around the child and stood her on a stepladder before weighing out the granulated sugar. An hour and a half later, the butterscotch was set hard and Fiona broke it into squares. She handed a piece to Emma who crunched it noisily.

'It's delicious,' she said.

'Yuk! Butterscotch!' said Becky, and stuck two fingers in her mouth, miming being sick.

'Becky doesn't like it,' Fiona explained needlessly. She handed another square to Emma.

'Thank you, Mrs Carr.'

'Fiona,' Fiona said.

Emma took the tin into the crook of her arm and wandered into the garden, intent on eating the batch. Fiona decided not to make an issue of this. The exercise had gone so well, and, after all – she cringed a little at the disparity of her concern for the two girls – they weren't Becky's teeth.

Half an hour later, Emma brought her back an empty baking tray.

'Don't tell anyone I let you eat it all,' Fiona said, smiling.

'I don't want any tea,' Emma said, looking pale.

'Fiona's been look aftering me,' Emma said. They were in the car. Annie saw her knuckle bones, white and round like marbles, as her hands clenched the steering wheel.

Of course Annie had realised, at the back of her mind, from where she chose not to remove the knowledge, that Fiona must be in contact with Emma to some degree or other.

'She taught me to make butterscotch and I ate it all and then I felt sick,' Emma reported.

Annie felt that Emma was telling her this for a reason and that, if she was a properly perspicacious sort of a mother, she would know why. Would be wise to the fact that this was a cry for help. That it was a maternal test. That it was a desire to hurt Annie because she felt abandoned. But all she was aware of was a tearing rage which stifled thought.

She said, in as controlled a voice as she could muster, 'I don't think it's a good idea to eat too many sweets in one go. That's why I only let you have one or two, on special occasions. They're kind of bad for you, in excess.'

She felt like a terrible killjoy. She felt as if Emma might be measuring her against Fiona Tart and finding her wanting. She writhed at the idea of her baby making such a comparison.

'I love you, Emlet.'

'I love you, too, Mummy.' Was it Annie's

imagination or did she reel this off parrot-fashion? Annie tried, very hard, to be composed.

Thereafter, the day had not been quite so honeyed to her. They had passed it at a riding stables close to the village. For two years Emma had badgered her parents for riding lessons and, because there was no money for such things, Annie had had to fob her off with maybe-onedays. When she told Emma that she had booked them both into an 'own a pony for a day' course, Emma was bug-eyed with excitement.

'Becky'll be green, Mum,' she said. 'She's like me. Pony mad but pony-less.'

'Well, I'm not taking *her* along,' Annie replied tartly.

Funnily enough this went down well. Emma lost the sad cunning in her glance and giggled, whether because she understood some of the reasons for her mother's vehemence, or because of a new chilliness between her and her friend, Annie could not be sure.

For the remainder of the day, Emma was entirely happy, bouncing around on the back of a hairy Shetland, grooming it until its coat would surely squeak. But even as Annie watched, behind Emma's face with its brimming smile, there hovered Fiona Tart with her bag of butterscotch, like a stranger luring her into a car. And there was sweet F.A. Annie could do about it.

The anger flared within her during Sunday at the flat, as she washed and ironed and read the papers and worked on an article on the office portable, and throughout Monday, at work. It was hardly dissipated by the shock of hearing that Stella had made Al redundant.

'What a cow, eh?' said Tony. 'Said the budget wouldn't stretch to a staff photographer. Only using freelances now.'

'Well, that's not her fault, is it?' Annie couldn't stop herself sticking up for her friend, though she knew it would make her suspect in the eyes of the staff, one of them, rather than one of us. It was amazing, really, how juvenile office men could be.

'Ah, you're just sour with Al because you two fell out,' Tony said.

'That's not true,' she protested, but he simply walked away. She turned her eyes to the ceiling. It wasn't worth worrying about. She had plenty on her mind that was.

That evening, there was to be a party. James, the new editor, had invited senior staff, together with key people from the newspaper's advertising and PR agencies, to drinks. It was a pleasant gesture of introduction, diminished a little by the stinginess of the board, who had stretched only to dubious plonk and uninspired canapés on paper plates. Nevertheless, by seven o'clock, the room was chock-a-block. Annie walked into the expanse of the third-floor newsroom, preoccupied, but she came to upon spotting Tony at the centre of a huddle of review staff, raising his glass and saying loudly, 'Here's to absent friends.' Poor dork. He missed his male mates. Try as he might to pretend otherwise, Callum just wasn't his type.

Annie followed the ebb and flow of bodies through the room, landing close to Stella, who had had her hair cut into a bob and dyed mahogany brown. She was wearing a very simple and almost prim beige suit. No wonder men were frightened of women. Like a protean species from some sci-fi thriller, women reinvented themselves with such ease at the most opportune moments. Tony and Callum thought they'd pinned Stella to a board and labelled her; only now did they realise how wrong they'd been.

Stella wheeled around. 'Oh, Annie. Come and meet James,' she said. She was adopting the voice she normally used on the telephone. A thin, aesthetic-looking man in his early forties shook Annie's hand.

'And this,' Stella continued the introductions, 'is Rick Kinsala, an account director at our ad. agency.' The man from the encounter by the lift shook Annie's hand. She smiled but the nerves between her brain and her vocal chords seemed to be paralysed.

As the group resumed their conversation, Annie took a gulp from the glass James handed her. The wine was like vinegar and she gasped, began to splutter and to redden. Stella hammered her on the back. When she had recovered somewhat, she blinked, patted herself on the chest, and exclaimed, 'An ill-tempered little vintage.' Fortunately, they laughed.

'I know your writing, Annie.' James was saying. 'And I must say that it has developed enormously over the last few months. The last piece you did, the interview with the minister, was excellent.'

Annie was flattered. With one sentence James had earned her undying loyalty, particularly as he had helped her redeem her dignity in front of the Adonis from Wallis, Stephens and Wade. Stella jumped in with some political insight; the conversation floated off on a new current. Annie listened. Every now and then, mindful that she was in the company of the editor-in-chief and must not disappoint, she interjected an opinion. But she was even more conscious of trying to impress Rick the ad-man, whose low purr of a voice was so erotic he must have practised and practised in order to perfect it: no natural diction could be so sensuous. Plainly, Rick Kinsala fancied himself, which was fine, because who wouldn't? Annie shot him a look and she caught his sudden awareness of her, the aroused interest in his eyes.

During the next half hour she learned how he would sell the two major political parties to the electorate, that he watched rugby and that he frequented a list of fashionable restaurants, presumably not on his own. More importantly, she read from his body language that he thought her attractive and that he had the inclination to develop this thought further. It seemed to her to be a very long time since she had flirted – properly flirted – with a man. It was a very long time: fifteen and a half years. It was no surprise that she found the experience so heady. She was aware that her manner and her tone were becoming more animated. She was casting a spell and unwittingly James, too, strayed within its circle. She spotted the admiration in his appraising glance, try as he might to hide it. She drew the two of them closer. For half an hour, fuelled by bad wine and long sadness, she played the eternal woman. She was enjoying herself.

And then the chairman entered the room. James, shadowed by Rick, made off abruptly to intercept him.

Annie watched their backs recede. She was piqued. Let that be a lesson to her. These men followed their ambitious brains, not their crotches. They were on the trail of a scent more powerful than pheromones.

She turned to Stella. 'Rick is The Most Beautiful Man I've Ever Clapped Eyes Upon, the one I told you about, the one I saw by the lift that day.'

'Ah,' she said. 'I can tell you on the basis of the business meeting I had with him this afternoon that although he has the hunkiest pectorals in Greater

London, he has an under-developed sense of humour.'

'Oh.' Annie felt a silly sense of disappointment but she rallied. 'I'm not primarily interested in his funny bone.'

'I know,' said Stella, dryly. But then she added, and she sounded almost sad, 'I was watching you. You looked so beautiful and neither of them could resist you. Please don't be angry with me for making this highly insensitive statement, but I almost envied you being single.'

'You're looking wonderful,' Annie said. 'You know that. You're flying high.'

Stella mustered a grin. 'But I'm not seducing anybody,' she said.

'Well, since the chairman entered, neither am I. It's such a waste,' she chirped, 'when nature abhors an empty bed.'

'Just don't forget that nature tends to fill empty beds with rampant weeds.'

'Oh, I have no romantic illusions about Rick Kinsala. Frankly, I'd just like a bit of wild and re-creational sex. And I am fed up with being a victim, of having things happen to me, of not being in control. Be it Chris's wanting a divorce, or Fiona Tart trying to steal my baby, or,' she lowered her voice, 'getting drunk and having Callum leap on top of me.'

'Well,' said Stella, 'if you're going to take an executive decision you better do it quickly.' She gestured to the other side of the room.

Through the throng, Annie saw Rick's expensively suited back slip through the swing doors. She stood, poised in a moment of indecision. Then she put her glass on one of the desks nearby and turned for the lifts.

'Atta girl,' whispered Stella as she went.

She jabbed at the button and it illuminated. Above the metal doors, the number nine glowed red. She jabbed again. Nine faded. Eight, seven, six. The lift remained on the sixth floor for thirty seconds, forty, fifty, a minute. Someone was holding it, while a colleague ran for a coat or a forgotten item of work.

Annie laughed quietly. Well, what won't be won't be. She wasn't going to act like a teenager, except, she remembered ruefully, that teenagers today were not so suggestible.

The lift announced its arrival with a chime.

On the ground floor, she stepped out, so completely self-possessed that when, through the plate glass, she saw Rick on the pavement hailing a taxi, she was unflustered. She strode across the marble hallway and intercepted him.

'Rick,' she called. He turned, and then asked the taxi to wait. He wore the slight and confident amusement of a man who is used to being pursued.

'Are you gay?' she said.

'No. I'm a little surprised you find the question necessary,' he added evenly.

'Are you single?'

'Yes.'

'Are you free?'

'Also yes.'

'You'll do.'

At that, he threw back his head and laughed.

She took him by the tie and led him into the taxi, which throbbed expectantly, like their groins.

They went to his place, a flat, in Notting Hill, which was done up in the manner of the Conran shop. It was punctilious in its tastefulness, all bare boards, Memphis chairs and modern art on the walls.

Rick disappeared into the kitchen which opened from one end of the living room, and reappeared with two glasses of a very cold and delicious Sancerre. Annie sipped at it, examined the paintings, but neither of them wanted to spend much time on preliminaries. They began to kiss and to pull at ties, jackets, shirts.

Rick emerged from his concealing clothes, chest first. He was very beautiful. She wanted to stroke the rounded muscle under the smooth skin. She heard their breathing, the greedy sucking at air, the musical inhalation.

He was not yet naked, but she was, when he took her through to the bedroom. He fumbled in a drawer by the side of the bed. She saw the package in his hand, heard him tear at the foil. He handed her a condom and undid his belt, his zip, peeling off his trousers and his underwear in one graceful movement, the curve of his buttock, the length of his leg revealed. Then he turned round and Annie saw that this beautiful man possessed the smallest penis she had ever seen.

Rick did not seem self-conscious. He cupped her hand in his around his slight organ and rubbed it, up and down, up and down, until she slipped the condom, with its faint, unpleasant, artificial odour, upon it.

Rick was adroit at foreplay. Perhaps he had had to be. Annie lay while he worked on her with his fluttering tongue and long, clever fingers. It was pleasant, luxurious, some sort of compensation, but she couldn't come. She didn't mind this. He lay on her, within her, the contours of his chest moving above her. The pang between her legs, however slight, was sweet to her. It was comforting, but curiously unerotic. For politeness' sake, she panted, tightened, faked, so that he would feel able to come himself, which he did, with a little groan. And then he kissed her neck, before slipping from her. There was something about this that was respectful and almost boyish and it endeared him to her.

Afterwards she watched him in the half light, a Greek statue. He was perfection with a small penis. She giggled. His eye opened. He smiled at her, sleepily.

She rolled on her back. She was glad of having done this. Of feeling again the warmth of flesh. Of observing another human at their most vulnerable and when sleeping. Beside her, Rick's lungs filled and emptied, slowly and peacefully. How odd it was to know that she would never feel more for him than a lukewarm benevolence. What are the tiny differences of gesture, timbre, the way a muscle lies on a bone, the way a quality overlies a fault, which makes us love someone or not? What was it about Chris that at their first meeting had triggered the frantic, psychological dance?

Annie thought she might like Rick present in her life for a while, though not perhaps, for long. This was a new sentiment for her. Between her first, brief meeting with Chris and her marrying him three years later, she had had two relationships. These had winded their course through the months, eventually dying away, but their time span had not been set in her mind at their beginning. But foreseeing the end at the outset was a relief. Annie was conscious, too, that somehow, privately, though not completely, she had evened the score with Chris. And that this was her chief satisfaction.

Chapter Fourteen

The vicar wore Jesus sandals. This tickled Chris: the woollen socks, the bony ankles, the thin cord trousers, threadbare at the knee and a little too short, and the buckled sandals themselves, all seemed to sum up the Reverend Robbie Cartwright to a nicety. Emma had wanted to call a fledging robin they had tried to save Robbie, but try as he might Chris hadn't been able to associate the name with such a bright and rotund species of bird. Chris had suggested they call the robin Bob instead. The word Robbie was attached to the vicar who was tall and thin with reptilian eyes, whose colours were subdued: beige hair, beige eyes, pale, translucent eyelashes, sludge green clothes, grey socks, greying skin.

Unexpected as it was, he had a kindly manner. 'Come to my study,' he said, waving Chris into the hall, as if he were waving him towards a spread table.

The vicarage was Edwardian, the rooms as high, wide and cold as caves, with their scraps of carpet centred in the middle of dusty floorboards and their odds and sods of strange furniture, each piece unique in its dilapidation and ugliness. The

209

curtains, the carpets, the chintz on the sofa, all were as faded as the vicar and his garments. But in the study, from among dunes of dusty books, their covers also in muted shades, of rose and gold and green, rose the vicar's gleaming, state of the art computer.

'You wanted to have a play, I believe?' he said.

Robbie turned the statement into a question by the inflection of his voice. He habitually did this, just as his speech frequently sidled towards the bawdy. Like Mrs Thatcher, the vicar had a gift for artless double entendres. These were, in fact, his tools of ingratiation. He danced nervously around the inhabitants of his parish, this and the neighbouring three villages, ever defensive, determined never to offend by pressing God or morality upon them. It was one of the reasons Chris had felt quite sanguine about visiting him. When he had suggested to Fleur that they investigate the possible advantages to the arts barn of a computer link to the Internet, she had been encouraging.

'Go and see Robbie,' she'd said. 'He's a wizard at all these innovations, so I hear.' And Chris had telephoned and invited himself around, confident that the vicar would not steal an opening to counsel him on his marriage.

Robbie knew, of course, that Chris was nominally Catholic. But Chris's lackadaisical search for some spiritual conviction had taken him sporadically into the village church. And Robbie would rather see Chris in a pew once, maybe twice a year, than risk alienating him. The truth was that Chris, the only baptised Catholic in the village, and a man creeping towards atheism, attended the parish church more often than most of the villagers who claimed on hospital forms to be Anglicans.

Robbie sat down in front of the screen, shifted a couple of piles of papers to make a space for man-oeuvring the mouse, and began to click on icons. As he did so, he rattled on about access providers, modem speeds and local connection points.

'We're on,' he announced. 'Now,' he sat back, a smile playing on his lips, 'where in all of cyberspace shall I take you?'

There was a thrill in the expression, the priest guiding his neophyte towards a new and limitless reality. Chris propped his elbow on the desk. Robbie navigated to a programme devised by NASA for chil-dren. An image of Mars, red and angry, appeared line by line, before them. As he clicked and steered, his hand cupped comfortably around the curve of the mouse, the vicar chattered on. The enthusiasm in his voice was quite equal to that which infused it when he dared to talk of God.

'Originally, I was interested in the potential for religious and ethical debate on the Internet, you see. Some churches use it for proselytising.' He sounded disapproving. 'The American churches were very quick to see how they could exploit it. The Catholic church has a site on the web. And the satanists. Then there's E-mail, of course. Everyone will be sending E-mail within a couple of years.'

He handed the mouse to Chris. 'Have a go,' he said, getting up but hovering behind Chris's shoulder for ten minutes, poised to offer help, or maybe just reluctant to leave this glorious other world. 'Dive into a news group or two. You'll find that they're like a meeting place where people from all over the world who are interested in a certain subject can swap ideas. You can read what others have to say and add your own messages. Like a club in cyberspace,' he added.

He seemed like a clubbable type, Chris, who was not clubbable in the least, thought to himself. 'Yep. I remember reading about them,' he said. For some reason, he did not want to appear totally ignorant. It was like admitting you didn't know who Blur was. It declared that you were out of touch. Chris had worked in advertising long enough to feel that this was the beginning of brain death. He began to scroll through an index of 'club' names.

'There are thousands of them. Read the postings,' said Robbie. 'Don't try to send anything. There's an etiquette which you won't know about.' Just call me when you've finished.'

It was dusk and the gloom outside seemed also to be gathering in the corners of the vast and icy study. Robbie's footsteps creaked over the floorboards, down the corridor and diminished to silence. Wherever in the house he, and presumably his young family, was, they were entirely inaudible. Chris turned back to the bright screen. The click of his mouse was as friendly as a cricket's chirrup. The names rolled upwards, one after another in a seamless flow. There were groups whose purpose was clear and serious, some amusing, some ridiculous. The enthusiasms of techno-nerds seemed boundless. They would debate philosophy and politics, food, health, soap operas. They taught each other to cook, to make patchwork quilts and they played games. He was spoiled for choice, and his hand began to click on the scrolling device automatically, like a man who dithers in a restaurant because the menu is too extensive.

But suddenly, he stopped, with a jolt, his fingers poised. He stared at the name on the screen, hesitating for a moment. Then he clicked. The name was highlighted. The computer prompted him:

Subscribe? it asked. He clicked again. The hard disk whirred. He was in.

Click. Click. Chris was mesmerised, lost in messages sent by scores of unknown people from around the world, bound together only by their common experience of divorce and its aftermath. Bound together by pain. Many wrote of losing their children, and most of these were fathers. There, on the vicar's computer screen, might be Chris's own future.

Click, open the posting, read, close. Click, open, read, close. Conflict and revenge.

There were terse, embittered attempts at humour. Occasionally, there was an account intended to encourage, written by some rare man who had beaten the system, or by some kind, reasonable woman who had arranged for her ex to enjoy unfettered contact with their children. But mostly he read his way through cries for help.

The fact that there were so many similar accounts gathered together may have added force to their impact on him. And it was, perhaps, the immediacy of the communications which affected him, also, because there was, in fact, nothing in the content that surprised him. He had heard it all before. With a divorce rate of 40 per cent, everyone does. A friend at the office, a neighbour, a member of the family perhaps, each has their own personal tale of injustice and grief that is fresh and raw. Chris suddenly remembered a client, sitting in a smoky bar once, apologising for his distracted state.

'My ex-wife has custody of our kids,' he explained. 'She moved two hundred miles away shortly after the divorce to live with her new boyfriend. Every fortnight I get in the car and drive down the motorway to see my kids, and the last couple of times I've got there and she's told me they don't want to see me. She's poisoning their minds. She wants them to think of her new bloke as their dad.

'I feel so helpless. I think, should I give in? Give up? It's what everyone else seems to want.'

'No, no,' Chris had cried. Though he hardly knew the man, his sense of fair play had been wounded. 'You mustn't. This is so unfair. Take her to court. If she's reneging on a court order.'

And the client had smiled, rather superciliously, at his naïvety. 'I've been to court. They don't do much, you know. What can they do? They can hardly imprison a mother . . .'

Funny how it came back to him now, after all these years. At the time it had seemed so remote from his own experience. He remembered thinking, thank God that will never happen to me. He had been so sure of his marriage.

Chris could imagine them all, these faceless, universal men. How many of them, like him, had always supported the drive for female equality – and with enthusiasm, recognising its justice? How many had been happy to adapt to the new dynamic in the home? Even before the collapse of his business, he had cooked his share of the meals, changed nappies, and more importantly, cradled Emma in his arms when she was tired or frightened or simply contented. But the involvement of the much maligned new man seemed to be something which could be shrugged aside when it later became inconvenient. Thank you very much, you didn't do quite well enough, so eff-off, you who only produced the sperm. The one with the ovaries still gets custody.

How could these fathers forget the moment when they kissed the soft down on the top of their children's heads? Inhaled the smell of these beloved children? Held their fragile bodies within the circle of protective father-love?

Not that Annie would act badly. If she won – he thought in these combative terms, without being aware of it – if Emma lived with her, then Annie would never hinder his seeing his daughter. He knew that. He would not be neatly excised from their lives, as if the divorce ended everything, including paternity. But to see Emma once or twice a week? It could not be enough. Not now he had been with her, day by day, listened to her chatter, helped her learn to read, held her when she sobbed over dead robins and snails. He might have failed as a businessman and as a husband, but as a father he was premier league.

Emma would be as happy with him as she would with her mother, and as well cared for. When he picked her up from school, she hurtled across the playground with a cry of 'Daddee', her whoop of joy at his being there, once again, at the appointed time and place. He could not *not* be there. Whether it had happened during the vigil in the labour ward or in the years he had spent being, in the social jargon, her prime carer, he was now as bound to Emma as Annie was. There was wanting, there was winning, there was hurting. The story could only come out one way.

His resolve hardened. He had a good case. He could see that. Jobs for white middle-class males had crumbled away, a silent, sad erosion, and now the landscape was quite altered. The working woman walked upon it, unscathed, but she hadn't looked behind her, caught the man sneaking up unnoticed, holding a piece of paper in his hands, the price to be paid, the residence order for their children.

'I'm sorry, Annie,' he told the computer screen.

He closed the windows on the screen, left the

group, scrolled to another area altogether. For some reason, he was covering his tracks. He did not want the vicar to know what he had been doing. It was quite ridiculous, but it was as if he must maintain the element of surprise. Or maybe it was simple guilt, as if he had been caught stealing by a maiden aunt.

He was not, he realised, any nearer knowing if the Internet would be a useful business tool. What the hell! He decided to tell Robbie and Fleur that it would be because that was the answer they were expecting and would react well to, but he would add that it was not a priority for funds, so that Fleur did not part with money needlessly. He highlighted a group with a particularly outlandish name and, because he was not sure how to do it himself, went to fetch the vicar to break the connection.

Stella looked at her reflection. The new black wool trouser suit, with its high collar and long jacket, was discreet, fashionable and slimming. She had paid more than eight hundred pounds for it, and she had not told Phil. The fact that she hadn't irritated her. It was her money and she could afford it. But that would not stop him grumbling and mumbling. Did he have any right to tell her how to spend her money? she asked her unusually elegant reflection. Of course, not.

That was what she had said to Annie, yesterday, when she had returned to the office with the thick, glossy bag swinging heavily in her hand, like a conscience. And Annie had gone very quiet and looked out of the window and faraway and said, 'Ah, but Stella, if he were the big wage earner and he did something like that – spent eight hundred on a boy's toy without consulting you – would you object? Of course, you would.'

Stella had felt rather exasperated with Annie. 'Friends,' she had said, 'are supposed to tell you what you want to hear.' But Annie, of course, was still looking out of the window at some scene from her failed marriage, wondering if she had played it differently, would the result have turned out differently, too.

Stella tossed back her bevelled dark bob. She strolled downstairs. Mark was feeding Thomas in his high chair in the dining room.

'Wow! Look at you!' he exclaimed. 'Give us a twirl, then.'

She rotated before him, lapping up his encouragement even as she thought his camp expressions were all grist to Phil's dark, satanic mill.

Phil himself wandered in, cup of coffee in one hand, cigarette in the other. He looked at Mark with undisguised contempt, and blew a stream of smoke from his nostrils, malevolently. Mark flapped his hand in front of Thomas's face, wafting the fug away.

'Don't smoke in the same room as the baby when he's eating,' Stella wailed.

Phil beat a retreat as far as the doorway. 'Black!' he drawled. 'Why do you always buy black? You look like something out of the Addam's Family.'

Annie's lawyer was called Dominic Frazer and he was a senior partner in a firm which was situated on the tube line between her flat and the office. This turned out to be less convenient than she had anticipated. Her first appointment was scheduled for late morning and she had to be in the office beforehand and return afterwards, so shuttling back and forth proved a bore.

She was nervous before that appointment though she did not know why. The offices were shoe-horned into a fine Georgian house which had not adapted well to the change of use. On the right-hand side of the door there was a waiting room, into which she was shown, lined with cheap green leather chesterfields. There were a number of leaflets and pamphlets with titles like 'Know your Rights' and 'Family Law Explained'. She did not think she could face reading these.

From the piles of magazines arranged on the table, she extracted a copy of *Country Life* and played the English game of pretending she could afford the houses in the property advertisements. A small black and white photograph towards the end of the section caught her eye. It was of an enchanting cottage in Wales which she realised, with a thrill, she could buy outright if she sold theirs, and she was soon flying high on a fantasy of living there quietly with Emma – the schools were good in Wales, weren't they? – while running a cottage industry. Then she thought to check the front cover and discovered the issue was six years old.

She replaced the treacherous copy, although it did occur to her that it was possible the cottage's price had dropped since then, the housing market being what it was. She spent the remaining time flicking through another glossy magazine. As there was no one else in the room, she tore out a recipe page that took her fancy. It had been a long time since she had felt like cooking, like proper cooking, probably because she had no one to cook for. The thought of concocting some of these recipes for Rick crossed her mind. Somehow, though, she could not place him in her ghastly bedsit for an entire evening, the social prelude as well as the going to bed. And the invitation would seem a little cosy, a little girl and boy, for such a young and casual relationship. Rick was taking her to the favoured restaurant of the moment on Friday – she imagined the list in his Filofax, the crossings out as he updated it, frantically keeping pace with fashion – and she was looking forward to being spoiled.

The receptionist popped her head around the door. 'So sorry to keep you waiting,' she lilted. 'Mr Frazer's ready to see you now. Would you like to go up the stairs? Right to the very top.'

Annie's anxiety returned. She was getting so good at distracting herself. She would concentrate so hard on some peripheral that the dreadful pain which was at the centre of her life became bearable. She did it now, climbing the three flights, noting that they were broad and with an imposing oak balustrade at first, then narrow, with plain pine rails. The carpet was a virulent shade of green, and as Annie ascended it, she wondered who else would buy such a colour save for a huddle of paunchy English professional men. Did the manufacturers make it especially for fusty London lawyers and Harley Street doctors?

Dominic Frazer, who was wearing a very sober suit and a bow tie with a pink pig motif, rose from behind his desk and shook her hand. He was a very nondescript sort of a man – balding, half-rimmed spectacles, of medium height, medium weight – and the flamboyant bow tie was probably an attempt at becoming noticeable. He wore no wedding ring. That did not signify much because many married men chose not to – Chris hadn't – and a photograph of a rather elegant woman and two teenaged children was prominently positioned on his large, wooden desk.

She perched herself on the seat of an armchair, this one in brown leatherette and velvet. The nap of the seat was shiny with use and the arm rests were cracked and crumbling. She picked at a flake of fake leather. She imagined her predecessors in this chair, over the years. Men and women coming to consult Dominic Frazer about their divorces, all of them digging their nails into the same spots, all of them on a knife-edge. All of them seeking his comfort and being confronted, initially, by the impassive shiny head with the rows of books behind.

Dominic Frazer frowned at her from over the top of his spectacles. 'You are the petitioner in the divorce, I believe,' he said, at once. 'I take it there is no chance of reconciliation.' He looked rather mournful, as if he wanted Chris and Annie, whom he did not know, to walk off hand in hand into the sunset, though this would deprive him of his fee.

'No chance,' Annie said.

'No. I did not think there would be,' he said. 'A woman like you does not come to a solicitor if there is a prospect of it. Well, very rarely.' He had a very educated English accent, very correct pronunciation, except that he rolled the r's around his mouth with a flourish. It might have been the strategy of someone with a tendency to lisp.

'A woman like me?' Annie asked.

'Of, if I may say so, a certain intelligence. Well, well, let us see what we can do to make this as painless as possible,' he added. It was a nice phrase and she warmed to him further.

Annie had done her research. She had gone down to the library and to the Citizens Advice Bureau and read the reports and the guides, marshalling the facts. She knew that the terms she had thought in – custody and access – were outmoded and that she must try to refer to residence and contact. She knew that she might use Chris's adultery to show why her marriage had broken down, beyond repair, and that if she did, the divorce would proceed quickly, within a matter of months. She knew that the government was tinkering with the law even as her own went through, so that it might be one of the last of the 'quickie' divorces. She had read how they wanted to extract what remained of the concept of right and wrong, of blame and regret, from the system. A 'no-fault' adultery. How truly stupid they were!

For what Annie required was retribution. The law threw up its hands and ran screaming at the very idea, but retribution was what was wanted; by the family of the murder victim, by the pensioner bloodied by a lout, by the raped woman, and by the woman abandoned by her husband. She wanted divorce to include a ritual marking of bad behaviour, and she knew that she was not alone, thousands expected it and were reduced to petty arguing over bitter details because the law remained mute.

So, she had quite deliberately made herself a cup of tea, and curled in the most comfortable chair in her bedsit, calming herself, before she made out a list of points in a reporter's spiral notepad; her proposed divorce, her plan of action. She did not want to inflict upon Emma the business of moving house. Nor did she want to obstruct Chris from seeing Emma, not for his sake, particularly, but for hers. She did not want Emma to suffer as she had done, in those early days and those long years after her parents' divorce. She was determined to do this better. She was determined to quench that angry voice in her that sounded like Mom's.

She extracted the pad from her bag, and read aloud, so that she wouldn't forget anything. She filled Dominic Frazer in on the history of events which had led to this moment, a history she started with the collapse of Chris's business, for she saw that as the beginning of it all, with subsequent events acquiring an inevitable momentum.

'As far as the division of property goes, I think it would be fair if the house is sold when Emma leaves full-time education and the proceeds divided equally. I envisage living there, with my daughter, until that point.' She ticked the subhead with her pencil too firmly and the lead snapped.

'I would want to set out minimum access terms for my husband. Say, one night a week, one day at the weekend. But my daughter could see him whenever she wished. I'd want to encourage that . . .'

She faltered for a moment, because she had noticed how brusque her tone was. She knew she was adopting the guise of the professional woman because it was the only way she would endure this unravelling of two intertwined lives. She had lost her place. She swallowed and searched her notes again.

'My husband, freed from childcare, would be able, I'm sure, to find a job to support himself. I would be happy to pay him a monthly sum until he was on his feet, say, for six months to a year?' She did not know quite how she would afford all this but she knew she had to help Chris rearrange his life.

'And what are you planning to do about child care?' Dominic asked.

'I'll hire someone,' she said. 'A child minder? Some of them aren't very good but I don't think I can afford a nanny. Is that important?'

'Have you considered,' Dominic shifted his weight in his chair, 'have you considered that your husband may want your daughter to continue residing with him?'

'Yes. No.' She put her notebook down. It was as if, in the middle of a calm conversation, he had reached across his desk and slapped her. 'I haven't wanted to think about it, if you want the honest answer.' She had to clear her throat. 'What are the chances he might win?'

Dominic sat back in his chair and made a steeple of his fingers. Annie recognised it as the stalling tactic of a man with bad news to break. She found herself springing to her feet and pacing to the window, where she looked down on the street, dull and grey under a heavy autumn sky, where people with fewer troubles, of that she felt sure, made their way, oblivious to her. Her mouth was working, taking on the slant of anguish, which is an echo of the slant of laughter. She didn't want to look at Dominic while he said what he had to say. But he began, very softly, 'Mrs Greene. Annie. I don't think you need worry so much. I think the balance is tipped in your favour.'

There was a small noise as he spoke and she saw, from the corner of her eye, that he was fiddling with a propelling rubber, pushing it out – *clickety, clickety, click* – as he spoke, pausing in thought, and pushing it back – *clickety, clickety, click* – when he resumed. He added in a most kindly and avuncular tone, 'We're here to help you. I'm going in to bat on your behalf.'

She dared to turn and look at him properly, and he tipped his chair forward again, and adopted a no-nonsense tone. 'It's been what, five months since you left home? Mmm. This is the main obstacle for us. Judges are a cautious lot. They are rather reluctant to upset the status quo. The theory goes that if the child is relatively happy as things are, why risk changing them? You are working full-time, your husband is at home with your daughter . . .'

'But I'd only be working full-time for the present,' she said hurriedly, returning to her chair. 'I aim to go back to freelancing, which would enable me to work from home, you see. It's just that at the moment the future of the paper is a little dicey and it would be mad to pitch myself into the freelance world without so much as a retainer. I've read about those cases in America. Career women losing custody of their children. But I'm not like that. I'm not a real career woman. I'm a fraud. I'm just pretending for a while because I have to pay the bills.'

He smiled. 'As do most of us,' he commented. 'I wonder if that would make a difference,' he mused, leaning back in his chair, *clickety, click, silence,* examining an abstract that interested him for a moment. 'You know most women with children prefer the idea of part-time work. They do these surveys and the reply always comes out the same. But now that there is no job security any more, we may see huge shifts in working patterns. Two partners with two part-time jobs between them, perhaps. Career women with house husbands, like yourself. Interesting to think what effect this will have on divorce. On maintenance payments. On residence orders for children – custody as you would probably call it.' He drummed his nails on his notes.

'Well, as I say, you and I have to deal with the status quo. We can't really apply for an interim residence order with any hope of success.' He glanced at her and realised she was confounded by the jargon. 'If you lived close to the marital home, I would have suggested that we go to court and ask for your daughter to be resident with you. But you don't. To have her live with you in London would mean your daughter changing schools. No judge would grant it.'

'I wouldn't want that,' Annie said. 'I don't want her uprooted.'

'Of course. Well, the simple way to maximise your

chance of success is to move back into the family home.'

'You're kidding.' It was so simple and so unthinkable.

'Nope. I'm very serious. Indeed, I would urge you to take this course. Unpleasant as it may be, many divorcing couples are forced to share the family house until matters are resolved. Separate bedrooms, separate meals, icy silences,' he waved his hand to encompass the whole gamut of domestic awfulness. 'It's very nasty. But because of the way the law works, it's what happens in numerous of the cases I deal with.'

'Can he stop me? My husband, I mean.'

'Of course not. Nothing he can do about it. Just pack your bags and move yourself in. It's your house as much as his.'

Annie slumped back in the chair and exhaled, a long, slow breath, *oohh*. She put her chin in her hand, covering her mouth, which was twitching once more, while she tried to imagine what he was describing. 'It will be awful for Emma, won't it?' she said finally. 'I mean, the atmosphere will be terrible and there'll be no way she'll escape it.'

'No,' he said. 'But it's not for ever. We could push this through quickly unless he opposes.'

She thought about this. 'He may be more likely to oppose if I move back. It sort of ups the emotional temperature.'

Dominic shrugged as if only she could anticipate how Chris was likely to react. He was looking at her very intently.

'Dominic, can I think about this, please? I want to do it but I don't want to, if you see what I mean. I can't bear the thought of damaging Emma any more than she . . .' Her voice tailed off and she dropped her head, looking at her lap. She had realised what she had been about to say, a truth she was not yet ready to admit even to herself.

'And we don't know that Chris will contest custody – residence,' she continued, finally. Her voice sounded very small and unconvinced, even to herself.

Dominic got up, walked around the desk and from somewhere produced a handkerchief, on which he blew his nose noisily. 'Of course you must think about it. I have rather dropped a bombshell on you. But Annie, a word of warning. Don't think about it for too long. The longer the system operates the less any court will want to disturb it. However, I will be honest with you. I'd be more worried if your child were a son. The fact that your child is a girl makes me optimistic. It will be very hard for your husband to argue that he is the natural parent to explain menstruation, to deal with the difficulties of adolescence. No, it would be very difficult for them to argue that . . .'

Annie found that she could raise her head again.

'Right,' he announced loudly and suddenly, as if he had made up his mind about something. 'In the meantime, let's get this petition sorted out. The simplest tack for us to take is to say that the irretrievable breakdown of the marriage was caused by your husband's adultery. I'm going to try to move things very quickly just in case you decide against moving back.'

Annie got her things together.

Dominic was examining his notes. 'I must say I think you're being eminently reasonable about the division of property, maintenance and paternal contact,' he said with satisfaction.

'I don't want to be reasonable,' she said. 'I feel so

bitter, Dominic. Raging. Vindictive. I have dreams in which I kill my husband's . . . the other woman. I just don't want my daughter to be . . . I was an only child and my parents got divorced.'

'Aah.' He shook her hand. 'We'll get things moving. Let me know what you decide.'

Chapter Fifteen

In the end the decision was taken away from her. She was still weighing it in her mind, and it was the subject of lots of long, circuitous conversations with Stella or Rachel, but she could not quite steel herself to the unpleasantness. She kept imagining Emma's initial joy at her moving back, her hope that this meant her parents were reconciled, and then her guileless face falling as the truth became clear in studied silences, resentful looks. After all, Annie had left her home for Emma's sake, because of tears and scrawled notes and listening on the stairs.

In the meantime, the forms were sent off, the replies arrived. D8, D10 – they each had a number, these documents, though not consecutive ones. The D stood for divorce presumably. There had been an extra copy of the form D8, sent to Fiona Carr, named as co-respondent. Annie had looked in the phone book to check her address. It had been that simple, but she felt sullied, like a voyeur, as she did so. And when Chris's affadavit arrived in response, the facts of adultery stated, without emotional embroidery, on a document that seemed to carry all the self-importance of the legal system, she had felt worse. This is my husband saying this. He was my best friend, I neglected my girlfriends because I had him, and I thought I always would.

Chris's lawyer was the local man who had handled their conveyancing six years earlier. When Annie learnt this, a feral hope leapt in her throat. This little provincial backstreet solicitor could not compete with her city expert. But nothing was certain. Don't count your chickens. Don't walk on the cracks.

One day, Chris called her at the office. She was surprised, because their informal pattern for her Saturday access – or contact, as she must learn to call it – was established. She dreaded rain. Other women, hearing the thrumming on the windows, tut-tutted over ruined washing or fractious, cooped-up children. But to Annie, rain meant something else, an anxious search for an under-cover attraction where she might take Emma. In the listings, there were a limited number of suitable museums, skating rinks and indoor swimming pools within easy reach, and Annie dreaded that they would exhaust them before next summer, and that Emma would grow bored with the visits.

There was something in Chris's voice, that day, that alerted her. It was edgy, a little hang-dog. She heard a trace of the tone he had used when he had denied there was anyone else. He was telling her about a new business venture he was embarking upon with Fleur Manningtree and she had trouble listening to the words because she was wondering why he sounded defensive. She stood up, phone pressed to her ear against the office cacophony. And then he said, 'Annie, I've got something else to tell you,' and there was a pause, during which she could feel her pulse quicken as her heart pumped blood, the automatic reaction, fight or flight.

'Fiona has moved in with us,' he said.

Us. It was the term which had once included her but now slammed a door in her face. She could hear someone breathing thickly, as if they were thrashing in a smothering sea, and then realised it was she. When she managed to speak, her words sounded like a sibilant whisper: 'You bastard,' she said, 'you bastard,' and put the phone down.

Then, she was sitting once more, sipping at a plastic cup of water which she had no memory of fetching or of anyone else bringing to her. Her computer was beeping again and again and after a while she realised that her hands were shaking wildly, not just the faint rustle of pre-interview or first-date nerves, but an uncontrolled, spastic jerk; as they did so, they jogged the keyboard, sending incomprehensible instructions to the hard disc.

Susie, the secretary, walked around the bank of desks. Without a word, she took Annie's hands, pressing them together, holding them between hers. They looked as if they were praying, or in the middle of a service of healing. And, indeed, the office fell silent, watching them, guessing at personal pain.

Dominic, whose number she already knew by heart, exhaled noisily when she told him, blowing out his disappointment.

'Can he do this?' She caught a whine in her voice.

'Well, yes. Of course, you could apply to exclude her but we would have to prove that she's likely to harm your daughter, which, as I understand it, isn't the case. So, that is the short answer. But, Annie, you are still perfectly within your rights to return. His girlfriend's being there doesn't alter that.'

'Ah, but it alters everything,' she said. 'You know that, Dominic. I want to kill her. I dream of harming her. How could I live with her? What would that do to Emma? What would it do to me? I can't move back there now.' She rested her head in her hand.

'That's what they may have been hoping for. They may have worked out what we would do.'

'This is war, isn't it?' she said very softly. 'And we've just lost a vital battle.'

'No, no, no, no, no.' She could hear the click of the rubber in the background. 'You mustn't think in those terms. I think you should come and see me and we'll plan what we do next.'

So she did. She went to see him the next day. His room, its shelves of law books, its intellectual's disorder, already seemed comforting. Her file was open on his desk when she went in and she had the impression, as he spoke, that he had spent much of the evening thinking of it, running through options in his mind, strategies for the next round, though he preferred not to use these terms. She was warmed by his involvement but she also felt a twinge, imagining his wife as she watched her husband fretting over yet another in a parade of nameless women. Did she grow jealous? Was it galling to see him playing the gallant to others whereas, when she needed him because the wind had blown the tiles off the roof, or the children's headmaster suggested an ominous meeting, he simply shrugged and expected her to manage?

Dominic laughed when she told him what she was thinking. 'It's not so far from the truth,' he said.

Dominic liked her being whimsical, she could see that. He liked her attempts to be brave. But he knew full well how her happiness balanced on his skill, as a lover's would. It was a strange situation in which to be. She had never been so dependent on a man. And although he was a stranger in many ways, with her knowing so little of his history and his life, in other ways, he was her closest confidant. He knew even more about her emotional landscape, her desperation, than her friends, Stella and Rachel. It was a professional relationship with a curious, fierce, personal reliance, quite unlike anything she had experienced before. She thought it might be a little how you felt about your therapist.

'So, your husband is disputing nothing really except the crunch matter. He wants to continue to live in the matrimonial home and to have your daughter reside with him.' He was tapping with his pen at a document before him. It was his copy of Chris's lawyer's reply to the divorce petition.

Annie leaned forward, looking at him. She wanted to extract the truth from behind his eyes. Her voice was very husky; she seemed to have a permanent sore throat these days, as if her body were echoing her sickness at heart.

'Dominic, as I see it, the system is pushing me to act in a way that would harm Emma. If I move back home, making it a God-awful place for her to be, the law will reward me. But if I think of her, and what that will do to her' – her voice was trembling and she struggled to control it – 'I may be playing into their hands but I can't subject Emma to that. I cannot do what would benefit my case.'

He smiled at her, sadly, kindly. 'I knew you wouldn't change your mind,' he said.

'So I've tied one hand behind your back when you go into box?'

'Bat,' he corrected. 'I bat on your behalf. Stop thinking about prizefights and battles. For your own sake.'

'No, I see it how it is. You use the euphemisms, Mr Lawyer. But this is Chris Greene versus Annie Greene. You can set some rules – no low punches, no butting – but it's still going to be bloody . . . I sound like a cheap script.'

He said, 'I like cheap scripts. I much prefer them to arty ones. I like the endings sewn up. In high falutin films they always leave you hanging.'

'Chris used to say that. You should meet him.'

'I will,' Dominic replied.

A couple of days later, Dominic Frazer's first bill slipped, together with a circular, onto the coir mat at her bedsit. Its arrival was so much sooner than she had somehow expected. She could barely afford him. She shredded the envelope into wisps as she sat at the oak table and stared at the winter-flowering pansies which had replaced the busy lizzies in Karen Harris's narrow borders. She wondered how she might pay for her lawyer and for all the munificent schemes in her proposed settlement. She wouldn't stand a chance of getting Emma unless she could afford first-class child care. She needed more money.

There was a solution. Promotion. She had been too preoccupied to consider it further; now she had no choice but to apply for the features editorship. She dressed quickly, gulping great draughts of scalding coffee as she hurried from bathroom to bed-sitting room. Within an hour, a clever letter of application was sitting on Stella's desk.

Two hours and a long, cordial meeting later, she had the job. Annie could hazard a guess as to why Stella had been initially reluctant to promote her, but it was obvious that no one better had come along. She hung firm on a big pay rise and she got it.

By the end of the morning, the word was out. There were congratulations, genuine from people like Rachel, and insincere from people like Callum.

Callum and Annie affected to have forgotten their tawdry moment of sexual intercourse and worked alongside each other with studied tolerance, with less enmity than ever before. The staff pretended not to know a thing, though Annie realised, with a sinking feeling, that any new recruit, even a temporary secretary or a holiday-cover sub-editor, would be told the tale within days of arrival – over a glass, through a snicker.

Stella took her to lunch, which was less a cele-bration than a conference. Annie had to perform, to justify her fancy new title and its matching salary. But inside, she felt herself wither a little more. She had no one now to whom she could boast. No one whom she could ring excitedly, to say, 'I've been so clever,' who would reliably react as they were supposed to.

The residence application acquired a pace of its own. A court hearing had been set, for 13 December. It was a Wednesday. She had always hated Wednesdays. She warned Stella. Everytime she flicked through the monthly planner of her heavy personal organiser, she saw it there, with a grey circle around it. This date would never again be insignificant to her, one in a seamless flow of busy days to be spent shopping and sending cards in anticipation of Christmas. This day would now be one of the most significant, possibly the worst, days of her life, and she would always on that date in years to come, stop, looking back, spinning round the vortex.

In the meantime, while she waited for time to rush her into a face-smacking collision with this Wednesday, a court welfare officer would make a report. This was the person, Dominic explained, who would meet the three of them, the trio that had once been the Greene family, to 'help the court decide' with which of her parents Emma should live. This omnipotent being would observe Emma with Annie and, separately, with Chris. Dominic used words like impartial and not to worry. But of course Annie worried. Worry was the nausea against which she struggled in the morning. She saw the meeting as a test, as the ultimate test, the one that determined whether you were a fit mother, or an unfit one. And oddly enough, the only person who would understand how she felt was Chris. But neither of them dared to raise the subject during their sporadic telephone calls or on the steps of the cottage on a Saturday, in case they gave something away, some evidence that might be quietly noted and later used against them, because whatever Dominic's code of practice said, however often he repeated his catch phrase, 'This is not a conflict,' they still saw themselves as adversaries.

The lady with the short blonde hair and the pale tired eyes had a very soothing voice. It lingered over certain words like a caress. She said, 'You're six, are you, Emma?' and she said the word 'six' slowly, and the rest of the sentence was like music as her voice swooped down and up.

Emma was so busy concentrating on the lady's funny voice that she didn't pay much attention to the question. 'Yes,' she said. Sitting next to her on the sofa, Mummy nudged her. 'No. I'm seven now,' she added. 'I had my birthday quite soon ago.'

The lady put her head on one side and smiled too much, the corners of her eyes crinkling up like tissue paper.

'I had two birthdays, really. On the Friday, my daddy and . . . my daddy took me and my friends to

McDonald's. That was my actual real birthday. And on the Saturday, my mummy took me to see the ballet in London.'

'What fun!' said the lady, clasping her hands around her knees. 'I wish I had two birthdays, like the Queen.'

Emma looked at her with more suspicion. She knew this lady was helping to decide something about Mummy and Daddy, something about them not living together any more, and whether she should stay as she was or whether Mummy should come back and Daddy go. Emma imagined this as involving Daddy moving to London and taking over Mummy's job.

Firstly, the lady had turned up and talked to Daddy and then they had called her in and they had all talked together. Now Daddy had gone out for the day with Fiona and Becky, and Mummy had come to the cottage to see the lady. Emma sensed her mother's awkwardness.

Mummy had muttered to herself, 'This is crazy. She's got to see me here but actually there's no place I feel more uncomfortable,' and then, seeing her listening, 'she's going to talk to me and then to both of us together.'

'Why?' Emma asked. 'Who is she?'

And Mummy said, 'Oh, she's to help us get things sorted out and all stay friends.'

Any divvy could tell that the lady was make believing that it was so much fun to have two birthdays you wouldn't mind your parents not living together anymore. Emma decided to tell the truth, which was what both Mummy and Daddy had told her to do.

'I would rather have one birthday like I used to, and have Mummy and Daddy happy again,' she said.

Mummy turned her head away and Emma thought she'd made her cross. Emma had told Mummy that she wanted to live with her. She had said that last Saturday. The trouble was, she had said the same thing to Daddy, too.

The lady with the blonde hair was looking at her with a friendly but slightly sad face. 'I thought you'd say that.'

Perhaps she wasn't quite such a divvy after all. 'Divvy's my new favourite word,' she volunteered. 'And eerie. Ee-rie,' she added, extending the sounds.

The lady laughed. 'I thought it was spooky,' she said. 'As in spoo-kee.'

'It is,' said Emma. 'For my friends, it is. I prefer eerie.'

'What about brill?' said the lady. 'Is there anything that's brill in your life?'

Emma considered. 'Mummy taking me to brill new places,' she said. 'The stables. Thorpe Park. Have you ever been to Thorpe Park?'

'No. But I've seen pictures of Princess Diana taking her sons there.'

'Oh,' said Emma. 'I'm a 'publican, like Daddy. That means we don't like the Royal family.'

'I know.'

Mummy took her hand, rubbing it with her thumb. She could tell from this that Mummy wanted her to act calm and confident and polite. She put her head on Mummy's shoulder and said, 'I want a cuddle,' and was scooped up onto Mummy's lap. Somehow, she had known she would be, though in the old days, in company, Mummy would have whispered, 'Be a big girl. We'll have a cuddle later.'

Emma felt very loyal to Mummy, because she sensed that she was frightened of this lady, which was rather frightening to Emma herself. Emma

wanted to say the right things which would make
Mummy happy.

Her mother's arms tightened around her. Emma
peered out from the enclosure of woolly sweaters and
familiar scents at the lady. On her last visit, she'd
told her how much she loved Daddy. She'd also said
that Fiona was her big friend. Would the lady tell
Mummy what she had said? Emma squirmed and
buried her head in her mother's neck.

'I don't want to talk any more, Mummy,' she
grizzled. 'Send the lady away.'

Mummy shushed her, gently. 'She seems rather
tired,' she told the lady in a stern voice. 'I don't know
what time she was allowed up till last night.'

'I take into account things like that,' the lady said
in a low voice, as if trying to pitch it below Emma's
hearing.

Emma raised her head. She was frowning. 'I can
hear you,' she said.

'Emlet!' Mummy said, but softly, and with a reassuring rub of her arm.

Emma knew she was being rude and naughty. She
also knew that for the first time ever she wasn't going
to get told off for it.

Annie called Dominic Frazer the next morning. 'I
think it went quite well,' she said. 'I mean, she can't
have doubted that Emma turns to me for comfort, or
that she loves our time out together. I told her about
my promotion and that I'll be able to afford a proper
nanny. Oh, and she asked me whether there was
"anyone else in my life". Can you believe that?'

'What did you say?'

'I said there was someone but it was too early to
tell if he is going to remain there for long. I rather
thought not. I mean, I didn't want to seem like I was

rushing into a heavy relationship. Like I was the sort of mother who'd inflict a stream of stepfathers or "uncles" on my kid.'

'Mm hmm.'

'What happens next?'

'There'll be a lull for a while. Then it will all happen quite quickly. We'll get the report. It won't be that much in advance of the hearing. I'll take you to see the barrister who'll argue our case in court.'

When Annie put the phone down, she sat for a long time, staring into space, rubbing her cheek which was breaking out in a rash for some reason. 'Stress,' Rachel said. 'Allergy,' said Stella. She was thinking back to that evening when Chris had told her his business was collapsing. If she had not done the right and proper thing, gone to work to pay his debts off, the house might by now have been repossessed and she might be living in a shabby bed and breakfast, but she would be living there with Emma. As it was, by doing what was honourable, she was in any case living in a drab little place, but without her child and under the threat of losing her, an officially endorsed loss against which she was powerless.

She had adored her childhood home; oh, not the second one, the bungalow in Daly City, but the first one, the old one, in San Francisco proper, when Dad was there. It was stupid. All these years, she had thought that what she had missed were the high ceilings, or the way the light flooded into the ground floor rooms, the personality of that house, but it was something much simpler: what she had missed was living in the family house, the place where your parents both were, so that you felt safe within an eternal certainty. She had worked so hard to avoid the repossession of the cottage and, indeed, she had spared Emma that. Instead, there was the greater loss.

At lunchtime, she went to the post office and bought an air letter. That evening, she sat at the oak table and wrote to her mother for the first time in months, finally to tell her the news. She hadn't told Mom the reasons why she was working in London, she hadn't told her about leaving Chris; there was a great deal to cramp into the confines of a crinkly-thin blue rectangle. She wanted to write, 'I am beginning to forgive you,' but she couldn't, because she had never told Mom that she blamed her.

The next morning, she saw the letter on the table and wondered how Mom would react to it. It seemed so abrupt. The phrasing could be a little softer in places. She could well imagine her mother in indignant histrionics at receiving the news – 'Why didn't you tell me? Whaddya mean, you forgive me?' Annie needed comfort and she was only too aware that she might be required to give it instead, so rather than risk such a heavy disappointment, which would weigh her spirits with yet more lead, she neatly folded the letter and placed it under the cheap straw basket that Karen Harris thought appropriate for the centre of the table. Over the weeks, as Annie dusted, or sat reading newspapers, or eating, it remained there, unread.

The mornings were growing duller, misty. The rain held off but the skies were heavy and the lights were switched on from morning through to night. It became harder to rise from anaesthetising sleep to wakefulness and cold reality. She went to work, she occasionally saw Rick for an evening meal during which they discussed the things polite acquaintances discuss – the latest Tarantino film, the new bestseller – before they returned to his house and the real business of their friendship, the shedding of clothes, the rolling and interlocking of bodies, the steady grunt, a mating without emotions. But she still didn't come.

It was the beginning of December when she thought again of sending the letter to Mom, whatever its faults of expression. But the question was driven from her mind because Dominic telephoned that day and said that the court welfare officer's report had finally arrived, and would she like to come in and discuss it with him.

She felt sick. She felt nauseous both before and after. The report made no recommendation. It didn't recommend Chris, and it didn't recommend Annie. And yet there was something about it, so clinical and bland, which disturbed her utterly. She thought perhaps that she had expected the court welfare officer to support her, as another woman, and she hadn't. And also that everything was happening so quickly, and it would all so soon be settled, by a judge who was a complete stranger, who knew nothing of her, who had never met Emma, and who would soon decide whether Annie would remain a whole and entire woman or whether she would have something vital ripped from her so that she must walk through the rest of her life injured and in pain. And all of this to be resolved in a court appearance, which would take, at the outside, a day or so, and very possibly less.

Chapter Sixteen

On 11 December, Dominic met her at his office and took her, in a black cab, to meet the barrister; her barrister, he said, and it seemed so odd and formidable to have acquired one. The driver dropped them on one of the city's busiest thoroughfares, and said, 'Thanks, guv, Merry Christmas,' as his tip clinked in his leather pouch. There was red tinsel in the window of a tobacconist's; fake snow sprayed in a triangular shape in the bottom right-hand corner of each pane. Beside the shop ran a dank alleyway, through which Dominic led her, single-file. 'An ideal lurking place for footpads in former days,' he called with false joviality, and his voice bounced from the walls – *ho, ho, ho*.

They emerged into a different London. A wind blew. It was bitter cold and Annie shivered. Buildings huddled together on either side of a narrow street. Grassy squares and gardens opened out at irregular intervals between the patrician edifices which they passed. Wooden boards with the names of lawyers painted in black script were fixed outside each entrance. Dominic and Annie dodged the parked cars eased onto the edge of the pavement. A shining

Mercedes thrummed softly on the cobblestones as it inched past, its wing mirror ricocheting against another so sharply that it made Annie jump.

It fell surprisingly quiet, the only sound the rush and puff of the bullying wind and the faint, suppressed roar of the traffic and the hurrying people in the city beyond. Dominic also was silent, perhaps understanding that Annie was too lost in thought for his lame banter to reach.

Up two flights of stairs, in a beautifully proportioned room with views overlooking a square of grass and a contorted mulberry tree, they found Annie's barrister, a tall, broad, substantial woman in a printed wool tent of a dress. She had a Richard III haircut, a brisk manner and an Oxbridge accent as thick as heavy cream. Dominic greeted her as Laura, but to Annie she introduced herself as Mrs Thackeray, and she addressed Annie by her surname, too.

They sat around the wide, immaculate desk in the corner furthest from the windows. Various papers, including the court welfare officer's report, were lined up neatly on top of it. There was the usual busy-ness of offers of coffees and preliminary pleasantries between the two lawyers, which Annie longed to shush. Eventually, Laura Thackeray, fingering the edge of the report in one hand, announced, 'We better get started,' as if she was reluctant to, and Annie, dreading bad news, put her cup in her saucer with a clink.

'I wouldn't be fair to you, Mrs Greene,' Laura Thackeray said, sucking at her bottom lip, so that the beige lipstick dissolved, remaining only in a line at the edge, 'I would be failing you if I pretended that your husband doesn't have . . . a good chance.'

Dominic's head bowed. He began to pick at an

imaginary speck on his knee. 'Good or better than good?' he asked. Annie could not speak.

'Good but not certain. You know, Dominic, that we can never be certain what an individual judge will say on the day.'

'I see,' Annie said. 'Then we fight on.'

For once, Dominic did not bother to correct her adversarial language.

On a low bookcase, directly in the line of Annie's vision, was a school photograph, still in its cheap brown and gilt cardboard frame, of two boys, one about thirteen, the other a little younger, with metal braces glinting in his grin, both in crisp, white collars and navy blue ties. Annie addressed them. 'When my daughter is older, when she's a teenager . . . it's important that she knows I didn't just give up. I want her to know how much I want her.' Her voice shook.

'Annie, we haven't lost the case, yet,' Dominic said. 'We've got a chance.'

Her face screwed itself up into the furrows it assumed when she was trying not to cry. Emma's face did that, too. 'She wants to live with me. She told me so.'

'She wants to live with both of you,' Laura Thackeray corrected her gently. 'Or so she told the welfare officer. Children always do.' Then she added in a different tone, 'The court welfare officer has avoided making a recommendation.'

'I know. I was disappointed.'

'Oh, you shouldn't be. I find the better ones don't. They present the facts and leave the judge to decide. That, incidentally, makes my path run smoother. I don't have to persuade the court to disagree with an existing opinion.'

'I didn't think it helped me,' Annie said. 'It's that

bit in there' – the words were burned on her brain,
'"Mrs Greene says she plans to return to freelance
journalism which would allow her to work from
home. However, she has recently applied successfully for a major promotion." What does she mean by
that "however"? It makes me sound as if I don't know
my own mind. She's planting an impression by the
subtle use of words.'

'As a journalist, you'll know about that,' said Mrs
Thackeray, her mouth lifting at one corner in amusement, though it was not unkind. 'Don't worry, Mrs
Greene, I can make it clear that your intentions are
sincere. Can you give me any sort of date?'

'You mean, when I'd be able to go freelance again?'
Laura Thackeray nodded. 'I don't know. It's very
uncertain. Hypothetically, I could resign tomorrow.
But then we – I – couldn't really be certain of meeting
the mortgage. I'm trying to do the right thing here.
And every time I make a move someone says, sorry
girl, you just shot yourself in the foot.'

'I mean, we're talking about a daughter here,'
Dominic interrupted. He sounded upset, personally
upset; he was not using the voice of professional
pique. 'A young girl who needs her mother.'

'Mmm hmm.' Laura Thackeray nodded again. 'I
shall certainly make that point.' There was a faint
shake of her head. It was the nearest Laura
Thackeray came to expressing any hidden indignation, any emotional involvement in the case, for
otherwise her manner seemed fixed in a kind of
vague impartiality. By that one gesture, Annie could
see through her. It became easy to imagine her
applying layers of detachment over the years, as
protection to her idealistic self, the one who, at the
beginning of her career, had wept for her clients
when she lost a case, perhaps, taking her failures too

heavily, empathising too keenly. Even now, it did not take much to scratch the surface. Understanding this made Annie like her.

'Now,' said Laura Thackeray briskly. 'Let me tell you what to expect. I want you to be prepared. But have you any questions?'

The first question Annie wanted to ask was silly and incidental, but it had been bothering her so she asked it anyway. 'You know I had to send in my marriage certificate – well, do I get it back?'

Laura Thackeray leaned back in her chair with a very sober expression. 'Why do you want it back?' she said. To which Annie did not have an answer.

In the event, it was like childbirth, or the death of a close relative; you could not be fully prepared for the experience. The county court was a bog standard, modern, concrete building on a busy street, so nondescript that Annie walked past it twice thinking it an empty office block. Inside, there was a vinyl-tiled foyer and four cramped lifts. It was quite empty and silent, so that, when Annie emerged from a lift on the first floor, she was taken aback by the activity. A barrister in a very crumpled silk robe, the pigtail of his wig unravelling gently, cannoned into her and took the stairs two at a time.

A formidable woman, wearing a badge on her lapel, was directing a man in a grey suit. 'Are you waiting for Mr Taylor?' she said. 'He's been held up because of a problem in the magistrate's court. I think Mrs Carter is down there. If you prefer you can wait here.' She indicated two plastic chairs wedged between the lifts and the stairwell, and Mr Carter looked so relieved to avoid Mrs Carter that he sat down upon one, thanking her profusely, and put his briefcase on the other.

There was a list on the wall behind the woman's shoulder. Annie examined it. Her case was there, for Court One, at ten twenty. Clutching her handbag in front of her stomach, she made her way to the waiting area, down a corridor painted blue, with watercolours of local beauty spots tacked at regular intervals, past the robing room, past a door with sliding metal signs that read 'Court Welfare, Engaged', to a small area, fitted with airport lounge chairs and grey carpet tiles. Dominic and Laura Thackeray were already there, sitting under a notice, Sellotaped to the wall, that read, 'Users of this area do so at their own risk.' So, too, amongst the hubbub, under the harsh lights, a metre away, not more, was Chris, his solicitor, Mr Clough, whom Annie recognised because of the house purchase, and Fiona Carr.

Chris was wearing his one and only suit, the one he had bought for Emma's christening and worn to his sister's wedding. He was also wearing the tie Annie had given him as one of his Christmas presents three years ago. Had his mind summoned up these family associations as he dressed that morning?

There was the business of pretending not to have seen them, as she shook hands with Mrs Thackeray and Dominic settled her in his seat. Laura Thackeray was wearing a rather severe black suit with a wide A-line skirt of unfashionable length and a white blouse with a ruffled collar. She said, 'All right?' as they sat down.

'Very much as we discussed,' she added, gesturing to the room. And indeed, it was. Mrs Thackeray had described all this to Annie, the discomfort, the lack of privacy, that one might not be able to avoid hearing what the other side was saying, how the most intimate details of your life might be the matter of discussion in a room full of strangers. 'These are not user-friendly places,' she had said. And Annie could see that the users, the ordinary men and women who found themselves here to argue over children or money or houses, to defend themselves or to sue others, were intimidated. One or two were being loud and over-confident to try to compensate. The only people who seemed relaxed were the lawyers.

A young man with an earring standing by the window said very loudly, 'Well, I didn't know they was stolen goods, did I?' and then a red head in a sky-blue suit walked in, declaring to the two men who followed in her wake, 'You're telling me that she can go out any day she wants and we've got to stay in Friday, Saturday and Sunday. Well, bloody think again. And she can listen all she likes,' she said, voice rising, making a rude gesture in the direction of a small mouse of a woman who sat in the corner.

Annie read the notices on the board opposite one by one. Domestic violence, don't stand for it. Make Legal Aid Your Next Move. She examined floor and lap and the brushstrokes in the magnolia paint on the wall, as she avoided looking at Chris, Mr Clough and Fiona Carr. And at the same time, the three of them ignored her with equal concentration.

Annie could hear much of what they said.

'Don't look so worried, Fiona,' Mr Clough cooed at one point. Once upon a time, he had been as avuncular and deferential to Annie.

Five minutes later, Fiona said, 'Darling, do you want a cup of coffee?' which jolted Annie physically, so her head cracked on the wall behind her, and Laura Thackeray, with her pale, sharp eyes, turned to her and Annie knew that she knew.

Annie got up. She whispered, 'loo' to Laura, as an excuse, and retraced her steps down the corridor. When she came to, she realised that she had mounted the stairs to the next floor. This was much quieter. She leaned her head against the cool, impersonal wall, closing her eyes, listening to the sounds of her breathing and the thump of her own heart in her ears, until gradually, she became aware of the sensation, the inkling, that she was being watched. She opened her eyes.

Leaning against the jamb of the panelled court door with a list of cases pinned to it, husband versus wife, wife versus husband, was a girl of about twelve or thirteen. She was thin and pale with a pointed chin and long, straight, brown hair that fell from a central parting, and because she was so angular, and her clothes – a flared, navy mini skirt and a powder pink, cropped cardigan – seemed so skimpy for winter, she reminded Annie of a Victorian urchin. She stared steadily at Annie, as if there were something about her which called out, soul to soul, as if the child recognised in Annie's behaviour, the same erratic, pulsing despair she detected in herself.

They were knowing eyes. Annie saw the scabs that lay behind them, the ones that grew to block the well of tears. I know those scabs, Annie thought. I have them, too. And she began to see the girl almost as a mythical creature, some insubstantial being her imagination had conjured up. Standing in the corridor, Annie expected the child to dematerialise at any second, her personal imp from hell, her nemesis. The seconds ticked by. It was quiet as a coffin.

'There you are!'

Both Annie and the girl jumped. Dominic's head appeared at the top of the stairs. 'Are you all right?'

he asked, and he looked from one to the other, a question on his face, so that at that point, Annie knew that the girl was real, that someone else saw her.

The door to the court room swung open, and two groups emerged, the two camps, a man with a hasty step and his legal team, and a slight, pale woman in an aquamarine skirt, with hers. They swept past as Dominic took her elbow. 'Conciliation appointment,' he said, and Annie vaguely remembered the term, a chance to sort things out with skilled help. But they looked, the whole party, so grim and preoccupied that Annie could not guess if they had succeeded, and rather suspected they hadn't.

They trooped past, these fellow players, the girl falling into place behind them, unnoticed, as if they had all forgotten the child they were squabbling over, and Annie never knew who they were or what happened to them, and a second later, she forgot them completely because Dominic was urging her down the stairs. It was her turn, now.

The courtroom felt empty. It wasn't a big room, maybe twenty feet by forty, but it was too big for the number of people using it today. When Laura Thackeray had told her that the court would be closed to the public, Annie had felt a sense of relief, but now the space in the room unnerved her. On one side, a wall of windows overlooked the street and Annie could see, in the block of flats opposite, a young man in jeans chatting on a telephone, looking back at her as he spoke. She sat, at a pale wooden table, with Laura Thackeray and Dominic. Next to them Chris and Mr Clough arranged themselves. She and Chris had still not acknowledged each other. It was bizarre, as if the normal courtesy they had maintained so far had been drained from them. Fiona Carr had not entered the room.

Although she had been told that the judge would not be wearing a wig, Annie had still imagined him in full fig – the black robe, the grey sausage curls – so that for a moment she wondered who the man was with the receding grey hair, in the dark suit, who entered and took his place at the large table on the dais before them. They all sat down, and Annie examined him. He had a pleasant, humane, pouched face, purple veins sketched on his cheeks as if in fine felt pen. Annie observed him as he arranged some papers; she wanted him to look up so that she might induce some connection between them, however fleeting or fragile. But when he raised his head, he looked first at her and then at Chris and smiled reassuringly at both of them. He wore a gold ring on his third finger.

At first, Annie heard very little of the proceedings because she was only aware of her own primal fear. She wrapped one ankle around the other, tightly, because she could feel them trembling and she did not want her heels to tap a tattoo on the floor as her hands had, that day, on the computer. When she was able to concentrate, Laura Thackeray was questioning Miss Miller, the court welfare officer, whose lilting, mellifluous voice had a hypnotic quality, as if sound could tickle the folds of the brain. Mrs Thackeray was standing, and Miss Miller was in the little wooden pulpit of a witness stand.

Laura said, 'As I understand it, Mr Greene is in the process of establishing himself in self employment as an artist. One effect of this would be that at least some of the responsibility for caring for the child would fall to his new partner, Mrs Fiona Carr?'

'Yes.'

'Do you feel that Mrs Carr would offer better care than that which could be given by a trained,' she strung the word out, rolling the r faintly, 'a trained nanny, as proposed by my client?'

'Better?' said Miss Miller. 'No. Probably not better than a trained nanny.'

Annie's heart leapt.

Then it was Mr Clough's turn, and he said, 'But you mention in your report that the child seems relaxed, er, comfortable, in the company of Mrs Carr?'

'Yes.'

'There is a good relationship already established?'

And Miss Miller answered, 'Yes.'

But there won't be, Annie screamed silently. Not when she knows. Not when Emma knows Fiona Carr's part in all this. And I'm going to tell her. When she's older, I'm going to tell her. But then she realised that she wouldn't, couldn't, because she could not bear to hurt Emma further, to twist her into a bitter, angry shape like the mulberry tree by Laura Thackeray's chambers.

Chris's side had said something, which she had missed. The judge turned to her. They wanted Fiona Carr in the courtroom. She could see in the judge's eyes that he was going to refuse. He felt sorry for her, sitting there, alone but for her legal team. She found her voice. 'I don't mind,' she said, and she registered the surprise on his face. But she wanted Fiona Carr there. She wanted to read her face. She wanted to see her enemy.

Fiona Carr looked pleased as she entered the court. She sat down next to Chris and her hand, under the table, squeezed his knee. Annie turned her head away.

In fact, Fiona was the next in the pulpit. She

fiddled with the end of her plait as she spoke. She had a small voice, a girly whisper, and said 'Pardon?' when she didn't quite hear or understand a question. Emma had done that recently. Annie had suspected from whom she'd picked up the habit and had shouted at her. She curled her nails into her palms.

'Mrs Carr,' said Laura Thackeray, 'you yourself work, I understand?'

'Part-time,' Fiona said. 'I'd never have taken a full-time job when Becky was little.' She sounded so smug.

'Can you be sure that your employers won't alter the terms of your contract?'

'Pardon?'

'Can you be absolutely certain that your employers won't, at some stage, ask you to work longer hours? Many are.'

'I don't think so.'

'Mr Greene looked after both your daughter and Emma during these last summer holidays, is that so?'

'Yes.'

'What will you do in future, if he is working again?'

'I don't know.'

'Thank you,' Laura said politely, and sat down.

Mr Clough now stood. 'What did you do before Mr Greene helped you out?' he said.

'My mum had Becky. Oh, I see what you mean. I suppose my mum could have Becky for a bit and, er, Emma's mum could have Emma. And then either Chris or I or both of us would take time off. After all, Chris can work the hours to suit himself. It's not like a proper job, if you know what I mean.'

Annie squirmed in her chair and the judge threw a glance at her. Mrs Thackeray had warned her that he would be able to observe her from his vantage point and would form an impression of her. But it was impossible to appear composed in the face of her rival.

It was Fiona Carr's extreme ordinariness that struck Annie now, perhaps because she was wondering what the judge's impression of Fiona would be. There was nothing exceptional about her, not in her appearance, her manner, or Annie realised suddenly, her personality. She was a vague, insipid being about whom it would normally be hard to work up much liking or anger. It would have been easier somehow for Annie if she had been more striking. It would have explained Chris's defection in gentler terms. As it was, Annie could only assume that she herself was so repulsive to him that he preferred this unintelligent nonentity.

Chris had had a haircut recently, which made him look younger and more vulnerable. Standing in the witness box, he brushed his hand through his hair once, so that you were aware of his nervousness, that there was nothing cocksure about him, but at the same time he looked directly at whoever was speaking to him. He was bound to come over well.

'This is quite a young relationship,' Laura Thackeray said. 'I have to ask you, Mr Greene, are you quite confident that it will stand the test of time?'

Chris's mouth curled down at one corner. 'You're asking a man who's in the middle of a divorce? I was confident my marriage would last, Mrs Thackeray. The honest answer must be, I cannot be certain, but I am certainly hopeful.'

'It was shortly after the emergence of this disagreement over the residence of your daughter, that Mrs Carr moved in with you. That did actually make it inconceivable for my client to move back to the marital home as would have been to her advantage, didn't it?'

Chris frowned. 'That wasn't the motive,' he said. 'To be honest, it hadn't crossed my mind and no one else mentioned it. No, not even Mr Clough. You see, my, er, my, Annie moved out because we were rowing so much it was upsetting Emma. She wouldn't have risked disturbing her some more. I, er, whatever has happened, Annie is a good mother. A very good mother. And I, also, am a very good father.'

'I don't doubt it,' said Laura Thackeray. There was a pause and Annie knew that in other circumstances they would have liked each other, Chris and Laura. 'But Mr Greene,' she said gently, as if reproaching herself more than him, 'do you not think a little girl needs her mother? Will you be able to guide Emma through menstruation, through puberty, through the hazards of early relationships with boyfriends, with the same sensitivity as her mother?'

Annie saw Chris's Adam's apple move. Both she and Laura Thackeray knew she had touched a raw nerve.

'I hope I could react with sensitivity,' he said.

'With the same sensitivity as her mother?' Laura repeated.

There was a pause. 'I don't know.' He sounded very sad. From the corner of her eye, Annie saw Fiona Carr's hands fly to her mouth.

And then it was her turn in the witness box. She tried to speak slowly, as she had been schooled, keeping pace with the judge's pen. She tried to look straight at Howard Clough, to treat him with the grave courtesy which the principal at high school, whom he resembled, had once inspired. She felt she must make her sincerity manifest, as if the judge, upon feeling the weight of her love for Emma, could not resist its force.

Mr Clough was defeatist, at least his questions seemed designed to play into their hands, allowing her to underline the doubts that Laura Thackeray had just planted.

'Have you, Mrs Greene, found that your daughter wants, at the age of seven, to discuss anything to do with the facts of life or issues, er, connected to puberty?'

'Yes, I have actually,' Annie said clearly. 'She'd heard playground whispers – boys being "rude", you know what it's like – and she asked me whether they were true.'

'When was this?'

'This autumn.'

'Recently?'

'Yes,' and then she couldn't resist adding, 'after Mrs Carr had moved in, actually. So she clearly didn't feel that she wanted to discuss it with *her*.'

Both Dominic and Laura Thackeray shot her pointed looks. Shut up, those looks said. Don't be antagonistic.

'And you were able to have a full and frank – as far as her age would allow – discussion with Emma?'

'Yes. A simplified version of the truth. As I felt was appropriate.'

'Then, Mrs Greene,' he said, leaning forward. 'Doesn't it seem as if you are skilled enough to be able to exercise the kind of maternal guidance she needs during the existing contact that you enjoy with her?'

A white blindness settled behind Annie's eyes. When it cleared, she saw the intensity in Dominic and Laura's faces as they willed her to revoke his claim.

'As she gets older,' Annie heard her voice say, 'I think these matters will raise themselves on a daily basis. This is just the start of the questions she's going to want to ask me.'

Dominic and Laura both breathed out and sat back. Annie was free to step down.

There was more of it. This was just what Annie remembered afterwards. The seesaw of our point scoring and their point scoring, the accompanying up and down of emotion. But eventually, the judge went away, through the door by which he had come, as if he could not make decisions with the anxious appeal of their eyes pulsing on his skull. But he did not take long, fourteen and a half minutes by the sweep of the black needle on the wall clock which Annie watched revolving. The funny thing was that within that quarter hour he somehow appeared to have grown older, as if placing the judgement of Solomon upon him had taken its toll.

'I feel that I would be lacking in compassion to the two parties to reserve judgement to another day,' he said. 'Moreover, considering the matter further would not change my mind. But I must say, that although in the family court I have to deal with many sad cases, this one leaves me particularly heavy hearted.

'Mrs Greene,' and he turned to Annie, so that she gripped the table. 'It is clear to me that you have acted throughout with the best interests of your daughter uppermost in your mind. Your decision not to return to the marital home, for example, and risk provoking further upset. I am perfectly satisfied that if and when you feel the moment is right to return to freelancing that you will do so if that means you will see more of your daughter.' Hope bubbled up from some deep wellspring, treacherously, against her will.

'However, I must bear in mind a number of factors. It is clear that you have not formed a settled relationship whilst Mr Greene has, and with a lady whom the child knows and accepts. She is adapting to the separation of her parents, partly because her mother had been working, and therefore largely absent during the week, for the previous two years. On balance, therefore, I feel that the status quo should not be disturbed at the moment. I am consequently making a residence order in favour of Mr Greene . . .'

A cry of 'Yes!' escaped Fiona Carr's throat.

Annie felt her heart break. She heard her chair tumble backwards as she stood up. She felt Dominic's hand supporting her elbow. Then, she was in the hall by the lifts, and she remembered shaking his hand, and Laura Thackeray's, and she heard herself saying, 'We almost did it. Because of you we almost did it.' And she said thank you to them, and she tried to comfort them, because they were so downhearted.

She has no memory of the next four or five hours.

Chris walked up the corridor, briskly, Fiona almost skipping to keep up with him, Howard Clough slowing them by refusing to alter his pace. Chris stopped by the coffee machine while Howard fiddled with change and plastic cups.

'Will they appeal?' Fiona asked.

'There's very little chance of a successful appeal against a residence order made by an experienced judge,' Howard Clough replied.

'Really? That's wonderful! How do you feel, darling?' Fiona said, like one of those gauche television reporters to the survivor of a disaster.

Chris turned away. He could not give her the answer she anticipated. He should have felt elated, relieved at the least, but like all those who escape disaster, his thoughts were with the victim.

He wondered what Annie was doing. There had been a moment, just a beat of the heart, when he had seen her rushing pell-mell to the cottage, to snatch Emma from the arms of Dora who was babysitting, an Annie determined to frustrate the court's decision, but just as quickly he had known in his bones that she would not do this. Only the selfish snatch children. Annie loved Emma too much to deprive her of Chris.

How do you feel, darling?

Ashamed. He could see, very clearly, a scene from their past. They were in the kitchen, the three of them. Annie had called Emma 'baby', as she sometimes did.

'I'm not a baby. I'm four,' Emma had said, self importantly.

Annie had pretended to tweak her nose. 'Look,' she said. 'Get this into your head now, ratfink. You'll always be my baby. When you're twenty, thirty, forty even, you will be my baby and I will worry about you and nag you if you're not taking care of yourself, and generally be a pain in the backside.'

And Emma smiled and put her arms around Annie's waist and buried her head in the soft curve of her stomach. 'I love your podgy tummy, Mummy,' she said. 'Don't go on that diet.'

Annie had looked at him, over Emma's head, pulled a face and said, 'Wow! Thanks for the compliment, ratlet.'

That was what he was remembering, under the

neon lights in the corridor, after they had performed their final ritual together.

They reached the hall. Through the glass swing doors they could see sheets of rain, the wild leap of water hitting pavement, beneath an iron sky. Annie's lawyers were climbing into a cab. Chris wondered if she was with them.

'You wait here,' Howard Clough said, 'I'll go and get the car and bring it round.' He flung himself through the doors and out into the drumming of the storm. He had driven them up and now he would drive them back in undoubted triumph. Chris supposed he should invite Clough in for champagne and celebration.

Fiona linked her arm through his. For a while, he suffered standing there, watching the pedestrians caper past, the snakes of rain darting and hissing at their ankles, then he disentangled himself.

There were three sets of swing doors leading from the hall: the pair on the left led to the stairs, the pair on the right were blocked by a group talking animatedly. Chris walked aimlessly through those at the back, behind the lift shaft, into a small, cold, inner lobby. There was a large coir mat on the floor. Two glass firedoors gave onto a paved courtyard which the rain lashed like a sadist.

He was turning away when he saw her. She was in the far corner. Her coat was lying on the ground in an inch of dirty water. Her head was tipped to the sky and the rain poured over it, so that her hair, the short hair he had never quite grown used to, was pasted to her skull, and mascara puddled her cheeks, inky black. Her smart navy suit was soaked and he could see her pink skin through the fabric of her cream silk blouse. If he had not known her, he

would have thought she was one of those
unfortunate mentally ill cases, let out into the
community and unable to cope.

He could see her mouth working, her hands
clenching. Her head fell back and her mouth fell
open in a cry. It was just a bleat, really, there were
no words. She stepped one pace, drew back. Her
arms folded around her belly, as if she were in pain,
fell limp, crossed over her breasts, plucked at her
keening mouth so that lipstick was smeared on
her chin, bright as blood but more humiliating.

Back and forth she swayed, one step forward, one
back. Up went the hands to her breasts, then
dropped to cup her womb, the pounding of water on
concrete slabs muffling her occasional cries. So she
rocked in this strange dance of lamentation and the
rain washed her, cold and vicious, but still it did not
bring her to her senses.

'Darling!' Fiona's voice, bright as a stewardess's,
called him from the door. 'Come on! It's Howard.'

Chris hesitated for a moment. He did not want to
leave Annie, but he did not believe that he, of all
people, had the power to quiet her; nor did he want
to expose her to Fiona's curious and hostile stare. He
stepped back into the hall and said, in a low voice,
to a surprised court usher, who stepped from the lift,
whose badge proclaimed him to be Mr Tyler, to
please take care of the lady outside who had had a
terrible shock. Then he sprinted across the pavement and climbed into the back of the car after
Fiona, but he was gripped by a sharp and terrible
guilt, and the dawning knowledge that only the crass
can be serene in the face of another's anguish.

Chapter Seventeen

It was even worse, this time. The pain of the previous months was as nothing compared to this. Perhaps it was cumulative, like a little poison ingested over a long period, building in the system towards agony.

The rash spread: red bumps on her cheeks which made her look as ugly as she felt, red lumps on her arms and down her torso, so that the touch of winter woollen clothes was an itch without relief. Several times a day, she had to race from her desk to the lavatory, shut herself in a cubicle and rub and scratch at the coarsened skin. The doctor shook his head when she returned to him. He offered her tranquillisers but she refused.

A little burst of grey hairs appeared quite suddenly at either temple, speckling the dark. She, who had always taken pride in the glossy swing of her hair, no longer cared enough to dye it. Permanent colour, the boxes of dye in the chemist's declared, the words positioned above photographs of improbable women, gleaming, smiling, untroubled women. Permanent grey suited Annie fine. It went with permanent loss.

She was on the top floor at the local bookshop one lunch hour, searching for books to read in the long hours of dark, for her insomnia had returned, when a dog pushed past her and trotted down the long room. It was a long-haired, tan-coloured dog, with a curved back and a loping stride, a greyhound or a mongrel with greyhound blood. As it made its way, panting, it turned its head from side to side, peering down the aisles between the tall shelves. At the far side of the floor, it turned around, neatly, on a sixpence, and paced back. Annie watched it as it leapt down the stairs, its nails tapping on the bare wood.

She followed it. On the floor below, it traced the same path, hunting urgently, but with an edge of fear about it now. It was oblivious to the people it encountered, who reacted with delight or irritation. Veering deftly to avoid the arms of a man crouching to catch it, despite the reassuring noises he made, it headed for the stairs once again, a thin whine escaping with each exhaled breath. Annie knew that it was looking for its master, the somebody who had smuggled it into the shop, taken it to the top floor and then left it, escaping its unwanted dependency by dodging down the fire escape, perhaps, or by the lift.

It padded through the doors and out into the street, lost in the marching army of Christmas shoppers. She barged through the swinging door, searching for it in despair. But it was gone.

'Excuse me, madam.' A woman in a thin suit stood shivering next to her. A badge on her bosom said 'Mrs Helen Carr, Manageress,' and for a moment Annie stood transfixed, imagining her to be some relative of Fiona Carr's who knew of her and had materialised in order to torment her.

'Excuse me, madam, but you've walked out with one of our books. Without paying for it,' the woman said. And there, in her hand, was the novel Annie had been considering before she had spotted the dog.

'There was a dog,' she said and the sentence sounded unlikely even to her own ears. 'I followed him because I was worried.' She looked straight into the woman's nondescript blue eyes, willing her to understand.

'I thought that was what you were doing,' the woman said. 'Poor thing just left to fend for itself on these streets. But I had to come to remind you. I'm afraid you can't be too sure nowadays.'

This was a relief, such a relief indeed, that Annie, accompanying Mrs Carr inside the shop, bought the book, though she hadn't fancied it. And once outside, in the tug and tussle of the crowd, the stifling heat of the shop exchanged for the bruising cold of December, she found herself frowning, worrying about the dog which was so faithful and which couldn't accept that it had been abandoned.

That day was the worst of all. She returned to the office feeling battered and found she couldn't settle to her work. The dog padded around her mind. It felt as if the rash had crawled on to the surface of her brain, encrusting the soft, damp folds. She made her way, with some difficulty, feeling the way, as if she were drugged and could scarcely remember where to go, to the cubbyhole by Stella's office. This was a cramped closet that housed a miniature stainless steel sink and some cupboards to hold the paraphernalia for making coffee and tea. Stella's secretary used it when visitors came, carrying in trays with the cafetière and enormous chunky cups. The staff used it for instant soup and never washed their mugs out.

Annie put water in the kettle and picked up an

unwashed teaspoon from the draining board, a half moon of brown liquid coagulating within it. She stood for several minutes examining it. She had intended to make a cup of tea, but she had forgotten what happened next. Spoon in hand, she waited for the information to reassemble itself in her brain, except that it didn't, and instead, after a brief interval, the teaspoon launched itself across the corridor, ricocheting from the opposite wall. She supposed she had hurled it.

Stella came out of her office at that moment. She ignored the spoon on the carpet tiles and the viscous smear of coffee on the wall. She put her hands on Annie's shoulders.

'You need a holiday,' she said.

'I can't remember how to do it,' Annie said.

'How to do what?'

'How to make a cup of tea.'

'You need a holiday,' Stella repeated.

It was on the shortest day that Chris completed the sculptures. The barn was almost finished, too, just the last of the panelling to erect at the other end, the remaining halogen spotlights to fix up, which the builders promised they would do after Christmas.

It had just gone half past four but the dark outside the windows was as thick and smooth as a coating of black paint. Within Chris's compartment the lights were on, a bright room within the shadows that gathered in the rest of the barn. It was silent, the sort of sacred silence that is supposed to grip the world at midnight on Christmas Eve. Chris pressed the back of his legs against the inadequate storage heater, examining the figures on the plain table in front of him. The clay was drying slowly, so that in the folds it was a deeper red than on the broad, smooth surfaces. Robbie, the vicar, had asked him to craft something for the church that would be displayed during the festive season, this year and in years to come.

'I saw the lights were on.' The voice was disembodied but it was Fleur's. She padded into view, wearing green wellington boots and her old cord gardening trousers. She was swaddled in a thick cardigan, each hand inserted into the opposite sleeve.

'Almost there?' she said, jerking her neat head towards the dark rafters.

'A few finishing touches,' Chris said. 'They promise to finish off after the Christmas break.'

Fleur walked around the table, gazing at the figures on their wooden boards. They were small, no more than nine inches high, little vignettes of mother and child, roughly carved, proportions slightly distorted, dressed in shapeless, sexless clothes, like sacks. Chris had hacked them out of the clay. He had not wanted them to look twee.

In one, a woman crouched, an exuberant child diving against her back, its feet kicking free of the ground, its arms round her neck. In another, a child buried its head in its mother's stomach, the taller figure stooping to place its arms around the smaller, one hand resting on the child's backside. In the last, the mother cradled the child, who was slack with sleep, head hanging back, a suggestion of the pietà in their pose.

'The bartering system still operates in this village. The vicar called in his favour,' Chris said. He gestured to the table. 'So, here you have it. Madonna and child times three. What do you think?'

Fleur extracted one hand from a sleeve, picking up

one of Chris's carving tools, which she proceeded to jab into a lump of raw clay at the edge of the table. 'They're exquisite,' she said evenly, her feline eyes looking at him from above her thick, knitted collar. 'But they're not the Madonna and child. They're Annie and Emma, aren't they?'

Chris blew out a puff of breath. 'That obvious, huh?'

'I think so,' she said.

For a moment, he leaned on the table. Then he picked up a ball of red clay and began tossing it from palm to palm, where traces of it immediately dried, tightening the skin. Eventually, he said, 'Emma's started wetting the bed. Hasn't done that in years. The dog's gone a bit incontinent, too. That's just old age. Fiona wants to put the dog down. I could interpret Emma's bed wetting as anxiety about the dog, couldn't I? If I wanted to.'

Fleur moved away from the table and sat down, on a stool, opposite him. 'Do you know,' she said, 'years ago, Hugh almost left me.'

That jerked Chris's head up. She was sitting at the edge of the light, the left side of her face in shadow, but her eyes gleamed and her pink lipsticked mouth, which was always slightly curved at the corners in a faint smile suggesting self confidence, smiled still. Her voice was very low, and Chris knew that what she was telling him now she had probably told no one before.

'I always thought of you as having one of the rock solid marriages of all time. An English couple. Comfortable.'

'Unemotional,' she suggested. 'Not likely to feel the highs and lows of torrid passion.' She was amused. 'Actually, I think he was having an affair,' she continued, with a sigh, looking to one side, past

Chris, conjuring up visions from her past. 'I can't be certain – I never asked, and he never told me. The children were young, I was very preoccupied, we were – fractious, is the word – we niggled at each other. Do you know what I mean? Of course, you do.

'And then, I was suddenly aware that Hugh wasn't *there* anymore. Oh, he was there physically. He came home from the City and ate his supper with me. He pottered in the gardens on Saturdays. Went shooting. Followed the same routines. But essentially he was somewhere else.

'I remember very clearly: I looked out of the window one evening, when he was due home, and I saw him walking up and down the lane, just outside the drive, pacing back and forth. And I realised that he didn't want to come indoors. He was gathering up his will, or his strength, or whatever it was, and he had to do that in order to bear my company. Which was terrible. Can you imagine how terrible that was?

'Every evening after that, I would watch him and he would pace, and I knew how much he didn't want to be at home.' Her voice tailed off and she sat, looking into the darkness, still calm, still with her faint smile.

'What happened?'

'Mmm? Nothing. Nothing happened. That is to say, nothing that was admitted openly. But at some stage, I believe, his affair ended, whether because he decided he must think of me, or more likely the children, I don't know. Perhaps the woman ended it? But he became more solicitous. He came back. And eventually, in time, I forgave him. I realised I didn't care any more about what had or hadn't happened.'

'How long did all this take?'

'Five or six years?' she said, with a questioning tone, as if Chris would know.

He put the clay down. 'That's a long time when it's measured in daily grudges and irritation.'

'Yes. A very long time. But you know – this is going to sound like a frightful cliché – it made me re-examine my marriage vows. You think you know what they mean when you take them, don't you? For better, for worse. And I imagined the worse being some disaster visited on us from outside. A life-threatening disease to be fought, side by side, perhaps. A Down's Syndrome child. But some threat against which the pair of us would unite. There is a romance to such a scenario.

'What I had not realised, until then, was that the worse might be self-inflicted. That the worse might be his being grumpy and unappreciative; my being tired and frustrated. The worse might be that petty, and it might go on, for year after unrelenting year. But it was a part of what I'd signed up for. I'd said that I would stick it out, unsure as to whether we would feel any happier together in the future, but hoping, grimly, that we would.'

'And are you?'

'Happier? Yes, very. It isn't a sham. We are as happy as we seem. It was that simple, you see. We acquired a dignity and a mutual respect simply in sticking to it. But people don't these days, do they?' She paused. 'And who am I to say that my recipe would work for others?'

'Oh, Fleur. Don't humour me. We both know, you and I, what you are saying to me.'

Chris picked up a kidney rubber and began to scrape dried clay from the table, slowly, rhythmi-cally. 'You see,' he said after a while, during which she sat, patiently, 'I thought there would be a period, turbulent but relatively brief, during which Emma would react badly to our breaking up. I also thought she would recover. That it would be better for her not to have to listen to the never-bloody-ending arguments. But I am only just beginning to realise that it actually wasn't bad enough for her to want that. It has to be very bad, doesn't it? – physical violence or near physical violence – for a child to feel relief when her parents part.'

Scrape, scrape went the rubber. Chris paused, because it wasn't until this moment that he himself had realised the truth. Then he blurted out, 'You know, there may have been stupid, noisy, pointless scene after scene, but the reason they upset Emma is because she was afraid they meant we were splitting up. Jesus! How can I have been so stupid? How can I not have realised that?'

He sat down and placed his head in his hands. 'Jesus Christ, Fleur. What a basic piece of analysis. And we both of us missed it. We gave her what she most dreaded.'

There was silence, during which Fleur seemed to jump from her stool, and then he felt her hand on his shoulder. He could imagine it, slim, elegant, with the large sapphire and diamond ring weighting her fourth finger. She didn't offer any platitudes, for which he was grateful.

'Anyway,' he continued, and his voice was muffled by his cupped palms, 'it's done, now. I brought a third party into it. The *coup de grâce* that killed the marriage. The decree nisi will come through in the New Year. A fresh beginning. Except that, for Emma, it's not going to work out like that, is it? I'm happy, Fiona's happy, Annie is happy. Well, she has a new bloke apparently. But Emma? Emma's buggered up for years.

'That's what that's about,' he said, sitting up, gesturing to the trio of models. 'That's my lament to

271

Emma, my apology to her. This is how happy she used to be until her father and her mother screwed up.'

Fleur patted his shoulder. 'I think you're going to come indoors and have a drink with me,' she said. 'What's the time? Only five? Well, it's after dark so it doesn't matter.'

Chris managed a smile. He held his smeared palms towards her. 'I'm not dressed for it,' he said.

'Chris, in all the years I've known you, you've never been dressed for it,' she retorted, and she slipped her arm through his as he switched the lights out, locked up, and they picked their way up the brick path towards the welcoming windows of the manor. But when they reached the kitchen door where Hugh was sitting, reading *The Times*, they wordlessly disentangled their arms. As she pushed open the door, she said softly, 'Don't let Fiona put the dog down,' and then, in a louder voice, 'Hugh, darling. Here's Chris come for a Christmas drink. Will you do the honours?' And everything seemed to return to normal.

Sitting in a taxi on the way to a dinner party, Stella worked out that Phil earned something like £1.25 an hour. Since Mark had arrived to look after Thomas, Phil and a friend of his had been importing specialist food from Spain, a business which entailed long hours, twelve-hour days, and countless trips already across the channel. He was there, now, was not due back till tomorrow, which was Christmas Eve, the selfish pig.

A week ago she had said to him, 'There seems to be an awful lot of effort for very little return.' And he'd said, 'Well, it's early days yet, babe. Gotta get it up and running.' But Stella was beginning to suspect that Phil did not actually care whether the business made much of a profit – thanks to her salary he had little need to make one – keeping himself occupied was enough for him.

He was happy, she should be happy. God knows, splitting up was no walkover for the working woman. Annie's custody battle had shaken Stella. The researcher had told her Annie's case was indicative of an as yet small, but growing trend. Stella wanted to do an article on the phenomenon but had some qualms about raising the subject with Annie. Yet they had to cover it: this was true equality. Women were marching into boardrooms. Men were tied to the kitchen sink. And who was going to get custody of their children if the stresses got the better of you? It had made her fearful of splitting up with Phil, which was what she had been considering. She rued the day she had given his name on the birth certificate.

The cab halted, rattling. Handing a fiver to the driver, she picked her way in her high heels up icy steps to a glossy black door, kissed the perfumed gel on her hostess's hair – *smnch, smnch* – and in her accustomed posture for dealing with unnerving situations – shoulders back, bosoms out – strode into the dining room where everyone else was seated. 'So sorry to be late. Nanny problems,' she breathed. 'His love life's not the best.' If there was one thing Stella did well, it was making an entrance.

She had the impression, which hardened as the evening wore on, that her hostess had been so pleased to see her because she was cast as the character who would enliven the table. It was not hard to see why: the other guests were uniformly stuffy. She found herself performing for them, becoming steadily more provocative. When she heard her voice declaring, 'Oh, let's not knock Diana! Charles is so anally retentive he could perform colonic irrigation without the tubes,' she thought it was time to subside. In past times, she wouldn't have cared too much, but since becoming editor she was always aware that she had a position to protect. Although she had not a flicker of genuine interest in any of them, she decided it might be politic to ply the guests near her with questions. She could not quite face interrogating the stuffed shirts on either side of her. The woman opposite, whose short blonde hair and designer cocktail dress defined her as a trophy wife, but one with real distinction, was eager to talk. There was something appealing in the brazen way she assessed Stella's use to her. 'So you're an editor,' she drawled, stressing the last syllable. 'My daughter wants to be a writer. She's so talented. All her English teachers say so. I don't know where she gets it from. Do you, Simon?'

Her husband, who was a big cheese with one of the privatised utilities, was sipping at his claret and ignored her. She didn't appear to mind.

'My only creative talent was artistic,' she continued. 'I used to work for Charlotte Sackworth, the interior designer. Do you know her?'

'Of course. She's very good.'

'I loved that job,' she said wistfully. 'Loved it. But it was very demanding and for peanuts, frankly. And Simon wanted me there. He didn't want to come home at eight after a hard day and me not be there.'

'So you gave it up.'

'Mmm.'

Stella took a sip of mineral water. 'Do you know, I never thought I'd live to hear me say this, but I can quite see your husband's point.'

'You do?' said his wife. 'I mean, I do, but I didn't expect you to.'

'Men,' said Stella, 'expect to be accommodated. And women are very good at giving way to them. But you reverse the roles. You make the woman the big earner. You ask the man to make a few adjustments, to curtail his two-bit job just a fraction, so that he can be there when she gets home. And do you know what happens? Sweet F.A., that's what happens. He goes off to Spain just before Christmas when his parents and his sisters and his uncle Tom Cobbly and all are expected for Christmas lunch. That's what happens.'

'Oh.' There was a pause. 'Do I take it you're talking from bitter experience? Darling, what do you think Stella should do?'

'What?' The husband turned reluctantly, his lower lip projecting in a disagreeable way. His face was fat and florid. He seemed, Stella thought, a most unrewarding person to flatter and flutter around. The size of his share options must form his main attraction.

'Stella's husband has a job a bit like my old one,' the wife explained. 'Teensy weensy salary. Long, long hours. And he won't cut them down.'

'Puh!' Simon said. 'I know what I'd have done if you hadn't left that stupid designer woman.' He paused for effect, wanting Stella to prompt him. 'I'd have had an affair. Traded you in for a new model. Hah, hah, hah.'

His wife laughed, too. 'Are you saying that Stella should cheat on her husband?'

'Partner,' Stella said in a small voice. 'We're not actually married.'

'Oh!' hooted Simon, who was now quite animated. 'It doesn't even count as adultery, then.'

'Oh, but surely it does, darling.'

'What are you? Turned into a lawyer, have you? Become an expert overnight?'

'I mean, morally, darling, if not literally.'

'Brian! What do you say?'

A man looked up from his end of the table, straining around a forest of crystal glasses.

'You're a solicitor. Can you commit adultery if you're not married?'

'Of course not,' Brian replied, bemused. 'You mean if you're co-habiting. No, the definition of adultery assumes marriage.'

'There you are then. Told you,' he said to his wife. He nodded towards Stella. 'Nothing to stop you.'

'How comforting,' Stella said archly. She tapped her spoon into the crust of her crème brulée, and glanced at Simon's wife who was smiling brightly. This is a useful reminder, Stella told herself. There are far worse fates than being a bread-winning woman.

It was Christmas Eve. Steam misted Karen Harris's kitchen windows, puddling the tiled sill beneath. Annie sat in a chair trying to make herself as small as possible as Karen bustled around her. She had called in with the Belgian chocolates she'd bought Karen and been hustled into a chair to sip Asti Spumante and eat a supermarket mince pie.

Four large lumps of turkey breast rotated within a roasting bag in the microwave oven.

'Are they for tomorrow?' Annie asked.

'Yeah. I cook 'em now, slice 'em and re'eat 'em tomorrow.'

'Don't they get dry?'

'We 'ave gravy wiv 'em, of course.'

'Oh.'

'Saves all the palaver this way. Can't be bothered with a whole bird no more. None of us likes the dark meat. Year before last I threw it all away. Well, who wants to pick it off for the cats or make it into pies and things these days. Who's got the time? I ask you. And the way all the little bits get under your finger nails . . .'

All the family were expected tomorrow, Karen said. Tiffany's boyfriend was coming over. Daryl and his girlfriend and her children. 'It's our turn this year. It'll be nice to have the kiddies here for Christmas. Not the same without kiddies, is it?'

'No,' said Annie.

Karen shot her a look. 'When you seeing yours? Boxing Day? Ah, well, love, I just wanted to say, I know I said when you came that I wouldn't hold with kids staying 'ere, but at Christmas-time, like, if you want to, long as it doesn't set a pressie-whatsit.'

'Thank you, Karen. That's very good of you. I've actually arranged to take her round to a friend's. This girl I work with, Rachel, she's invited us round. She's got children of roughly the same age.'

'Oh, that's good then. And what are you doing tomorrow? You can come round to us if you like.'

'Thank you. I've got some plans,' Annie said. She didn't, but she couldn't face Christmas Day with the Harrises. And she didn't think they could face her: she wouldn't make very good company.

Chapter Eighteen

On Christmas morning, Annie woke at seven, as usual. The sky was dull above Karen Harris's prosaic little patch of back lawn where the winter flowering pansies had grown leggy and bedraggled.

She drew herself a very hot bath and poured a stream of extremely expensive bath oil under the churning taps. This had been a present from Rick, who was spending Christmas at his sister's but who had taken her out to dinner before he left for the country. He had been very chivalrous about pretending not to notice how awful she looked though she noted that now he avoided kissing or touching her bumpy cheeks and breasts. She hadn't talked much to him about the case: it meant far too much to her for that, and their friendship was certainly not at a stage where he either wanted or had the power to comfort her.

She dressed in sweat pants and a baggy jumper. In her fridge there were her favourite foods, smoked salmon with eggs for scrambling, vintage Krug champagne. She had thought she had better try to tackle the day as if it provided a welcome occasion for pampering herself. She switched on the television in the corner, which was a mistake, because the programmes were frantic in their family jollity. When she switched it off, though, the silence was terrible.

The pop of the cork and rush of champagne was cheering. She poured it into a tumbler, which was all she had, and sipped at it. It was now ten o'clock. She could ring Emma.

She dialled the number, praying that Fiona Carr wouldn't answer, and someone, for once, was listening to her.

'Mummy! Happy Christmas, Mummy.'

'Happy Christmas, sweetheart. Do you like your present?'

'I got a bike.'

'I know. The bike's from me.'

'Is it?' Had they not told her? 'It's fab.'

Annie could hear Fiona's voice in the background, laughing with her daughter, and what sounded like a balloon popping.

'I've got some more presents for you tomorrow,' Annie said and thought how pitiful she was.

'What are you doing, Mummy?' Emma asked.

'I'm just . . . sipping some champagne and having a quiet day, and looking forward to seeing you tomorrow,' she said, which was the best she could come up with. She had to monitor so much of what she said now. Even on Christmas morning, she was trying to find the middle ground between telling the truth about her low spirits, which might put a damper on Emma's own mood, or lying brazenly, which might give Emma the impression her mother did not miss her.

'I'm looking forward to seeing you, too,' Emma said.

When Annie put the receiver down, she discovered there was no longer any point to her day.

TWO INTO ONE

She occupied herself for another hour or so with wrapping Emma's additional presents for tomorrow, the book on ponies, and the realistic, malleable pony and rider with its complementary stable set. She stuck bows to the bright parcels, and tags with loving messages, and then, sitting back on her heels, she thought, 'This pretending is useless.'

She pulled on her coat, took her purse from the table, and pulling the door behind her with a soft click, walked to the car, furtively, as if she were doing something criminal.

The streets were empty, the shop faces blank and shuttered; there was something sad and redundant about a city street on a bank holiday. Without people to distract the eye, the grey tarmac, litter and billboards became especially stark and ugly. She took the main roundabout towards the motorway, changed down on the slip road, and accelerated fast, going north. Three quarters of an hour later, she turned off the main roads onto the lanes which dissected the rolling fields, green with some new-fangled winter crop.

It was lunchtime when she got to the village and no one was out and about to spot the car, to say, 'Isn't that Annie Greene?' as she slowed and manoeuvred it onto the farm track and into the field behind the church, parking it behind a thick hedgerow.

There was an afternoon carol service at their church, requested by the village women who were too preoccupied by tyrannous turkeys to enjoy the morning service. Annie and Chris always came. Had come. She was still adjusting her tenses. She remembered last year, when they walked up with Emma, the first year she had been fully able to read the words in the hymn book, her voice, slightly off key, wavering between them, as the organ wheezed through 'Away In A Manger' and 'Silent Night'. The WI had festooned the sills and the nooks and crannies with holly, ivy, pine, mistletoe, and fat unbleached candles, which Pammy Henderson lit at the start of the service, turning down the lights.

She checked her watch. One and a half hours to wait. She was shivering. She got out of the car and walked briskly up the bridlepath, over the stile and down to the copse. It was all so familiar to her, the black patch where the rotted stump had been burned, the two dilapidated white beehives old Cecil had placed at the edge of the wood, the smooth dip between trees where the village children freewheeled their bikes with whoops of fear. Thick waves of fungus rose like a crest on a fallen tree. She stamped her feet, blew on her hands, jogged back to the car. A long hour to go.

At twenty to three, Robbie walked across from the vicarage, his black robes flapping around his legs. She had positioned the car so that she could see, through a small hole in the hedge, the path that led from the lane, through the graveyard, to the thick oak door. Shortly afterwards, the villagers, in twos and threes and fours, in groups, in families, appeared through the lych-gate, laughing, greeting one another.

She saw Emma first, riding her bike, wearing a red woollen hat with white fur trimming which was new and strange, but suited her. She hoped Fiona Carr had not chosen it for her.

Close behind came Chris, with his hands in the pockets of his old waxed jacket, and Fiona, in a pink padded coat, holding the hand of her daughter. As Annie watched, Fiona quickened her pace, slipping her hand into Chris's pocket, too, laughing. They looked so happy.

Emma dismounted the bike uncertainly. She looked back at Chris and Fiona. 'Prop it on the wall there,' Fiona said. She extracted her hand and jogged towards Emma, taking the handlebars, helping her, ruffling her fringe and cracking a joke. And then, as Annie watched, Emma put her arm around Fiona's waist.

Smiling, they disappeared through the oak door, following Chris and Rebecca.

Emma loved Fiona.

She had lost. Annie lay her forehead on the cold window. Long ago, it seemed, she had grown this child in her belly, felt the first soft flutters of new life, had birthed her and nursed her and gently set her towards independence. She had thought the job unfinished, that there were many more years to be spent in watching over her. But in a fundamental way she was wrong. She was no longer needed. The judge had known what he was doing.

The faint strains of the congregation breaking into 'Once in Royal David's City' were audible. She turned the ignition key, reversed onto the bridlepath, and slipped away towards London. She had to come back tomorrow, to collect Emma. She must keep coming back, to show Emma how much she cared. That was all there was to the great task now. It had become so simple and so ruinous.

The next day, when Annie woke, she felt a little better. Today could not be as bad as yesterday. She packed the presents, dressed with care and applied several layers of make-up. The bumps on her cheeks were fading slightly, which was a mercy; she wanted to look good in case she had to meet Fiona Carr.

There was frost on the windscreen. She chipped it away with the plastic scraper, turned the heating up full blast and retraced yesterday's route with the sound system playing Bruce Springsteen at full volume. At nine o'clock she pulled onto the gravel in front of the cottage. There was an artificial wreath on the door.

Chris looked tired and as if he had lost weight. 'We're behind,' he said as he opened the door. He would normally have said, 'We're late,' and Annie knew that he was unconsciously adopting Fiona Carr's idioms, just as Emma had done.

The dog waddled past and launched himself at her, wheezing and squeaking so that his whole body shook. 'Late night, trouble getting her up. You better come in.' He read the look on Annie's face as she crouched over the dog. 'Fiona's in the kitchen with Becky. You can't wait out here. It's freezing.'

She followed him into the hall. There were cards strung from ribbons hanging from the beams, which was not as Annie had displayed them, and there were perhaps more than last year. Annie wondered if all those who sent them knew it was now not Chris-and-Annie but Chris-and-Fiona. When he went through to the kitchen – she heard his voice though not the words – she took the opportunity to tweak open the nearest card. 'Dear Fee', it read, 'Don't do anything I wouldn't, Love Gilly.'

'I want to go in to the lounge. I want to,' Becky was insisting loudly.

Annie saw Chris, across the dining room, closing the kitchen door. He rejoined her, showing her into the sitting room, as if it were not her house.

And it wasn't, not really. When she entered the room, she saw that quite clearly. Fiona Carr had changed the furniture around: the sofa had been pushed back, the books removed, and a collection of miniature china teapots had appeared in their stead. All the photographs, of Chris and Annie and Emma, had been removed from the desk. In their place, at angles to each other, were a basket of dried flowers and a plastic model of two cutesy figures entwined above the inscription, 'I'm bugs over your hugs and there's nothing missin' in your kissin'.'

Chris was removing newspapers and a tin of sweets from the sofa. He gestured to her to sit down. 'Where are my photos?' she said. 'I'd like some of them.' She sounded peremptory even to herself.

'I'll, erm, I'll look some out. Fiona wanted to make some changes.' He looked embarrassed. There was an awkward pause. 'Do you want a coffee?'

Annie didn't, but she thought of saying yes just to be rid of him, her husband, who was now so bumbling and obviously discomforted by her presence. Thankfully, the door behind them opened. 'Mum-mee.' Emma hurled herself into Annie's stomach. The joy of the greeting, the softness of her hair and skin, the very scent of her, broke Annie's composure. She buried her face in Emma's neck. It was a few minutes before she managed to say, 'Hello, ratfink. Ready to go?'

She chivvied Emma through to the hall and helped her in the battle with her overcoat. 'Come on, don't dither like a zither,' she said, one of her nonsense rhymes, though what she meant was, 'Let's get out of here.'

Chris opened the door for them. She saw him standing, watching as she drove away. And she realised that he was as glad to see the back of her, as she was of him. How extraordinary that a marriage could come to this . . .

*   *   *

It was in this way that Annie began to hate Fiona Carr. The emotion she had previously felt for her was lukewarm compared to this new lust to do her harm. All the old clichés to express anger – white heat, blood boiling, all of these Annie understood perfectly. She thought often of Fiona and her posture was distorted by her thoughts: teeth held in a rictus clench, her hands balled into fists. What a ridiculous and ugly spectacle she must present! But there was nothing she could do about it.

In the New Year, she returned to work for three days and then, on the fourth, she woke up one morning and knew she had had enough. She telephoned Stella and told her she had the 'flu. She kept busy all morning, taking clothes to the dry cleaners, sewing on buttons, polishing windows. In the afternoon, in plenty of time, she wrapped up warmly, for she had learned her lesson from the wait outside the church, and drove up to Cambridgeshire once again. The journey was now irritating in its familiarity, so she took the A10 to vary the scenery, though the road was tedious and trying as it crawled through the suburbs, until it crossed the M25, whereupon it sped through villages, the ancient houses at its edge lurching to one side, as if blown by the slip stream of so much traffic. Finally, when it neared Cambridgeshire, it undulated over the hills where, on either side, the frosted fields sneaked off to lap the toes of the bare trees on the horizon.

Annie kept her thoughts within the present, within the car, within the tunnel of air through which it rushed northwards. She was conscious of a sense of wrong doing but as long as she did not examine her actions she could continue, right foot depressed, to her destination.

In town, she parked in the pay and display car

park, cast a shawl around her head, and walked through the back streets to the high street. The library was opposite the estate agents where Fiona Carr worked and when Annie entered, the librarian smiled in recognition. For some reason, this greeting made Annie feel ashamed.

She sat at a table by the plate glass window, a reference book open before her. She watched the estate agency. In the forty-two minutes that she sat there, not one potential customer entered, though a woman with a pushchair stopped and read the details of one of the houses displayed in the window. Finally, she saw the figure she now knew so well, tall, on the heavy side, the inappropriate plait flicked over her shoulder, the deep set eyes, the cheap clothes, Fiona Carr. Through the open door she called something to someone inside and then laughed. She had so much to laugh about.

Fiona Carr turned up the high street and Annie went after her, at a slight distance. She followed her to the school and watched, from the opposite side of the street, near a bus stop, as Fiona Carr chatted to others of the waiting mothers, women waiting for their own children. Annie had never felt at ease with the playground small talk, the boasting about children, the prattling about mundane life. She suspected that most of the women considered her aloof. But Fiona Carr was quite at home, as easy picking up Annie's daughter as she was rearranging Annie's house, or sleeping with Annie's husband.

Fiona Carr took Emma's hand as well as her own daughter's when they eventually trailed across the playground. She walked between them, chatting easily, on the way to the car park. She stopped at the newsagents and bought both girls a sherbet dip. And when they were all strapped in Fiona's hatchback,

Annie slipped into her own car and trailed them back to the cottage, slowed outside it and wound her window down. She heard Emma shout, 'I'm frozen,' as Fiona fumbled for the key which she now possessed to Annie's house, and saw Ben emerge, wagging, to greet all three of them, the two intruders as well.

She was close enough by then to hear Fiona say, 'This dog smells gross,' and for Rebecca to shout, 'Ur! Go away, you yukky animal!' She was close enough to see Emma's face crumple as she patted Ben and planted a kiss on his fur. But no one turned and saw her. They went into the house and lights went on.

Annie drove past the cottage, turned and parked near the drive. She could see figures through the window, dark against the light, but by their size and shape she knew them. In her mind, she knocked at the door and threw the acid into Fiona Carr's eyes, plunged the knife into flesh and bone, again and again, the expression of surprise and disbelief on the woman's face turning to knowledge, fading to life-lessness. Nemesis on the doorstep. Annie had no weapon with her, and there was none in her flat. In her imagination, she was now at the wheel of the car as it mounted the pavement and mowed Fiona Carr down, heard the thud of her plump body on the bonnet, saw the wild angles of shattered arms and legs.

Teeth clenched, fists clenched, Annie came back from her bleak flight and found herself sitting in her car. She heard ragged breaths, someone sobbing, and as so often recently, there was a time lapse before she realised who was sounding so broken.

You're sick, she said to herself. You're obsessed. How many times are you going to do this, Annie?

She remembered – a year ago, was it? perhaps

two – a world away, in any case, when she was a rational human being who had thought that whatever her difficulties, her life would remain firmly on its course, she remembered her reaction to the odd story of Princess Diana supposedly making silent telephone calls to her friend Oliver Hoare. Poor cow, she had thought. Silly woman, as if the noun were perjorative in itself, so complete was her acceptance of the male stance that overemotional behaviour was both female and despicable. Ah, but I understand you now, she told the blonde head in her mind's eye. Here I am, reduced to this same degradation.

Losing your child would drive anyone mad. Taking away your child took away your reason for remaining whole and healthy and sane. There was no dimension to Annie's day any more, no sweetness or purpose. The rightness of being a mother belonged to Fiona Carr.

Once, years ago, she'd had that scare, that lump which had turned out to be – wonderful, warm, unthreatening word – benign; and during the weeks in which they'd waited for the appointment and the all clear, she had wondered what would happen if she died. Would Chris remarry one day? Would Emma be brought up by some faceless, nameless woman? Now she had no need to wonder. If she were snuffed out, as Susan Boyd had been snuffed out, no central light would die in Emma's life, just a kind flame at the corner of her life, the absent mother who turned up on Saturdays, whose visits meant treats and presents certainly, but also disruptions, having to refuse invitations to see friends, having to do something each week at the same time. If I drive this car off the motorway tonight, Annie thought, distracted by my anguish, how little difference it will make. Emma might remember me, just a faint recollection that might even be distorted, but essentially she will be Fiona Carr's creation.

Ah, the malignant stepmother of fairy tales! How wrong the men were who wrote them! For the benign, warm, unthreatening stepmother inflicted equal pain on the woman she replaced. Emma might even turn to Fiona one day, at her wedding perhaps, and pay tribute to her kindness. 'You could not have done more for me had you been my mother.' 'You brought me up. I don't think of you as a stepmother, Fiona.' 'I owe so much to you.' Might still feel all of this, even if Annie lived to be old and hale, the visiting mother, the parent to whom Emma did not feel equally close. There would be grandchildren and split Christmases and awkward arrangements to be made. 'I hate to think of her on her own but we simply can't have Annie this year, we're having Dad and Fiona.' There would be twee titles – Nanna F and Nanna A perhaps – and fixed smiles under picture hats at christenings, weddings and funerals.

None of this would have been any different had she won the glorious, inalienable right of a mother to be with her child. But the pain would have been distributed differently. It would have been Chris's rather than hers. And whatever he had done or not done in the years of their marriage and the months of their splitting up, she would not wish this pain on him. Nor this humiliation, this finding out how low you could sink.

What am I going to do?

There was a moment of stillness, a pause in the mist her breath cast on the cold glass. She could feel the world revolve as she came back to herself. She was suddenly aware that, without having thought anything through, she had decided.

It was dark. Slam of the car door, crunch of the

gravel, rat-tat-tat of the old iron knocker. As she peered around the front door, Fiona Carr's face froze, and Annie realised she had the power, by her mere presence, to frighten her. What was *she* imagining? The acid? The knife? Or perhaps something more prosaic: that Annie had returned to stake her claim to the family home, as perhaps she still had the right, for the decree nisi had not been granted yet, though it was sure to be shortly.

'Hello.' Fiona Carr's voice wavered slightly.

Annie found it in her heart to wish to reassure her. 'I'm sorry to trouble you,' she began and continued with a white lie. 'I was driving back this way after an interview and I just wanted to pop in to see Emma. I'm, erm, I'm going on vacation very shortly. I've decided I need to after . . . everything. I wanted to tell Emma and Chris.'

Fiona opened the door wider. 'Emma's in her room,' she said tersely. 'I'll phone Chris.' As Annie climbed the stairs, she heard Fiona, who hadn't lowered her voice, saying to Chris on the telephone, 'Come home now! Your ex-wife is here . . . I don't know! Some cock-and-bull story about going away.' Annie realised it was the first time she had felt that she, not Fiona, was in charge of events.

It was a long time since she had been in Emma's room. As Emma hugged her in delighted surprise, Annie glanced round. The yellow bedspread, the row of toys, the posters of horses were unchanged. But on the little pine table by Emma's bed stood the family photographs that Fiona had moved from the sitting room.

'I rescued them, Mummy,' Emma told her.

Together, Annie and Emma sat on the bed and looked at them in turn, laughing over the shared memories. But when Annie explained that she was going away for a fortnight or so, back to the States, Emma's face fell.

She turned away and began to pick at the ribbon tied around her teddy bear's neck, her lower lip jutting out. Finally, she said, 'Are you taking Thomas?'

'Thomas? Who's Thomas?' Annie could not think she knew anyone by that name.

Emma looked at her suspiciously. 'Thomas the baby. Your other baby.'

Annie's hand darted out to capture Emma's chin, to stop the pouting face from turning away again.

'I don't have another baby,' she said, looking directly into her daughter's eyes, knowing how important this declaration was. 'What was it I used to say to you? When you wanted a brother or sister . . . ?'

'I never wanted a brother.'

'. . . You're the only baby for me. That was it.'

There was silence. Annie stroked the soft cheek with her thumb.

'I thought you had another baby in London.'

'Oh, Emlet.' Annie had not thought her heart could crack any further. 'Of course, I don't have another baby. Can't you read the label on my heart?' She took her hand away, pointed to her chest. It was another old joke of theirs. 'This heart belongs to Emma Greene, Tudor Cottage . . .'

'Cambridgeshire, England, United Kingdom, Europe, the world, the solar system, the universe,' Emma finished the chant. There was a pause. 'I'm glad,' she said.

'I've been trying to be so brave, Emlet. Trying not to show you how much I miss you. But you needed to know, didn't you? You actually needed to know how I miss you. You needed to see my pain.'

'I've missed you terribly,' Emma said and her voice wobbled and her eyes and nose began to stream. Annie took her head against her breast, where she felt warm saliva soaking through her sweat shirt. She rocked her back and forth, kissed the silky head.

'There, there. I love you. It's all right,' she murmured. And all the while, Emma's hand tapped her on the back, trying to comfort her, also, as if she finally understood how Annie had suffered, too.

Chapter Nineteen

Annie saw Stella the next Monday and arranged a three-week break.

'I'm glad you've seen sense,' Stella said, turning immediately to practicalities. 'Who am I going to get to cover for you? Even running on empty you've been better than most. Do you know of anybody?'

Callum was in his windowless cubby hole opposite Stella's office. The previous Friday, he had resigned. He had a new post on a daily newspaper.

Annie knocked on his open door. 'Congratulations,' she said.

'Yes!' He punched the air. 'I'm going to a real newspaper,' he crowed. 'Where the men are men and the women have to act like men or suck my dick.' He made a one-fingered gesture, presumably to some imaginary woman.

'Wow! You'll be in your element,' she said and made to leave.

'Oh, Annie?'

Reluctantly, she turned, anticipating a put-down. He was twiddling with a pen self-consciously. 'Sorry about your kid. Huh, well, I'm sorry *for* your kid.'

Callum's life story flitted back to her mind. 'Good luck,' she said, softly.

It was four o'clock, early morning in San Francisco. She hadn't spoken to her mother in over a year, and it was only now that she thought to wonder that Martha had not herself called in all that time. Their relationship was now so spiky that they dared not communicate too often, for fear of sparking a scene. It reminded Annie of her last weeks of living with Chris. It was time to do something about it.

'Martha Bradshaw.'

'Mom. This is a cheek but will you pay my air fare for me?'

'You got it.'

'I've got a lot to tell you.'

'I know. What? You think I haven't phoned my only grandkid on her birthday?'

'Ah.'

'Ah to you, too. Put the flight on a charge card and call me back with the details.'

So she did. That night, she saw Rick for the first time in a fortnight. He had grown a sharp goatee beard and did not look himself. In fact, he looked faintly ridiculous, as if he were practising metamorphosis: seemingly he was changing into Bob Geldof. Even after two hours over dinner and a further hour in his bed, Annie could not grow accustomed to it. She lay on her side watching him as he slept, thinking how physically unattractive he had become with this one, small, and probably temporary addition to his face. He had once looked almost immortal in his beauty; now he was uncannily Mephisphelean.

She was used to intimacy, to influencing Chris's appearance, from his clothes, to his haircut, to his aftershave. How odd it was for her opinion not to count. She had been afraid of being single, but now she was more dismayed by being one of a pair. To be half of a lukewarm partnership did not suit her. She had always wanted commitment, full-blooded and onerous. She was not of the next generation, as she had encountered them, with their easy, jogging companionships defined by undramatic sex and a lack of demands. She wished, indeed, for someone to demand something of her.

In the morning, she got up and was ready to leave while Rick lay, snoring gently, under his duvet.

From the bedroom door, she called softly, 'Good bye, Rick,' and he sat up suddenly.

'See you before you leave?' he said.

She shook her head.

The penny began to drop. 'Not when you get back?'

'No,' she said. 'Take care.'

'I'll miss you,' he said, but he exaggerated almost as an act of courtesy. He had always been so polite.

Five days later, she crossed the Atlantic flying Virgin for comfort, swopping her shoes for the funny slippers, lathering her face in moisturiser and drinking gallons of bottled water because she knew that Mom was going to comment on her appearance. And there she was, at San Francisco International airport, standing by a white pillar, her hair still slicked back into its severe bun, her lipstick still the same shade of peach, her jewellery still chunky and golden, worn even with the slacks and sweat tops in pastel colours which she habitually chose for everyday. But there were new lines crisscrossing her forehead and the soft pouches under her eyes.

She said, 'Hi,' extended her hand and tugged

fiercely at Annie's earlobe. It was the nearest she would come to a hug.

'Hi, yourself,' Annie said, 'And please don't rip my ear off. I'm falling to pieces as it is.'

'So I see.'

Annie was home.

Martha had moved, three years ago, to another house on another suburban estate, much further south of the city, so this was not a house which Annie recognised, nor was there a room which was defined as hers. And yet, the furniture and the books, the pots and plates were there, and the ambience of the place was Martha's.

Suddenly, Annie was bone tired. She was as weak as if she'd had the 'flu. She did not think she had the strength to crawl out of bed in the mornings and face the awful unpredictability of another day.

'So who's forcing you?' Martha said. She had not, and this was totally uncharacteristic in its tact, asked too many questions.

So Annie spent two days in bed, slumbering or with her nose buried in a book, while Mom was out at her job, an administrative role for an import-export company. Somehow, Annie did not think her mother found it especially fulfilling.

In the evenings, Mom cooked and they sat in that part of the L-shaped living room designed for dining – there was a hatch in the wall through to the kitchen, on one side of which hung a spider plant in a coir basket which Annie remembered from childhood. Mom prattled on, with determined vigour, about everything that had happened since Annie had left, the friends who had divorced, or got breast cancer, or moved to hicksville, until Annie's head swam with the details.

On the third day, which was a Saturday, it was

mild enough for them to take their coffee onto the deck, although they had to swaddle themselves in down jackets and lay towels on the wet teak chairs. The house was on a hill so there was a view, if a tame one, of other houses and other yards fringed with trees, of men in checked shirts gathering leaves from empty turquoise pools, of a boy bouncing a basketball, one, two, three, pound, pound, pound, then aiming it for the net fastened to the carport wall. The sky was a paler version of the drained swimming pools, was the colour of Martha's slacks, but scattered with a benevolent flock of clouds. Annie squinted, trying to see as far as she could, as if her sight would focus on the point where the earth met the sky and curved away. She took a deep breath.

'I've made a complete mess of my life,' she said.

Martha lent back in the chair. She chuckled, a low, emphysemic sound. 'Like your mother before you,' she said.

This was a surprise. It was not a surprise when Martha was feisty or impossible or generous or angry. But sadness did not go with her, nor did reflection. 'Don't tell me you're mellowing in old age?'

Martha's match flared and the tip of the cigarette glowed brighter, fainter, brighter, as she puffed. She had tried to give up a dozen times but had merely succeeded in swopping brands, to menthols, which she told herself were safer.

'Am I mellowing?' she repeated. 'Not too much, I hope.'

'Tell me about you and Dad.'

'But you know it. We met in 1958 and married three months later. We had you in 1959. We divorced in 1970. I think he married me for his green card.'

'Surely not? I'm sure you had some lovable qualities, Mom.'

'Maybe he didn't realise his own motives? Nah, I think he did. You always gave him the benefit of the doubt and more. I was worried when you said you were gonna marry an Englishman. But then, when I met Chris, I thought, it's OK, he's as far away from your father as it's possible to get. Your father was hungry. He was gonna climb his way out of the English class system and nothing was going to stop him. And where better to do that than in the land of opportunity?'

'Chris was never hungry,' Annie said. 'But he was kind to dogs and children. If not wives.'

Mom wheezed her breathy laugh. 'It didn't take me long to realise about your father,' she said. 'I remember being so shit scared. I was twenty-four.' She pronounced it as twenny. 'I was Mary Tyler Moore. I had a baby and I polished the house for a living. And the man on whom I depended, body, soul and bassinet, wasn't in love with me. As you know, I'm not good at being frightened. I'm shit at being frightened.

'I remember the first time I read Betty Friedan, it was like a light coming on. There were other women who felt like me. Other women who did not trust the deal they'd made, who were making a profession of whiter than white sheets and neutralising pet odours. They gave me the words with which to fight your father.'

'Your husband.'

'I thought of him as your father, by then. I hated him. Probably the fear factor.'

'You were a she-bitch.'

'I am proud of having been a she-bitch.'

'You drove me to college wearing a dirndl skirt with a rip in it and hairy arm pits.'

'So tell me your daughter isn't mortified by you.'

300

'Ah, but she's too young. And when she's older I will be the parent of choice, the glamorous and tolerant one, the one who isn't there. My daughter will be embarrassed by Fiona fucking Carr.'

'Don't be bitter, my little Anna Louise,' Martha said, leaning forward to squeeze her hand. 'I never figured Chris for an affair, either.'

They stared out at the boy with the basketball.

'That kid is so noisy,' Martha said. 'He's always practising. *Ber-doing. Ber-doing.* Drives me nuts.' Her face was sad. 'I thought you two stood a good chance. You picked him because he was agreeable, compliant. He was never gonna boss you around like your dad tried to with me.'

'No, you're wrong,' Annie said. Her hands were cold and she wrapped them around the coffee pot. It was funny how clearly she could see it now. 'I picked him because he was the exact opposite of *you.* I was fed up of being bossed, Mom, I was fed up of you ruling me, telling me what to do and how to do it, making me aim high, for a Magna if not a Summa, pushing me to achieve all that you hadn't. Chris didn't do any of that, and I thought I was free. I thought no one would ever be niggling me again. It was such a relief to be allowed to score B-grades in life.

'And then I became the sole earner, and everything changed. My success mattered. I remember last year, when I was being given a real rough time by the editor, I used to get chewed off everyday, and when I trailed home in the evening, I'd go to Chris for sympathy but he just didn't want to discuss it. This barrier descended. And why? Because he had such a stake now in my buckling down, in my putting up with it. It was far too frightening for him to say, "OK, no job is worth this." But he was only doing what thousands of wives have done before him.

'And finally, he reacted to being economically dependent just like you did. He began to try to control the emotional temperature. I guess because it was the only power he had. You know that, you've done that, too. The difference is that you chose to do it by tantrums, and he chose to do it by silences and depression. And, eventually, by an affair. Very male.

'But it was all classic stuff. I regulated the purse strings, he tried to regulate the domestic mood. He was going to prove he wasn't mentally dependent. That took me right back to childhood. So what did I do? I ran away.'

They sat silent for a moment. Annie topped up Martha's coffee.

'God,' she said, 'I hope I don't have to listen to Emma laying her bad stuff on me, one day.'

'It's preferable to her not,' Martha said.

'Yeah. I'm sorry about the silence. I was mad at you.'

'So shoot me. Don't ignore me. Promise?'

Martha stood up, piling the mugs and ashtray noisily onto the tray, disappearing through the sliding glass door, but Annie rammed her hands deep into her pockets and sat on. Eventually, the chill forced her to get up. She walked back and forth along the deck, examining the shrubs and potted plants which lined its edge. A hebe in a sheltered corner was already showing signs of budding. The spiked heads of some as yet unrecognisable bulbs had emerged, clean and shiny-green, from the earth. In Cambridgeshire, the snowdrops, hanging their heads gracefully, like ballet dancers, would soon be grouped in the dark humus beneath the ash trees, each year the same.

Here she was. In that same year, less than a year, she had lost everything that she cared for most keenly, and it was only now that she could see all the reasons why. The pattern of her life had been so artlessly drawn. She saw herself in the kitchen at home, almost three years ago, saying to Chris, 'They've offered me a job.' They had hugged each other in the relief of knowing there would be a regular wage, and made optimistic plans as to how they would work it. She could hear their discussion, their deciding how she must give her spare time to Emma.

So, she had become the model of a working mother, her weekends concentrated on her child, baking together, walking, reading, playing on the swings, packing into Saturday and Sunday all that she thought she was missing because of the weekday commute. How glad she had been to do this.

But Emma had been her excuse. Devotion to Emma was the stainless motive behind which she hid the grubby truth; that she did not want to be with Chris. Emma stood between them at the carol service, she swung on their hands as they walked down the street, frequently she pattered in after a bad dream and inserted herself between them in bed. It had been so comfortable to have her there. It meant that each could avoid the other.

What was it that Chris was always saying during that time? That she was so much more relaxed on a Sunday evening, that she gradually became herself again during the course of the weekend. At the time she had interpreted this as he did. That being with Emma made her revert to a truer, nicer self. But he wanted the impossible. He wanted her to be tough enough to stand up to Alec's bluster, but to revert to a feminine archetype as she walked through the door and took off her coat. He wanted her to be armoured for the workplace, sweeter, supine, at home. Like a puppet with interchangeable heads, she was supposed to switch easily between the job and the home, the city and the country, the male and the female in her life. The strain of trying had made her sour. And so, she had semaphored her message to Chris: 'Get a life,' she had told him, and he had.

So they were both to blame and yet now she did not have the will to reproach either of them. It was so understandable. The bill landed on the mat. The tax collector knocked at the door. You dared not look up from your bank balance long enough to consider the great and eternal questions.

Annie didn't do much during those three weeks. She went to the city a few times. Martha gave her a thousand dollars, in cash, for the pampering of herself only, which was touching, and to her surprise she found spending it easy as she wandered through the heavy swing doors of the big stores on the square. She prowled the floors, from boutique to boutique, until her feet ached. She tried on the designer outfits, habitual thrift leading her to the reduced price rails. It had been almost a year since she bought herself clothes, since that wretched halter neck dress, in fact, but shopping was plainly not something you lost the skill for. And she found a rich, deep maroon velvet scarf which she bought for Martha, whatever her instructions.

'I told you to spend it all on yourself,' Martha wailed predictably.

'I'm not an obedient sort of a child, Mom,' Annie reminded her.

They ate out a few times, Korean, Chinese. They went for Sunday brunch at one of the touristy hotels. Martha took time off work and they drove down the coast, where the twisted pine trees kept their heads down in the face of the stiff ocean breeze.

One day the doorbell rang and it was her friend Jim come to collect her. He drove her very fast to the city and pulled her up the wooden steps of a house where five of her better friends from her teenage years were waiting. They embraced her shrieking, but all the same she noted the pause in the greetings, where they would normally have said, 'You haven't changed a bit.'

'I know,' she said, tapping her cheek and her hair. 'It's stress. It's misery. It's a man.'

'Oh but tell me,' Lisa said, 'I'm on husband number three, and he's the last. I swear!'

She pushed Annie into her front room and the others whooped and clapped again.

'Isn't this just great?' they said. 'After all these years?'

All these years and it was astonishing that some of them still had the same hairstyles. Annie was bemused by juxtaposing today with her memories. They sat on the rug, and her girlfriends brought out their photos of their children, some older, some younger than Emma, and their husbands, or second husbands, or boyfriends or none, just the big gap where the male was expected. Six women and only one of them had escaped without a major heartache, but all making light of it when reunited with the gang.

She went to dinner with Jim, who returned for her at six. His hairline had retreated over the years but he had grown a moustache and a marsupial tummy in compensation. He dressed still in denim shirts and denim jeans, a red scarf tied around his neck. Jim had had one great love in his life, for a seemingly prosaic man, an accountant called

Dennis, with whom he had lived for the best part of ten years, until Dennis's car had been skewered by a truck speeding on a rainy night, when waves of water sloshed over windscreens and under wheels. Jim affected not to grieve. 'Life is too short,' he would declare. 'I only remember the happy moments.' But Annie knew that Jim sometimes locked himself away, in solitude, for weeks on end, and that since Dennis's death, there had been only desultory and volatile affairs.

'It's so good to see you,' she told him and leaned over the table to plant a kiss on his cheek.

'My poor, poor girl,' he said. 'I was so certain you were going to live happily ever after.' He poured her a glass of wine.

'Oh, Jim,' she said. 'This is so nice. I can get drunk and not have to worry about you taking advantage.'

'Are you speaking from experience? Things done in the bleakest months of your life? You know that's typical of you, Annie; even your sins are little league. They don't score many points on the scale of human wrong doing. You should aim higher, like me.'

'You have very deftly made me feel better about bedding a slimeball,' she said, and he raised his glass. 'You sound like a warped version of Martha, by the way. I guess she told you I was here, huh?'

'Your Mom told me before you got here. Actually, she called me last fall. She'd called your house and Chris had told her you'd split up. She wanted to ask my opinion.'

'In what way?'

'Whether to let you know she knew.'

'And you said, no.'

'I said, "Wait, Martha, and she will tell you herself. And then you will be in such good odour for having not interfered." And I was right, wasn't I? Uncle Jim is always right. So good at arranging his friends' lives. So clumsy with his own. But aren't we all? It's so much easier to see straight without a big, beating heart getting in the way.'

'I can hear your heart, Mummy,' Emma used to say when they lay on the sofa to watch television, head on breast.

It was another of their jokes, another piece of silliness in which Annie wrapped the recklessness of her love. For Annie would say, 'It doesn't go *ber-boom, ber-boom*. It goes, "I love Emma. I love Emma."' Stupid, private, family stuff – stuff that couldn't be told to Martha or Stella or Jim because it would simply sound mawkish. Stuff of pain, stuff of joy.

Martha sat opposite her, burrowing into the old rose armchair. It was late, the lamps were switched on and the light gleamed on her square gold brooch and on the two fingers of whiskey which she nursed in a beautiful, crystal glass. It was Annie's last night and they hadn't felt like going out.

Martha had been tetchy all day, Annie's going playing on her mind. But now that it was almost upon her she had grown as near to tranquil as she would ever be. She took a long, hard drag on her cigarette. 'Do you know something, Annie?' she said. 'When I was pregnant with you, I used to hope and wish that you were a boy. Tcheuch! I must have been nuts.'

Annie smiled. 'I don't remember caring. I just wanted a baby, any baby; at one stage in my "trying to start a family" saga, I'd probably have plucked one out of some poor, unsuspecting woman's buggy.

'You know,' she added, 'when I seriously doubted I would ever get pregnant, I went one day into the Roman Catholic church in town.' She had almost forgotten she had done this. 'I lit a candle. I had no idea if it was the right thing to do, but I lit a candle beneath the statue of Mary holding her infant son, and I knelt and . . . I didn't exactly pray, I just said, please, please, please, please, please, again and again. Like a kid. I figured if she were there she'd know what I meant.

'And the funny thing was that I felt much better. Immediately. As I straightened my back. It wasn't that I'd had an answer, it was that I felt strong enough to cope whatever happened. I said to myself, "You were happy before you started trying for a baby and you'll be happy again. There's more to life than having a child." And it was shortly afterwards that I became pregnant with Emma.

'But I was wrong, wasn't I? There isn't more to life than having a child. It is the purpose of your body. It is the reason why.'

There was a silence between them; the only sound the low rumble of the boiler in the next room and the busy-ness of Martha's smoking, the inhaling, the light tapping of the butt on the porcelain ashtray.

'I knew you'd make your peace with me,' Martha said. 'I knew you wouldn't be mad forever.'

'But all those years, Mom, all those empty years. I'm so sorry.'

Martha waved a hand dismissively, sucked in smoke, blew it out in a white stream.

'When I was a kid I used to think you had dragon blood in you because of your smoking. A dragon lady. Very apt. I wish you'd quit.'

'Don't you start.'

'It's my role. At a certain age, a daughter gets to do this. How much did you nag me? You're going to reap it all, Mom. Hear me and shiver!'

'Jeez, Annie,' said Martha, 'I'm going to miss you like crazy when you've gone.'

She nearly managed to make it sound ironic.

Chapter Twenty

During the melancholy early weeks of January, Chris interviewed the first applicants for places in the barn and allotted space to four; a woman who wove dramatic, colourful tapestries, and three men, a middle-aged artist, a twentyish ceramicist and a pensionable wood turner. There was an immediate camaraderie between them. By Easter, he hoped the remaining five places would be filled so that he could stage the first exhibition, an introduction to all their work.

A handful of villagers had approached him after seeing his mother and child sculptures for the church, interested in buying any similar studies, and in fact, he found that the need to mould and press and carve his emotions had not lessened. He did a series of six more, and one, of a woman grieving, her head thrown back, which he would not sell. He decided to switch to abstracts for a while.

He organised art lessons; for the village children and pensioners and also for the handicapped children from the local residential home, which he did for free and which proved especially rewarding. It was also good to be earning money again, not a fortune, but a steady three figures a week. He had his eye on an old brick stable behind the barn: if all went well he would ask Fleur if he could expand into it, as an area where he might tackle more ambitious sculptures in different materials.

So, he was busy, and he should have been happy. Instead, he felt flat. The improvement in his working life did not cancel out his deep sorrow. And it was there, all the time, within him, this steady, quiet sense of loss.

One night, returning home in the late afternoon, he heard the murmur of the television as he stepped into the hall. The dog blundered towards him, tail swinging violently, whining with pleasure. He bent to cuddle it, then, frowning, clicked the latch and looked in. Emma and Becky were sitting on either ends of the sofa watching teenaged soap operas.

'Have you done your reading?' he asked.

Becky scowled. 'We do it in bed.'

Chris walked in and pressed the on-off switch. 'You'll be tired by the time you go to bed. I know you. Do it now.'

'Aw!' Becky wailed. It was her favourite soap. 'You can't do this. You're not my father.'

Emma was hastily burrowing in the transparent zippered plastic envelope which the school issued, extracting *The Lion, The Witch and The Wardrobe*. Fiona appeared in the doorway. She had an apron on, and was holding her right hand vertically: traces of raw mince and fat clung to the fingers.

'What's the matter?' she said. Becky ran to her and buried an outraged face in her left hip.

'Oh, Chris, it's only kids' television. It gives me some peace while I'm cooking.' She stretched to the button with her left hand and Becky returned to the sofa, radiant.

'My mummy never let me watch television before homework, you see,' Emma explained. She was trying to stick up for her father.

'Well, we all have our different ways of doing things,' Fiona said, rather sharply.

Picking up on her mood, Emma grew nervy, and started to prattle. 'My mummy used to watch *Inspector Morse*,' she said.

'Put a sock in it, Emma,' Fiona said. 'We've all had quite enough of your mother.' And rolling her eyes to the ceiling, she returned to the kitchen.

It was cruel and unnecessary. Chris looked at Emma over the top of the sofa. Her cheeks were bright pink. 'Get on with your reading, sweetpea,' he said gently.

She retreated to the chair by the inglenook, book open.

Becky pulled a face at her: 'Swot!'

Chris wished he hadn't come home. He took Ben's leash from the peg and clipped it to the collar. 'I'm taking the dog for a walk,' he called to Emma. Outside, in the gloom, he thought of Hugh Manningtree and for the first time saw the story from his point of view. He thought of how he and Annie had turned down childminders because of their ever-blaring television sets. And he finally acknowledged that the flat feeling was not simply caused by his remaining anxiety over Emma.

They made it up. Chris felt he should learn from the mistakes of his marriage, so he waited until his irritation had waned before raising the subject that night when the children were in bed.

'Fee, I don't think Emma meant any harm by rabbiting on about Annie, you know. I thought you were a bit too sharp with her, don't you agree?'

'Oh, Chris, she's too sensitive. You're always fussing round her.'

'She's seven. She's been through a rough time.'

'Haven't we all?' she said cryptically. 'Haven't we all?'

For the moment, he let the matter drop.

The next Saturday, Emma saw Annie for the first time since her break in America. Through the cottage door Emma ran that evening, rustling with exciting parcels containing a touristy sweat shirt and a baseball cap, inexpensive items but redolent of a land of sun, pleasure and attitude, and proof, too, of her mother's thinking of her. She was full of it. Then, Becky flushed the baseball cap down the loo. Chris shouted at her but really that was no consolation to Emma.

Fiona intervened. 'Becky didn't mean any harm,' she insisted.

At supper, Emma was crestfallen. Fiona told her to stop whingeing. To Emma, this was the final straw. She picked up her a plate of spaghetti bolognese and catapulted it in slow motion across the table. It struck Fiona on the shoulder spectacularly.

'You're a bitch and a whore and I hate you,' Emma yelled.

She had to be sent to her room, of course, though Chris was torn, angry himself at Fiona's continuous siding with her own daughter. At last he admitted it. In the last few weeks since the residence application, Fiona had begun, slightly but perceptibly, to snipe at Emma. It was as if her former warmth had been forced, to some degree at least.

But Emma's outburst shocked him, too. He had not been aware that Emma knew such words, and certainly not that they were attached to infidelity, or

314

that she knew that infidelity was what had been done.

Fiona, in a clean blouse, said that it was obvious, wasn't it, it must be Annie. Emma always returned from her visits to her mother hyped up or difficult.

'Well, what do you propose? She doesn't see her mother because you can't cope with a bit of cheek?'

He heard the measured malice in his voice. It reminded him of something; a row with Annie over jobs he'd seen in the local paper, or that time he'd told her to shut up. All his hopes of a fresh start and it had come to this.

He took the dog for another walk.

Two days later, Chris had an appointment with Emma's teacher. It was a routine talk, a substitute for the parents' evening before Christmas which he had not been able to attend because he had been so deeply involved in the court case.

Miss Carroll was reassuring. 'She showed some signs of upset initially through the change in the family circumstances,' she said, smoothly, and Chris imagined her picking her jargon from some teachers' handbook on dealing with the modern nuclear family. 'But she's quite settled now. She's doing fine. Absolutely fine.'

Chris unfolded himself from the child-sized chair on which he was perched. He felt that Miss Carroll meant well, but at the same time he distrusted her bland comments.

Stretching his legs, he made his way to the scaled-down desk, to examine Emma's work laid out on the lid.

He rifled through the exercise books, growing uneasy. As Miss Carroll had indicated, the standard was adequate. It was certainly not poor. And yet it was not Emma's best. He knew the sort of stories she wrote – had written, for she no longer did them – at home. It was Annie who had encouraged her to write stories and poems and played fanciful games of the imagination, who had got wildly excited reading books with her. He sighed. This work was perfunctory. Chris could imagine Emma rattling off the exercises, doing just enough, her mind elsewhere, her mind, perhaps, with her mother. He dealt the half dozen or so paintings onto the desk one by one and on each he read the same dedication: To Mummy and Daddy, Love from your Emma.

It was so pathetic; his heart stung.

'Thank you very much,' he said and left, somewhat swiftly.

It was sheer coincidence that Mike who lived in one of the sixties-built cul-de-sacs at the other end of the village, whom Chris knew vaguely from the days when he, too, had commuted to London, bumped into him on Saturday morning. They were queueing to use the National Lottery station which had been shoe-horned into the tiny village shop. An incongruous addition to the lurching shelves of tins and faded packets, and the boxes of wine which stole across the uneven brick floor, it was the modern village's meeting point.

Mike's children were at a private school in Cambridge and Mike was full of their progress. 'Best money I've ever spent,' he said, drawing his downstrokes on the card and dreaming of a win which would render school fees mere small change to him.

Chris took the pen from him. He had never, in all his fortunes or misfortunes, envied another man his greater earning power, but he envied Mike now.

It was sheer coincidence, too, that his mother rang

while Fiona and Becky were out shopping that afternoon. Or perhaps not. Marjorie usually called when Fiona was out; she seemed to have divined their routine. Chris told her some of his concerns about Emma.

'It's good for a state school,' he said. 'But this woman's got a class of thirty-three mixed ability pupils and she's not going to care that much if Emma isn't doing as well as she possibly can. To her, Emma is better than average, so what's the problem? She doesn't have the involvement. The trouble is, Emma needs a bit of geeing up, now more than ever.'

'She's taking the divorce badly, then,' Marjorie said, a resigned statement not a question.

'Yeah,' Chris said baldly. That and the fact that Fiona thinks *Grange Hill* comes before homework, he thought to himself.

Half an hour later, Chris's father called back. 'Look, son,' he said, the word indicating his embarrassment. 'We've got a bit of a nest egg and we'd like to pay Emma's school fees. Silly you having it when we're gone when you need it now.'

Chris was moved. He had never told his parents the true extent of their former debts, had never asked them for money – it had been a point of honour to him and Annie – but for his daughter he would take it gladly.

Marjorie came on the line. 'You'll have to clear it with Annie, of course,' she said. 'I mean, you'll have to tell her.'

She seemed unduly anxious. Chris, as he replaced the receiver, wondered why. He knew that Annie would have no problem accepting any scheme that benefited Emma. No, his problem would be in telling Fiona.

By the evening, he knew he was right. Annie, dropping Emma off, listened attentively to his account and was full of joy and relief when he reached his parents' suggestion. Fiona, on the other hand, hit the roof.

'What about Becky?' she wailed. 'What about her feelings, being left behind? What about my feelings? Emma's doing OK.'

'But she's not doing as well as she could . . .'

'Why is Emma's education more important than Becky's feelings? Answer me that!'

In the middle of this, Marjorie rang back to find out what Annie had said.

'Er, she was really grateful,' he said, picking his words carefully, hoping Fiona would somehow not guess what he was referring to. He had developed an allergy to ill-argued rows. Fiona banged a saucepan on the Aga and ran from the kitchen in tears.

'Is there a problem?' Marjorie asked disingenuously.

'Fiona's upset. She thinks Becky will feel left out.'

'Sorry, darling,' Marjorie said, bridling. 'But you surely don't expect us to pay for Becky's school fees, too. After all, she means nothing to us, so to speak. She's not a relation or anything.'

It took him five minutes to assure her that he had not been fishing for more money in telling her this. Wasn't it all just typical? He decided not to press the matter at the moment, hoping that emotions would settle and Fiona would come round to the idea. After two days, she stopped sulking and began to look more cheerful, replacing the plain curtains in the sitting room with a swirl of pastel chintz she had bought in a sale. She sold an antique stool without telling him. It was like a power game. She had interpreted his silence as compliance. But he had no intention of letting his daughter's future slip away so easily.

As it began, so it ended. It was still dark when Chris was woken by Fiona's hand pulling on his penis, up and down, squeeze, squeeze, crude but efficient, as if she were milking a cow. She wriggled closer to him and blew in his ear. Why did she think that was erotic?

'Will you see to me with your tongue?' she whispered.

In the darkness, he closed his eyes. He loathed her girly euphemisms in bed. Annie had never . . .

He had no intention of doing as she asked. He fiddled with her manually for a while, then, with as much self disgust as a Catholic schoolboy needing to masturbate, he rolled atop of her, the necessary in and out. His eyes were still closed when he rolled off.

He opened them and stared at the ceiling. He must be the only man in Britain who made love to his mistress while fantasising about his wife.

As it grew light, he rose and pulled on his jeans and sweat shirt. The dog whined and under his breath he told it to be quiet. Fiona stirred.

'Where are you going?'

'Dog needs to be let out.' It was the one reason she wouldn't question.

Downstairs, he put his Barbour on, manhandled the dog, who was too arthritic to jump, into the back of the car, and reversed across the gravel. He put his foot down and took the bends in the lane too fast, sliding onto the wrong side of the road, stabbing on the brake as he encountered the milk float. On the back seat, the dog swayed precariously.

Leaving the next village, he slowed, coming to himself. He parked at the base of a footpath that crested a slight hill. The way was muddy and it was heavy going: he was panting slightly by the time he reached the top. A storm of crows took off from their twiggy platforms in the trees nearby, wheeling as they laughed their sad, bitter caw at him, this pitiful, struggling figure.

It was over. He sat on a damp stump and the dog capered round him blindly, drunk on smells. What a twat he was! What a dork! What a prick! He ran out of rude names with which to berate himself. They had absolutely nothing in common, he and Fiona, except that when they met they had each been bruised, and feeling like failures. Apart from that, there was nothing. They did not even have a child in common. Indeed, their children separated them. Curiously enough, it was winning custody of Emma which had hastened the end of his relationship with Fiona. Fathers didn't, or hadn't in the past. If it was difficult for a stepfather to cope with a ready-made family, it was going to be even harder, in this brave new world, as Britain hurtled towards the turn of the century, for a stepmother to embrace another woman's children. The matter of manners, of upbringing, the notion of hers being brighter than yours, all this was enough to choke any magnanimity.

He could not condemn Fiona for not caring for Emma; why should she? A cuckoo in her nest, and the child of a woman she was jealous of. For his part, he had tried to feel fond of Rebecca but hadn't done too well, either. They were not a family nor ever would be. They were a surrogate family, patched together, an imitation of the real thing.

Chris was ashamed of feeling glad that there was

an escape route. Fiona could move back to her old house, which she had not been able to sell. Each Saturday, after shopping, Fiona called in and checked it over, her forlorn ex-council house that no one in their right mind would want to buy in this of all markets, save some desperate divorcée, perhaps, as Fiona had been when she had purchased it.

When Fiona had begun to rearrange the cottage, it had occurred to him – a rogue thought, quickly quashed – that his house – his wife's house really, as Annie paid for it – was part of his attraction to Fiona. She had wanted him, he now realised, because she wanted to regain what she'd lost: a pleasant home and within it, the reassuring presence of another adult, a father for Becky. But Chris himself? He thought not. He suspected she would get over him very quickly, particularly if she met someone else. She was one of those people who need a partner and almost anyone easy-going will do to fill the empty spaces.

For what had they represented to each other but sympathy, stability, domesticity? The chance to do it all again and this time to get it right? In mid-life you cease to believe that there is a one and only, intended for you. You know that there only are chances to take and to spurn.

He had made a bad choice. It was that simple.

It was as simple as realising that the numbers which he picked for his lottery ticket were based on the dates that celebrated his life with Annie. Not Fiona's birthday, but Annie's. Not the date on which he'd met Fiona, which he could not, in fact, remember, but the date on which he first saw Annie, at a party, in San Francisco, and thought her incredibly beautiful and sad. His lucky day as he had always thought of it thereafter. Annie had shaped fifteen years of his life and borne his child.

They belonged, he, Annie and Fiona, to a generation which scoffed at marriage, which, when young, parroted, 'It's just a piece of paper', as if the cheap sentiment were bold and shocking. But they had been wrong. It was divorce which was a mere document. Marriage was a mingling of time, the creation of a common past that could not be completely undone.

Below him, the first commuter train of the morning rattled along the track, glimpsed through the bare trees that lined it. The sky pressed its bulging breast of dove-grey clouds upon the earth. A cold wind blew up the hill and through him, and he wished it would blow him clean, like the river Jordan. He wanted to go home, but not to Fiona.

He saw himself, and it seemed a long time ago, in the quaint garden of the Cambridge college, watching *Twelfth Night*, with Fiona; pale flesh of her legs, rounded, tarty, lonely, lame duck Fiona. Gawky Fiona getting everything, from a picnic to a love affair, slightly wrong. His emotion towards her had always been a degree away from love. He had been sorry for her. She was someone to protect when Annie no longer needed protection. With Fiona, he was playing at being the sheltering male.

He must go back and face her at once. He got to his feet. It was all crystal clear. He must see Annie, too. He must say sorry.

No fault divorce! That was the buzz word of the moment, the new way of splitting up, the new way of thinking, which was to be introduced, controversial though the measure was, during the life of the parliament. But he could tell them, the government ministers with their fatal, good intentions, the Lord

Chancellor with his, the meticulous lawyers who drafted the bill, he could tell them all that it was nonsense. It may lie on both sides, but there is always fault when a marriage fails, which is why there is a need to apologise and, especially, to receive the apology. You cannot take away the pain by pretending it was nobody's fault, just one of those things. You can only lessen its sharp tang by looking, much as you do not wish to, at the grubby, petty things you did, and owning them as yours, and seeking absolution.

But there was more. Chris wanted his wife back. He wanted his family whole. He wanted to reclaim his past. But Annie had someone new, someone he did not know, a shadowy lover on the edge of his fretful imaginings, who might by now, have insinuated himself into her affections. And even if not, he rather feared that Annie had moved beyond him now, separated from him forever by silly quarrels, by his regrettable affair and by the final battle over Emma.

When Annie returned to the office, she realised, very quickly, that she was supposed to be completely healed and firing on all cylinders, and that she had better bring in a few exclusive stories fast to prove it. She realised more slowly, after two weeks, that Stella was having an affair. There were rumours. Someone in publishing, they said. Long lunches, a new giggle in her voice. But to Annie, the proof was in Stella's distance. They had grown so close through Annie confiding in her during the past year, had maintained a personal warmth even when observing the constraints of the new balance of power, but now, with one of them needing to hide secrets, they grew apart.

Rachel said that Stella was behaving like a man, she wanted a trophy husband, and she was lining him up, Phil's replacement. But Annie couldn't join in the general condemnation. She went off at lunchtime and got herself an air letter and wrote to Mom to thank her and tell her how much she loved her. Rick rang to see if she had a nice time in America. Dominic rang to say did she know, they had a date for the decree nisi?

She put the phone down and her heart turned over. That was it then.

Daddy picked them up from school and Emma knew immediately that something was up. He was tense and hardly said a word in the car home. Becky asked where her mother was and Daddy said, 'She didn't go to work today. She's rather upset about something. I'm trying to calm her down.' It was all so ominous.

When they got home, he told them to go upstairs and they both went, quickly, without bleating about it. And then came the sounds of a fight, one which seemed to have been going on for a long time previously. Emma hid in her room, for as long as she could, listening to voices, Daddy's at the same level, calm, murmuring, but Fiona's changing to a shout and then to weeping. Once, when everything went quiet for a stretch, she opened the door and peered out and caught sight of Becky in her room, the room that had once been Mummy's and Daddy's, sitting on her bed, holding her fluffy moose to her chest. Becky looked as scared as she felt.

She had been about to venture across to her when footsteps came racing up the stairs and Fiona hurtled around the corner, her face all red and white, and snot pouring from her nose. It was frightening to see a grown-up looking like you looked when you fell over or were throwing up and you wanted your mummy and she wasn't there.

Fiona stopped outside Becky's door and said, 'We're going back to our own home. We're packing up and we're going,' in a tight, angry voice and Becky immediately began to wail.

'But I prefer it here . . .'

'I know, darling,' Fiona said, walking in and hugging her, 'I know. It's just . . .' and she caught her breath and began to sob on her daughter's shoulder.

Emma shut her door, and drew for a long, long time, but all the while she was listening. There was a lot of scraping of drawers, and eventually the sound of a heavy suitcase being dragged down the curve of the stair. Then there was more opening and closing of drawers and cupboards. They certainly had a lot of stuff.

She jumped at the low knock on the door. It was Daddy, looking tired but underneath it, almost happy, with a tray of toast and eggs for her. She wasn't hungry but she tried to eat while he sat at the other end of the bed and said that Fiona and Becky were leaving because he and Fiona weren't getting on any more and it just wasn't right, and he wasn't making a very good job of explaining this.

'I'm sorry, sweetpea,' he said. 'I know you're fond of them and this is another upheaval you could do without.'

Emma was now so used to grown-ups telling her how she felt that she tried always to summon up the emotion which they ascribed to her, but on this occasion, try as she might, while she could manage pity for Fiona and Becky's red-and-white faces, she could not manage much disappointment on her own account.

'I don't mind,' she said.

Daddy looked at her with a question on his face.

She was fed up with saying what they wanted her to say. 'I don't mind. I don't like Fiona and Becky much.'

He sighed and stroked her hair. 'Because of Mummy?'

'Because of Mummy and just because. Becky is a bit of a bully, you know, and Fiona always takes her side, and while she was here Mummy couldn't come back.' She swallowed some egg. 'Does this mean Mummy will come back now?' she asked, and her face screwed itself up though she had tried not to let it.

Daddy got up from the bed so suddenly that the tray lurched and a splash of Ribena plopped onto the bed cover. 'It may not be as simple as that, sweetpea,' he said.

Why? Emma felt like yelling. Why isn't it simple? It seemed very simple. A thought struck her. 'Doesn't she want to come back?' she asked.

Daddy began shaking his head and, she knew, was about to say what he and Mummy always said, that she mustn't think that, that it was nothing to do with her, that they loved her very much and always would do, but they had grown apart, when Fiona's voice, low and angry and right outside the door, said, 'We're finished and we're going,' so instead, Daddy, shooting her a look, dived out of the door.

There was a murmur of voices downstairs, the sound of a car. Emma looked out of her window and saw the hatchback, the back seat laden with cases, driving away, Fiona and Becky in the front seats, each face pinched and furious-sad. 'They didn't say goodbye to me,' she told her teddy. And then she took the tray downstairs, past Daddy having a drink, standing in the dining room, and plonked it in the kitchen.

The house felt quiet and empty and Emma felt glad.

Chapter Twenty-One

It was Emma who telephoned at eight the next evening, secretly, while Chris was washing up. She interrupted Annie in the shower. 'Mummy,' she stage-whispered, 'Daddy told Fiona to go. You can come home now.'

The room circled Annie once. 'Could you get Daddy please?' she said.

Chris came on the phone. 'Little monkey!' he said, amused. He really was remarkably sanguine, she noted.

There were so many questions she wanted to ask him and couldn't. It was a necessarily brief and frustrating conversation. All the same, she thought as she replaced the receiver, she knew the salient point. Is gloating bad for your moral fibre? she asked herself. Well, too bad! She was going to gloat.

The radio was on and Annie pranced inexpertly around the room in her towel, opening it at strategic moments, flashing at the inscrutable cats. Crooning to the music, she tied the towel above her bust and jumped on the bed, go-go dancing, using a thumbing a lift movement she had absorbed from re-runs of *Rowan and Martin's Laugh In*.

The knot loosened and the towel began to slide towards her waist so that she was dancing topless. Shortly afterwards, she realised that the curtains were open and the neighbours opposite had full view of her if they should happen to glance out of their bedroom windows. She bounced down and drew them quickly.

At that, her mood punctured. In the bathroom, she pulled on a robe, hugging it round her. Did this news make any difference? Only in so far as Fiona Tart was no longer influencing her daughter's life, which was something, some sort of comfort. Little Emma thought Fiona's going made everything all right. How did you explain that life and the big, beating, human heart are not that simple?

She was not expecting him when he turned up at her flat, the next evening.

'May I come in, Annie?' he asked while she stared stupidly down at him from her front step.

Under the harsh central bulb of her hall he looked much older, drawn and tired, not the losing-of-a-night's-sleep tired, but deep, bone-weary, soul-sick tired. There was a deep line that ran from the inner corner of each eye, across his cheekbones, and away. Her heart, which was no longer set against him, softened further when she saw this. It was unimaginative of her to have thought he hadn't suffered, too.

She showed him into the bedsit and while he inspected the plates and the feline portraits, she spooned instant coffee into mugs and sniffed frantically at her cartons of milk, searching for one that wasn't questionable. She wanted to act normally and to make him feel welcome, to show him that she had grown up, that there were no hard feelings, while all the time she was desperate to know why he had come.

'You didn't exaggerate, did you?' he called through the sliding door, straightening the Anne Boleyn in the Tower plate. He could never bear to see a picture even slightly askew. It was the artist in him. It had always driven her to distraction when he started fiddling with paintings which to her eye hung perfectly plumb. People said marriages broke up over such accumulated tiny irritations – the cap left off the tube of toothpaste, they said. What rot! Many an evening she had sat in this flat, spotted a lurching picture, and been caught with the sharp-sweet wish that Chris were here to straighten it.

'Foul, aren't they?' she agreed, nodding at the decor. She indicated a chair. He was still wearing his battered waxed jacket. 'You can take your coat off,' she added. They were so full of exaggerated buoyancy.

He sat on one of the hard oak chairs and accepted the thick green mug, taking a sip and clearing his throat. That nervous gesture told her he was going to come straight to the point. She knew him so well.

He put the mug down and leaned forward, propping his elbows on his knees. 'Annie, I came to say sorry to you,' he said, quietly. 'I know it sounds completely lame . . .' He looked at her sadly, as if expecting her to concur '. . . But I just had to tell you how sorry I am.'

'There's a date for the decree nisi,' she said. His head drooped. 'I'm sorry, that's a stupid thing to say. I don't know what to say to you.'

She paused, trying to muster her thoughts. 'I accept your apology, I throw it in your teeth. A bit of both. I don't know what I feel. I'm terribly glad it didn't work out with Fiona Tart whom I loathe as I have never loathed anyone before. Unfair to her, you may say, but there it is. Actually, I hate you, too. And I forgive you. And I apologise to you, too.' She waved her hand as if encompassing the whole mess and flinched when he caught it. 'I do, I do forgive you actually. I forgave us both as I sat on my mother's deck in Belmont and thought about it all.'

'Did you? I forgave us sitting in a barn sculpting figures of you and Emma.'

'You sculpted me?'

'Yeah. You popped out of the clay unbidden.' His smile was still lop-sided.

'Annie, will you come back to me? I don't want this divorce. I don't think it's possible.' He raised his hand, almost a plea. 'Please, hear me out. I know I don't deserve it. What I want to explain, what I want you to understand, and I'm not the best with words, is that the terms have changed.

'How can I put this? I want nothing of you, Annie. I used to, you see. In a funny way, I saw our marriage as some kind of fast track to self-fulfilment. You were the woman who would make me happy. I expected you to make me happy. I had an unstated list of what a good marriage should consist of – companionship, love and contentment. A rising standard of happiness. I required that of you. We expect so much, don't we? We are the greediest generation in history.' He was gripping her hand so tightly now that her wedding ring, which she still wore, bit into her finger. The tears were standing in his eyes.

'But now all I want is that you come back and be there. And I will love you, Annie. I will love you as you are, with all your inadequacies, with all your faults and your tempers. I do not require you to be perfect for me. I don't want an easy ride from this marriage. I will take it with the highs and the lows and abrasiveness. I will take it as a more difficult course, looking for no compensation. I will take it with the long years of nothing but the striving.'

She got up. She was very moved. She walked to the window and back again. 'I don't know,' she said. 'I'm scared to.'

'Exactly,' he said, and he gestured fiercely, inadvertently sweeping the straw basket from the table top. 'We should have been terrified when we married. We should have been terrified at each sea change in our lives. We should have guarded our marriage ferociously. Not asked what we were getting out of it.'

They were silent. Perhaps he was waiting for an answer? She could not give one. Even had she known what she felt at that moment, her throat hurt too much to speak.

He looked her straight in the eye and added very quietly, 'Annie, if you can't do this, I understand. There's so much that's happened. But,' and his voice gave way completely for a moment, before he struggled to control himself, 'I want you to live in the cottage with Emma. I can't bear you two . . . You must be with Emma. I realise that now. It's not that you would look after her better. It's because I have to stand by my vows. I promised you, didn't I? All that I have, I give to you.'

Annie sat down immediately and took his hand. 'Emma? Me and Emma. Do you mean it? You're going to give Emma to me?'

The black night coated the window with a gleam like ebony. The light in the room was yellow as cream. She heard the tick, tick of a fin of the radiator fidgeting as it warmed up.

He drew an unsteady breath and nodded. 'Yes,' he said. 'I love you, Annie, I don't want to hurt you any more. I saw you in the rain, grieving.'

She sat back. She believed him. She believed he would do it. She saw the depths of his emotion and it stretched as far as the inky night.

'Look at me,' she said, pulling at her greying hair, pulling it away from her scabby face. She wrenched at her suit so violently that the top button popped off and rolled away, but she didn't notice, simply parting the jacket to reveal the red weals on her chest. 'Look at me. Look at what's become of me. I'm ugly. I've got the looks to match the feelings inside, all those ugly, twisted feelings. I wanted to kill, you know, to kill Fiona Carr. I followed her in my car. I lay in hiding behind the church hedgerow on Christmas Day, watching you. Did you know that? I watched you going to church. I was that degraded. This is the person you say you love. I'm not that vulnerable girl you met on Jim's lawn. I'm fierce and warped and grey and ugly.'

'I don't care.'

He took her gently by the shoulders and leaning forward, very slowly and deliberately, he kissed her unsightly cheek – she felt the light sting of his lips on the red-raw skin – and then he lowered his head, almost reverently. Her hands flew upwards, pulling her jacket together, but he took them away, gently, and kissed her disfigured chest through the open jacket. Finally, he brushed back the hair at her temple and pressed his lips to where it was most grey. She felt his familiar smell, of soap and skin, and it smelt like home.

'There are no conditions,' he said. 'I've realised. Our marriage wasn't a deal – I'll stay if you make me happy. It was a sacrament. There may be long years when we do not make each other happy. And only a married couple could inflict the misery and humiliation which we have on each other these last months. But if there is more of that, I accept it, too. You're my vocation, Annie Greene. You are the course of my life.'

She cupped his face in her hand, brushed back the hair from his forehead.

'Then I accept,' she said and she smiled.

Karen Harris was torn when Annie appeared at her kitchen window and said she was moving out, tonight, because she'd patched things up with her husband. She was not an unkind woman but she had her finances to think of.

'Keep the deposit – it's a month's money – in lieu of a month's notice,' Annie said.

Karen looked dubious at this, not that she could own up to the reason, but she had spent the deposit long ago. Somehow she hadn't ever really thought that she would have to give it back. It was hers, like, by rights.

Annie read her thoughts. She wrote out a cheque for an extra fortnight's rent on top.

Karen cheered up immediately. 'Thanks, love,' she said. 'I'm glad everything worked out for you.'

Chris was packing, throwing clothes into the two suitcases with which she came. She had not acquired much. She hadn't made the room cosier.

'It was like a cell, really,' she said, looking round it.

'Prison or monk's?' he said.

'Bit of both.'

He stuffed the luggage and a trio of carrier bags into the trunk of her car. She went to give the keys back to Karen.

'Duration ended,' she said, and held them up

before placing them, ceremoniously, on the centre of the kitchen table. Karen fetched two glasses and a bottle of Cyprus sherry from a cupboard.

'Here's to us, love!' She raised her glass high. 'May all our menfolk come back to us, if only so I can knee mine in the goolies,' and they both began to giggle.

Chris knocked on the glass of the back door. 'Ooh, you're a piece of all right,' Karen exclaimed. She was the only woman Annie knew who could get tipsy on a few sips of cheap sherry. 'I wouldn't knee you in the goolies, neither.'

Under the streetlight, Chris put his arms round Annie and kissed her on the forehead briefly, and on the lips. 'Let's go home,' he said.

It was way past Emma's bedtime when they reached the village, but she was awake. Dora, who was babysitting, came to open the door and when she saw Annie she said, 'Well, and I'm glad to see you,' in her lovely, rolling accent, with her big crooked smile showing all her uneven teeth, and Emma, who had been in bed, pretending to be asleep, came hurtling down the stairs.

'It's my mummy! It's my mummy!' she whooped, as she took the steep steps recklessly, two by two. 'I knew my mummy would come back to me!'

And then she buried her head in Annie's stomach, their arms wrapped tightly round each other, and Annie bowed to kiss Emma's head and pat her bum; the old, familiar pose.

So it was that Annie came home. They slept, that night, on the sofa bed, all three of them, with Annie in the middle. For hour after hour Annie lay, listening to Emma's even breathing on her right, her left hand in Chris's hand, which tightened every now and then so she knew that he, too, was awake and happy and thinking his thoughts. And in the small hours, he got up and lit a pile of logs in the inglenook so that she finally fell asleep to the sound of the merry chatter and hiss of the fire.

Annie should have gone to work that day and Emma to school, but Chris phoned them both in sick. Later that morning, Annie unpacked, sliding her clothes back into drawers, placing her tooth-brush back in the mug, while Emma trailed her, watching her, as if she did not dare to believe that what she had so long wanted had finally come true.

And while they were doing this, Chris burned the bed he had shared with Fiona, putting a flaming wad of newspaper to its petrol-soaked bulk at the bottom of the garden, so that Annie was reminded of Diane Boyd. Their bed, their old bed, had been stored in the attic, and Chris moved it back to their old room, and Annie always felt peculiarly comforted that he had never slept with that woman in their bed in their room, that he couldn't bring himself to do that. Because of course, the old jealousy, and the burning memories, returned from time to time, and some-times escaped her in a dig or a bitter look.

Within days, the village knew. Ian Henderson spread the news. Emma spotted him wheeling his bike up the drive, the paper under one arm, and she raced from the door to tell him, as if the telling, too, would make it all absolute, real.

Annie went out to see him. 'How are you, Ian? I've been thinking of you.'

'I'm managing,' he said, 'I miss her. It's been five months and it hasn't got much better. My sons tell me to pull myself together. They think I should be getting over her by now. But we were married for twenty-five years, Annie. I lost my job. I lost my wife. That's a big gap to fill. Sometimes I travel to the depths of blackness, the bottom of the pit. I'm so lonely. But there's nothing I can do about it,' he added. 'It's just something to be got through. I shall learn, I shall heal.'

'Oh, Ian.' She rubbed his arm and he managed a smile.

'It's good to see you, Annie. And back for good? That's wonderful. You've given me something to brighten my day.'

She asked him to supper in a fortnight's time which he was pleased about, then she went indoors and called Dominic, who was out, but she left a message with his secretary, and Chris telephoned Mr Clough, who was there, and somewhat thrown by Chris's fresh instructions.

Dominic called back a day later, when they were both at work, but he recorded a message on the answering machine. 'Annie, I have never been so happy to cancel an instruction in my life. My wife, who knows you only by hearsay, as the nice woman who, in the middle of her own troubles, spared a moment to think of her, said especially to send you her best wishes. I was so pleased, I called Laura Thackeray and she said . . .' But Annie never discovered what Laura Thackeray said because the machine cut him out with its rude beep and Dominic never called back.

Annie was moved by the reaction of these well-wishers. She watched the world and in it she saw people whose lives brushed others' but lightly, yet who bound themselves to their fellows by goodwill.

'Do you remember when I told you I was pregnant?' she said to Chris.

'Of course. The man who gave you his buttonhole.'

'Tell me, tell me,' said Emma, who had heard the story often but who never tired of hearing it again.

338

Annie ruffled her fringe. 'Now reminds me of then,' she said. 'Everyone's so pleased that our family is reunited, such an everyday matter, people we hardly know . . .'

'Not so everyday,' he said.

And he was right, because they lived in the age of the disposable marriage. All over the western world, people were being replaced, even before they were aware of it, as Stella knew in her guilty heart. They were replaced during and after divorce, and immediately after death, like Susan Boyd. But there were still some who clung to the old ideals, to the notion that pain must be endured, quiet people whose lives would never be sung, and now Chris and Annie were among them.

It was Chris's birthday in February. He filled the remaining spaces in the barn. Annie's rash faded, but she decided not to dye her hair. Chris said she was more beautiful than ever. Emma gained a place at a top flight private school and fortuitously there was a vacancy for her to start immediately. That worried Annie a little. She imagined some poor parent whose luck and money had run out.

They had a row, which was half-hearted, but made them both feel better because it proved the second honeymoon was over, and they were coping with the steady core of marriage, the daily irritations as well as the underlying contentment.

Once, Annie saw Fiona Carr in town. She and Emma were in a gift shop, buying a present for Marjorie's birthday, when Fiona and Becky walked past the window. They looked so suburban, so nondescript and unthreatening. Odd to think of all the stories to be told of all the similar people on the pavements, the passions they aroused, the wanting and the hatred.

Emma saw the Carrs, too, and examined her mother's face as if anxious about her reaction, but Annie smiled at her and all Emma said was, 'It's funny but I don't miss my old school at all.'

In the morning, when the light was gentle as a smile, Annie woke and watched Chris sleeping. With the tips of her fingers, she traced the curve of his chest and the roundedness of his shoulder and arm. He was naked, beautiful, curved, flaccid. She drew her finger over his cheekbone and his fine nose, over his thigh and around his flat belly. He opened his eyes and kissed her.

He knew her body, the drowsy kiss and the imperative touchings that aroused it. He stroked her and she was pliable. He kissed her body and she was content and deeply breathing. Those books, they lie: the ones which tell of shattering sex between new lovers. It is within the bonds of a familiar love that the slow rhythm builds best. Her little grunts and cries and groans of sex moved him. He knew the places and the pleasures. Annie's hands tightened on his shoulders, her legs wrapped around his, locked together until the coming, and the tenderness beyond.

It was March and it was fine, though they were wrapped up against the chill as they walked up the bridlepath behind the church; the dog who was frail and stumbled from time to time, clipped to the lead in Chris's hand. They knew Ben couldn't last much longer and maybe that was why Annie was so alert to her happiness that day. It was a common matter, the family out, walking the dog on a Sunday afternoon, their breath smoking in the air as if they had all turned into dragon ladies.

340

TWO INTO ONE

Emma splashed through a puddle in her new and too capacious green wellingtons. She had homework to do later, and so had Annie, copy to read, a pile of newspapers to peruse. Chris was planning to cook supper, traditional, organic roast beef and Yorkshire pudding, which would be a theatrical event, involving all the saucepans and most of the cutlery. But none of them was thinking about later. They were each, in their way, inhaling the moment.

On one side of the flint wall, the women whose names featured on the rota for decorating the church – Audrey Benbow and old Dora among them – had left a pile of discarded greenery. On the top, at an angle, were two graphic palm leaves, clipped from one of Fleur Manningtree's indoor plants for last week's dramatic green and white display.

Annie pounced on them. 'Look!' she trilled. And she wafted them before and behind her, in a parody of a fan dance, head over chin seductively. 'How can you resist me?'

Emma, who didn't quite understand the reference, was nevertheless caught by the mood. She began to do the sand dance next to her, back and forth, all angular arms and ostrich gait. 'Look, Mummy! I'm being a mummy!' she cried, like all children a sucker for lame puns.

Chris stood, head on one side, smiling. 'The vicar's watching you,' he said.

Emma gasped. Her hand flew to her mouth as she turned to spot Robbie. But Annie pretended to swipe Chris with one of her palms. 'I know you too well for you to be able to pull that one.'

'Rats.'

She tucked her arm through his. Emma spread her arms obliquely and ran down the path ahead of them. 'Wheeeee!' She was merry as a young animal because her parents were together once more and that was all that she wanted.

Annie's heart was full, and with what? With stupid, private, family stuff that you'd never tell anyone else. Simple stuff that she, too, wanted. Stuff of laughter. Stuff of joy.